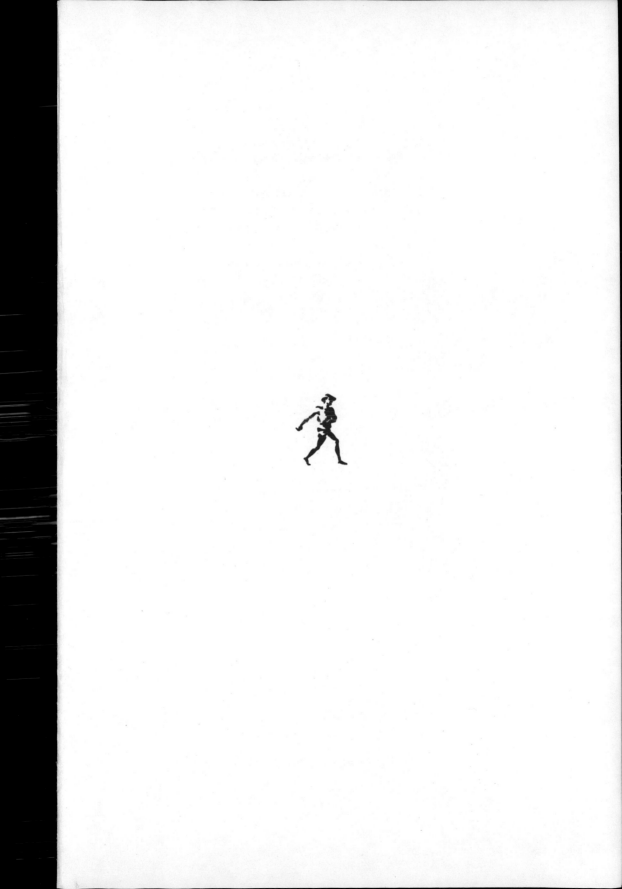

MASTERPIECE

Thomas Hoving

SIMON AND SCHUSTER • NEW YORK

Copyright © 1986 by Hoving Associates, Inc.
All rights reserved
including the right of reproduction
in whole or in part in any form
Published by Simon and Schuster
A Division of Simon & Schuster, Inc.
Simon & Schuster Building
Rockefeller Center
1230 Avenue of the Americas
New York, New York 10020
SIMON AND SCHUSTER and colophon are registered
trademarks of Simon & Schuster, Inc.
Designed by Eve Metz
Manufactured in the United States of America

1   3   5   7   9   10   8   6   4   2

Library of Congress Cataloging in Publication Data

Hoving, Thomas, date.
Masterpiece.

I. Title.
PS3558.08755M3   1986   813'.54   86-15522

ISBN-0-671-61099-6

To my wife,
Nancy

No painters in history surpassed Diego Velázquez, even the divine Italians. With his incomparable skills he created truth in art. He rendered true homage to his king, who justly loved him. He preserved for eternity the beauty and laughter of the royal children. He brought the Bible to life. He recorded the lasting virtues of victories and triumphs. Velázquez ennobled all that he painted, even dwarfs and buffoons. Above all, he knew feminine beauty and in daring to bring truth to that beauty, surpassed the artists of Greece and Rome.

From the biography of
Diego Velázquez by Antonio Palomino (1724)

1 A WORLD PRIZE

By God, he had done it!

Sir Peter Grundy, milk-skinned and portly, at fifty-three years of age dedicated to comfort and guile, carefully replaced the telephone receiver on its ornate stand and sighed in contentment. Lord Richfield, that most curious man, had actually instructed his solicitor to award the sale of his masterpiece to Grundy's firm, William's Ltd. Grundy's first impulse upon hearing the news was to shout in triumph. But it was better to be restrained. To raise his voice, to make a fuss, would mar the sanctity of his coup. It would be almost like deliberately scratching the polished veneer of a Chippendale console.

Sir Peter chuckled. How fitting! Only six months before he had —to the surprise of the art world—gained the chairmanship of William's auction house. The word had been received among his colleagues with puzzlement. Not that Grundy didn't deserve the post, they said. He was clever, owed little to art dealers and private collectors, was a scholar of English Romanesque sculpture and a capable administrator, had the ability to gauge prices of works of art to the farthing, and was adept at massaging the egos of potential bidders. Yet could he really take a second-rate auction house and elevate it to the stature of Christie's or Sotheby's? Most people in the art world thought he could not. "Peter Grundy's basic problem," one jealous observer had commented, "is that, with him, the jury is always out."

Having landed the spectacular *Marchesa*, Grundy knew that they'd continue to talk that way about him. No matter. He eased his ample body deep into his overstuffed leather chair and gazed out the window at the rows of Georgian townhouses flanking the street like ancient sphinxes. A momentary silence hung over the gathering London twilight. It was the time between the departure of the local shopkeepers and the arrival of disciplined squads of gentlemen returning to their homes from the Temple Bar or the Exchange. The serenity of the street, void of people for a magical instant, conjured up for him the memory of those photographs of a deserted Paris which, although a bit contrived, always managed to impart the mood of poetic bliss and approaching threat.

But there was no threat looming over Sir Peter's life; only bliss and victory, even if temporary. Hadn't he destroyed the bastards? The hell with restraint! He allowed himself a muted cheer of victory, but then grew reflective. His rivals would counterattack when they heard the news. He could just hear the president of Christie's remarking in his smooth, bland voice, "We were not all that interested in the Richfield Velázquez—at least on His Lordship's severe terms." And he knew exactly what the chairman of Sotheby's would say to the press: "To have won it, we would have had to give, ah, far too much away."

The customary language of defeat. The words sounded responsible and yet cast, ever so cleverly, a taint upon the victory. Grundy could easily repair that. The fact was Christie's had lost the prize because its usually alert chief had succumbed to arrogance and assumed he would automatically be given the painting to sell, the way a duke's firstborn son automatically inherits the title. How embarrassing! Particularly since Christie's had been consigned the flamboyant canvas the only time it had ever been sold in history, in 1788, fetching eight pounds ninepence. A high-pitched laugh escaped Grundy's lips.

No, it was not often that William's, a stunted palfrey compared to London's two thoroughbreds, Christie's and Sotheby's, could gallop past its more exalted rivals and win the race for one of the most uniquely beautiful and historically captivating paintings ever created.

How to account for the failure of Sotheby's, with its juggernaut of publicity, its almost obscene amounts of American capital, and its cadre of young highborn men and women? Sotheby's couldn't by chance snatch the prize away from him now that he had gained it? No! Never!

Perhaps Sotheby's had made its principal mistake, Sir Peter mused, in having failed to hire the one titled young lady he had prudently signed on just a year previously in hopes of just this outcome—the niece of Lord Richfield, Lady Eleanor Swift. But it had taken much more than that. Almost too much.

No one at Sotheby's would have bothered to sit through weeks of arm's-length discussion with the eccentric peer, patiently reassuring him through his solicitor, the unbending Harold Greenway, carefully placating him, gently placing one discreet argument on the table after another—it had been like playing eighteenth-century whist—gradually capitulating on the percentage His Lordship would have to pay for an unprecedented twenty-four pages of advertising in magazines in America, Great Britain, and Switzerland, and giving in to his bewildering, almost irrational, demand that no prospective purchaser be allowed to examine the painting with any instrument more technically advanced than a pocket magnifying glass. How would that bizarre impediment hurt the sale, he wondered. Ah, well. And he also had to bow to Lord Richfield's singular request that only his own security man guard the picture—the very military Mr. Field. No one would have suffered through all of that and, in addition, listened hour after hour as the peacock-proud Greenway read in his grating monotone every line of the two-hundred-page agreement. Finally, there was the humiliation of having to initial his agreement to every paragraph on every page —like a surrender document!

But, overall, it was a triumph, wasn't it? There was no doubt the sale would cause a sensation. The entire art world would rush to ogle the sensual masterpiece which for close to two hundred years had been all but inaccessible. What price should he assign to the sexy lady, he wondered. Not one to believe that the worth of unique works of art could be estimated by any rational means, Sir Peter, within seconds of learning that Lord Richfield might auction off his fabulous Velázquez nude, had assigned to it the figure of eleven million pounds. Since the dollar and the pound had been fluctuating close to equality for six months, he assumed that parity would be maintained; quoting the assessment in pounds was more gentlemanly. His evaluation was quite arbitrary, of course, being simply twice what another great painting by the master had managed to fetch nearly two decades ago. That was all there was to it.

But now that he'd won the picture, how to achieve a complete triumph? How to excite potential bidders to reach for such an incredible price? How to place the *Marchesa Odescalchi* into the auction record books as the most expensive painting ever publicly sold? By manipulating, cajoling, pressuring, flattering, assuring, lying a little, and, above all, by struggling.

So let the battle begin. Sir Peter plucked the telephone receiver off its stand like a ripe plum and began to make the first of a dozen calls to museum directors, trustees, curators, and private collectors around the world.

It took him two days to reach everyone on his list of potential bidders, and in each case Sir Peter quoted his evaluation, waited for the gasp of surprise, and gently launched into a lyrical description of the "world-class" masterpiece. No matter whom he talked to, he assured them that everybody he had just spoken to had confided to him that they would "most certainly" examine the picture and would "most likely" place some sort of bid.

The going was not entirely placid. Ayn Steyne, the chairman of the board of the Metropolitan Museum and its self-appointed pro-tem director, had coolly pointed out that the Metropolitan already had a number of paintings by Velázquez, so why was another needed? "With the beauteous *Marchesa Odescalchi*," Sir Peter had assured her, "the Met's collection of the master will rival the Prado's." After that she had warmed up. So it seemed.

Frobisher of the Getty Museum, as usual, had sounded like a frightened rabbit and had predictably intoned that "with an evaluation of those dimensions, even the Getty's resources are not inexhaustible." After the proper cajoling, Frobisher promised that he'd at least take a look.

Grundy had counted upon keen enthusiasm from the private collector Baron Otto von Thurn, who had started off with a noteworthy collection of masters assembled by his father and cleverly had quadrupled it in excellence.

"I have coveted that Velázquez for years, as you well know, Peter," von Thurn told him. "But that is a very high price. Oh, I could borrow the money, but then I'd have to pay it back. I spend my income or I sell a painting or two. I don't have a hundred or so million like the Getty, but a fraction of that. Yes, I can raise that with a phone call, but it would finish me. I'll surely come for the fun, but count me out on the bidding."

Discouraging. Or was it a ploy? On the bright side, the German industrialist Kurt Krassner, when told by Sir Peter that his archrival Baron von Thurn would be "definitely bidding," growled that he expected special considerations in examining the painting before he would even think of making a bid. Grundy assured him that he would be accorded the usual VIP treatment. At that, Krassner said he would come to see the Velázquez as soon as possible.

Grundy had no idea what to expect from the idiosyncratic American private collector Robert Symes. He had to discipline himself from laughing out loud when he heard the millionaire's latest quirk. Symes insisted upon speaking in a falsetto whisper, sounding very much like a mezzo-soprano with laryngitis. He explained reedily that his psychiatrist had warned him that certain powerful men unconsciously lowered their voices, attempting to sound as basso as possible, in order to project their "power image"—to the serious detriment of their vocal cords. Symes further surprised Grundy by trying, in breathless, high-pitched whispers, to convince him to remove the painting from sale for "eight million dollars—cash!"

Sir Peter declined graciously, convinced that Symes would bid to ten million, minimum!

After a half-hour of aggressive electronic clickings and broken connections, Grundy was finally able to get through to the chief curator of the Prado, Don José Sánchez. It was merely a courtesy call. The Spanish government would never raise the necessary funds to capture the divinely beautiful mistress of the greatest painter in the history of the country for the Prado—where it properly belonged. Don José confirmed that fact sadly and asked, "How much will she fetch? Only eleven million? She's worth much more. She's on a par with our greatest Velázquez, even *Las Meninas*." Grundy asked if he could use Don José's opinion in publicity releases. Sánchez was reticent, but quickly agreed after Sir Peter told him William's Ltd. would "naturally see to the question of your passage to and from London—and perhaps a few days' sojourn."

One of the most delightful conversations was, as usual, with Count Ciccio Nerone in Naples, who even if rumored to be involved with the Mafia and possibly even the mastermind of a gang of particularly devilish—and successful—art thieves, was scintillating. Whatever else he was, Grundy counted him as one of the most charming and brilliant individuals in the art world. The Count's clear, silvery voice at once brought to mind the physical impression of the man. A strikingly handsome dark face with hair of the deepest black and flashing blue-green eyes, all the more striking because the Count stood barely four feet tall—almost like one of those incredibly handsome dwarfs that Velázquez had portrayed with such a sense of humanity.

Count Nerone seemed to know more about the *Marchesa* than he did. But that was to be expected from Don Ciccio. He of course knew—almost everyone who entertained the slightest interest in the history of art did—that a nude portrait of the same gorgeous woman seen from the back was in the National Gallery in London. He was cognizant of all the details of the attempted theft of the masterpiece from the Richfield estate, and he asked the penetrating question why His Lordship, instead of auctioning the painting, had not made a tax arrangement with the government.

"His Lordship was never tempted by that rational move," Sir Peter explained. "His great-grandfather bought the picture at auction and he, a man obsessed by tradition, was convinced that the next buyer must also go to the free market." Don Ciccio had then quietly asked if the National Gallery would move to block the export of the painting if a foreigner won out at the sale. Sir Peter had hoped that that troublesome question would not arise, but if it did, he had intended to be less than frank. But with Don Ciccio he found it difficult not to be candid. Peter had to admit to the Count that he believed that the director of the Gallery, Roy Bentley, would "move heaven and earth to keep it in England."

Grundy hesitated several minutes before calling Bentley at home. Since school days the acerbic art historian had been jealous of him. Was it Sir Peter's fault that Bentley had failed to receive a knighthood in the most recent list of honors? Why one had been bestowed upon Peter a year earlier was, truthfully, puzzling and perhaps a little unfair. After all, Grundy's two slim volumes on the remnants of English twelfth-century stone sculpture were hardly as significant as being in charge of England's most prestigious picture gallery. But honors lists, as the adage went, were as capricious as changes in high fashion.

"What? Richfield actually is going to sell? Through you?" Bentley responded tightly. "Thanks for the news." It sounded as though he were talking through clenched teeth. "We shall consider our moves, if any. By the way, how much is your assessment? . . . Eleven million pounds?" At this he cackled like a parrot. "Quite ludicrous!"

After Bentley, Grundy called Andrew Foster, the young head of the other National Gallery, the one in Washington, D.C., with far more monetary resources. Foster, who had always reminded Sir Peter of a Cary Grant, was, he was told, "out in the galleries, escorting a delegation of senators." How American! Grundy replaced the telephone and eased back in his chair to reflect upon what he had learned and accomplished by his calls. By God, he muttered delightedly to himself, we might be developing a truly historic sale! He was startled a few minutes later by the harsh jangle of the phone. Andrew Foster was on the line.

"Peter, what's up?"

"I've landed the one you've long been waiting for. You and your distinguished patron," Grundy purred.

"That can only mean the *Marchesa*. What does she really look like? Would I run off with her, as Velázquez did? When can I see her? What'll she bring?"

"Yes, it is the *Marchesa*. Condition, superb. Price? Are you sitting down? You will win it for sure if you are willing to go to twelve million pounds. Then you can run off with her. At least that's how the financial situation appears to me right now."

"My God! Even Jonathan Cresson may not be rich enough for that. You really think the picture will go for more than double the Met's *Juan de Pareja*? That was the only Velázquez we ever wanted. We lost it . . . I shouldn't be telling you this . . . because back then, Mr. Cresson refused to consider paying a dollar more than we'd paid for Leonardo's *Ginevra dei Benci*. That was, confidentially, five million six. But maybe times have changed. Who else will be in?"

"Everybody."

"Even the Metropolitan?"

"Yes."

"Jesus! Why the hell would the Met need another Velázquez? They don't know what they're doing up there. Olivia Cartright's just the acting director. Does she have the clout to pull off something like this? I doubt it. I just can't see the Met in this one."

"Throughout the history of American museums," Sir Peter gently intoned, "as you should well know, young people wanting to make their mark have striven for the finest treasures. I know Olivia Cartright. I'll wager she has the ambition."

"Maybe. But will Ayn Steyne allow her? She calls the shots. And so does Roland McCrae."

"A few minutes ago Mrs. Steyne made what seemed to be a commitment."

"Peter, you're getting to be a master manipulator. When's the sale? . . . Three months? Not much time. I'll let you know when I want to examine the picture. I might fly over on the morning Concorde . . . What? Not before two or three weeks? Why? What do you mean I won't be able to examine it the way I might want? . . . Lord Richfield insists that we can only use a hand magnifier? That sounds somewhat naïve . . . Oh, he'll change his mind. I'll persuade him. See you soon."

How American of Foster to suggest that he fly over on the next Concorde and dash to William's to examine the painting! But, Grundy thought, it was that type of unflagging, matter-of-fact optimism that would take Foster a long way toward winning the prize. Although he abhorred predicting outcomes when it came to auctions—no one knew better than he the complicated twists and turns in the labyrinthine process of a great sale—if he had to choose who the final contenders would be on that tense day so many months away, aggressively bidding each other to the stars, they would have to be Andrew Foster, the Louvre, the Metropolitan, and the German industrialist Kurt Krassner. He hoped so. What theater!

Proceeding from the electrically charged Andrew Foster to a phlegmatic auctions reporter of the London *Times* was like sailing through a summer squall into the tranquil waters of some lagoon in the British Antilles.

"Let me repeat what you told me, Sir Peter," the reporter said in his gravelly voice. "Lord Richfield has consigned for sale, quote, the greatest work of art of the entire seventeenth century still remaining in private hands—the portrait of his lover, the Marchesa Odescalchi, by Diego Velázquez, painted in 1650 on the painter's second visit to Italy, close quote. Richfield's is Velázquez's lover from the front, right? Might I assume that the back's the Rokeby *Venus* in the National Gallery? . . . I expected so. And you say he painted an identical pair for the Pope? And the Pope's pair disappeared, which explains why Lord Richfield's is so valuable . . .The Prado says it's better than any of theirs? Now, there's a nugget! Good. And it is expected that, quote, being the last work of any significance by this grand master available in private hands, the picture—which appears to be in matchless condition—will easily reach the plateau of thirteen million pounds, close quote. Do I have that correctly? . . . Good. Would you consider answering three questions? . . . How did you win out over Sotheby's and Christie's?"

"I worked very hard."

"Will the Americans get this?"

"Not if the others, including Great Britain, work very hard."

"I see. Final question. What's this nude really worth?"

"For the right person, the world."

2 THE CONTENDERS

Tears of anger and frustration welled up in the eyes of Roy Bentley when he finished his conversation with Peter Grundy.

"How I loathe the luck of that man!" He cried softly to himself and sniffled into a silk handkerchief. But by the time his companion had entered the living room with a glass of sherry, he had begun to regain his composure.

"I have the most awful news," Bentley wailed, observing with a penetrating eye the entrance of his lithe young friend.

"What in God's name has happened?" the youth asked in alarm.

"The finest painting still in private hands—a world masterpiece despite its meretricious subject—is going to be sold at that third-rate auction house, William's, Ltd., where that devious Grundy holds sway. I hate him. The painting's a Velázquez, and I'll have to work myself to death convincing the authorities that we must save it for the nation. Just when we were off to Greece. Damn!"

"Why meretricious?" the youth asked, his mouth slightly parted in fascination. "What? No Greece?"

"The picture is of a young woman, said to be the painter's lover."

"And?"

"She's naked, stark naked. An exercise in feminine sensuality."

"Now that *is* meretricious," the young man trilled. "And *you* want this 'masterpiece'? Isn't one nude female by Velázquez enough?"

"It's the same creature. The Rokeby *Venus* is viewed from the back. This one is from the front . . . and, furthermore, it shows her in her bed, getting ready to be porked! But despite all that, the painting's a masterpiece and shouldn't leave England."

"Oh, put up a show to try to get it for the nation and then . . . you know, let some rich American buy it, as usual. How much will it cost?"

"That fat pig Grundy is trying to puff it up to eleven or twelve million."

"No painting of a naked woman is worth *that!* Go through the motions and let someone else buy it—that vulgar, awful Getty Consolidated. Then everyone will scream at them again and it'll soon be forgotten. And on to Greece."

"But will being forgotten bring me closer to the knighthood I deserve? Never!"

"Oh, the hell with this Italian whore. Buy something nice, something Greek—a Greek cherub."

"I run the National Gallery, lovey. Not the British Museum."

When faced with a difficult decision concerning an acquisition, James Waters of the Cleveland Museum invariably withdrew from human contact and closeted himself in his office. In the evening after the museum had closed and the curators had departed, he emerged to wander for hours through the lonely galleries along the exact same route, studying time after time the treasures they contained, as if appealing to the mute works of art for guidance.

He had the full backing of his board and he had the money, but he would need enormous resolve to pursue the Velázquez. Thinking about Grundy's initial evaluation, Waters groaned, the lugubrious sound echoing throughout the empty, bone-white chambers.

Eleven million pounds—and probably more by the time Grundy had stirred up the art market. It was an outrage! Waters could remember a time in the museum profession when the top prices of even the most splendid treasures were in the hundreds of thousands of dollars—certainly not millions. The damnable Metropolitan had ruptured forever the delicate alliance that had long kept prices at their genteel levels. There had been an unwritten, gentlemanly understanding among American museum directors that no one would try to buy any painting, no matter what, for more than one million dollars. The unspoken concordat had worked until the Metropolitan shattered the pact in the 1960s by winning Rembrandt's *Aristotle Contemplating the Bust of Homer* for the record sum of $2.3 million. To Waters, that had been a monstrously stupid— and selfish—act.

But Jim Waters was a hypocrite. He had clandestinely been the underbidder for the *Aristotle.* How he loathed having been sucked into that nouveau riche game!

Painfully, wearily, wheezing from shortness of breath, Waters eased himself onto a wooden bench in the Dutch gallery and contemplated the two Rembrandt portraits he had purchased fifteen years before. They were mediocre. He should have gone all the way on the *Aristotle.* He sighed as he lifted himself to his feet and continued his slow circumnavigation of the empty galleries.

He halted once again, this time in front of a life-sized painting depicting a nobleman holding a glass of wine. *"Unknown Portrait by Diego Velázquez,* Spanish School. Ca. 1638," the label read. It was the only painting by the master in Cleveland's collections. He poked his aquiline nose near the dull, dark brown surface of the large canvas, squinting as he moved his eyes over the surface. The picture had been a bargain at only $560,000. Although the art press had proclaimed it a great discovery, his colleagues knew better and behind his back mocked his attributing the flabby picture to Velázquez.

Deep inside, Waters had to agree. After looking at the painting hundreds of times, he had recently begun to admit—and only to himself—that the canvas lacked the depth of the genuine article.

As he shuffled to his office, James Waters mulled over what he should do about the *Marchesa Odescalchi.* Despite the terrifying evaluation, he had plenty of money. Eighteen million dollars sat in the bank, quietly waiting for acquisitions. Few knew of the wealth of the Cleveland Museum. Being wholly private, the trustees of the institution had been able to keep their financial holdings confidential. He could easily afford the $12 million. But should he spend such an obscene amount? Since he would retire in less than two years, the prudent course would be to avoid the sale and publicly raise his voice against the excesses of his colleagues—as he had always done.

But since his illness James Waters had grown more and more anxious about his reputation. He knew that his peers accused him —never to his face—of not having the courage to pursue a work of art with a passion that transcended any consideration of price. And the bastards were right! Still, had the moment come to relax that conservative image he had maintained so responsibly over the decades of his prim stewardship? Was this the way to enter the history books?

Waters turned the corner leading to the galleries of Japanese painting. In front of him, as if intended to be a message, was a landscape painted by a classic Edo master. He saw instantly how the painter had emphasized his series of deft brushstrokes with a single stroke placed in the opposite direction, making the sinuous movement of the primary strokes compellingly vibrant by the appearance of the reverse stroke. Ah! The *Marchesa Odescalchi*—if it were any good, and if he were to win it—might be that master counterstroke of his career. Yes, why not go all the way? He could afford it.

He smiled with satisfaction as he entered his drab beige office to retrieve his overcoat. Only when he nodded good night to the security attendant did he feel the sharp pang of doubt. Did he have the guts?

Robert Symes settled himself into his favorite deck chair on his patio in Newport Beach, luxuriantly planted with hibiscus in gaily painted Mexican vases, and gazed fondly out toward the Pacific Ocean placid at ebb tide. A pair of bodyguards, stationed like bookends at the flanks of the immense redwood terrace and armed with machine pistols, saluted him. Confident that his universe was in order, Symes stretched back his arms, cupped his hands behind his neck, looked out at the waves, and conjured up an image of the Velázquez.

When was it he had seen it? Nearly fifteen years ago, during a whirlwind visit to the grandiose estate of Lord Richfield with the board of directors of Telecontrol International. The peer, who at the time was serving on the company's British advisory committee, had dragged him off to a dark landing in the country house and pointed brusquely toward a large painting, muttering, "I'll wager that not even your Telecontrol holdings are equal to the value of this beauty."

Symes had squinted in the gloom. A veil of yellowing varnish seemed to mute the surface of the picture like wisps of smoke. Within seconds, however, Symes's eyes had grown accustomed to the darkness, and then the painting came alive. He was taken aback at the animal energy of the young woman, depicted at the moment when her lover was entering her boudoir. He'd turned to Lord Richfield and challenged him, "I'll give you six million pounds for it."

"That's a good offer," Lord Richfield had said. "But it's not for sale—at least for now."

As soon as he had returned to the States, Symes tracked down the man who was considered to be the preeminent expert on the works of Velázquez, Professor Howard Broadbent of the Fogg Museum in Cambridge. Broadbent had listened to Symes's description of his encounter with the Richfield Velázquez and told him, "It should be very, very good. Velázquez painted two pairs of his mistress. The second pair for his patron Pope Innocent X. That spectacular portrait of Innocent in Rome was done at the same time. The Richfield picture must be Velázquez's version for himself, because the Pope's nudes have vanished. The Church probably burned them."

Symes looked at the horizon and sighed. To obtain the painting he knew he would have to go to $12, perhaps $13 million. It was an insane amount of money. But for the man who had everything and who could afford almost anything, why not?

Within moments of receiving the news from Peter Grundy, Kurt Krassner began to pace up and down his suite of offices overlooking the cathedral in Munich, swirling a glass of bourbon and barking orders to his chief aide. Finally he reeled off the names of the world's leading art scholars, curators, and museum directors who would know about the Velázquez and demanded to be put through to them at once.

With each, Krassner lingered on the phone for at least ten minutes. A few of the conversations continued for almost an hour. The German industrialist phrased and rephrased dozens of questions about the picture, ranging from its condition to the nature of its "soul." When he received either a summary answer or an answer he deemed incomplete, he would begin the interrogation again. In posing questions, as in negotiating, he was formidable, which accounted for his meteoric rise as an industrial and communications czar.

Two days later, when Krassner had analyzed the comments, he thought he knew as much as anyone on earth about the *Marchesa* and he vowed to acquire it. The only information he had not been able to pin down was the condition of the picture. Those who had seen it, however briefly, hinted that it was filthy. Yet everyone assumed it was in prime condition—perhaps simply because it had not been in and out of the art market and subjected to a scrubbing each time it was to be sold. Was there anyone who could tell him the true facts?

Suddenly Krassner had a brainstorm. "Get me . . . I have her home phone . . . get me Ludmilla Tcherninka in Moscow, the curator of paintings at the Pushkin Museum. How could I have overlooked her? She was there with Leonid Ermenentov at Lord Richfield's during a state visit to England just before he became Party Chairman. And she once told me about examining the picture for hours. Get her, even if you have to wake her up."

Tcherninka was no longer the curator of paintings but the director of the renowned Pushkin. Her lover had promoted her a week after he had assumed the Party leadership.

Tcherninka was surprised, and flattered, to be called by the German capitalist and was even more surprised when he asked her bluntly, "Where would you place the *Marchesa Odescalchi* among the works of Diego Velázquez?"

She chatted with him for a minute or two about its qualities until, suddenly becoming suspicious, she inquired, "But why do you want to know all this?"

Krassner confided to her Sir Peter Grundy's phone call and the upcoming sale.

"Well, in that case," she said, lowering her voice to a conspiratorial tone, "I must be frank. The condition worried me. It seemed less than impeccable. I suspect the picture may have been relined, rather ineptly, and possibly seriously damaged. I would be very wary."

"I thank you deeply," Krassner replied with feeling.

"Are you going to try to purchase it, Herr Krassner?"

"Your words have given me pause," he admitted.

As soon as she had finished talking with Krassner, Ludmilla Tcherninka slipped out of bed and walked through her spacious living room to a breakfront imported from France by Catherine the Great—a gift from Leonid—and opened a small drawer on the right side. Inside was a telephone with a single red button, which she depressed three times. In a flash the phone crackled and her lover was on the line, speaking in a hoarse, concerned tone.

"Is everything all right? Good. I'm working straight through the night. We are still trying to decide how we should indicate to the new American President—I hate working with the instability you get with democratic governments—what he has to do to bring us to a summit. It's very delicate. I want some advanced technology, but they'll refuse. What do we want that they can give us to persuade us to return to the conference table? I know what I don't want. Remember that wonderful capitalist joke? 'Never accept anything that has to be fed or repainted.' Ha! You have an idea? Something that has been painted very well once and does not need to be fed? Come over at once. What time is it? Only one-thirty? Fine. I'm starved. We'll have a late supper. And I'm starved for you."

As her limousine raced toward the southern gates of the Kremlin she ordered her chauffeur to halt for a few minutes in Red Square so she could watch the final moments of the changing of the guard at Lenin's Tomb. She never failed to be moved by the perfection of the ceremony when the goose-stepping soldiers, bundled up against the chilling wind in their bright crimson-and-gray uniforms, exchanged salutes at the precise moment when the great chimes started to ring in the clock tower. It was theater, of course, but just right. Not too many soldiers, not too many moves. The walk from the gates of the Kremlin to the half-open door of the tomb was a full half-mile. In that was the emotion. How marvelously Russian it was, she thought, snuggling back into the lynx wrap in the backseat of her car.

Over a Kiev stew and a bottle of Georgian wine, she warmed up the cadaverous Ermenentov by describing the sad status of the Pushkin and other art museums. How they were understaffed, never received their fair share of travel coupons to France and Italy, and worst of all, had not in the past decade under the grim late Minister of Culture, Piotr Ilycka, been allowed to acquire a single work of art other than the insignificant remnants of private collections within the Soviet Union.

The Chairman watched the slim, beautiful woman hungrily, only half-listening to her animated words. "I planned to promote you to Minister of Culture this evening. But with this petty tirade, I'm not sure I shouldn't demote you to art lecturer again—where I found you."

He reached up to take her hand in his. She slipped into his lap.

"Do you remember my expression when I looked up from my feet on that tour I had to make when they opened the new museum building and saw your lovely face? How many years ago was it? Fifteen, already. Hmm. And our trips together? Ah!"

"Dearest, England was still the best of them. Remember that vast estate belonging to the Earl of Richfield? And the painting of the nude woman you fell in love with? It is still the only work of art you've ever appreciated."

"That was because she looked exactly like you!" He stopped to laugh and embrace her. "That Gauguin!"

"It's by Velázquez, darling. And you could own it—or at least it could belong to the Soviet Union."

"What fantasy is this?" he rumbled.

"It's for sale." Snuggling closer to him, she described in whispers the impending auction, leaving out for the moment the question of price. "Your industrial reforms are well under way. You have cemented relationships with India and Egypt. The farm problems are being ameliorated. Your secret missile program is flourishing. Now is the time to make achievements in the arts, too."

He kissed her left ear.

"I want the *Marchesa Odescalchi*," Tcherninka crooned softly, yet in her voice there was an echo of steel. "Especially as the new Minister of Culture. It has come time for our great country to compete on the world market for masterpieces. There's not a single painting by Diego Velázquez in Russia."

"Sometimes I think we have too many art museums, too many paintings—most of them dark brown," he growled, then laughed.

She pulled away from him and exclaimed, "What else do our

people have, other than culture? Long lines, bitter cold, hardly enough vodka to drink since your reforms, years of mandatory military service, small and ugly apartments? Where are the longest lines in the Soviet Union? For fresh fruit. And where are the second longest lines? To get into our cultural events!"

Leonid Ermenentov's long face broke into a smile. He relished her anger. He embraced Ludmilla tenderly. Her face was flushed and beautiful and her dimpled ears looked as if they were about to burst into flame. He kissed one, then the other.

She didn't attempt to wriggle free of his powerful embrace. She laughed merrily and nipped him suddenly on the neck. "So, Mr. Chairman, do something 'kulturnyi' for once. Give our people this treasure!"

He stroked her silky brown hair. It was a gentle touch. "Well, how much is it going to cost?"

She told him, expecting an explosion. But he didn't react at all, merely laid his head between her ample breasts.

"We don't have to spend any money to have it," she purred. "Not a cent of our preciously hoarded dollars."

He grunted amorously and a large hand moved to the front of her dress.

"Get the Americans to buy the Velázquez secretly and give it to us. The *Marchesa Odescalchi* can become one of the presents from the Americans to show us they are truly serious about wanting to talk."

His other hand stroked her right thigh under her dress.

Ludmilla hurried on. "Remember what your uncle Leonid Brezhnev used to do with the National Security Adviser? A vague hint and they would give him cars, once even a helicopter, and that splendid yacht. Those gifts were expensive."

He began to unbutton her blouse.

"The gorgeous *Marchesa* will cost them a mere eleven or twelve million dollars. And when you eventually give it to the Pushkin—I absolutely insist it not go to the Hermitage—"

Abruptly he stood up, lifting her effortlessly. He carried her to a large couch and gently put her down. He began to undress her and, as he did, mumbled what sounded like an offhand question. "Are you sure it's as good as you once thought?"

"I trust so!" Ludmilla whispered and then gave out a delighted gasp as his familiar hands caressed her tenderly.

"Trust is for fools." Ermenentov gazed lovingly into her eyes and his voice dropped to a barely audible whisper. "I shall have one of our agents in England ordered to study this masterpiece."

She returned his kiss and reached up for his belt. "Who?" she asked absently.

"Sir Michael Fairless, the art expert."

"Oh, God," she sighed, and planted a long kiss on her lover's mouth and pulled him down beside her.

He pushed himself up on his elbows and looked at her adoringly. "And tomorrow I shall order Ambassador Dvorkin to talk discreetly to William Bass about your Velázquez. We have received some interesting overtures from the Security Adviser in the past month. He seems willing to be kind to us peasants."

Whereupon Chairman Leonid Ermenentov sighed contentedly and turned toward a more pressing agenda.

Andrew Foster did not even attempt to remain cool when he spoke on the telephone to his patron, Jonathan Cresson.

"Well, sir, I just got off the phone with Peter Grundy in London. He's landed the sale of the Richfield Velázquez. Now's our chance!"

Foster paused to listen to the reaction from the philanthropist whose family, second only to the munificent Mellons, had forged the National Gallery of Art into one of the greatest picture collections on earth. Staying very much behind the scenes, Jonathan Cresson had poured $127 million into acquisitions, endowments, educational funds, and conservation laboratories. But to his surprise Andrew found himself listening to a man who clearly had reservations.

"I agree with you that we have to be prudent," Andrew commented smoothly. "I'm afraid the picture—if it's really any good, and no one knows yet since it's been stuck off on an upper floor of that country house for over a century without any responsible art historian being allowed to look at it—I'm afraid the picture is going to bring a lot more than ten million pounds. Grundy says we might get it for twelve . . . Yes, unfortunately, twelve. I agree it's high. Of course we cannot make any decision until we've looked long and hard . . . The competition? I'd say the keenest among private collectors will be Baron von Thurn and possibly Kurt Krassner. I simply don't see Robert Symes at this level. As far as institutions are concerned, we'll have to watch London. Their Rokeby *Venus* is the other half of the twin portraits. Having both will make their collection fabulous . . . Cleveland? Never! Jim Waters spends most of his time attacking those of us who believe in reaching for greatness. I'm convinced that our most serious competition will be the damned Metropolitan. Peter Grundy told me confidentially—not in so many words, but I read between the lines—that Ayn Steyne is committed to buying the picture. The acting director, Olivia Cartright, plans to build her career on this one . . . Yes, I agree we have to be cautious until we've actually seen the picture, but then be decisive."

When he finished the conversation, Foster felt a small wave of anxiety. After years of hearing Jonathan Cresson express his hopes of laying his hands on the Richfield Velázquez, he now sounded fainthearted. It could not be a question of money. The Cresson Foundation earned money faster than Cresson and his trustees could dispense it. Was it simply a failure of will? Or something else? Foster pulled himself up in his chair and straightened his shoulders. He would pull it off. He had never failed before.

Olivia Cartright nervously checked her collar and smoothed her hair into place as she strode from her office down the long hall with its illuminated vitrines displaying objects from ancient Byzantium. The fifteen-year-old fabrics lining the cases had long since faded into an unpalatable streaked yellow-brown. At least a third of the fluorescent lamps were flickering. No one in the department of medieval art had bothered to respond to her month-old memorandum to start cleaning up the mess. That was what happened when you were merely the acting director, she thought wryly. But she smiled to herself when she turned the corner into the Great Hall of the museum. The grand entrance, at least, was still looking fresh. She quickened her pace; as usual she was going to be late. But Don

Ciccio Nerone had called just as she was leaving her office and she couldn't simply tell him she'd have to call back.

His very first words had made her fall back into her chair in surprise. There seemed nothing in the world of art that he didn't know—and long before anybody else. In his lilting voice he had informed her that Lord Richfield had just placed his famous Velázquez for sale at William's auction house and that Peter Grundy was contacting "everybody." He then listed the parties, giving the gist of what was discussed with each one, including the evaluation of $11 to $12 million. The Met chairman had seemed to be particularly interested, he told her, and warned her to expect the subject to be brought up soon—at which time she must be sure to stress that Andrew Foster at the National Gallery wanted the painting badly. Don Ciccio confided parenthetically what Foster thought of her, that she was simply a "librarian" who would go nowhere at the Metropolitan. Olivia bristled. She hurriedly told him that she had to rush off to see Ayn Steyne, thanking him profusely. Once again the Count had come to her aid. What an enigmatic—and manipulative—genius he was!

The chairman of the board of the Metropolitan Museum of Art, and temporary director, was perched at her secretary's side in the outer office, poring over the place settings for the forthcoming gala. When Olivia entered, she looked up, folded her reading glasses, and placed them carefully into their gold case. She gave Olivia a businesslike smile.

"It is so courteous of you, Olivia, to drop everything and come up here. You must be overwhelmed trying to get everything in order for the UNESCO conference. As I am for our gala. God, how I abhor this day-to-day administration. It will be such a pleasure to drop these temporary chores, turn them over to our next professional director"—she shot Olivia a stiff smile—"and go back to my duties as chairman of the board."

"How daunting it must be to arrange these society affairs," Olivia said with a nervous edge in her voice. "With all the politics involved." She waited dutifully while the chairman tended to a few final details with her aide.

"Yes, yes," Steyne said to herself, distracted. "Ah, Olivia, there's a slightly awkward circumstance. I know you will understand. I was going to seat you at my table at the gala. But since we haven't actually voted the directorship, I began to wonder that it might be more prudent—for the moment—for you to be placed elsewhere. Of course, I can count on you to understand."

"Of course."

Steyne ushered Olivia into her spacious office. Olivia was surprised to see that every single vestige of decor that the former director had so cherished had been eradicated—the furniture, lamps, paintings, even the wallpaper. The once-cluttered and cozy room had been transformed into a clinical chamber with a severe desk, only four chairs, and low travertine bookshelves into which a host of files had been crammed. The only leavening notes were a pair of resplendent street scenes by Childe Hassam. Almost without thinking of it, Olivia rapidly committed to memory the complex and variegated brushstrokes. One never knew when such visual information might become useful. It was that sort of unceasing inquiry, seeming like casual study, that distinguished Olivia Cartright from almost all her colleagues. When they seemed to be scrutinizing a work of art, they were missing many of the fine points. When she appeared to be looking at a painting in haste, she was committing every inch of it to memory.

"Make yourself comfortable, Olivia. The news is good—possibly fantastic." Steyne leaned forward in her chair. "But first, are you all prepared for the Paris meeting? You go off within the week, don't you? If you still harbor any lingering anxieties, please dispel them. You'll be fine. I remember the first time I had to face a group of inquisitors—fellow congressmen, actually—at my first hearing. Frightening. But you're well armed; I assume you've done a superb job gathering the facts. These so-called Third World representatives are cowards, deep down."

"I've got most of the facts. But still, I'm a bit nervous," Olivia replied with a wan smile.

"My advice is to prepare, prepare, prepare. Write down and memorize every statement, every possible question, every feasible reply. Make a script. Stick to it."

"I'm afraid my style is more . . . free-flowing."

"Impulsive. That is one of your strengths and occasional weaknesses," Steyne said with a quick smile. "But you'll be fine, my dear," she added. "Now for the news. You of course know of Lord Richfield's Diego Velázquez, the *Marchesa Odescalchi*, the one that was almost stolen a few months ago?"

Olivia nodded. Count Ciccio Nerone had been right on the mark.

"It is said to be one of his best works, painted in Italy," Steyne intoned, her brow furrowing.

Olivia waited patiently. She knew the picture very well, although only from reproductions, having committed the greater part of a semester to studying the *oeuvre* of Diego Velázquez for a graduate seminar. However, with Ayn Steyne it was not politic to appear too well informed.

"As you know, this picture has been sitting in the collection of the Earls of Richfield, inaccessible to outsiders, for several hundred years. Because of that bizarre attempted theft the Earl has decided —rather suddenly, it seems—to put it up at auction. The sale comes up in three months at William's in London. I was told this morning by Sir Peter Grundy and that's why I insisted you rush up here."

"This is incredible. Everyone's been after it for years. I mean, we —the Met—offered to buy this painting from the Richfield family more than once and were always spurned. The story of the picture is very well documented, the Marchesa being Velázquez's lover. The 'verso' image is generally agreed by scholars to be the Rokeby *Venus* in London's National Gallery. The picture has always been high on our 'most desired' list. How thrilling!"

"What do you think the estimate is?" Steyne asked dryly.

Olivia waited.

"Grundy says, and I assume he is exaggerating, that the price may exceed eleven million pounds."

Olivia turned away and gazed out the low arched window onto Fifth Avenue, watching the crowds slowly making their way in the fall afternoon up and down the sweeping steps of the museum. She chose her words carefully.

"The painting has to be classed with Velázquez's greatest—I mean works like *Las Hilanderas* in the Prado. Our *Juan de Pareja*— my God, at half the price, that one shocked the world—is superb, but this is one of the grandest depictions of humanity in all of art. We should fight very hard for it."

"But why do we need six?"

"The oldest museum adage of all is to collect to strength. Six great pictures by Velázquez would make the total far greater than the sum of the parts. It's an exciting prospect."

"Shouldn't the Brits have it?"

"They already have their half. After all, Velázquez painted it for himself, not the National Gallery—either of them," Olivia remarked with a grin.

"Our acquisition funds are seriously depleted, as you know, after the purchase two years ago of those Japanese paintings and sculptures," Steyne said ominously.

"Haven't we almost always been able to raise the funds—even astonishing amounts—when the work of art is incomparable? This is a world-class . . . a Metropolitan-class painting. We have to pursue it. We have a lot of rich trustees," Olivia mused, half to herself.

"And I am one of them, my dear?" Ayn Steyne asked. There was an inkling of frost there. "Well, it *is* a challenge. I'm a little worried, though, considering that last series of acquisitions, which many on the board thought were exceedingly expensive, and our continuing city funding difficulties, plus that boring situation of having to increase staff salaries. Maybe, if we don't increase them too much, they'll understand."

"The staff is loyal. They'll understand. Despite the occasional complaint, they'll all realize the heart of the museum is the strength of our collections. I think I can handle them."

"I do hope that chance will come," the chairman said, patting her on the arm.

"And if we get it, just think of what this will do to the National Gallery! They've been after a decent Velázquez for years. I've heard that Andrew Foster wants to beat us out of this one badly."

"Oh, where did you hear that?" Steyne said, looking keenly at her.

"I mean, I'll bet he does. But this time that famous charm will get him nowhere. Wouldn't he be livid!"

"Assuredly. I have given very careful thought to him," Steyne said with a determined nod.

3 THE "NAKED TRUTH"

LATE SEPTEMBER in Washington can bring days of softness and luminosity unlike any other place on earth. Certain afternoons give birth to cool zephyrs that gently bloom and fill the city with the promise of a spectacular fall. This was such a day. The freshening air found its way into the sun-filled, almost deserted hearing room of the House Appropriations Subcommittee. To Andrew Foster, who had just been called by the clerk for his testimony on his forthcoming budget, a fanfare from nature seemed fitting.

He would easily obtain what he wanted. He had the chairman of the committee in his hip pocket. Leaving nothing to chance, Andrew had spent days assembling the facts for his crucial budgetary presentation, positioning each item carefully on his elaborate checklist. Foster couldn't live without his detailed lists and schedules. He prided himself on his addiction to them, for they helped slow down his hyperactive mind and made his decisions more effective. The only times in his life when he had encountered trouble was when he had reacted in haste or without adequate preparation.

Foster was wearing his "Congress" suit for the hearing, a dark gray pinstripe which his London tailor had assured him had been cut "tight enough for a crisp bit of business, yet loose enough for the scholarly impression." He sat down quickly, locked his eyes onto the faces of the committee members, and began speaking in a firm, well-modulated voice.

"Gentlemen, I apologize for making you turn out just to hear me. But I'll be brief, because by now you all know the gist of my testimony fairly well. Last year the National Gallery was visited by more people from more places in our country—and the world too —than ever before in our history. Our exhibitions did better than the year before, which itself was a record year. Our budget is virtually balanced. Out of the thirty-one million dollars we were voted by this committee last year, we spent all but twenty-seven thousand eight hundred.

"Why did we have a surplus?" he raced on. "Because I insist upon lean-and-mean management. I'm proud to be able to return this sum to the Congress." He paused for effect. "We worked hard to be in the black. You know, just enough to earn your favor—and get good press." He laughed. "And not so much that you'd have to slash our budget next year. I hope you agree with me, 'Put good money after good.' "

William Bulligan Leonard, for fifteen years the senior member of the powerful committee, had been scrutinizing Foster with a look that managed to convey sleepy distraction and alertness at the same time. He twisted in his lofty chair and spoke in a mellifluously hoarse voice.

"Any more revelations like that, Dr. Foster, and the Department of Justice will conduct an investigation. In this town, if you're that straightforward, you've got to be covering something up."

Andrew Foster allowed himself a short respectful laugh. "Something I do not intend to cover up, sir," he added silkily, "is the report about other, nongovernmental funds. All special grants and acquisition funds—two and a half million dollars—were raised from private sources. One remarkable donor must be singled out and that is our chairman, Mr. Jonathan Cresson, whose donations, unique in philanthropy, have ensured that the Gallery will never become a burden for the taxpayer."

"Give Jonathan the blessings of the entire committee, Foster," Leonard murmured in his gruff voice.

"I'll be happy to. Sir, my request for next year is simple. I ask for an increase of only seven percent. We can keep to that. I shall not take any more of your time. I've already given your staff supporting documents. Naturally, I'd be pleased to answer any questions."

The chairman pulled his elephantine frame to the edge of his seat, looked penetratingly at Andrew, and intoned, "The committee thanks the witness for his candid remarks. We've already made our decision based on the material you sent in advance—material which we always receive more quickly from you than from any other branch of the government, I might add. We have a question and a comment. The members of this committee have noticed that a series of highly popular art exhibitions have somehow managed to come to art museums in their districts, generating a lot of good press. Any idea how this came about, Andrew?"

"None at all, Mr. Chairman," Andrew said, chuckling. "Perhaps it was luck. Or maybe someone figured that if each member of this crucial subcommittee received a small but superb art show, it would be tough for him to turn down our budget request—if it was legitimate, of course."

"Second, the statement," Leonard said. "In the thirty-seven years I have had the honor to serve in the House, I have seldom encountered a more forthright spokesman than you. For the record, the committee wishes that the federal government had more like you, even if the government and the fine arts don't often understand each other."

"Sir, I'm honored." Foster scarcely paused before continuing. "The committee members should know that their chairman has shown such knowledge and genuine love for fine art that with a little bit of training he could succeed as one of our curators."

"Well, Mr. Witness, thanks for the flattery. I do believe that great art is the illuminator and preserver of civilization. But back to business. The committee will not vote an increase of seven percent in your operating funds for the forthcoming year."

Andrew's deep brown eyes darted to Leonard's rotund face. What the hell was this? He had observed all the amenities. Kissed all the asses. Flattered. Cajoled. Sent—at considerable expense—the exhibitions to the congressional districts. Had he made a blunder in strategy? Overkill? Was there something in the political winds he had failed to sense? He disguised his confusion with an even greater nonchalance. At the last second, his instinct told him not to comment, but to wait. It would work out as planned. It always did.

"You see, we've already agreed to increase your budget," Leonard said soothingly, "to eight percent. Maybe a few more beautiful shows will come to our constituents. Hearing adjourned."

With that, Congressman Leonard set his ivory-and-silver gavel carefully into its ebony box and began to saunter from the chamber.

Andrew bolted from his seat like a sprinter, slipping through the tangle of empty chairs and past the vacant press table to Leonard's side.

"Sir, I want to thank you warmly—and I need to talk to you."

"Come along, Foster, to my private rooms. I'll be pleased to listen—over a bourbon or two."

"Sir, again I'm honored," Andrew said eagerly. He had heard of Leonard's famous hideaway but had never before been invited. Only the most influential people were allowed in. Congressional hideaways went back to the beginnings of Congress and were parceled out to the most important power brokers, including some whose powers were highly creative. It was said that in the 1920s a bootlegger named Cassidy had been given his own hideaway in order to hand out booze to the appropriate members of the power structure. Later on, Sam Rayburn had one to which he would slip off at the end of the day to discuss affairs of state and sip bourbon with a set of cronies who called themselves the "Board of Education." When Lyndon Johnson became Majority Leader of the Senate, he got his hands on no less than seven offices, a truly imperial enclave that became known as the "Johnson East Ranch."

Chairman Leonard's hideaway, although no "ranch," was by no means a cubicle tucked behind some remote staircase. His was a suite of rooms with vaulted ceilings and a massive window draped in beige satin damask. At one end sat an early American sofa and a pair of Philadelphia side chairs, a Regency coffee table, and two Hepplewhite dropleaf tables worthy of the Smithsonian. There was also a Wooton rolltop desk, a Chippendale gaming table, three television sets, and a nineteenth-century French Provincial armoire. The chamber had beige wall-to-wall carpeting and was decorated with prints of Louisiana wildflowers and a prime Currier and Ives print, *Vermont in Winter*.

Leonard motioned Andrew to the sofa, lumbered over to the bar, and splashed out two sizable bourbons on the rocks. He deposited himself next to Andrew and gazed at him with eyes the hue of prehistoric ice.

"Sir, at the end of November—the twenty-first to be precise—it may be necessary for the Gallery to purchase, at auction, an important painting," Andrew explained smoothly. "It may be expensive."

Leonard sipped delicately from his glass and looked at Andrew Foster noncommittally. "What is this work?" he asked.

As the congressman worked himself more comfortably into his sofa, Andrew edged himself forward and spoke rapidly, not bothering to disguise his excitement.

"Most discriminating people," Andrew said, "agree that the world's most gifted portrait painter was not Rembrandt, or even Leonardo, but Diego Velázquez, who in the mid-seventeenth century under the patronage of Philip IV in Madrid created portraits of the king, his children, dwarfs, workers, and soldiers—all so full of vitality that they pulsate with life."

"From what I have been privileged to see at the Prado, I tend to agree," Leonard commented dryly.

"Of course. Well, Diego Velázquez went to Italy two times. He revered the place because of its antiquity, because of its art, and because he wanted a vacation from Philip's rather somber court. The second time was in 1649, when his reputation in Europe was lofty despite the fact that no one outside Spain had seen his work. But he didn't go to paint. He had been dispatched by Philip with a fortune in gold to buy what he wanted for the royal collections. The best Italian pictures in the Prado today are his choices. When he arrived in Rome artists like Bernini and Poussin were aching to find out what Velázquez himself could do. They tried to get him to show his work, but he always claimed he was too busy to paint."

"Timing, in politics or art, is everything," Leonard observed, getting up to replenish their glasses.

"What Velázquez was angling for," Andrew went on, "was a commission to paint the portrait of the Pope, Innocent X, a member of the Doria family, a middle-aged, imposing man with an exceedingly suspicious personality. But, obviously, no artist could just say, 'Holy Father, I want to paint your portrait,' and snag the commission. These matters were controlled by the most influential committee of the Curia."

"Something like my committee," Leonard muttered.

"Exactly, sir," Andrew hastened to say, amused by the chairman's pomposity. "But how to land that coveted commission? Velázquez decided the only way was to paint a portrait of someone that would be so compelling that Innocent would be enticed. So he turned to his traveling companion and apprentice, a Moor in his early thirties by the name of Juan de Pareja. Juan, with his full face, black-velvet complexion, and eagle eyes, seemed to be a young buck with extra juice flowing in his veins. The portrait would therefore brim with vitality. And, most important, it would be carried off with just a few colors—flesh tones, a deep green doublet, a touch of white for linen cuffs, and a dove-gray background. The best portraits on earth have a limited color scheme. Mr. Congressman, forgive me for straying . . ."

"Young man, this is a vacation compared to the bullshit of politics and compromise that I normally get up here."

"Thank you, sir. Well, Velázquez announced that, like a concert pianist stretching his fingers, he'd dash off a portrait of his companion. Now Velázquez never painted anything quickly in his life. We know from his biographers that he spent days, sometimes weeks, on one tiny fold of clothing, or a nose, or a part of a horse's mane blowing in the wind."

"You don't suppose he'd started on it weeks before, do you?" Leonard asked.

"Right!" Andrew responded enthusiastically. "Then Velázquez pulled off what we'd call a public relations coup. He got Juan to carry the life-sized painting from one artist's studio to another in Rome. Juan would enter striking the same pose as his portrait, keeping his upper body very erect and turning his head and sharp eyes to the onlooker. The reaction was just what Velázquez expected. One report holds that people didn't know who to talk to— the picture or the man—or who would answer. The word spread like wildfire through the city right to the highest echelons of the Vatican. Shortly after, Velázquez landed his hoped-for commission to paint Pope Innocent. And that portrait is close to being the single most thrilling and penetrating portrait in the world. Innocent kept a superb palazzo in the heart of Rome. Today his descendants still live there, but several floors of the palace are now a museum, open a few days a week. The magnificent painting is still there, isolated in grandeur in its own alcove lighted cleverly by a special skylight.

And the pontiff is *alive!* He glowers at you, questioning you, challenging you, humbling you. Magnificent."

"My only regret, my boy, is that we are not just now walking into that museum. This is far better than even your best testimonies," Leonard mumbled, wondering when young Foster was going to bring up the *Marchesa Odescalchi.* He decided to toy with him. "What are you planning to do? Purchase this fine *Juan de Pareja?"*

"Oh, no. It was snatched up some years ago by the Metropolitan Museum of Art for what was then a world-record sum, five and a half million dollars. Damn them!"

"Maybe they didn't play it fair and square."

"They didn't. Somehow—I've always suspected that one of our employees was bribed—they got wind of the precise amount one of my predecessors had decided to bid. The damned Met placed a bid one increment above ours and won. Seems unfair."

"Is the art world really like that?" Leonard exclaimed in a tone of mock surprise.

"Lamentably, yes. Whatever happened, I don't want it to happen again. That's why I need your counsel. Just after Velázquez painted his spectacular *Juan* and his Pope, he painted a double portrait that makes even those masterpieces look a bit lifeless. He had met a woman, a young noblewoman of Rome, the Marchesa Odescalchi—Fiona Maria della Tempesta di Grazia Odescalchi— who at twenty-five was in the sweet ripeness of life. She was gorgeous and sexy, tempestuous, willful, and just a tiny bit dissolute. Fiona was the rage of Rome. Every young noble was panting over her. Dark, velvety hair, startling azure eyes, an ivory complexion, and a body that makes Botticelli's Venus look as dry as an Egyptian mummy."

"How do you know about the body?" the Chairman asked, suddenly coming to life.

"I'm coming to that, sir. Fiona went bats over Velázquez and his remarkable talent. They became lovers. He painted two pairs of unbelievable portraits of his mistress, one pair for him and a second pair which he gave to his patron the Pope. One of the pair—no one knows whether it's Velázquez's or the Pope's—still survives. One picture is in the National Gallery of Art in London and is called the Rokeby *Venus* after the nobleman who acquired her centuries later.

That one shows Fiona lying nude on a bed. Her lovely back is toward the viewer. An angel holds a mirror and you can see her moody face reflected somewhat dimly in the glass."

"And the other?"

"The other one shows Fiona Odescalchi from the front and . . . well, I'll tell you, Mr. Chairman . . . take the most beautiful and sensual and erotic image of a woman you can conjure up in your mind—arousing instant lust, but imbued with great taste—and you have the Marchesa. She's alive. She pulsates. Glows. Her curving neck. The creamy shoulders. Those perfect breasts. The hungry eyes! The soft round belly. The thighs. Ah!" Andrew lapsed into silence, caught up in his own fondest hopes for the picture.

"And?"

"And this painting has also been in England for a couple of hundred years—in the Earl of Richfield's family collection. It's hardly ever been seen. I've only seen it in a photograph. The family, I guess, may have been slightly chary about it, since it is so powerfully earthy. Anyway, it's about to be sold at auction—in a little less than three months from now. The question is, should the Gallery try to buy it—assuming it's in good condition?"

"Why should a nude—even if a bit suggestive—by Diego Velázquez worry you? These days? Pshaw! It seems to me that after what you've told me, it would seem irresponsible *not* to."

"The nudity doesn't worry me at all. That's why I want it. That's why it's great. The same writer who so praised the *Juan de Pareja* wrote privately about the pair, the front and back *Marchesa*s, the so-called Venuses. 'These alone,' he said, 'are the objects of pure desire, the glory of both sacred and profane love, the pristine beauty of the naked truth.' "

"She sounds irresistible," Leonard drawled. " 'The naked truth,' eh? Not bad!"

"But she's bound to be expensive, sir. All the great museums of the world and most of the rich private collectors are going to be in the competition. I want your sage advice on what the reaction might be from the Hill—and the members of your committee—if we do go for it. Of course, all the purchase funds would be privately raised. Not a cent of taxpayers' cash would go into this. But still I'm a bit concerned. I would like you to tell me what the political reaction might be. I'd never do anything to jeopardize our smooth relationship."

"Roughly what kind of money are you thinking of, son?"

Foster had sedulously considered the way he would break the news and had decided on a firm, matter-of-fact approach, a decision arrived at through his conviction that the Congressman would interpret even an astronomical sum to be insignificant compared to the billions he spent annually.

"We plan to bid up to eleven, maybe twelve million dollars," Foster said, almost offhandedly. "We're confident of victory."

Congressman Leonard sat rigid for a moment, as if his image had been hacked into Mount Rushmore. When he spoke, his voice was cold.

"Twelve million dollars for a painting? Even if it is the most artistically naked lady in the world's history? Andrew, you surprise me. I thought you were politically attuned. After spending that kind of money on a single picture—a front-page price—what do you think your prospects from my committee might be next year? Our relationship is strong, yet fragile. Such an impetuous act would never be forgotten. Remember, in politics it's always that one negative move that's indelible. All the good you do is forgotten. You want my sage advice about this painting? Back away from this silly idea. Twelve million bucks for one painting? It would seriously damage the Gallery—and you, my boy."

Andrew thanked Leonard as politely and diffidently as he could and beat a quick retreat from the chilly atmosphere in the room. Jesus, what an unexpected reaction! What the hell was going on?

No sooner had he departed than Leonard splashed himself another generous portion of bourbon and picked up a light blue telephone.

"Roger Bass, please . . . Yes. It's Congressman Leonard . . . Thanks." That was all he needed to say. The boys surrounding the National Security Adviser were always on point. He waited less than ten seconds and there was Bass talking in a low, smooth voice.

"Bill, what's up?"

"Roger, let me tell you about a meeting I just had with Andrew Foster." He spoke rapidly for less than two minutes, then said goodbye. Leonard swirled the bourbon in his glass as he reflected carefully about what he was going to say in his next call. Then he dialed the number of Count Ciccio Nerone at his villa in Naples. The *Marchesa* was just the kind of treasure that would tempt his friend. If it was, perhaps he could talk him out of participating in the sale.

A hush surrounded Jonathan Cresson's mansion as Andrew walked a little gingerly up the meticulously tended brick path. Why was it that wealth and silence always seemed to belong together? Andrew had always been impressed with the quietude which surrounded his patron's immediate environment. It was a serenity that seemed to be associated with not just old money, but the oldest money. The doorbell could scarcely be heard, and the butler opened the door without a sound. The retainer spoke in whispers; even his receding footsteps had a muffled quality. When the front door closed, Andrew heard no slam or click, only a smooth meshing sound of perfectly finished wood against perfectly tooled metal.

Jonathan Cresson himself seemed to speak in a voice of such perfect modulation that Andrew thought he could be listening to a recording of a shadow. It was difficult to become impassioned in the presence of the philanthropist.

Andrew gave a straightforward account of his testimony, at first not mentioning his confidential meeting in William Leonard's hideaway. Then he changed his mind, figuring that Cresson might meet the powerful congressman and hear of his reaction. The decision was fortunate. Cresson listened attentively to his low-keyed description of the exchange, which Andrew had prefaced with the casual question, "Perhaps *you* know, sir, but is Chairman Leonard losing his grip on things?"

Cresson somberly told Andrew that Leonard had telephoned a few minutes before he arrived and had told him the news "sternly and somberly."

"Leonard's negative reaction mystifies me," he admitted. "I admire him for many things. His leadership in the House has been, overall, exemplary. But why should he care to involve himself in the private side of the National Gallery? I hope you'll understand, Andrew, when I say that I do not agree that it was altogether a good idea of yours to discuss with Leonard our possible interest in the Velázquez and the question of money."

"Ah, what do you want me to do now about the Velázquez, sir?" Andrew asked, not quite knowing what to expect.

"We have a professional, even a moral, obligation to explore judiciously—dispassionately—the pedigree and the condition of anything painted by an artist of Velázquez's stature. If the *Marchesa* compares with what some art historians have written over the decades, then we should seriously consider a go at it. The money involved should be the farthest thing from our minds."

"Great!"

"But we should not be impetuous, either," Cresson added somberly. Then he looked up at Andrew and smiled. "This time, though, it would be nice to beat the Metropolitan."

"We simply must!" Andrew burst out. "They have no right to this one. Why do they need another Velázquez? They already have five, plus a possible sixth, a badly damaged sketch. Why are they bothering? They don't have the money. They should get their house in order before they go chasing after another masterpiece. It's pure grandstanding."

"Would it help if I were to talk to some of my friends on the Metropolitan board?" Cresson asked gently.

"I fear that might make them want it more. They're so sensitive up there in New York. Inferiority complex, I think. I would like to suggest spreading a few rumors about the painting."

"Rumors?" Cresson said in alarm and edged back in his chair.

"You should not be weighed down with the details, sir, but I'll get word to Miss Cartright and the Met trustees that the picture is in questionable condition and is dreadfully overpriced. My conservator, Erich Saffern, is exceedingly clever at creating smokescreens. When I get through with them I bet they'll step aside from this particular masterpiece."

"Do what you feel is necessary, Andrew. But don't tell me; don't ask for my specific approvals. It is best that I hear nothing about it. I truly would like to beat out the Metropolitan. Can you make that possible?"

"For sure," Andrew said, feeling elated.

4 FRIEND OR FOE?

THE NEXT MORNING precisely at nine a rolling table, laden with a silver coffee service, croissants, butter, and a crock of orange marmalade, was wheeled into Andrew Foster's spacious office on the second floor of the National Gallery. Besides Foster there were two people—a heavyset man in his early sixties, Erich Saffern, the chief conservator of the National Gallery of Art, and a slender, pretty, auburn-haired woman in her late thirties, Rebecca Holcomb, the director of public relations.

Andrew poured coffee for his colleagues without a word. Finally he looked up and said with mock petulance, "Isn't anybody going to ask how I handled myself at the budget hearing yesterday?"

The two others smiled indulgently.

"Brilliantly. We got our operating money," Andrew said gaily, and then, with a hint of irritation in his voice, continued. "But I utterly miscalculated how Leonard would react to our possible acquisition of the picture. When I mentioned the price he turned frigid. He told me—no, *commanded* me—not to attempt to buy it. He seemed put off by the evaluation. But thank God, Mr. Cresson appears to be staunch. At least he wants us to get to London and study the work. So we've won the first round, I think."

He knelt down before the door of a small refrigerator and extracted a bottle of champagne. Rebecca sauntered over to a closet and pulled out three tulip glasses as Andrew opened the bottle with a whisper of a pop.

"Cheers!" Rebecca said, then turned somber. "I can understand Leonard's reaction. The press will react the same way. In confusing economic times, the price is . . . well, difficult to rationalize."

"But you'll do it, Rebecca," Andrew remarked.

"Of course!" she responded.

"Other than public relations, my concern comes down to two things," Andrew said crisply. "Is it a great work of art, and is its condition superior? That's all I really care about. I suspect that no one in the Richfield family ever called in a restorer to fix it up and thereby ruin it. Presumably William's Ltd. is not planning to clean it on their own."

Foster turned to his chief conservator. "Erich, you've got to get to William's and subject this glorious naked lady to the most intense physical examination possible. As you know, I've got to be in Paris for the UNESCO conference. You'd better get to London and take a preliminary look before I do."

"With the Andrew Foster patented checklist, of course," Saffern replied with a glint of amusement in his eyes.

"Never make up your mind about a work of art without it." Andrew laughed a bit self-consciously.

"Boss, I've committed it to memory," the conservator said, and quickly ticked off the dozen steps. "First, write down your immediate impression of the work. Two, describe it in painstaking detail so that your description will force your eyes over every inch of its surface. Three, find out about its condition, wear, age. Four, did it have a specific use? Five, what's the exact style of the piece? Six, subject matter. Seven, iconography. Eight, the history of the work. Nine, its bibliography. Ten, obtain outside advice. Oh, Andrew, I hope you avoid that step in the case of the Velázquez. Anybody we ask will probably lie to us."

"Right." Andrew nodded somberly. "This time the stakes are too high. But I should interrogate Ulrich Seitz."

"Don't!" Rebecca cut in. "Didn't I read that he was Olivia Cartright's professor?"

"True enough. Well, I'll avoid him too. Let's keep this one totally to ourselves."

"Eleven," Erich Saffern continued. "Scientific analysis. Name the results obtained from all scientific investigations, including microscopy, chemical tests, X-ray, infrared, ultraviolet, spectographic analysis, thermoluminescence. Then, finally, twelve, go back to your first impression and if it holds up, go for it!"

"Bravo!" Andrew said, raising his glass.

Saffern's face fell and he added gloomily, "But this time it looks like item eleven will have to be scratched. I just got some rotten news about an hour ago. The Earl has confirmed to William's Ltd. that *no* prospective client may examine the picture with anything more sophisticated than a . . . a Boy Scout magnifying glass. And when you told me about the sale I pored through all the literature on the picture and there's not a published word about its condition."

"Erich, we'll have to get around that restriction. It's downright ludicrous."

"Unhappily, it's serious. The Earl told Sir Peter Grundy—with considerable relish—that nobody is to be allowed to get his 'grubby scientific equipment near my picture.' " Saffern allowed a fleeting smile to cross his morose face. "We'll all feel a lot better if we can study the painting thoroughly—every millimeter of it."

"What do you think of the story that Velázquez painted two nearly identical pairs of portraits of his mistress? One pair for him and another for the Pope?" Andrew asked.

"The story may be nothing more than a tantalizing legend. Who knows? It's always been said that there are no replicas made by anyone else, the portraits being so spectacular that copyists avoided them. Can we believe that? Anyway, whatever the Richfield painting is, it won't be some obvious copy."

"But has it been wrecked?" Andrew probed.

"Unlikely," Saffern replied. "But I'd sure like to clean enough— or you do it—to be sure that nothing's been repainted. And of course it'd be nice to get the painting out of its frame to be sure it's never been relined. If it has, you don't want it. Who needs a flattened Old Master—even if she's got nice thighs? How the hell are we going to accomplish this with Richfield's stupid ukase?"

"Perhaps I can make a stronger appeal to Peter Grundy," Andrew said brightly. Then his voice fell. "No. That won't work. He'll keep his word to Richfield. He would have agreed to anything to land this picture. I know the Earl is regarded as something of an eccentric, but this is downright bizarre! I'll just have to deal with his Lordship face to face."

Erich Saffern edged toward the door. "I've got to X-ray one of our masterpieces—it has a runny nose." He paused. "Look, Andrew, so much will be riding on the condition of the *Marchesa*. Without substantial time and the right equipment, it'll be like conducting a heart bypass operation by candlelight—with a spoon."

"We'll find a solution," Andrew said soothingly. "If not, I may have to do it his way. On second thought, perhaps I'd better go to London first and pave the way for you. If the damned restriction holds up, I may have to examine it myself."

"Maybe so," Saffern said with resignation.

"Erich, I could try a trick. Is anything available on the market which looks like a simple hand loupe but is actually exceptionally powerful?"

"I think—"

"You'd get caught," Rebecca interrupted anxiously. "My God, the publicity!"

"Yeah, better not to play games," Saffern agreed, and winked slyly at Andrew. "Andrew, I'll brief you carefully on what to do."

Andrew smiled broadly at him.

When the door had closed Rebecca burst out, "You must be careful! Please! Frankly, I'm worried. But . . . it's not about the Velázquez. I'm worried about the Met directorship . . . that you . . . After all the years of working with you here, I think I deserve to know if you're about to leave us. Has their search committee approached you yet?"

"No, and I doubt it ever will," he replied casually. "It's obvious that they want Olivia Cartright. Anyway, I bet there'll be no decision until after the sale."

"I hear a lot of talk that they've got you in their sights and the auction will be the proving ground between you and her. Would you consider directing the Met, Andrew?"

"Sure," he said candidly. "And you know it. I like my job; I love the Gallery. I adore working for Jonathan Cresson. Yet . . . "

"Getting restless after ten years?"

"Unchallenged. When you think of how slack the Met had become under that Brit! Imagine what I could do to jazz the place up!"

"They'll be in touch, I'm sure of it. Of course, it might be only a maneuver, a game to get you to back off from the Velázquez."

"I've thought of that too. But I'm on my guard, I assure you."

"Ha! Those three little words. Whenever you say 'I assure you,' I know you're worried."

"After so long, I guess you do recognize my quirks. You see, I want two things—very badly. I want the Met, and I want the Velázquez. If it's the picture it's supposed to be, getting it will be the capstone of my tenure here. Oh, why didn't I just go over a year ago to England and offer Lord Richfield the world? Damn. Yet I fear both the Met and the picture may be out of my reach. Too many uncontrollable factors."

"Not for you. That nimble mind of yours will come up with something." Rebecca sensed it was time to go. She became kittenish. "I have a neat solution. Entice Olivia Cartright into buying the painting at a frightful price. You know, just bid her up and then let her get it. They'd throw her out of the Met and you could take over."

He chuckled. "Not bad."

"Better than if you win it for us and then go to the Met," she added.

Andrew grinned.

"Or you could seduce her. She's actually pretty attractive, deep down there somewhere. As a pro I can tell you, she's marketable."

"God, Rebecca! I've met the woman only once, two years ago or so, at one of those boring museum conferences. She seemed mousy to me. I've always thought of her as kind of a librarian. But she's smart, I'll give her that, and she's got a good eye. She's lucky too, and enigmatic! One of the biggest mysteries in the museum profession is how she tracked down—while only a graduate student at Berkeley, for Pete's sake—those two incredible miniatures by Antonio Pollaiuolo, the ones that had, apparently, been stolen by a member of the Wehrmacht during the German retreat from Florence in 1943. Somehow she heard that some guy in California—he later turned out to have a pronounced German accent and had come into America through Canada—had these two paintings. She tracked them down, then told the FBI, who returned them to the Uffizi."

"A P.R. dream," Rebecca mused.

"She refused to talk to the press. Puzzling."

"Shy? Can't be."

"I wonder."

"If I were she I'd be shy and avoid going to the UNESCO conference," Rebecca said. "Will she really show up?"

"She has to. And it's going to be rough for her. One of the Third World delegations—India, I think—is going to take her apart for some works of art the Met supposedly imported illegally. There's a move afoot to nullify that retroactivity clause in the old treaty against smuggled art."

"A great story! Should I exploit it? Andrew, where did you hear it?"

"From one of the Met's trustees who happens to be Olivia Cartright's strongest ally. Let's think of a way to use the story to embarrass the Met. That will make it more difficult for them to chase after the Velázquez."

"Andrew, I find it surprising that a trustee of the Met—and her confidant—would talk to you."

"He's a friend of our family and a hopeless gossip, that's all. Bruce Thompson's his name. I'm hoping that in an unguarded moment—he's always unguarded—he'll spill to me what the Met plans to do about the Velázquez. With a sense of keen anticipation, I wait. Maybe he'll even tell me tomorrow night at the gala. All set for it?"

"Am I! It's the most chic party of the season!"

"The perfect place for me to sow a few seeds of doubt about the Velázquez."

"Watch out, my friend. You are not what I would characterize as a consummate schemer."

"Just you wait. Maybe I'm not as pure as you think I am. People in art seldom are," he observed.

With a laugh Rebecca slipped out the door. "That I can assure you," she said gaily.

Andrew Foster didn't relish telling lies to Rebecca Holcomb, but he had pledged not to say a word about the secret visit from Ayn Steyne. The contact had been made only two days before through his family's lawyer, Oscar Brentwood, an elder statesman and fixer in Washington's legal circles. When Brentwood had politely summoned him to his elegant offices on Constitution Avenue for "discussion and a cup of tea" Andrew figured it was a routine matter —probably nothing more serious than updating his will, a chore that Brentwood attended to flawlessly every six months, for Andrew's good and for his own. As principal executor, his stake in the estate was considerable.

When Andrew strolled into Brentwood's private suite, he'd been astonished to hear the lawyer intone, "Andrew, there's someone to see you. Ayn Steyne. Of course, you know her. She wants to have a little chat. Take all the time you want, son. My assistant will stick around to see you out."

To Andrew, Ayn Steyne—pronounced Staynah—in her early sixties had to be one of the most imposing-looking women on the scene—a testimony to what presentation could do for one. Hers was human theater without bombast. Her carriage, the way she entered a room, delivered a clarion message, one that trumpeted, "I am wealthy, powerful, and confident, the majority stockholder and chief executive of the largest privately owned oil company in America. Socially, I stand on the summit. I am an author, former member of Congress, connoisseur of art, and a widow relieved never to have to submit to marriage again."

"Dear Andrew, delightful to see you again." She spoke the formula with convincing warmth. "Was fun dining with your father two evenings ago. Regaled me with your triumphs at the Gallery. Told me you've forged a close relationship with my former colleague, Bill Leonard. Bill's aging. Parkinson's disease. Didn't you detect it? He has hidden it so well all these years. It's accelerating. So sad. Have you ever considered a career in politics? You'd be good. You seem to have just the right mixture of boyish charm and Machiavellian cunning to capture the voters."

Andrew listened, amused at her telegraphic manner of speech. People had made fun of the affectation many times, but never to her face.

"Politics is what I'm here for now," she went on. "Call it an interim assignment for you. What I am going to say is unofficially official. You will hear my words, but they were never uttered. You know the rules. The search committee of my board wants to know if you would consent to a serious interview for the job of director of the Metropolitan."

"Mrs. Steyne, I've heard fairly recently that you've already decided upon Olivia Cartright," Andrew responded stiffly, annoyed with himself that he couldn't sound at ease. "Why another interview?"

"Olivia *is* still a candidate. I'd guess that the eternally indiscreet Bruce Thompson has already broadcast the word about her status to you. He has become a little . . . well, taken with her. But frankly, some members of the search committee have doubts about her. And I do too. They raise questions about her social background. They are not sure about her ultimate effectiveness. You see, she . . . she lacks those invaluable family contacts—the grease for the museum wheels."

"And I have 'grease'," he said, unable to suppress a grin.

"And I personally worry if Olivia has the proper administrative skills. Having had to take day-to-day charge of the Met has taught me that it's thousands of nagging, petty, administrative details every day. She strikes me as being more, in a sense, creative. A perfect curator. Perhaps she should be relegated to a warm, friendly place on the academic shores of the institution."

"Banished?" he asked.

"Oh, that sounds awful. I don't mean it to sound like banishment."

"It does a bit," Andrew observed.

"You see, my board wants someone antithetical to our former director, that highly praised, self-destructive British fool. Many of us are not altogether unhappy he died. The board wants someone capable of infinite toughness. Someone skilled in . . . well, the right sort of manipulation. With all the scholarly degrees, of course. And a politician to boot, a canny guide to lead us through these hard times of art popularization and museum marketing—in the right way, you know, bending, not bowing to the public. Above all, someone with what the French call *grand goût*."

"By *grand goût*," Andrew drawled, "do you mean someone who can acquire the *Marchesa* for you? You can't be serious about making a play for it."

"We're always keenest when it comes to quality," she answered.

·51·

"I'd be cautious about being tricked into spending such a ridiculous sum for a questionable picture."

"Questionable?" Ayn Steyne's eyebrows lifted.

"What else can you call a canvas that every conservator who knows anything at all swears has been severely overcleaned and possibly overpainted in the decades it's been in the possession of the Richfield family."

"Goodness. I hope we will always exercise caution. Are you sure?"

"Things are not always what they seem to be in the art world. Just ask Olivia Cartright. See if she's totally convinced that this painting's in matchless condition."

"Fascinating!"

"Do you personally want me as director, Mrs. Steyne?"

"It's not only up to me. I wish it were," she remarked. "But what you just said about the Odescalchi portrait would convince the trustees you'd be the perfect leader for the Met. The picture is very much on our minds. I assume it's on yours and Jonathan's minds, as well. We have made no firm decision about it . . . perhaps except for one."

Andrew cocked his head in interest.

"That's, in part, why I'm here. In an unusual procedure, the three steering committees of our board—the executive, the acquisitions, and the ad hoc search committee—convened together. They've decided the following. Unless intense examination proves the Velázquez to be a disappointment, we will attempt to buy it. At the same time—during the attempt—we shall examine the conduct of the two people who are on our 'short list' for the directorship— Olivia Cartright and you. By the way, Olivia knows nothing of this plan."

"Not telling Dr. Cartright? Is that an ethical thing to do?" Andrew found himself asking.

"I find it painful to go around her back, to talk to you and others. But I excuse this behavior by telling myself that we already know she wants the job. She even sent us an official letter. I admire that. That was politically skillful. Made her candidacy a women's rights issue. The board does not yet know of your interest. That's why I was instructed to meet with you."

"Mrs. Steyne, Ayn, I am . . . very interested in the job," Andrew said a bit hesitantly.

"Good. All I want is to settle this. I want to go back to being chairman. I'm convinced you are exactly what we need, a proven connoisseur *and* administrator. It's my task to see to it that a new director is named—and fairly quickly. I'd look upon that as one of my major accomplishments. Whether you or Olivia. Truly."

"I must discuss this with my patron," he injected softly.

"Oh, please don't do that yet," Steyne implored. "Don't rock the boat. Talk to the committee. Then decide. Then tell Jonathan."

"Perhaps that is the way to handle it."

"I'm positive of it."

"All right."

"Andrew, I'm so happy that you're coming to the gala."

"Wouldn't miss it. Even if I know I'm not going to enjoy myself," he went on gallantly. "It's not much fun for a rival museum director to show up at an exhibition of treasures pledged by your donors and see what my institution can never have."

"The material pledged is satisfactory. Yet, frankly, it could be better. With the right person at the helm, perhaps more illustrious pieces could be garnered—even from your family's magnificent holdings."

"At the moment, that's for my father to decide."

"You must understand that, normally, I would have had you at my table. But under the circumstances, because of our professional interest in you, I must keep my distance. At a time like this, image is everything."

"Now that's the truth," Andrew mused.

5 PLEDGE NIGHT

Gaylord Smythe, the chief of operations at the Met, fluttered like a hummingbird among the tightly packed, ornately decorated tables filling the great Medieval Hall, darting his bony face nervously close to a napkin—was it folded just right?—or seizing a champagne glass to assure himself that not the slightest smudge cast a shadow on his well-deserved reputation for arranging the best parties in the museum world. All the while he chattered brightly to Olivia. She followed the tall, lean, birdlike man as best she could, cherishing his monologue.

"I look frantic, but I'm not," he was saying. "I'm like a racehorse waiting for that clang . . . I'm not nervous, just pumping myself up. The gala! The parties! Around here they say the museum's three missions are to collect, protect, and educate. No, no, no, no, no . . ." he muttered like a metronome. He paused as he spotted a fleck on a napkin. He clutched the offending napkin and, with more theatrics than real annoyance, threw it on the floor.

"Boys!" he screamed. "Replace *all* these napkins. Chop chop!" He smiled in satisfaction to see the team of three busboys hurrying over.

"No, it's not art, not exhibitions, and certainly not education that are the Met's most important duties. Olivia dear, parties are more vital than them all. I mean, one of our newest—and richest—trustees confided in me just the other day that 'the art may be a key part of the museum, but the parties are *serious*.' Absolutely said that, and what's more she's right. You'll learn, my dear, that our august Metropolitan excels in everything—it has three million works of art and a million and a half square feet of building, et cetera. But the very best thing it does is throw parties. That is my—and now your —sacred duty. It's my job to see that not an exhibition is opened, acquisition made, catalogue published, article printed, gallery refurbished, wing constructed, lawsuit settled, painting cleaned, pot repaired, fund raised, curator promoted, or employee retired without a party—masterfully arranged by me."

Suddenly seeing that a waiter had brushed a tray against one of the towering floral displays, Smythe dashed over and with the help of an assistant inched it a few centimeters away from the path leading to the kitchen.

"And our gala. What can I—or any poet—say about it?" His voice rose to a triumphant contralto. "In America—no, in the whole world—there's nothing grander, more devastatingly chic, elegant, arrogant, slick, and famous than our Pledge Night Gala!" His voice fell to a whisper. "The gala, as Cole Porter put it, is 'the tops, it's the Tower of Pisa'! And *I love it!*"

Bathed by searchlights and the multicolored spotlights cleverly concealed on the roofs of the apartment houses across Fifth Avenue, the imposing Neoclassical façade of the Met shone like the setting of an opera at the Baths of Caracalla. But the museum's gala was even more grand than opera, combining music, action, and a cast enlisted from every important level of high society, including a sprinkling of those who hoped to be and those who acted as though they were. Specially flown in at the museum's expense were two "Serene Highnesses" from tiny but currently fashionable kingdoms in Europe and Africa, a genuine prince of the Netherlands, albeit a junior one, and hordes of British lords and ladies. In addition, there was, at their own considerable expense (since they would soon be asked pointedly to contribute large sums), a platoon of captains of American industry and finance. Plus more national, state, and local politicians than anyone would care to know. And bands of actresses and actors, scores of fashion models, and an outrageously garbed rock star who also happened to have a Ph.D. in art history.

Every entrance was grand. The chosen swept up the stone steps, past crowds of gawkers, and through the brightly polished bronze portals of the museum. Dozens of photographers and television journalists lined the "route of honor" to record the pageantry. Who had been invited, and who had not, was reported with portentous seriousness by a New York City weekly magazine which touted its special insert as "the only reliable Social Registry in the United States."

Assessing the throngs of guests with a knowing smile upon her face was Connie Winthrop, anchor of United Broadcasting's top-ranked morning show. She stood directly in the center of an empty circle among the anonymous onlookers carved out by a pool of sun-guns. She listened intently to the instructions from her producer, nodded, and waited for the commands that would initiate the ritual.

"Do we have speed?" the producer called out.

"Rolling," the sound man responded.

"In three, Connie dear," the cameraman said. "Dear heart, just move a couple inches to your left. Super! Now the arch and that banner frames your gorgeous face. Okay, give it to me. Three . . . two . . . one . . ."

Connie Winthrop nodded her head slightly, licked her lips, looked down for a split second at her script written in Magic Marker on a large cue card placed in front of her feet, and gazed into the camera with a grave expression.

"In the most exalted worlds of high art and high society, there is no pinnacle higher than the gala reception and dinner for the donors at the prestigious Metropolitan Museum of Art here in New York City. As an arbiter of the city's social life confided to me earlier this evening, 'If you are invited to the grand opening of the opera, you know you have arrived. If you are invited to the reception at the Donors' Gala at the Metropolitan Museum of Art, you know your children have arrived.' "

The journalist paused. The producer felt the chill of pleasurable anticipation. It was the beginning of her signature move, a physical "ad lib" adored by her audience. She looked down as if in reflection, turned back toward the towering façade, and then, languidly, faced the camera.

"But if you are invited to the reception *and* the dinner of the Metropolitan Donors' Gala, then you can be certain . . . your *grandchildren* have arrived."

The last words came out in a throaty, intimate whisper, as if she were speaking to a lover in the confines of her bedroom. It was a devastating performance, made even more stunning because, after waiting a few seconds, the camera still rolling, she repeated the routine precisely the way she had first done it, down to the most minute moves—"just to be sure," she said to her producer.

"Beautiful, Connie," he said in genuine awe.

"See you," Connie Winthrop said perfunctorily. "They're starting to come in. I've got to change for cocktails, do some interviews, and change again before dinner. I am a bona fide guest too, you know," she added archly.

The producer turned to his crew and drawled, "Follow her closely inside, for maybe three, five interviews. Get some close-ups of the artworks. Then the *pièce de la pièce*."

"Will I get the hell outta here by two or three in the morning?" the assistant cameraman piped up.

"Sure, sure," the producer assured him.

"What's this *pièce de la pièce?*"

"The dinner!" the producer brayed.

"I eat?"

"You don't eat. You film. The cream of New York society."

"Where are you going to be?"

"In black tie. Along with Connie."

"Any hard-news stuff?"

"Forget it. This is strictly a society bash."

Within ten minutes Connie Winthrop had changed into a black cocktail dress and was studying her notes for an interview with the chairman of the Metropolitan.

Ayn Steyne greeted the television star warmly—and a little warily. "Connie, seeing that you were able to come to our little affair assures me of a success."

"Ayn, how sweet of you! How proud I am to be at the party of the year! Now let me explain what's up. I want to run this tomorrow morning. It's a pure puff piece. Are you ready?" She cocked her head at the cameraman and ordered, "Now!"

Turning to Ayn Steyne she said smoothly, "It appears that anybody who has attained great stature not only in the world of art, but in politics, literature, science—I recognized two Nobel Prize winners entering your portals a few minutes ago—has been fighting for an invitation to the Donors' Gala for a year. Do you agree that this is the event that virtually defines today's high society?"

"Ah, Connie, thank goodness 'high society' no longer exists in our egalitarian world. I, for one, am delighted. When I entered the Congress that part of my life was set aside forever. We at the Met are not concerned with society. What we stress at this function—which we call 'Pledge Night'—is the profound responsibility of individuals who have earned a certain position in life and the unselfish obligation of our great friends to share their treasures with the people. You see, the people really own this institution. The common man . . ."

"Cut," Winthrop said. "Ayn, give me that once again. Be more succinct, faster. I need to come back after a sentence or two. You needn't refer to your term in Congress, I'll handle that in my voice-over intro. Also, Ayn dear, stay away from the term 'common man.' Seems a touch condescending."

"I understand," Ayn Steyne replied metallically, and after a nod from the correspondent faced the camera confidently and spoke in a lively tone of voice. "Connie, this is the night that we in the museum call our 'Pledge Night.' It is when all the closest friends of the institution—old and young, wealthy and of modest means—pledge to donate beautiful works of art to this, the people's museum. So generous. So unselfish."

"What are the highlights?"

"A divine Monet that we've been hoping for years to acquire. And a magnificent Rembrandt drawing that a member of our Junior Council purchased for practically nothing last summer in England."

"If it is possible to say, Madame Chairman, what would be the approximate value of all the works of art given this Pledge Night?"

"Let us say, many millions of dollars. I always cringe when I have to translate fine art into monetary terms."

"Thank you, Mrs. Steyne," Connie Winthrop said, then turning toward the camera with a dazzling smile: "I agree. When it comes to creativity, money does seem so vulgar. Art exists to enrich our lives, move us, and make us all better human beings. I thank you, Madame Chairman. And best of luck for your next Pledge Night."

She turned to Ayn Steyne. "That's it."

Then she leaned over to whisper something in her ear and stealthily signaled the cameraman to start rolling. "Oh, I must ask a private question of Mrs. Steyne, who's also a member of the museum's prestigious board of trustees. I'm sure that the whole world would like to know if you are going to be a contestant in the sale of what is, I suppose, the world's most risqué masterpiece, Velázquez's now world-famous naked lady."

Steyne, taken aback, managed nevertheless to disguise her reaction. She gave a small shrug and, in a stage whisper, replied, "She is amazing, isn't she? I imagine there's not a front page of a newspaper on earth that hasn't shown her—"

"*All* of her . . . or a television program that hasn't, either," Connie Winthrop interjected. "And I'm proud to have been part of the scoop we at United Broadcasting achieved. Are you going to bid on the painting?"

"There have been discussions," Steyne said contemplatively. "But I'd be rather surprised if my board felt that strongly. You see, we already have five paintings by Diego Velázquez. But we shall see."

Winthrop turned to the camera. "So, folks, we wait. Whatever happens, you can be sure you will get the news first from UBC. Now let's have a look at some of the works of art at Pledge Night."

She smiled into the camera until the cameraman said "cut," then turned toward Ayn Steyne. "I hope you'll forgive me. You pulled it off so brilliantly. As you always do. Please forgive a girl doing her job."

"Darling Connie, if you hadn't asked me a few of your tough questions I would have thought you'd lost your touch."

"Seriously, what about the painting? Of course, I'll tell no one. And what about the next director of the museum? Have you made up your minds?"

"The board's still working away. It's so terribly difficult in these hectic times. We're still ruminating. But just between us, we are going to let the Velázquez go by. The price will be horrendous. We are deeply concerned about what will no doubt be frightful publicity regarding the price."

"Of course, dear Ayn. But be sure to call me when you've made up your minds. See you at dinner."

Andrew Foster and Rebecca Holcomb had walked the gauntlet, smiling at the frantic efforts of the throngs of photographers and television crews to commit them to posterity. The guests, Andrew had to admit, were the most dazzling group of real and fake achievers he had ever seen gathered in one place. He was proud to say that he knew most of the authentic ones personally. As he wended his way through the Great Hall he cheerily greeted America's most gifted cancer surgeon chatting with Brazil's most prestigious plastic surgeon, who, Andrew knew, quietly devoted most of his prodigious earnings to operating on the deformed poor of his nation, waved familiarly at a recent Pulitzer Prize winner in nonfiction, laughed at the jokes of the garrulous executive director of Off Broadway's most sophisticated theater ensemble, conversed for several minutes with a painter who was touted as the "hottest talent to hit SoHo in years" and who was virtually dead to the world from cocaine, and halted to exchange a few words with Bruce Thompson of the board of the Metropolitan.

"Andrew, always nice to see the competition writhing with envy at our treasures," Thompson said with a sly smile. "Heard of any fascinating things on the art market?"

"By fascinating things on the market, do you mean the Velázquez?" Andrew challenged. "They say it's incredible. Yet I have my doubts. I truly wish it is as it seems to be."

"Meaning?"

"How could I dissimulate with you? I'm very, very keen on trying to acquire the picture, but I'm edgy about its physical condition. You've heard about the restrictions Lord Richfield has placed on its examination? Why, I ask you? Is there something wrong with the painting? You know our conservator Erich Saffern. Well, Erich has an old friend at one of the other auction houses—I can't reveal the name—who swore that after examining the picture, he advised his company to pull out."

"Something a loser would obviously say," Thompson said with a small sigh.

"My first thought too," Andrew said in a tone of sincerity. "But, then again, what if there really is some sort of hidden problem? But the Met doesn't have to worry. With your strengths in Veláz-quez."

"Strength to strength, as they say in the collecting world."

"How's Olivia doing?" Andrew asked abruptly, to Rebecca Hol-comb's surprise. "I understand she's your candidate, Bruce. When are you guys going to make the announcement?"

"I consider her one of the more brilliant young persons in the museum business—along with you, Andrew," Thompson intoned.

"Indubitably," Rebecca muttered.

"It's just a matter of weeks before the search committee makes the formal announcement," Thompson added casually.

"Really. I thought the board was still looking," Andrew said breezily.

Thompson's face turned the color of faded vermilion and, abruptly excusing himself, he hastened away.

Ayn Steyne really has managed to bottle him up, Andrew thought with pleasure.

"Well played, Dr. Foster," Rebecca whispered into his ear. "The doubt you just injected into Thompson's brain might just last for-ever."

"Bruce is sure to pass along the good word."

They threaded their way through the series of chambers jammed with art treasures. Andrew scowled at the massive accumulation of works, muttering that "numbers alone don't mean much." He re-marked to Rebecca that if he were in control, he'd put the brakes on accepting every gift that came through the doors of the mu-seum.

"For example, why did they bother with that!" He pointed to a bronze ewer in the shape of an eagle. The label claimed it to date to the High Renaissance. "That's crazy! It's late seventeenth cen-tury—and third-rate. Hmph!"

"Is this any good, Andrew?" Rebecca asked, gesturing to a pair of small gold earrings in the shape of antique ships, each with full sails pulling a single mast forward and a dozen minute crew mem-bers struggling to maintain equilibrium.

Andrew peered closely at the two pieces. His lips pursed. "Magnificent. I'll bet they were recently smuggled out of Greece. The Met is walking a very fine line with their antiquities."

The galleries were all but empty as Andrew and Rebecca Holcomb strolled through. At truly grand openings, almost no one bothers to look at the art. The need to be seen at the reception and to exchange rumors is far more compelling.

"Why the hell would the Met be interested in yet another Corot?" Andrew snorted, and ambled over to examine the painting of the Isola Tiburina. "Damn! It's very, very fine!"

Out of the corner of his eye Andrew noticed a tall woman stride into the gallery, and became instantly alert. Lean and athletic young women especially appealed to him. It was Olivia Cartright. He studied her closely as she walked toward him. Good carriage. Long, straight back. Long legs. Sleek. But merely a vision of sleekness. Otherwise the young woman was plain and pure. Purity and plainness. That could be a formula for a certain attraction.

"Olivia Cartright!" Andrew called out, and introduced himself. "We met several years ago at a conference. This is Rebecca Holcomb, our public relations officer. We've been studying some of your pledges. Nice Corot."

"Thank you very much, Mr. Foster," Olivia replied hesitantly. "That's one of the few things I personally had something to do with. I begged for months before the donor gave in. Would you have selected it?

"Frankly . . ."

"Andrew Foster!" The voice penetrated the gallery like a dagger. Connie Winthrop sailed into the room, decked out in an orange organza evening dress that teetered on the brink of gaudiness. "Andrew Foster, you must give me an interview!"

He grinned. Olivia watched the approach of the star with what looked like anxiety. Winthrop walked over to Andrew and gave him a peck on the cheek, keeping her back turned to Olivia. It was obvious that the network journalist had a fine sense of the museum power structure.

"And Olivia Cartright too," she trilled, turning and shaking Olivia's hand. "Here comes my crew. I hope I can have a double interview."

Winthrop jockeyed Andrew and Olivia into the position she

wanted, very close together, but angled in such a way that they seemed to be at odds.

"Perfect," she muttered to herself. "How's it look?" she asked her cameraman.

"Not bad. Tell the lady to cheat a bit to the left. Turn her to a forty-five-degree angle. And, lady, when you're looking at the guy, look past him."

In the blinding light of the sun-gun, Andrew was a bit surprised to find himself thinking that Olivia's skin was remarkably milky.

Facing the camera Connie Winthrop intoned, "I have with me two of the most brilliant—and dedicated—rivals in the entire world of museums, famous Dr. Andrew Foster of Washington's National Gallery and the brains behind the Met, Olivia Cartright, whose name comes up daily as the leading candidate for the awesomely important post as director of the Metropolitan."

Wheeling around to Olivia, she launched two arrows. "Do you expect to be named director? And do you feel you could do it? As a woman?"

Olivia replied nervously, "I'm afraid I am going to appear un-communicative, but that is a question only my board of trustees can answer."

Connie Winthrop quickly changed the subject.

"The Velázquez nude. Are both your institutions going to be rivals at the sale? What do you feel about a painting that is such a blatant sex symbol?"

Andrew hesitated, but Olivia plunged forward. "But is it? The strength, and the allure, of the portrait of his young lover is that it keeps you constantly off guard—unsure of what it really means. Sex symbol? Can one be sure? Couldn't she represent pure, inno-cent paganism? Perhaps she symbolizes a spiritual experience, seen through seventeenth-century eyes, of course. If this painting is in actuality as fine as it seems to be, then it is worthy of profound consideration."

Winthrop was impressed. The demure scholar had come up with a quote that would need minimal trimming in the editing room.

"As I've always said," Connie Winthrop cut in, bringing the interview to a close, "great art does have its mysterious side. Thank you both."

When Winthrop had sailed off in search of other prey, Andrew chatted for a few minutes with Olivia. He felt annoyingly inept, almost as if he had forgotten something important. For a man who prided himself on remembering every move, it was an uncomfortable feeling.

"I liked your words," he told her. "But I detest how the media treats every work of art as a scandal, a sporting contest, or a financial event."

"In this case, it seems to be building up to all three," Olivia observed.

"Right, right," he chuckled, feeling more relaxed now. "But will it, really? Those of us who are close to the situation are all suspicious, aren't we? After all, the condition, you know."

Olivia looked him in the eye and said evenly, "For a painting that's hardly been examined in modern times, there are a considerable number of sudden rumors about its being flawed. Just a few minutes ago I heard this ridiculous tale from one of the members of my board that several auction houses had summarily rejected Lord Richfield's proposal to sell the painting because it's a wreck."

"Imagine that!" Andrew exclaimed. "All I can say is that anyone who gets involved with the naked Marchesa had better watch out."

"I agree. But why must she be tainted with lies? She's supposed to be 'Truth.' "

"Not lies, merely rumors. That's the art business."

"It must be difficult to be in your position," Olivia suddenly remarked.

"How's that?" he asked, off guard.

"Having no Velázquez at all, and knowing that this one might be the last great example ever to come on the market. It must be a frightful temptation."

"Oh, not for me, I can assure you. The Getty has decided to go for it, I hear. And they can have it," he added casually.

Had he scored? He thought so, but wasn't sure. She made him uneasy. Why? Olivia Cartright had, he thought, a most intriguing ability to conceal what she was thinking. I'll bet she's had some acting experience, he said to himself. He had made the mistake of prejudging her. Now he found he was unable to read her.

It was time to go down to the dinner, but he was reluctant to end the conversation. "Congratulations on that Corot. Really. I would definitely have gone for it."

His charm touched her. A few minutes earlier she had been puzzled by his seeming nervousness. As she looked into his soft eyes, she realized he must have been playing a game, part of the game surrounding the Velázquez, no doubt. Be wary of this man, keep on your guard, she told herself.

"Will you be going to Paris?" she heard him ask. "For UNESCO?"

"Yes. I've been asked to address the plenary session," she said with a correct smile.

"So I've heard. I'll be there too," he said, studying her. "I'm an observer in the American delegation. I guess that means I'll be observing you."

To Andrew's surprise, Olivia blushed. So she wasn't so cool, after all.

"I've heard certain rumors about the meeting too," he said, allowing his voice to trail off at the end.

"Just routine," Olivia remarked. "If there's time, perhaps we can have lunch."

"Excellent!" he said, again to his surprise.

Why am I getting myself into this? she thought.

"At the meeting we'll talk about where and when. Good luck!" he said with feeling.

"You dazzled her, Andrew. But, then, you always do," Rebecca Holcomb observed as they walked to the gallery where the dinner was to be held.

Andrew shot her a quick look.

"What did you make of that performance?" Rebecca asked.

"Smooth," he replied.

"She may give us trouble."

"Oh, come on, Rebecca, Olivia Cartright's only a pawn in this game."

"You know what happens when a pawn reaches the other side."

"A queen? Olivia Cartright?"

"Could happen."

Andrew thought for a moment. "You know, you're right. She's going all out for that Velázquez."

"You may have put a few doubts in her mind."

He laughed. "None that worked, I'll bet."

The dinner was perfection. The select two hundred and fifty luminaries savored a meal prepared by no less than the three chefs of New York's trio of four-star restaurants. The wines were textbook classics, the champagne superb. And most cheering of all, the speeches were made at the beginning of the repast. Miraculously, from the opening remarks of Ayn Steyne to the closing toast by Roland McCrae, the statements were, if not witty, at least short. The only part of the dazzling evening that appeared unrehearsed was when Steyne praised Olivia Cartright for her "dedicated labors." She seemed to falter slightly over her name and introduced her as "Director Cartright," which she immediately—and rather too emphatically—corrected to "Acting Director Olivia Cartright."

Andrew smiled to himself at the slip. Freudian? Had to be. He glanced furtively at Olivia Cartright. She sat placidly. Had she been hurt by the slight? If the decision had been made, would Ayn Steyne have corrected herself? Of course not. Andrew left the Metropolitan with a sense of well-being.

6 OLIVIA'S DESIRE

As SHE PACED back and forth in her loft on Spring Street making final preparations for her trip, Olivia Cartright paused several times to stare at the portrait of the woman in the faded photograph. She pursed her lips. The Marchesa glistened like the kind of peach you can only find on Mediterranean shores. An Italian peach, sweet and delicately fuzzy, ripe and sexy, seeming to exude a tangible warmth. What else to expect from a refined young noblewoman with the body of a goddess and the demeanor of a courtesan? The image made Manet's Olympia look like a block of wood! Paganism? Symbol of purity? Nonsense! She was a pure and simple sexual magnet!

Olivia turned on the water taps of the tub, then paused before the mirror and studied herself. Her body was not like the Marchesa's at all, not like that soft piece of fruit. She was tall, athletically firm, perhaps a little too slender. And her face was not soft, but chiseled. Moreover, she kept it plain. Deliberately. No makeup graced her features. Not even a subtle hint of lipstick. Her hair was tinted a neutral brown. Olivia Alexis Cartright looked purposeful, responsible, scholarly, just the way the acting director of the Metropolitan Museum of Art had to be perceived—and wanted to be.

"Let's face it," Olivia mused out loud, "no one would ever confuse me with the voluptuous Marchesa."

Though sometimes called a "Venus," the painting had nothing to do with ancient Greece and was by no means an idealized portrait. Diego Velázquez had been incapable of softening or generalizing. The Marchesa was a hot, naked, and thoroughly realistic creature, Olivia thought with a smile. The creature didn't just throb; she steamed! The subject might have great appeal to at least two of the members of her board, the indomitable sexists Amos Fischbach and Bruce Thompson. But what about the rest of them, and especially Ayn Steyne? What did Steyne really think of the picture? Would the Marchesa's sensuality enhance or destroy her chances?

Olivia had already made up her mind to compete for it, assuming the picture proved to be as superior as legend had it. She realized that not even the exalted name Velázquez was sufficient to sell it to her board. Considering the staggering amount of money Grundy had mentioned to Steyne, Olivia had serious doubts about the Metropolitan's chances of ever getting it. In the ten days since she had been summoned to Steyne's office, Roland McCrae, the former president, had complained bitterly upon hearing that the museum was even thinking about purchasing the picture. He didn't care how "rare and important" it might be.

"God, I need it and I'm going to use everything I've got to get it," she whispered hoarsely. Then, hearing herself, she laughed.

Ready to step into her bath, Olivia saw that she was way off schedule. If she bathed for only a half-hour she would still make the plane—as usual at the last minute. Smiling to herself, she picked up a file of recent news clippings.

"Oh, no," she sighed a little self-consciously, reading the first paragraph of the short profile in the *New York Journal.*

Olivia Cartright is hard to pin down; yet, how do you secure a fresh, variable wind? She is thoughtful, demure, intelligent, slightly insecure, totally dedicated, and a bit impulsive. Surely such qualities will make her a distinguished leader of America's greatest art museum. Why don't they hurry up and elect the first woman in their history?

But the glowing words could not offset the sardonic comments of Howard Olines, senior art critic of the *New York Times*, who that very day had written his third article (as usual without having bothered to talk to anyone involved in his story) on the Metropolitan's "agonizing quest" for its eighth director.

Since the untimely death of Sir Edmund Prost an unseemly period of one year and three months has gone by without the Trustees of the Metropolitan making any sort of decision. If they have decided never to elect another director of this institution, why not come out with it? What they are saying is all too clear: no one can follow Sir Edmund. Most surely none of those frequently mentioned in the past six months—I call it "the short list of incompetency." François Gautier, curator of paintings at the Louvre, well known for his vulgarity and his utter inability to recognize quality in any of its more obvious manifestations. Raymond Fairing, head of the art department at Harvard, a distinguished but unspeakably dull academic. John Bradley, a competent banking executive and lawyer who should be put on the board of the museum and not be involved in running it.

I will not win any popularity contests in museum circles, but I must place on my list of unacceptables Olivia Cartright, the acting director. She is, I've been told, an effective, scholarly young woman who, some say, is too headstrong to be a true administrator. She is also tender in years and experience and should perhaps best remain on the solid, safe academic shore of the museum swamp. To my mind there's only one man who can do the job. This of course is the charming Andrew Foster, who has meticulously managed to bring a sense of tasteful populism to the National Gallery without having to cater to the mobs.

"Damn Andrew Foster!" Olivia growled out loud, wondering if the rumors that Olines's wife had been a National Gallery Fellow weren't true after all.

After a hot soak, she pulled herself smoothly from her bath, toweled herself with luxurious strokes, and dressed in a brown skirt and beige sweater. Then she dashed out the door of her loft and into the waiting limousine. She greeted the driver of the rented car familiarly, instructing him to take her as quickly as he could to the Pan Am terminal at Kennedy, and plunged into the backseat. How exciting it was still, after six months, to ride in luxury! She clicked on the reading light, opened her blue leather notebook, and extracted her pocket stereo from its leather case. She had chosen Rachmaninoff's Second Symphony; its familiar sweet melodies would help ease the angry sounds of traffic.

In the darkness shot with the menacing lights of the onrushing vehicles, a curious spasm of fear gripped her. Impulsively, she brought the little notebook up to her lips and just as quickly slapped it smartly into her palm. God, she was edgy! She shook herself in vexation and stiffened her back against the seat of the limousine. She had actually been about to kiss the notebook as if it were some precious treasure of childhood, a romantic diary inscribed with the most intimate fantasies.

But the notebook contained no romantic idylls. It held Olivia's random observations on how to overcome the seemingly insuperable obstacles in the way of acquiring the Velázquez and, in doing so, win the job she wanted. She perused the headings, her mind racing.

QUALITY. Was the portrait of his mistress truly as fine as the marvelous *Juan de Pareja* the Metropolitan had purchased back in 1971 for $5.5 million, setting a world record that had stood for nearly fifteen years? Much as she wanted the *Marchesa* to be its equal, from what she could tell from the photograph there seemed to be a certain softness not apparent in the *Pareja*. But perhaps that was only the photo.

CONDITION. This was the most puzzling issue of all. A world-class masterpiece, to be a worthy acquisition, had to be in prime condition. Was the *Marchesa?* Was Andrew Foster correct? Had he and his conservator of paintings discovered something? She had to admit to herself that the failure of *both* Sotheby's and Christie's to land the picture tended to condemn it. Olivia was thankful for the tip her former professor Ulrich Seitz had given her—that one of his students had been Lady Eleanor Swift, Lord Richfield's niece. She intended to follow up as soon as she got to London. What could she wheedle out of her?

COPIES. Then there was the confusing problem surrounding the subject of copies. Was it true that Velázquez's identical replicas of the pair of portraits had disappeared forever? Had anybody ever bothered to look for them? Probably not. Art scholars were so lazy. Olivia was proud of one of her own recent accomplishments, one that might actually solve the puzzle surrounding the copies. By chance—or perhaps unknowingly she had been looking for it—she had discovered in an obscure Czechoslovakian art journal a footnote that described, with copious quotes, a document chronicling the first time Velázquez had ever exhibited his four *Marchesa*s together. In the same footnote it was mentioned that in the archives of Saint Luke's Academy in Rome the precise measurements of all four paintings were to be found. Wouldn't it be thrilling to unearth even the measurements? The bare possibility that they might exist excited her. After all, none of her competitors knew of the information.

Her thoughts turned months ahead to the sale itself and the question of who would be the museum's representative. At the Metropolitan it was standard practice to hire the services of an art dealer or solicitor to bid at auction on its behalf. Curators—and directors for that matter—were allowed to attend the sale but were forbidden actually to bid. The policy had been formed twenty years before after an inexperienced curator, inflamed by auction fever, had vigorously bid against himself repeatedly, and won. Who would the agent be in the delicate case of the Velázquez? It had to be someone at the epicenter of the art world who could listen to, sort out, and interpret all the rumors. It had to be someone utterly discreet.

Who? Olivia smiled to herself at the thought of recommending Count Nerone. What a scandal that would make! The stories about him didn't matter to her. She had, of course, heard them all—the tales that he was the clandestine chief of the Cosa Nostra, that he was the organizer of an especially deft group of art thieves. There was even a tale that had Don Ciccio the mastermind of a ring of master forgers. Less romantic, and more likely, was that he was as he said, simply the last in a line of wealthy Neapolitan nobles who had inherited enormous land holdings. But, of course, Don Ciccio could never be the Metropolitan's agent. He belonged to her; he was her weapon, her inexhaustible source of information. He had promised to deliver an important message regarding a highly sensitive issue that was sure to be on the agenda at the UNESCO meeting. What if he didn't get it to her in time? No fear. Although Don Ciccio had never failed her, Olivia couldn't quite erase from her mind her concern over why he seldom revealed everything he knew at one time. Was that manipulation? No, probably just natural caution and an obsession to decide on the right timing for every move.

The obvious choice was courtly Jules Bramet, a Parisian art dealer whose family had been in the trade for six generations. Without question Bramet fit all the needs. But could he be fully trusted? Although she liked the gregarious dealer, she had heard stories about his duplicity that sounded plausible. And could she persuade him to bid for the museum without asking for too high a percentage? Olivia was convinced she could, but she would have to be very cautious.

PRICE. She looked at the heading and let her head fall back heavily onto the top of the seat. Horrible! Although Ayn Steyne had steadfastly assured her that Grundy's evaluation of $12 million was but a "transparent ploy," Olivia was growing more and more convinced that $12 million was merely the beginning. The museum had a purchase fund reserve of only about $5 million. The rest would have to come from private donations. It was a daunting prospect. Who should she approach first? Bruce Thompson, of course. But Olivia was worried about how to get him to make a significant pledge—something in the vicinity of a million dollars—without falling into the trap he was so obviously setting for her. Nothing but problems. Nothing ever turned out as it seemed to be. When Bruce first began showering her with attention she thought it was simple infatuation. Then she began to suspect that he really did want to marry her. But why? Was he manipulating her? she wondered. If so, what was he really after?

She closed her eyes, sighing. The biggest obstacle, she knew, would not be the price or even Bruce Thompson, but one of the trustees who had developed an irrational hatred for her, Roland McCrae, an arch, aging patrician with eyes that looked like dying oysters. He would probably veto the acquisition of the painting. Not a meeting of the trustees went by without an unspoken objection or a devastatingly negative nod of McCrae's head with the result that a vote was changed. McCrae had become an exemplar of how destructive it was for an institution to allow a member of the board to hang on virtually forever. He had been the president of the Metropolitan back in the late sixties and had held on to the post for nineteen years until he was gently—and oh-so-politely—edged to the side by the more progressive members. But he had forced them to name him chairman emeritus. And, even as his power seemed to have been diluted, it had gradually swelled. Roland McCrae may have been forced to give up his vote, yet he made his position clear on every issue, no matter how insignificant. Unlike any other trustee, he could be a member of any committee. A born conspirator, he knew that if he persisted and never failed to attend a meeting, he would eventually amass more power in semi-retirement than he had wielded as president. For one who is unembarrassed by or even relishes the role of "spoiler," such are the rewards, Olivia thought testily. McCrae was arbitrary, irresponsible, and immensely powerful. Even Ayn Steyne feared the man. That was, to Olivia, inexplicable. But then there was no enigma more inexplicable than the museum's chairperson. Why had she played such a silly game in not allowing Olivia to sit at her table at the gala, as was the custom? What did that portend? Olivia relaxed as she recalled the times Steyne had hinted—even if she had not actually said so in as many words—that Olivia was her choice for director. Buoyed by the thought, she turned to the final item in her notes.

COMPETITION. Fierce! She had listed the names of ten museums and five private collectors. But she realized that ultimately she had only one—the National Gallery's Andrew Foster, backed by the fabulous wealth of Jonathan Cresson. How could she neutralize him? By her own wits and the flow of information from Don Ciccio Nerone. Olivia shivered slightly when the Count's name came to mind. He was invaluable, but could he become a liability? What if even a part of the stories were true? Suddenly Olivia had a sense of the ominous, a frisson of real terror. Was she getting in too deep? The chill didn't leave her until she had boarded her plane.

Olivia walked briskly through the stark plastic halls of Charles de Gaulle Airport, down the precipitous pitch of the moving sidewalk toward the passport control booth, and felt like bursting into song. Being in Paris filled her with delight—even if she had to spend a day being tortured at a UNESCO conference which would delve into the export treaty, drafted years ago, intended to force art-collecting nations to return works of art to their "natural motherlands." It's going to be wretched, she thought.

Like so many documents issuing forth from UNESCO, the birth of the export treaty had been clamorous. The resolution had started off as a sincere attempt to put a halt to the illegal export of the cultural patrimony of Third World nations to the West but had soon degenerated into an ideological brawl between Marxism and capitalism.

The Western nations feared that once the treaty was signed, massive numbers of works of art in their museums would have to be returned to the countries where they had been created—even treasures acquired a hundred years ago. That would never do. So the West at first vigorously denied they had ever been the recipients of illicitly exported treasures; then retreated into silence; then announced pompously that what had come out over the years was "a drop in the bucket." The Third World reacted with hostility, branding all art collectors and museums in the industrial nations as "imperialistic despoilers of the people's artistic heritage."

Perhaps both sides had a point, Olivia conceded with a rueful smile. At any rate, the treaty had eventually been signed eagerly by all members of the Third World and reluctantly by the Western nations, excepting, of course, shrewd Switzerland, which had remained neutral throughout. The key element in the agreement and one that had, at last, quieted the anxieties of the Western bloc had been the insertion at the last moment of a fixed cutoff date on both accusations and prosecutions. Any work of art that had been clandestinely slipped out of a country prior to the date of the signing would not be subject to repatriation.

The agreement had seemed to work very well, but success was not enough for those agitators who demanded that all "highly significant people's treasures" be returned forthwith, no matter how many decades those works had been out of their countries of origin. And certain objects which had somehow entered the collections of the Metropolitan were going to be used as ammunition to shoot down the treaty. The attack was going to be spearheaded by India's Undersecretary of Culture, Ardagh Rashvapar, who Olivia knew was a seasoned demagogue.

She was confident that her testimony would mute the protests and blunt the attempts to alter the agreement, and in the process give a lift to her career. But she was far from being overconfident. Rashvapar had boasted of possessing "unequivocal information" that the museum had acquired a twelfth-century Nataraja that "had obviously been smuggled out of Bombay." Olivia knew she could explain every recent accession but the Nataraja. If the Count didn't come up with something to counterattack with at the last moment she, the museum, and the treaty would be in a dangerous situation.

A bored customs official waved her through the gate and Olivia guided her luggage cart toward the outstretched arms of a perspiring Bruce Thompson, who kissed her avuncularly.

"How was your flight? Good. Lucky you. Mine was a horror—three hours late. The weather is delightful; you'll love it. Are you prepared for UNESCO? Don't worry. Your problems aren't there. What do I mean? Oh, nothing much. I'll tell you this evening."

Thereupon he drove into Paris with a certain chaotic panache and deposited her at the Ritz, urging her to get some sleep before the "special dinner I've arranged for us at La Marée."

Olivia could hardly believe the luxury of her suite. Ayn Steyne had arranged it, asserting that a representative of the Metropolitan had to stay at a prestigious location. She consumed half an hour examining every nook and cranny, opening every one of the drawers in the dressing room. My goodness, all this for a poor girl from a small town in California! Being whisked around in limousines, flying first-class, sojourning for days in deluxe hotels thrilled her. Although she didn't like to own up to it, Olivia was aware that it was one reason she coveted the directorship. And with that her thoughts turned to the subject of her wealthy and lovesick friend, Bruce Thompson.

Olivia enjoyed Thompson's company because when his defenses against shyness dropped—usually after a quantity of the best wine —he gave forth an inexhaustible supply of gossip. She respected the same people he did and was wary of the same, especially Roland McCrae. Thompson had dedicated his life to living well and was rich enough to do so. But what concerned her was how to deal with him if he asked her to marry him. Was there a way to fend him off without losing his moral or monetary support?

Over and over she imagined herself taking his hand and saying ever so sweetly, "Bruce, you're the only man I'd ever think of marrying. You are gentle, intelligent, funny, and sensitive. But I don't want to marry *anyone*—not while I have a chance to run the Met."

She shuddered at the thought of actually having to say something like that. But at the same time she could not help wondering if he were wealthy enough for both his and her tastes.

She bathed, slept for an hour and a half, then, in corduroys and a maroon sweater, walked to the Café Ruc-Univers on the corner of the rue Bercy, where she dawdled over one, then another espresso. At last she strolled through the Tuileries Gardens across the broad sweep of freshly cut grass, stopping for a moment to admire the Maillol bronzes, and into the entrance of the Louvre at the Pavillon de Flore. The "Pyramid" main entrance ruffled her sensibilities.

Olivia wandered leisurely through the grand series of galleries, pausing before a dozen or so objects she found particularly emotional. Whenever she visited, she left for the last the same work—what she considered to be Rembrandt's finest painting, his haunting depiction of Bathsheba at the moment she read David's fatal love letter. Olivia had seen it many times, but every time she was moved by its poignance.

Bathsheba had the face of a madonna and the sensual body of a courtesan. She held King David's letter so lightly between her thumb and forefinger that it seemed about to slip from her grasp (somehow a terribly sexual gesture, Olivia thought). Bathsheba was contemplative, eager, prideful, and anxious. If there was one, precise moment when a girl changed into a woman, that must have been the moment Rembrandt was trying to portray in the painting. And, for Olivia, he had. There she was, a beautiful girl married by parental arrangement to an older man, one of David's generals, having resigned herself to live without love, who suddenly realizes that her king is infatuated with her. Instantly she knows her life would become a tumult of passion and sorrow, which she knows she can still avoid. Yet she embraced that perilous life with earthy pleasure.

"That will never happen to me," Olivia said aloud. She clapped her hand to her mouth, flushed, and looked about quickly. But no one was near. The gallery was empty.

It was the perfect moment to test her special equipment. Furtively she took from her purse what seemed an ordinary black plastic magnifying glass with a handle thick enough for two small batteries. She snapped it open with a flick of her thumb and focused it a few inches away from Bathsheba's face. She pressed a tiny button on the side of the housing. There was an almost inaudible click, then another in rapid succession. She was holding a minicamera, cleverly incorporated into a standard small illuminated loupe. An inventive technician in the museum's conservation laboratory had removed the bulb and batteries and substituted a minute camera.

On her way back to the hotel through the Place Vendôme her worries about Bruce Thompson returned. What an impossibly awkward situation! Back in her suite, she stretched out on the chaise longue and gazed at the fading sunlight glinting off the bronze column in the center of the elegant square. Why struggle through life? Why not just marry the man? If she became Thompson's wife she might never become the director of the museum, but she would be able to visit the Louvre whenever she wanted, reserve luxurious suites at the Ritz, read, write, study. Fashionable homes in New York and Palm Beach would be waiting for her with butlers, chefs, and gardeners.

Abruptly Olivia snapped herself out of her reverie. As she slipped into one of her discreet "scholarly" dresses she said to herself, "The hell with that!"

Dinner started off peacefully enough. She made it safely through the first course, a lobster bisque, which Thompson ordered, as he did the entire meal. Then came a dozen oysters and several sea urchins. Their very numbers were a distraction, throwing the agitated man off what he seemed to be struggling to say.

Next came veal paillards, sliced elegantly thin and done to perfection, accompanied by a Petrus '61. Nothing but the very best for Bruce Thompson! Olivia began to be persuaded anew that being utterly spoiled by a well-heeled bon vivant might be preferable to the agonies of running the largest museum in the Western Hemisphere.

"Wait until you see the Cézanne show at the Petit Palais. I think I am again in love with the master," Thompson suddenly blurted out, almost causing her to laugh. "My whole life since undergraduate days—not so very long ago, young lady—I have loved, hated, and loved this master in erratic turns. Why couldn't this dauber have drawn a straight line or fashioned a painting of elegant subtlety? For Cézanne it always had to be smash, smash. You know, brutal brushstrokes. Total insensitivity. But what a genius! What do you really think of Cézanne, Olivia? I want the professional point of view."

"Bruce, I adore you. Sometimes I wish what you call the 'professionals' could express themselves with a little more of your passion. I'm crazy for Cézanne. I've never been mystified or puzzled by his work. It's flinty, zesty, deliberately awkward perhaps, but not brutal. Subtle! Think of those incomparably light and sensitive watercolors where thin mists seem to hang over every part of the surface! There you have subtlety. His paintings are profoundly primitive. I think he himself said it: 'I'm trying to re-create the surface of the earth.' "

He gazed at her, enraptured. "Let's . . . I . . ." But his voice faded away. Then he caught the waiter's attention and ordered a green salad and a miraculously creamy slice of Camembert to accompany the last of the Petrus. Thompson began to squirm in his seat. His forehead began to glisten. Here it comes, Olivia thought, and she had half a mind to capitulate.

"There's a delicious little scandal going on at the Tate," Thompson said incongruously. "It seems that the Stubbs they paid such an exorbitant amount of money for is really in terrible condition—almost twenty percent restored. The curator had no idea. A student —yes, a student!—from some 'red brick' university learned the truth and wrote a letter to the *Times*. A frightful brouhaha! How very difficult it must be to have the responsibility for purchasing works of art that can't be studied properly." A pause. "Olivia, I wonder sometimes . . ." And once again his voice trailed off into silence.

Oh, God!

Dessert was *crêpes nature* with a piquant sauce made of steamed honey, butter, and lime juice. Had he given up? Thompson inspected the bottle of Château d'Yquem he ordered, rolled the golden liquid on his tongue for fully ten seconds, lifted his glass, and offered a toast to her . . . "intelligence." She thought of responding by toasting his "courage."

"Hey," he said, giving Olivia's hand what she took to be an affectionate squeeze. "I've got a great story about Ayn Steyne, which it's high time you heard."

"Bruce, I don't . . ." Olivia's protest faltered as she decided it would be better to listen. At least he wasn't going to propose—for the moment.

"I happened to be the Steynes' first house guest in that Hobe Sound place of theirs—it must have been twenty years ago. That smart old shark, Joe Steyne, had bought the *palazzo* for fifteen million from the Smithers estate. The gossips were cackling that it was an outrageous amount of money to have spent. But Steyne was shrewd. He had managed, very quietly, to alter a little-known local zoning regulation and got the okay to develop no less than twenty acres on the estate. Made twenty million in about twenty minutes.

God knows what the local pols earned! The mansion was architecturally handsome, but the house was full of junk—dried-out Frenchy furniture, some godawful 1920s Impressionists. The sort of traditional twaddle you always find in Florida. But there was one fine work of art. Mouth-wateringly fine! You know it well . . .''

"The wallpaper!" Olivia exclaimed. "The marvelous English chinoiserie wallpaper she gave to us last year? The IRS approved the evaluation of a million dollars!"

"That's it. Well, the first morning I stayed there, I strolled into the living room and there was Annie—which was what she was called before she became Ayn—perched up on a stepladder with a putty knife in her hand . . ."

"Doing what?"

"About to peel."

Olivia started to giggle.

"I said, 'Dear Annie, what are you up to?' And she said, 'Bruce, I want this wallpaper removed, and my decorator told me he'd do it for a thousand dollars. I suspect he was trying to gouge me. Anybody could scrape this off in a day and a half.' "

Olivia chortled.

"You see, Ayn is not what she seems," he concluded cryptically.

Now what did that remark mean? Did Bruce Thompson want her for some reason to distrust Ayn Steyne? What his own agenda was continued to elude her. It couldn't possibly be that he wanted to marry her so as to oust Steyne? Maybe nobody was what they seemed!

Then came the Cognac. Now was the time, Olivia was convinced. Thompson was a little tipsy and had quickened his fond touches. He set his face into a resolute expression, tightened his fists, looked directly into her eyes, and droned, "Olivia, I've got two difficult things on my mind to discuss with you. Please don't think I'm a fool."

She gave him a neutral smile.

"Okay. I'm fifty-five years of age and I feel like an adolescent. For the past three days I've been holed up in my suite at the Plaza Athenée agonizing over whether I should ask you to marry me. It got so bad that yesterday evening I drew a complete blank on how I had proposed to my wife, Gloria, over thirty years ago. In fact I couldn't remember if I *had* proposed. Here I am, a man of the world, in decent mental condition, and rich, a trustee of the most prestigious art museum in the world, infatuated with its acting director, a young woman twenty-three years younger than I am who insists on disguising who she really is. In short, an idiot. Don't worry—I won't. But I will tell you some sad news."

Who was the "idiot"? Olivia wasn't sure what to do. Impulsively, she reacted in the worst way. She laughed.

"I was afraid you'd do that," he said morosely.

She started to say something sympathetic, but he stopped her with an imperious wave of his hand.

"I'm trying to help," Thompson said somberly. "I'm sorry, but I have to dish this out to you—like a bucket of cold water. Will you forgive me?"

Olivia stared at him fixedly, incapable of predicting what he was going to say.

"Ayn Steyne has contacted Andrew Foster to meet with the search committee for a 'serious' interview. They're planning to dump you."

Olivia tried to remain calm. In a flash she took in what he had said and decided that whatever was going on, Ayn Steyne could not be a part of it. Olivia knew the search committee was interviewing others while continuing to consider her, but surely Thompson had either come to the wrong conclusion or was lying, at least about Steyne.

"Sorry for having to be the one to tell you this," he went on. "But I'm one of your last friends left at the Metropolitan with any influence—and by influence I mean money. You're brighter—and, I think, tougher—than Andrew Foster."

"I wonder," she said in a sad voice.

"Look, perhaps far more than wanting you to be my wife—a thoroughly unrealistic obsession," he said, shaking his head slowly, "I so wanted you to become the next director of the Met."

"Has the final vote been cast?" she asked.

"Not yet. I'm pretty sure Foster hasn't been interviewed yet."

"He told me he'd be in Paris for the UNESCO meeting," Olivia said. "That gives us a bit of time. What can I do?"

"I just don't know. My gut reaction is to say don't rock the boat."

"It might be better if I do, if it's true that my cause is virtually lost."

"The conservative members tend to appreciate peace and calm," Thompson objected lamely.

"What if I pull off several coups . . . manage somehow to come off brilliantly at UNESCO . . ."

"Not much chance of that," he said. "Thank God, I don't have to attend that sort of nonsense. Total propaganda. No one wins in UNESCO."

"Perhaps I shall come up with a surprise," Olivia said. "Or perhaps I can acquire the Velázquez, steal it away from Andrew Foster?"

"That's the spirit. Why the hell not? Keep the pressure on." His voice carried little real conviction. "I'll be working as hard as I can behind the scenes, talking to my coterie of pals on the board. Maybe now is the time to rock the hallowed boat. Come out shining."

"Bruce, I hate to ask this, but how much money will you pledge toward the Velázquez—if it measures up, of course? If it goes up as high as ten or eleven million, we're way short."

"I was thinking of pledging a hundred thousand," Thompson murmured sheepishly. "But now . . ."

"Ah, it has to be a million, Bruce. At least. Please?" She voiced the words firmly.

"We shall see. But promise me something, Olivia."

"Yes?"

"Foil that search committee, I don't know how. Beware of Ayn Steyne. Smash that son of a bitch Roland McCrae—who is obviously behind this move to shunt you aside."

"You want me to change totally? I can't," she answered, flustered.

"You'll have to. You're canny, you're tough. You have to change. You've nothing to lose."

Yet not even the bottle of vintage champagne Thompson had ordered up at the end of the feast could transform the mood into a festive one. They drove back to the Ritz in silence. Inside, he pecked her tentatively on the cheek and said, "Buck up. Perhaps all is not lost."

Back in her suite, Olivia stared out at the Place Vendôme for an hour and then spoke out loud. "I'm not going to lose. I swear! Either the painting or the Metropolitan. So no more Plain Jane disguise, no more 'librarian'!" No more scholarly drudge. No more worrying about what her museum colleagues might think. "I'm not going to look like a schoolmarm for another minute!"

Olivia stalked into her spacious bathroom and began to wash the dulling rinse from her hair, revealing natural golden blond. With a mixture of anger and daring, she picked up the telephone and asked the concièrge to book an early appointment with the best beauty salon in Paris. After that, it would be a round of boutiques.

Even as she was dropping off, exhausted, into a deep, peaceful sleep, her mind was still racing. "No more horn-rims! No more curatorial diffidence! I'm going to be manipulative, clever, confident, and aggressive. Am I not?"

A Jacuzzi filled with fragrance was how she would remember the day-long experience—almost six hours of combing, pulling, shaping, lotioning, and perfuming. There were times, though, when it felt like punishment.

To André Marchais, the proprietor of Paris's most fashionable beauty salon, Olivia was one of the principal satisfactions of his career. He personally selected and applied the make-up. When she was finally ready to leave, her straight blond hair had become a golden frame surrounding an ivory face, which he had taught her to accent with subtle tricks—echoes from ancient Egypt, Crete, the Italian Renaissance.

When a transformed and confident Olivia returned to the Ritz it was apparent that she had made a striking impression. The assistant concièrge, who up to that moment was cursing his evil luck in having to be on duty for a full twelve hours because his superior had acquired a new mistress, escorted her personally to her door and arranged for an enormous bouquet to be delivered within minutes. He then pattered off to call a friend in the press to gossip about a fascinating American beauty who might make a good picture story.

When Bruce Thompson came to fetch her for dinner all he could do was gaze dumbly at the apparition for almost a minute before he could speak. Then he sputtered in confusion.

"How? Why?" was all Olivia could understand.

"I was advised in my early interviews for a job at the Metropolitan," Olivia said stiffly, "that my career would prosper if I wasn't 'pushy' about my looks. I was told that if I planned to be in the scholarly world, I'd better look like a scholar, not 'something from California.' Sad but still true these days, a woman cannot be bright, serious, able, or worthy of attaining the highest levels of executive leadership and be attractive too. But after what you told me last night, I don't care. Bruce, this is a change of everything, not simply the surface."

"You should have done it before!" he said.

As they left the hotel, a reporter and a photographer who were hovering at the entrance caught them. When Olivia and a preening Bruce Thompson made their exit, they darted forward toward their prey. She made haste to explain that she was far from a celebrity, merely the acting director of New York's Metropolitan Museum, in Paris to attend a "routine" UNESCO conference.

The next the morning, the paper—a tabloid—published her photograph with the caption, "Olive Thompson, the golden-haired stage director of the Metropolitan Opera in New York who is in Paris to finalize artistic exchanges in Africa with the director general of UNESCO."

At dinner Bruce Thompson got pleasantly tipsy and twice proposed marriage—once jocularly, and once, she thought, seriously. Olivia was delighted with the impression she made on the diners at Taillevent, who had seen their share of attractive women.

Later, as she tried to stave off sleep, she kept posing the same question: If she had chosen earlier to cast aside her scholarly disguise, would she already be the director of the Met? Appearances were of paramount importance to the trustees, so might her real look command not just the attention but the respect of her superiors? And if it did, might it possibly also blunt Andrew Foster's blue-blooded and well-heeled advantage? When it came down to pure wits and connoisseurship, she was confident she could go head to head with the director of the National Gallery and win, if only she could buy some time. Yet what, really, were her chances? In the cold world of art museums there were no such things as pure merit or pure appearance. It was a world of illusions, so subtle that she feared she could not comprehend them all.

7 A MATCH TEST

ANDREW HAD AWAKENED JOYFULLY to a radiant Parisian dawn and had shrugged off the effects of jet lag. The morning was so spectacular he decided to walk from his hotel to UNESCO headquarters, a distance of three miles or so. He marched with his overcoat flung over his shoulder along the Avenue de Lowendal into the imposing semicircular Place de Fontenoy. When he caught sight of the concrete-and-glass shell of the UNESCO building, he snorted. The edifice looked even more like a series of shabby condominiums than he remembered. But as a symbol, the ugly building was inspired. What could be more fitting for the ideologically battered, politically compromised institution than the look of a third-rate housing development?

He took the elevator down to the level where the auditorium for plenary sessions was located. Having arrived half an hour early, he ducked into the delegates' lounge. A black security officer standing guard over the coffee urn scrutinized him sourly. "Name?" Andrew identified himself, explaining politely that he was a member of the American committee attending the export-treaty discussion group. The man set his face into a scowl and with studied insolence ran his thumb slowly down a list of names. He finally grunted with what Andrew interpreted as assent. Andrew flashed him a pleasant smile and asked if he could look at the list. The man spun the paper around so that it fell at Andrew's feet and stalked off. Andrew swore at him in German just loud enough so that the man could hear him, but not clearly enough so that the man could respond. He was convinced the black was being deliberately rude. But why? He shook his head to clear his mind; he was obviously imagining things.

Olivia's name was on the list. But would she really dare to show up? He wouldn't under the circumstances. The Met was going to be bludgeoned with propaganda. It would be hell. Andrew smiled to himself. Thank God the National Gallery didn't have to collect antiquities! Paintings, which had little to do with night excavations, subterranean pilferage, or smuggling, almost never got you in trouble. If she dared to appear, Olivia Cartright was going to get seriously mauled. Too bad. Anything that added to her problems and made it more difficult to chase after the *Marchesa* suited him just fine.

He settled into a well-worn couch and sipped the acrid coffee. Delegates and their aides had begun to gather by nationalities in the lobby outside the conference room. As Andrew watched them he smiled, thinking of how futile America's withdrawal from UNESCO had been. When, after several years, the United States had rejoined, it was just more of the same. *Plus ça change.* The more often international bodies were formed for the purpose of bringing nations closer together, the farther apart those nations actually became. Foster's law.

Andrew pulled his copy of the original treaty from his pocket: "The convention on the means of prohibiting and preventing the illicit import, export, and transfer of ownership of cultural property. The General Conference of the United Nations Educational, Scientific and Cultural Organization meeting in Paris from 12 October to 14 November 1970, at its sixteenth session." He perused it rapidly. Every paragraph of the document trumpeted a warning against the illicit removal of works of art from the signatory nations.

As he glanced through the complex legal language, it occurred to Andrew that there was an abundance of ammunition against the Western nations, constituting a considerable problem in what had been taken for so many years as an unbreakable promise of non-retroactivity. The small print actually said that a two-thirds vote of the members could change any "terminus," depending upon the seriousness of the case. So if anyone could prove that the Metropolitan had been involved in the smuggling of works no matter how many years before the treaty came into existence, the museum could be forced to return those objects and the whole treaty amended. So sad! he said to himself with a grin.

Andrew sprang to his feet and went off to the lavatory. It was likely to be a long, difficult morning for the Metropolitan and Olivia Cartright. He wondered how he could turn the events to his advantage. Surely by leaking certain juicy and embarrassing pieces of the testimony to the press. But what more to do for maximum damage?

When he emerged and began walking toward the doors of the auditorium, wondering if he shouldn't depart for more rational territory, he caught sight of a lean, attractive woman with short honey-blond hair standing off to the right of the entrance. Only in Paris could you see a woman like that—businesslike, chic, and sexy, tomboyish and feminine. She seemed suddenly familiar.

Only when he was almost upon her did he realize with a shock that the woman was none other than Olivia Cartright! He stopped in his tracks, momentarily befuddled. She was more than chic or an alluring image. She was radiant. Andrew stood transfixed. She was dressed in a modish beige suit trimmed in rust suede. A Hermès leather bag was slung carelessly over her right shoulder, and it was bulging with documents. Her head was cocked in attention, but there seemed to be nothing tense about her. She was expectant but by no means nervous. Andrew had the sudden impression he was in the presence of a jungle creature who was surrounded by enemies but was totally confident that she could keep them at bay—or even vanquish them. The changes she had made, he saw instantly, were far more than just clothes, hairstyle, or makeup; they had more to do with attitude than surface appearances.

In a fraction of a second Andrew Foster's feelings toward Olivia Cartright had changed. To his amazement he found himself sexually attracted to her—powerfully. How should he approach her? That he found her physically exciting didn't make his job of competing with her more difficult; it simply added another, more amusing, dimension. He would pour on the Foster charm, which had almost never failed.

Olivia had observed him from the moment he came striding down the long hall. And she had seen him look up, falter, and stop. His momentary confusion delighted her.

He approached her with a rakish smile and stuck out his hand. "Olivia Cartright, Paris seems to agree mightily with you. You look enchanting."

She met his gaze and smiled. "Paris can do that to one."

"I think I ought to warn you . . ." He paused for a few seconds. "I've heard there may be a few theatrical performances about to be sprung in there. You are going to be attacked—hard—by the Indian delegate." Andrew inclined his head toward the conference chamber.

She smiled. "I know."

"Aren't you concerned?"

Olivia nodded her head. "A little."

The sound of voices in the assembly room had quieted down. She looked intently over his shoulder down the empty corridor.

"Everyone's inside and ready. Shouldn't you go in?" Andrew asked. "You'll only make the bees madder."

Olivia suddenly grinned like a little girl. "They'll have to wait. I want to let them get their little stingers at the ready," she said, casting her eyes over his face. And to his astonishment, she abruptly pushed open the door and with a flurried motion of her hand beckoned him to pass through. He did as he was told.

A moment later the black security officer approached. "Sorry," he said softly, "I had to wait until that man had left. Here." He handed over a small light-blue envelope with her name written in the Count's elegant, almost nineteenth-century hand. Olivia tore it open eagerly, read it rapidly, and entered the packed chamber.

If Ardagh Rashvapar hadn't been concentrating so intently on how he was going to score a major propaganda coup in humiliating the United States, and thereby forcing the restructuring of the UNESCO treaty—a coup which would most assuredly be reported widely in the press—he might have noticed a certain assurance in the bearing of his target, and that might have given him pause. But perhaps not. Ardagh Rashvapar was far from perceptive and was incapable of easily changing course. In whatever he did, whether on the cricket field or when dealing with matters of culture, he invariably charged ahead like a water buffalo wearing blinders.

The reaction of the UNESCO delegates to Olivia'a entrance was varied. Some saw a tall Caucasian walking in with that take-charge attitude the breed affected. But more than one Western representative conjured up images that were far from the controversies of the moment—images of a languid stroll in the Bois de Boulogne or a late supper at the Pré-Catalan.

The chairman of the conference, a fortress of a man from the

Ukrainian Soviet Socialist Republic, hammered for order with a karate chop of his gavel. "Session hereby opens. Item number one on the agenda is the honorable representative from India, Dr.—"

Before the chairman could continue, Andrew Foster jumped to his feet and launched an objection.

"Mr. Chairman, I would like to point out that it is normal parliamentary procedure to distribute a written agenda several days before the meeting, accompanied by an explanation of why items are going to be discussed."

The chairman waved a piece of paper in the air and acidly replied, "An agenda has been already sent to all delegates, fully ten days ago." Andrew sat down, deflated. He turned hesitantly toward Olivia, who shot him a look of mild disapproval.

"Dr. Rashvapar, I apologize for this interruption. Please continue," the chairman said.

The rotund delegate from India slowly raised himself to his feet and spent some time adjusting his microphone to allow a sense of anticipation to build up. He pulled his hand through his jet-black hair and began to speak softly.

"Certain senior delegates and key members of the various subcommittees investigating the illicit trade in art and desiring to reopen the issue of the non-retroactivity clause of the treaty have asked me to act as their spokesman. We make particular reference to an American museum stewarded by a member of this assembled body. This museum must be charged with having committed most blatant and cynical infractions of our sacred convention to halt the illegal transfer of cultural properties from their countries of origin. The museum is the Metropolitan Museum of New York. And its representative, the acting director, is here. Dr. Olivia Alexis Cartright."

So Alexis is her middle name, Andrew noted, fascinated. It had character. He looked over at her again. She was sitting rigidly in her chair. Andrew detected a steely determination in the way she held herself and found it a compelling foil to her softness. She looked up to face the speaker, and Andrew saw that her expression reflected a mixture of guilt, anxiety, and vulnerability.

Rashvapar didn't bother to glance in her direction.

"Mr. Chairman, fellow delegates, allow me to list the specific examples. Item! Six months ago the Metropolitan Museum acquired an exceptional gilt bronze dancing Nataraja of the eleventh century created in the renowned school of the master sculptor Taki. That superb sculpture was most certainly smuggled across the borders of my country. It is one of the greatest in our history and must be returned at once."

Olivia lowered her head as if waiting for another blow. She examined her notes, shuffling and reshuffling them nervously.

Slowing his cadence. Rashvapar lovingly chose his words, selecting them like precious stones. "Item! The illegal, irresponsible, and heinous acquisition of a hoard of some two hundred magnificent pieces of gold and silver jewelry, plates, salvers, ewers, and ceremonial crowns—all of the fifth century B.C.—*all* excavated illegally in the middle of the night in February from the tomb of an unknown Eastern Greek prince some twelve kilometers west-southwest of Sardis in Turkey."

These too, Rashvapar insisted, had to be returned to Turkey "immediately, with abject apologies."

This was followed by yet a third charge. "Item! An outrageous example of imperialistic cynicism in stealing off with a majestic four-foot-tall, seated sculpture of an African priest in ebony made in the late eighteenth century for a tribal shrine revered by the Ife nation of ancient Nigeria."

Turning toward the section in the chamber where a host of African delegates were seated, Rashvapar played to his audience.

"Severe criticism should be brought to bear upon the Metropolitan and its capitalistic leaders, those wealthy private citizens whose money still encourages the worldwide pillaging of the archeological sites of undeveloped peoples, because of this flawed treaty. Fellow delegates, I am sure you will agree that the Metropolitan—whose acting director sits before us in shame—has arrogantly violated that sacred document by nefariously acquiring these treasures. We ask the museum's representative to stand before this group and admit institutional guilt and offer abject apologies. *For shame!* Then we shall vote to amend the treaty and formulate the list of great works that must be returned to their blessed motherlands."

Ardagh Rashvapar sank back into his seat as some of the delegates clapped automatically in a strong cadence. Only the British representative, the three delegates from Japan, and an elderly woman from West Germany kept silent. The French contingent clapped desultorily, having been too often a part of such drama. The Italians rolled their eyes. The Swiss observer concealed a yawn. A few delegates rose to their feet. The observer from Cuba began to whistle loudly through his gold teeth until the chairman quieted him with an icy stare.

Olivia had been stabbed by an expert. Andrew looked toward her in some sympathy—after all, she was an American. He wondered how he might have acted having been caught red-handed— churn up as thick a verbal smokescreen as he could, duck out a back door, and hire a team of international lawyers. But Andrew was amazed to see that Olivia seemed to be coolness itself as she stood up.

"Mr. Chairman, fellow delegates, I apologize," she began. "I apologize for what I am about to say. But first, does the delegate from India have anything more to say?"

Rashvapar rose halfway from his chair and cried out, "These three heinous acts are sufficient to blacken the reputation of your guilty institution forever and are enough to force a vote to redraft the treaty!"

"Then I heartily apologize for what I am going to say," Olivia said tautly. "You see, I personally feel that this forum should strive to eliminate embarrassments rather than to incite them. And there are times when public testimony hurts—unnecessarily."

Several cries of "Shame!" and "Get on with it! Confess!" arose from the members.

"If this forum will come to order, I will attempt to explain," Olivia said. "All I can say for now is that we purchased the Turkish gold and silver from a reputable art dealer in Paris who assured us that there was absolutely nothing illegal about it. I shall leave the name of the dealer out of this for the sake of brevity."

The French delegation sighed with relief.

"That is *all?*" Rashvapar shouted sarcastically.

"We had been assured that the gold and silver hoard had been out of Turkey legally for decades," Olivia went on in a voice that seemed to Andrew to be carrying an incipient quaver. "When we heard rumors that the hoard might have been smuggled out of the country, we launched our own investigation. We resolved whatever problems there were to our satisfaction."

Olivia paused and then sat down.

At this Rashvapar jumped to his feet shaking his finger at her. "But Mr. Chairman, surely this 'testimony,' this feeble assurance of propriety, will not be sufficient for this august body. We have here what is patently the case of a once-respected institution—the great Metropolitan—attempting to cover up behavior that is, on the face of it, clear fraud."

The delegate from Turkey waved his hand and was recognized by the chair. "I, too, demand a full explanation of the events surrounding what might be the most blatant art theft—the pillaging of the people's patrimony—in the history of my country."

"I assure you, that is not the case," Olivia protested.

"If not, then you will easily be able to explain these suspicious occurrences," the gentleman from Turkey bellowed.

"I'm not sure I should or—" Her words were cut off by the chairman.

"The chair must inform the representative from the Metropolitan Museum that although she does not have to say a further word, it might be in the best interests of her institution—and most certainly this world body—that she speak. Otherwise, her silence might be interpreted incorrectly."

Olivia stood up and in a low voice said, "Actually I think not, Mr. Chairman."

Rashvapar and the Turkish delegate again jumped to their feet, imploring the chair to force Olivia to "confess." Within seconds several delegations from Africa had joined the two, crying out for an explanation of the "stolen" Nigerian idol. As if orchestrated by a stage director, one by one more delegates joined the shouting throng. Andrew could feel that gathering electricity of the manic release one associates with lynch mobs. He felt another rush of sympathy for Oliva, who under the verbal blows had sunk into her seat, her head bowed. But he could think of nothing to do.

"All right, Mr. Chairman," Olivia said resignedly. "If I must, I shall attempt to give a fuller explanation. Although I'm not positive the chair will either like it or accept it."

"The chair will be the judge of that," the Ukrainian retorted.

"What possibly can be the explanation for the direct involvement in the rape of a member nation by another member nation and the flagrant violation of the sacred treaty?"

"From the investigation we learned," Olivia said calmly, "that this gold and silver hoard is Anatolian and was discovered shortly before midnight on the twenty-eighth of January of last year at a tumulus eighteen kilometers southwest of Sardis. The man involved in the illegal dig is one Maruk. He sold this Eastern Greek treasure to two members of the antiquities division of the Turkish Ministry of Culture who for the past twenty years or so have clandestinely engineered illegal digs in the vicinity of Sardis. Their names are—"

The Turkish representative leaped to his feet. "Of course, we know all this. We have launched our own investigations."

"But that is not the case," Olivia replied placidly. "Mr. Chairman, may I be allowed to state the facts?"

The chairman, incapable of stopping her, stared at her enraged.

"Actually there has never been a government investigation," Olivia said. "As is not known to everyone, we negotiated quietly with the Turkish government, which fully backed us from the start, knowing that we were an innocent third party. In exchange for the indefinite loan of the ancient treasure to the Metropolitan, we have agreed to send to Turkey an exceptional representation of American painting and sculpture on long-term loan. So much for 'heinous acts' in this case. I think it might be in order for the chair to offer me an apology."

The chairman coughed in embarrassment and managed to blurt out, "The chair will withhold judgment on such matters until the full facts are known."

Olivia smiled.

Before his colleagues could restrain him, the delegate from Tanzania, who had been dozing during the heated exchange and had not heard Olivia's riposte, arose abruptly and dared Olivia to "tell the whole truth" about the pillaging of the Nigerian carving.

"I shall be delighted," Olivia replied. Ardagh Rashvapar groaned and began to sink deeper into his chair.

"The 'pillaged' African carving is not owned by any nation," Olivia explained. "The piece came into the possession of a young tribal chieftain through inheritance five years ago. Having just received his medical degree at Oxford and eager to bring a measure of modern hygiene to his people, being well aware that the wooden idol had been used for decades as a fetish for 'cures' by witch doctors, he sold this symbol of the Dark Ages to a Swiss art dealer specializing in primitive art."

She stopped for effect, casting her eyes around the room.

"The gallery owner in turn sold it to an agent in New York," she continued to a rapt audience. "Certain forces attempting to bring about the humiliation of the young chief convinced a crusading reporter on a New York newspaper to write a series of stories stating that the idol was stolen goods. After half a dozen inaccurate and totally negative articles, the frustrated New York agent sent the sculpture back to the village, demanding his money back.

"The young chief was flabbergasted to see the fetish being paraded through town with considerable clamor—as he told me later —'by two jubilant members of the Peace Corps who had been sold a bill of goods by the newspaper reports!' Within a month the doctor—the legitimate owner of the sculpture—had once again peddled his idol, 'the symbol of Hippocratic darkness,' to another dealer, who, this time, did sell it to the Metropolitan without a fuss."

The members of the conference who had rushed to criticize Olivia began to fidget in their seats. The chairman fixed his cold stare upon Ardagh Rashvapar. "Thank you, Miss Cartright. I find the explanations—satisfactory," he said in a strangled voice.

"But Mr. Chairman," Olivia protested, "surely you will give me the chance to explain to the honorable delegate from India the circumstances surrounding the theft of the great Nataraja from his country."

Rashvapar scowled.

"I wouldn't want anyone here to think the Metropolitan does not conduct its affairs ethically," Olivia persisted.

"But we have so many items on the agenda," the Ukrainian mumbled lamely.

"I have one small question for Mr. Rashvapar, Mr. Chairman, just one," Olivia said teasingly. She held herself erect, her slim neck set at an angle which seemed to suggest an impending attack.

Yet, inwardly, Olivia felt herself trembling. What if the information her mentor had delivered to her through the UNESCO security officer—a man she presumed was one of his employees—was inaccurate? Quickly she scanned the note again.

Rashvapar's nephew, Tisvan Reddy, works in the art section of the Ministry of Culture in New Delhi and is responsible for signing off works of art for export. Clandestinely he works with his uncle. Together they have allowed the illegal export of 237 Indian treasures over the past six years. Mention his nephew's name and there will be no trouble concerning the Nataraja.

Every member of the assembly—with the exception of Ardagh Rashvapar—leaned forward expectantly.

"Is the honorable delegate from India acquainted with a certain Mr. Tisvan Reddy?" Olivia asked in the prim tone of a schoolmistress.

Rashvapar began to hunt from some papers in the depths of his briefcase.

"I would like the assembly to know and I would like to know," Olivia continued. "Is Tisvan Reddy one of his nephews? And if so, is he the same Mr. Reddy who, by chance, works in the Ministry of Culture in New Delhi . . . and is responsible for granting export permits for works of art from India?"

Rashvapar jumped to his feet, his hands seeming to make windmills in the air. "Mr. Chairman, I refuse to be unjustly accused. This is an obvious political attack. This is innuendo, false information, smear, and dirty tricks."

"Mr. Chairman," Olivia cried, "I'm not implying that Mr. Reddy had anything to do with signing the permit for the Nataraja to leave the country."

But Rashvapar shouted her down. "For the sake of cultural unity within our community of nations, I withdraw my suggestion that any action be taken against the Metropolitan Museum, and for the sake of unity want it to be known that I and my country . . . uh . . . seek a sense of . . . uh . . . cultural unity. Thank you, Mr. Chairman."

The furious Ukrainian called the room to order, bellowing, "Next item on the agenda!"

The chamber erupted in laughter, derisive whistles, and, in some sections, the discreet drumming of feet.

Andrew Foster stood up, shook his head in wonder, and ran after Olivia, who was striding toward the exit, accepting congratulations from a number of delegates. When he caught up with her, he touched her gently on the shoulder.

"Remember in New York you asked me for lunch in Paris. I'm ready."

Olivia hesitated. She really didn't want to. But then, seeing the look of genuine fascination on his face she cocked her head, as if in half-assent. "Where would you like to go?"

"To my club."

"Your club? How original," she murmured. "Well, I suppose so."

Andrew took her by taxi to the fashionable Cercle Interalliée Club on the Faubourg St.-Honoré, where they were served in the cavernous oaken library facing the lush English garden.

"I brought you here because I wanted to impress you," he told her. "The French don't allow many nonresident foreigners to join this club. Normally I can take or leave clubs—especially in Washington. But in Paris, it's frightfully chic. It drives some of my trustees wild to think I'm a member and they can never even cross the threshold."

Olivia raised an eyebrow.

"Item!" he cried out abruptly. "I choose to ignore this cynical and capitalistic and possibly even imperialistic comment because I want to preserve cultural unity." It was as if Ardagh Rashvapar had entered the room.

She could not suppress a laugh. Doing impressions was the last talent she expected from Andrew Foster.

He turned serious. "You . . . ah . . . Olivia . . . you were amazing at UNESCO. I've seldom seen such a combination of skills. You were part con artist, diplomat, prosecutor, and actress. You trapped them all flawlessly. I'm amazed, for I had heard that the

Met was having difficulties over the Nataraja's legal provenance. Is Rashvapar's nephew really involved with a smuggling ring?"

Olivia tried to smile in what she hoped was a convincing manner. She was stunned by his words. She glanced at him coldly for an instant. Charming though he was trying to be, Andrew was as dangerous as a rattlesnake. What he said about the Nataraja was the kind of insider's information he could only have received from someone on her board of trustees. The name Bruce Thompson came immediately to her mind. She almost wheeled around to see if Thompson wasn't sitting in the corner of the room in one of those overstuffed couches. But no. As Olivia gazed at Foster she disciplined herself to smile noncommittally. She was both infuriated by the man and fascinated by him. That she would have found him so attractive so quickly, and that he obviously was intrigued by her, puzzled her.

Coolly Olivia murmured, "As you have guessed, the Met was in a rather touchy situation. Rashvapar blundered. He's lazy—and, I think, corrupt. His nephew? I managed to find out that he had a nephew in the Ministry of Culture. I just gambled on the rest and I suppose I touched a nerve. Anyway, no one will ever bother to check. At UNESCO, they never do."

"So, you're a gambler?" Andrew exclaimed affably. However she had gained her information, it could not have been by chance. How could she have known about Reddy? Who was behind her? Certainly not Ayn Steyne. For a moment Andrew allowed himself to speculate wildly. Could she be in the CIA?

"At times, I do like to gamble. Yes," she replied, trying to sound matter-of-fact. He was slick but obvious, she thought, patently softening her up to try to get information on what she was planning to do about the Velázquez. Olivia decided that trying to charm the charmer was out of the question. So she opted for being reserved and slightly mysterious. In delicate sparring sessions in this first encounter it would be easy. Later, if there ever proved to be a later meeting, she knew her more assertive and candid personality would emerge. For the moment, acting the part of a junior Ayn Steyne was heady.

"What are you doing later this afternoon?" he asked casually. "I'm off to the Louvre. I've got a couple of quick appointments there. Then I'm going to wander through the galleries. Want to join me?"

"Sorry, I can't," she replied in a brittle tone. "I have an appointment—near here, as a matter of fact. And, though I hate to say it, I should go right now, lest I be late."

"Where are you staying?" Andrew asked urgently.

He wants to see me again, Olivia thought with a thrill. "I'm at the Ritz." She added hurriedly, "Official business."

"I'm just down the street—at the Hotel France y Choiseul." When he saw her look of puzzlement, he quickly explained. "Well, I know it's not ritzy, but since I first came to Paris as a student that's been my favorite hotel. Call it a sentimental reaction."

She laughed. "I know the feeling. In Rome, where I studied, there's a perfectly minuscule place I still adore."

"I have an apartment in Rome. It would be fun if you could see it. Tell me about Rome, your student days."

"I can't now. Please," she said gently. "I shall be terribly late. Thank you so much for lunch."

"We hardly talked," he said. "I mean, two rivals ought to argue, scream a little—at least gnash their teeth at each other."

"Rivals?" she repeated gaily. "Oh, I suppose some would call us rivals. But don't you agree that most of the time the talk of competition between art institutions is inflated—mostly pure theatrics?"

"Without a little drama, how could we poor art historians possibly get by?" he replied with a charming smile. "Come, then. Can I give you a lift?"

Olivia recoiled slightly. He would find out where she was going. That would never do. "It's a highly confidential meeting," she said stiffly. Oh, God, how awkward I sound, she thought. "I mean . . . if you don't mind, I really should go on my own."

"Oh, of course. I apologize," he said quickly in obvious embarrassment. "May I call you?"

Olivia smiled her assent.

As Andrew watched her dart nimbly through the dense traffic of the Faubourg St.-Honoré, he was tempted to shout, "Be careful, please!" And he even thought of running over to escort her across the dangerous thoroughfare.

As he walked the six blocks toward the France y Choiseul, he began to realize how vitally she attracted him. Amazing! The "librarian," clearly a very capable competitor, actually attracting him! He would have to be careful, for there was always the chance that she was trying to lead him into a trap. Like the unsuspecting Rashvapar. Black widow spider? Who was she, this Olivia Alexis Cartright? There was something about her that was too good to be true.

Olivia walked quickly down the fashionable street, her mind in confusion. What next? He was going to pursue her, she was positive of that. And he would also try to make a pass. To throw her off guard, of course. What should she do? Spurn him? Or weave a web around him and devour him? She smiled at the silly cliché.

8 STROKE AND COUNTERSTROKE

ANDREW STOPPED BRIEFLY at his hotel to put into the works a devilish little ploy that suddenly occurred to him. He called New York and chatted for fifteen minutes with the gossip columnist of the city's flamboyant morning tabloid, Candice Swanson, a dangerous harpy to some, and to a special few, including Andrew, an old and sympathetic friend.

He regaled her with the details of Olivia's tour de force at UNESCO and then, at the end of his description, confided how Olivia had boldly "gambled" and had come close—"possibly irresponsibly close"—to accusing Rashvapar of corruption. He urged Candice Swanson to write her piece so that Olivia would suffer just the right degree of embarrassment—not too much—and that she couldn't suspect that Andrew was behind the leak. But then, as he put down the phone, he regretted what he had done. He thought seriously of calling the columnist back and killing the story, but finally held firm to his resolve. He then phoned the art dealer Jules Bramet and asked for an appointment to discuss a "most fruitful" arrangement regarding the National Gallery and the *Marchesa Odescalchi,* which he took pains to outline in sufficient detail so that the dealer would have to agree. The dealer's reaction buoyed his spirits.

Before setting out for the Louvre, Andrew sat on his bed in the small, cozy room on the fifth floor of the France y Choiseul and brooded for a quarter of an hour before he picked up the telephone. He dialed a number which was answered by a woman who said simply "Red, seven" and cut him off. He started his stopwatch, waited until three minutes and fifteen seconds had gone by, and dialed the number again. The same voice asked coldly, "Identification?" Andrew gave his code name and number. In less than half a minute a male voice inquired what he wanted.

"What do you have on Olivia Alexis Cartright, the acting director of the Metropolitan Museum of Art and art scholar? Most urgent priority, if you please."

"Roger. Out." The connection was broken.

After informing the concièrge that he expected a phone call, Andrew retired to the tiny bar of the hotel and relaxed over a glass of champagne. No more than a half-hour later—that it took so little time always amazed him—a bellboy sought him out and informed him that he had a call.

"I'll take it here, at the bar," he said. "Hello, Andrew Foster here."

"Number, please."

Andrew whispered his code number.

"Okay. Olivia Cartright. Born in Newport Beach, California. Thirty-two years of age. Want the physical description?"

"I have that," Andrew answered briskly.

"Okay. Art historian. M.F.A., Ph.D. at Berkeley. Highest honors. Docent professor, Ulrich Seitz. Acting director of the Metropolitan in New York—"

"This I know," Andrew said rather impatiently. "Is there anything unusual? She's not in the CIA by any chance, is she?"

"No. Why do you ask that?" The informant sounded concerned.

"Nothing serious. But is there anything unusual on her record?"

"You ought to know she's flagged," the agent said, referring to a CIA designation on a person's file indicating that he or she had possibly been involved in suspicious activities or associated with questionable characters. He shrugged. In the voluminous files of the CIA virtually ninety percent of the people were flagged.

"Why?" Andrew asked.

"Five years ago she was apparently an informant in an art theft case in California. No one knows how she did it, but she tracked down and fingered to the FBI a former German Wehrmacht enlisted man who had filched two valuable Renaissance paintings from the Uffizi in Florence during the Nazi retreat of 1943. The FBI nabbed him and the paintings went back to Italy."

"This is the reason for the flag?" Andrew asked somewhat testily.

"Sure. You know she may be a part-time employee of the FBI, although the file says we're not sure. It's raw data only. I repeat, raw data."

"Anything else?" Andrew asked, amused to have confirmed again that the CIA's most serious opponent was not the Soviet Union or other external enemy of the United States, but the FBI.

"Nothing. We can continue the search if you like."

"Why bother?"

"In three days we can supply you with a list of all her acquaintances—domestic and foreign," the man said eagerly.

"Thanks, but not necessary."

"It's easy," he persisted.

Andrew didn't want to discourage the obviously gung-ho operative. "Well, go ahead. Why not?"

"Okay."

He should have known there would be nothing of substance. The tenuous link with the FBI was the usual fantasy one got from the unedited files of the agency. Suddenly Andrew felt foolish and a little cheap. Christ, all she was was an art scholar, not Mata Hari! Yet how had she found out all that stuff on the paintings—and about Rashvapar?

On his way to see François Gautier, the curator of paintings at the Louvre, Andrew took care to pay a courtesy call on the imperious director of the museum, Philippe le Grand, who, giving him a patronizing smile, spent almost the entire time looking down his nose at him. Several times Le Grand shot overtly bored glances at the clock on the mantelpiece as his visitor carried on a monologue of museum trivia. As Andrew moved to leave, he just happened to mention the Velázquez and confided to Le Grand that he had decided not to enter the competition for the painting. Le Grand seemed to notice him for the first time and motioned him back to his chair.

"Excellent! Confidentially," Le Grand said, bursting with pride, "I can tell you that the Louvre has become keenly interested in the picture. Only days ago I was summoned to the Elysée Palace for a private meeting with the President himself. He asked my advice as to what to do. I uttered one word: *Avant!* He, of course, agreed."

"Good hunting!" Andrew replied, astounded by what a little flattery could reveal. "I hope you can pin down the true condition of the thing," he remarked casually. "Doubts about that forced our decision to withdraw. And by the way, since I'm not in the auction I might as well tell you . . . I heard positively that the Met has already raised fourteen million dollars. Yes, fourteen! And they're on their way to even more."

Le Grand choked.

"But that's not much compared to what we could raise if we wanted to make a run for the painting," Andrew said offhandedly. "Our legendary patron, Mr. Cresson—if he wanted it—could . . . well, who knows? Maybe we'll change our minds."

Le Grand reddened as Andrew breezily said goodbye. Andrew climbed the narrow circular stairs to Gautier's cramped office in the rabbit warren of the Louvre's attic. Relating the story to his colleague he mimicked the pompous director with uncanny verisimilitude. The smile on Gautier's face changed to a scowl.

"*Merde*, that name-dropping idiot really believed you? Oldest ploy in the art game. *Merde!* I don't suppose I can talk you out of the auction, can I, my friend? That idiot! Sure, we're interested. How many Velázquezes do we have in the Louvre? Not one. And this one, Andrew, may be magnificent. If it is, it's one you desperately need too. Isn't it? I figure the Met won't be in on this sale. They've already got theirs. Yes, if it checks out, we go. To how much? Ten million. Perhaps a little over ten. I don't know. Will I let you know if we decide to bow out? Sure. And you'll tell me?"

"You know I will, François," Andrew assured him.

"Very good. Listen, are you going to get the Metropolitan job? Probably not? You think the girl is? You do? You saw what that bastard called me in the New York press? *Merde!* You seem to be the guy the Met wants. Listen, stay where you are, where you can call your own shots. The Met is like the Louvre—*Merde!* Good, Andrew, see you in the auction room. Don't forget to tell me—not *le grand* Philippe—if you're really out. You are sincerely worried about its condition? Have you seen it? You have? A private showing by the Earl? It's just like you to get there first—with your social contacts. I'm sure he hates the French. And you *are* worried? Truly? Yes, I can see you are. Oh, God!"

A tiny seed of doubt was all that it took. Of course, Andrew had absolutely no intention of telling his friend anything about his auction plans—anything accurate, anyway. His white lie about having seen the picture could never be traced, he was confident of that.

It had taken Olivia only a quarter of an hour to walk from Andrew's club to Bramet's house on Rue La Boëtie. Once inside the opulent late nineteenth-century mansion, she was greeted by an elegant-looking man, about five foot nine but seeming inches taller, who kissed her hand. He gave an approving nod of his head as he held her at arm's length.

"*Le tout Paris* has been buzzing about what by now the foolish press is calling a new diva of the Metropolitan Opera," he said lyrically. "But I knew at once it was you. I'm entranced. How beautiful you look! Olivia, you seem to have cornered the world market on radiance. You must be in love."

"Jules, if I had done this earlier, might I have become one of your legendary amours?" she asked, trying to keep a straight face.

"Olivia, I never . . ."

"You're right, I am in love. With the Velázquez."

"As soon as you called my office from New York, I knew," he said, sounding cagey. "What are your plans?"

"I intend to go for the picture. I'm confident I can raise a great deal of money. What few people know is that the Met was always after the *Marchesa* as well as the *Juan de Pareja*—for many more years, in fact. The dream was always to get both of these grand Roman-period pictures. Except for a handful in the Prado, Velázquez never painted better."

Bramet laughed. "*D'accord.* Let me tell you something. Each year for the last fifty years, a member of my family has paid a respectful visit to the Richfield country seat. Invariably, a curator of the Metropolitan would be there. Both were seeking the *Marchesa*. Both were hoping that the current Earl would lose his senses."

He went on, shaking his head in wonder. "There are some quite stupendous stories about how this picture affected certain people.

Back in the middle of the last century a Richfield cousin became so enamored of the naked Marchesa that he made off with the picture. What a scandal! He was about to be apprehended. He confessed his love, departed for Spain, leaving the picture behind, became an 'artist,' and changed his name to Velázquez. From then on, a fugitive, he aped every move that his beloved painter had made. He ended his life in Rome, trying unsuccessfully to obtain a commission to paint a portrait of the reigning Pope."

He shrugged. "And talk about obsession . . . my own dear grandfather when he visited would, each year, send in with the butler a check on a silver salver—increasing the amount annually. It was, I can tell you, an enormous amount of money for those days. And each time, the check would be torn up and the confetti sent out on the salver. Finally, in desperation, my grandfather sent in a blank check—signed. This, too, the Earl sent out in little shreds. But now the present Earl has given in—impetuously. Be prepared. The price will be unlike anything in the annals of art auctions."

"I'm prepared."

"Even at astronomical prices, others are bound to be interested in the picture," Bramet added. "Exactly what do you propose, Olivia?"

"When I was struggling with the problem of who could possibly bid for us, I thought of you because you've got the best information network in the world of art. I need that. And you are the most experienced art dealer on earth when it comes to bidding at auctions. So I wanted to get to you before anyone else could enlist you."

Jules Bramet strolled slowly over to the window and gazed for a moment at his spacious garden, stroking his chin. Then he turned to her. "But, my dear . . . I am so sorry . . . but I am already committed."

"Oh, God, I just hope it isn't to Andrew Foster."

"He called only fifteen minutes before you arrived. He assured me that his patron would pay a commission of five percent for my services."

"A little above standard, isn't that?" Olivia remarked evenly.

"It's in line," Bramet said reflectively. "But he said something else which you will find quite astonishing. If he ultimately decides to bid, Foster is willing to guarantee me, in advance, the sum of five hundred thousand dollars—whether my final bid proves to be the winner or not!"

"My God!" Olivia said.

"Naturally, I thanked him profusely," Bramet said, studying his fingernails, "and told him I'd consider the offer. But I have already decided to tell him that I am committed elsewhere."

"To whom?"

"To myself! I *must* possess this painting. I have no idea to what heights I shall go. Olympian, you can be sure. How amusing! Here we are—two good friends, two dedicated connoisseurs, clambering after the same grand prize."

It had to be a lie, Olivia thought instantly. Bramet might have made millions in the art business and his family must have salted away a fortune, but it was inconceivable that an art dealer would buy a painting that might go at auction for $10 million or more. The chance of selling it at the normal profit of fifty percent was obviously out of the question. Buy it for prestige? Bramet had all the renown he needed. What was going on, she wasn't certain, but she suspected Bramet had made the lucrative deal with Andrew Foster. How could he not have? What was there to lose? Or was there something else going on?

"Well, at least Foster didn't hire you as his personal mountain guide," she said with a wistful smile. "Bless you, Jules. Do you mind if I tell Foster—if I happen to run into him, of course—that you're thinking of bidding for us?"

"Fine. That will camouflage things nicely. You will be running into him soon?" Bramet asked, momentarily puzzled.

"I might," Olivia replied without changing expression.

Drained by her labors at the hearing and by her encounter with Andrew, Olivia retired to her suite looking forward to a solitary, light dinner. The quiet repast was shattered by the jangling of the phone. It was Andrew Foster.

"I do apologize for bothering you," he said earnestly. "But I've been brooding over my communication failure with you this afternoon. I didn't mean to press you. I thought you might enjoy going to the Louvre with me. Do come with me—say, tomorrow just after lunch? I mean, if two ardent art historians—even if we are rivals, we're genteel rivals—can't amuse themselves with some great paintings, what is happening to civilization?"

She had to laugh, his technique was so smooth. "I'd like that," she said warmly. "Make it the main entrance. Two thirty? Good."

Olivia was suspicious of his motives, but nevertheless could hardly contain her delight.

Just before going to bed she suddenly realized that she had neglected to brief Ayn Steyne on the UNESCO proceedings. That would be a mistake. She sat for a few minutes organizing in her mind what she was going to say to her superior, and was sorely tempted to come right out and ask what was going on with Andrew Foster and the Metropolitan.

Steyne came on the line at once and, uncharacteristically, gushed. "I heard that you've made yourself look simply marvelous. Bruce told me. I'm so glad. I don't want to sound like a gloomy Gus, but you'll no doubt receive some criticism. Pay no attention to critics. Appearances in the museum business can be misinterpreted. How silly. Now, how did we do?"

Olivia modestly described how she had blunted the attacks and had foiled the attempt to alter the draft treaty. Then she made a serious error. When Steyne asked if Rashvapar had brought up the awkward subject of the Nataraja, Olivia remarked casually that there had been no significant mention of the sculpture. And she couldn't resist adding a few words about Andrew Foster.

"I chanced upon Foster at the UNESCO meeting," she said. "He's charming, if somewhat laid back. I imagine at an institution like the Metropolitan he might be useful in some special area—fund-raising, for example. I don't think he's much of a scholar."

"He's said to be an extremely able administrator."

"Kind of casual, I'm told," Olivia replied, a little too sharply.

"You sound a bit on edge," Steyne remarked. "Relax. And I congratulate you for helping to defuse the UNESCO situation."

"There may be some press tomorrow," Olivia said.

"UNESCO matters tend to be on the back burner these days, but I shall let you know if there's a word or two," her superior said, her voice growing more distant. "What do you plan to do next?"

"Get to see the picture."

"Proceed," Steyne said patronizingly, and abruptly cut her off.

Could she be jealous? Olivia wondered just before nodding off to sleep.

They met the next afternoon in the modern, silvery vestibule of the Louvre and avoided the bank of bright new escalators sweeping the throngs rapidly to the galleries above. They were both uncertain if the massive program of refurbishment of the grand old museum had been successful after all. Olivia was more skeptical than Andrew, much to her surprise.

"One always has the suspicion," he remarked thoughtfully, "that fifty years after the 'modernizations' are carried out, the next group of officials in charge will restore everything back to the good old days."

"Only to be followed in several decades," Olivia added, "by a 'mandatory' freshening. I don't like that Pyramid outside, but I do like the interior. So many museums are dreadfully shabby. Better a little flashiness than grime."

He looked at her, smiling boldly. "Speaking of transformations, I want to know about yours. That is what I'd call a real freshening."

She was so caught off guard that all she could do was mutter hesitantly, "Perhaps—in time."

The fascination between them was growing. Olivia admitted reluctantly to herself. Their cautious relationship so full of doubt ("Why would he be interested in me?" "What is she really after?") seemed nevertheless to be inexorably deepening.

Within five minutes of their museum tour, Olivia recognized Andrew's line, and she was delighted with the creativeness of his approach. It was a most tactful propositioning, for that was what it was. He communicated his desire for her not with words, but by guiding her as if by chance to certain works of art. It was both an intellectual "show and tell" and a wooing.

Their visit became an effortless float through a series of evocative visual experiences, sometimes punctuated by a smile or a wary, glancing touch. Andrew had started with works of a severe didactic or hieratic nature and progressed slowly to masterpieces in which the human body was masterfully celebrated. Their path wended from the spirituality and awesome weight of the Romanesque to the soaring and uplifting freedom of the Gothic to the overt sensuality of the Rococo and Romantic periods.

They stopped to linger in front of Watteau's *Embarkation to Cythera*, silently appreciating the beauty of the young noble couples gathering together to sail back to reality from paradise. They paused before Ingres's *Small Bather* with her snowy mountain of a naked back. And they gazed for several minutes at the grandiose *Oath of the Horatii* by Jacques-Louis David as Andrew talked about the sanctity of oaths and loyalty. Now that is very clever of him, she mused.

To Olivia's delight Andrew paid special homage to Rembrandt's *Bathsheba*, confiding to her that this was his favorite painting by the master.

"Sometimes I wake up in the middle of the night, dreaming of this woman with that incredibly ripe body and that face . . . the face an angel, a harlot, a mother, a virgin, a saint, and a sinner."

Eloquent, Olivia said to herself. After that a lighthearted yet determined sexuality began to creep into his conversation. He directed her to Delacroix's monumental painting of King Sardanapalus lolling back on his ornate golden bed in the midst of his burning palace as his seneschals dragged in his worldly goods —his beloved horses and his most beautiful concubines. All to be destroyed. Andrew drew his finger in the air, following the contours of the nude concubine whose head was being pulled back so that the slave's knife could be thrust into her breast.

"That body!" he said in a stage whisper.

"Owes a great deal to Rubens," she replied, playing the scholar.

She allowed him to take her arm as they wandered into the underground galleries containing Greek art. He stopped in front of a dark brown bronze of a naked athlete, the Apollo said to have been excavated in the mid-nineteenth century near the village of Piombino in Italy. Facing her, he said in intimate tones, "I've always had a yen to be this guy, this Apollo, with those powerful sinews throbbing under that brown-purple velvet skin."

In keeping with his tone combining seriousness and mockery, Olivia stepped back a few steps and gazed at him playfully. He was exceptionally attractive, she thought. He had inky black hair, large, soft brown eyes illuminated by a few random hints of hazel. He was tall, over six feet, yet had the appearance of being stocky. Solid. Athletically chunky and well proportioned. Actually, not unlike the bronze youth planted with his low, powerful center of gravity on the sleek mahogany pedestal before them. She glanced fleetingly, now slightly embarrassed, at his face and saw clean strength.

"You are aware, I suppose," she said archly, "that this piece has been doubted."

"Oh, come now! It's clearly ancient," Andrew protested.

"Ancient, yes. But how ancient? That's the question."

"Do tell."

"The piece was cleaned a year ago and when they removed those sparkling silver eyes, the restorers discovered Roman—not Greek —writing on the backs."

"Everything I cherish is being shattered," Andrew wailed with a mock catch in his voice. "But"—he paused and looked into her eyes with a sly, triumphant grin—"I suppose you must know from a recent article in the *Zeitschrift für Archäologie* that scholars currently explain the little problem of fakery by claiming that it's an ancient fake, a Roman fake. I think they're all nuts. I think it's genuine Greek and those cheap, vulgar Romans forged just the eyes. The body is pure classical Greek and the soul is Roman. But body over soul, some say. Do you?"

Olivia smiled.

He walked her to the Ritz and in the lobby asked, almost begged, her to join him for dinner the following evening. With not a moment's coy hesitation, she agreed.

"Why don't you come to my suite, say, seven thirty?"

"Delighted."

In her rush to bathe and dress for dinner with the Met's curator of Islamic art who was passing through Paris after a trip to the Middle East, she almost overlooked the telephone messages on the writing table in front of the window overlooking the Place Vendôme. Ayn Steyne had called three times. Don Ciccio once. Olivia placed a call to Steyne immediately.

"Nasty little piece of press here," Steyne said without bothering with a salutation. "It's that bitch Candice Swanson."

"Oh, the gossip columnist?" Olivia asked.

"She's more than a mere gossip columnist, young lady, and you should know it. You should also know enough not to boast of your exploits. And you were less than forthright with me. Practically the whole story of your testimony is there. Including a most fascinating paragraph on how you 'gambled' in an irresponsible confrontation with Ardagh Rashvapar. What gave you such an idea? I feel I must tell you . . . I urge—no, I order you, Olivia—to hold your tongue with the press. From now on. But that's enough. I shall forgive you. Goodnight." And the storm had suddenly passed over.

"That filthy bastard!" Olivia cried out.

She picked up the telephone once again and put a call through to the Hotel France y Choiseul. The hell with him, his disinformation, his deceit! It was time to cut him off. She had intended leaving a curt message with the switchboard canceling their dinner, severing the dangerous liaison for all time. But the efficiency of the hotel defeated her. First she got the operator, then the concièrge, and just as suddenly, Andrew Foster himself. He must have just walked into the hotel the moment she placed the call.

"Miss me already?"

"I can't have dinner . . . uh, sorry." She cursed herself for wayering.

"You must. You promised," he replied, sounding amused.

"The fact is," she rushed on, "I am not at all sorry and I don't intend to have dinner with you. You told Candice Swanson. Damn you!"

What Olivia heard next could not possibly have been contrived.

His words came out in a sad whisper. "I did."

Olivia thought of slamming down the phone. Instead, she waited.

"I did," he repeated. "But that was yesterday and my mind was thinking thoughts of a day before yesterday. We must meet. You simply cannot turn down a man who has just made an abject confession."

"Seven thirty," Olivia said with a sigh.

As she replaced the receiver, she muttered angrily, "Why, why, why? Oh, why?" But, of course, she knew.

When she telephoned Don Ciccio, her emotions must have been

reflected in her voice, for the Count voiced his concern and within minutes had managed to extract from her the story about Andrew and what he had done. Sensibly, Don Ciccio made no comment on what he thought was not only a rather curious alliance but one that might cause unexpected complications, and launched into praising Olivia for her performance at UNESCO. He had been fully informed of her splendid job by the security officer who had transmitted his note. "It was a vital task, Olivia, and you carried it out perfectly. It was essential to stop in their tracks those who would have toppled the treaty. Think of what would have happened if the floodgate had opened and all those works had to return to their countries of origin! What a propaganda coup that would have been for the Left! So I salute you."

What Don Ciccio then said made her breathless.

"About Andrew Foster, I know his father—a rather intemperate and whimsical gentleman, not without wit, however," he said silkily. "Perhaps I can find out something about the son—you know, something that can help you in this, ah, complex situation in which you two have found yourselves."

"Oh, please, no," Olivia blurted, a little fearfully.

"Come now, what's wrong with having a tidbit or two of inside knowledge? Something to use in your struggle for the Velázquez? I mean, suppose he is using you."

"Well, I guess so. Yes!"

Count Nerone called her back within the hour with some information that depressed her and some news that startled her. Andrew Foster was not just rich, he was exceptionally rich—worth at least $50 million. My God, he could buy the Velázquez himself, she thought. To make matters worse, Foster was a connoisseur of women, usually only the most beautiful or the most exalted socially. His women entered and left his pampered life with revolving-door frequency. Predictable and all too depressing. Then Don Ciccio announced his surprise. When she heard what it was she said, "Are you positive?" And upon hearing him confirm the news, she burst out laughing.

9 A SEURAT IN THE BATHROOM?

ANDREW BUZZED THE BELL of the suite precisely at seven thirty, an immense bouquet of white and yellow roses in his arms. Standing tensely in her dressing room, giving a few last touches to her makeup and hair, Olivia stiffened and for a frantic moment thought of not answering. Then she took a deep breath and relaxed. Why not enjoy the game? Be aggressive and manipulative. After all, it was Andrew Foster who was on the defensive.

She ran to the door and opened it with what she hoped was a carefree smile. Andrew waved his flowers flamboyantly, kissed her hand, playing the role of cavalier, and walked over to the divan to lay his giant bouquet out with a flourish.

"Olivia, before you say a word," he said with a serious look, "I must know if you were in any way damaged by Swanson's piece. If so, I can persuade her to retract it, change it. I pulled a cheap, adolescent trick. Believe me when I say that as soon as I had put down the receiver with Swanson, I regretted—deeply regretted—what I'd done. I can be a one-track-mind kind of person. I had embarked upon an innocuous campaign of disinformation with the Metropolitan—and all other possible competitors too—involving the *Marchesa*, and you . . . well, you were just another official target."

He wanted to tell her that there was another reason for his actions, that he desperately wanted to know how she had managed to gather what had to be deeply confidential information on Ardagh Rashvapar and his corrupt nephew. But how could he? Since he had no idea, really, who she was, he couldn't begin to formulate the question.

"Target? Innocuous?" Olivia said. "I expected your sophomoric lies about the condition of the painting. But to repeat something I confided in you, when I was your guest at that club, to a gossip columnist . . . that was unconscionable and it hurt.''

"I'll call Swanson right now. With the time difference I can easily reach her. We're friends. I'll ask her to fix it up. What do you want her to say?''

"Nothing," she snapped. "Andrew, what you don't seem to understand is that I don't cherish your assistance. The damage—and it's slight—has already been done. You got my boss, Steyne, to chastise me. Is that what you were after?''

"No . . . I . . . I sound so awkward because I am. I apologize with all my heart," he stammered. "How can I make up for this? What I did was disgraceful.''

"Easily," she remarked with an edge to her voice. "By never again assuming that I am something 'official,' a fitting 'target' for one of your petty schemes. Face facts. We're competitors. Tough ones, I suspect. Opponents for a possible acquisition, and from what I hear from the rumor mill, rivals for the job at the Met. All I ask is the simple respect due a serious competitor. Some humanity. The truth.''

"The naked truth?''

It was said with such boyish delight that she had to laugh. Seeing it was time to stop belaboring her point, Olivia picked up the bouquet and started walking toward the dressing room in search of a vase. The Ritz must have a vase, and it did.

"They are, Dr. Foster, truly magnificent," she said warmly. She had genuinely shaken him, and that pleased her greatly.

The glow from the light in the Place Vendôme streaming in from the windows shimmered on the gilded lace of her Yves Saint-Laurent blouse and for an instant Andrew imagined he could see the curves and delicate movement of her breasts. He felt faint. A curious reaction for a thirty-five-year-old man, but preferable, he figured, to the other reactions his mind was churning up—curling up in her lap and whimpering, or tearing off his clothes and posing as the Apollo in the Louvre. What he was experiencing had never before happened to him.

At the restaurant he ordered the rack of lamb; she, sweetbreads. She was delighted to hear that his French was merely competent.

Their conversation at first was stilted, wary, idle chat about people they both knew in the museum profession. But Andrew poured on all the charm he could muster and was thrilled to see her melting. The talk warmed up when the subject of art critics happened to arise.

"Even though Howard Olines seems to prefer me for the directorship of the Metropolitan," Andrew said bluntly, wanting to see how she would react, "I deplore his writing. Never has there been a more opinionated or mindless critic of the arts!"

Olivia laughed. "I loathe him! He knows nothing about the process of scholarship, the demands of connoisseurship, the reality of running a large art bureaucracy. Nothing! All are mysteries to that priggish little man," Olivia observed in exasperation. "But the problem with him goes deeper. Olines, for all his artfulness, has never—deliberately, I suspect—conveyed an accurate impression of any work of art. I think that's irresponsible. I'm surprised to hear your opinion of him. From that article, I had thought you adored each other." Olivia paused for a few seconds. "Andrew, are you really interested in the Met directorship?"

"No, I assure you . . ." he answered haltingly, taken aback by her directness, again suddenly on the defensive. "There are, of course, so many opportunities there," he said soberly. "It wouldn't take much to get the place out of the doldrums."

"Hasn't the board approached you?"

"No. And I sincerely doubt that they will," he said too quickly, and was immediately furious at himself for lying so patently. Why was she so effective in putting him on the defensive? That she did it so well irked—and fascinated—him. He tried to sound casual and asked, "You want the job, don't you, Olivia?"

"Very much. I think I deserve it. Don't you?"

"Would you believe my answer?" He grinned.

"Try me."

"You'd probably be surprisingly good at it. I mean, from your background. I know about some of it—your skills in dealing with that budding staff union just after you were named acting director."

"I had no idea that was common knowledge," she said, not trying to disguise her pride at his remark.

"You know the museum world; nobody can keep a secret. I even know about that episode when you discovered in the deep storage of the Met that bronze which turned out to be by Giambologna. Was that skill—or luck?"

"Skillful serendipity," Olivia replied, even more delighted and proud. "At least your secret sources are accurate—and kind to me."

"I know more about you than you think."

And I about you, she thought, turning over in her mind whether she should confront him with the knowledge she had gained from her mentor—that Andrew Foster had two employers, one the National Gallery of Art, the other the CIA. No. Not yet anyway.

"There's nothing unusual about my background," she continued softly. "I attended the University of Southern California as an undergraduate, starting perhaps too young—at sixteen."

"I read that someplace. Of course, a child prodigy!" Andrew laughed.

"Just precocious. USC as an undergraduate, majoring in languages, especially French and German—my father was a German who changed his name to Cartright—and then after graduating and a year of doing nothing I was sort of discovered by Ulrich Seitz, the—"

"The greatest art historian alive. He discovered you?"

"Waiting on tables," she said without expression. "I suppose you have read the recent news articles."

"Not entirely. Sounds like there's a story hidden there. Can I hear it?"

"Someday, perhaps. Not tonight," Olivia replied, a bit on edge. "So I went to Berkeley to study with Ulrich. After a year and a half, I took two years abroad—Italy, France, Spain, and a summer as a docent in the National Gallery—the London one. Then back to Berkeley. Got my Ph.D. Thesis was on Caravaggio—the divine Caravaggio. I wrote the Met; they were seeking an assistant curator in European paintings. And I got the job. I've been there almost five years now."

"I know. Still precocious. Only five years and being seriously considered as the next director? I'm impressed. Truly."

"You're kind."

"Just interested," he said. "What about that strange episode when as a graduate student at Berkeley you tipped the FBI off to the Nazi who had stolen those superb Pollaiuolo panels? Was that luck or skill . . . or are you a witch?"

"I smelled a rat. How did you learn about that?"

"As I said, the art world is talkative. Tell me more," he softly challenged.

"I refuse to be unjustly accused. This is innuendo, false information, smear, and dirty tricks," she cried, mimicking the overwrought voice of Ardagh Rashvapar.

Andrew smiled. "Not half bad," he said. "I'm not trying to probe, but how did, how could, a young graduate student solve one of the major art theft mysteries since the Second World War?"

"By making friends." Olivia pursed her lips.

"How'd you *do* it? Tell me. Please!" he implored.

"I became a very close friend of a conservator of paintings—a commercial restorer—in Berkeley. One day he told me that some character had come in with two tiny wooden panels and left them for an estimate on how much it would cost to clean them. 'They're dynamite!' I remember him saying. I asked if I could take a look and he said, 'Sure.' From a distance of about twenty feet I could see the two thin panels, one depicting Hercules and Antaeus and the other, Hercules and the seven-headed dragon—what was its name?"

"The Hydra." Andrew said, mesmerized by the way her face had flushed in the excitement of telling the story.

"You see, I had just discussed these paintings, maybe two weeks before, in a seminar on the Florentine Renaissance and recognized instantly what they were. I asked Ulrich Seitz what to do. It was he who told me to call the FBI."

"With no publicity," Andrew remarked.

"Oh, no!" she cried. "He thought there might be other Nazis lurking around."

"You know, I think you're an FBI agent," he said, laughing.

"And you're in the CIA, I suppose."

Andrew feigned amusement at her remark: of course she didn't know. But was she lying? Her story could not be that simple. Someday he would have to discover the real tale.

"Does my record scare you enough to move out of my way and

leave the directorship of the Met to me?" Olivia asked with an inpertinent grin. He was a snoop and a dangerous one. Did the CIA have tabs on everything? What else did he know about her, her friends, Don Ciccio?

"I don't know how to answer you anymore," Andrew said somberly. "I feel somewhat like Ardagh Rashvapar."

"Does that mean you have something to hide?" she teased. "Or does it mean you're a 'gambler,' as what's-her-name Swanson would say?"

"Olivia, I told you I'm sorry."

"Say it again."

"I'm repentant—terribly, frightfully. I swear."

"What's your nephew do?" she joshed.

"Oh, God, I'm innocent," he wailed.

"What about *your* past, Dr. Foster? That is to say, your past that has not been revealed in spades by the press. Do you have any secrets?"

Andrew slouched down in his chair, took a sip of wine, and said, "The truth is simple and it's never been told—fully, that's to say, or with the proper flavor. I come from a humble patrician family which for at least five generations has owned most of New Jersey and a three-thousand-acre estate the size of an antebellum plantation along the Hudson River in New York. That came about because, three generations ago, some great-great-aunt of mine got into an argument with my great-great-grandfather and slipped across the river."

"Fascinating," Olivia murmured.

"The Foster clan controls major financial interests in banking, oil, uranium, timber, supermarkets, grain, and, in recent years, a surprisingly successful microchip company in Vermont. So, in a sense, there was nothing left for me to do but become an art historian. It was the only faintly creative thing left."

Olivia nodded in mock sympathy.

"I was eight years old when my uncle—the real art expert in the family—picked me up in his arms one morning and told me it was 'time to start looking at pictures.' It wasn't hard, really. In a corridor leading from my room to the salon were four of Monet's *Haystacks* paintings. One of the bathrooms in the mansion at Far Hills had a study for Seurat's *La Poudreuse* plunked on the wall, slightly off-center. We had, still have, thousands of pieces of Chinese ceramics and rooms full of English eighteenth-century furniture—"

"There was Seurat's first little *Poudreuse* hanging in the bathroom?" Olivia exclaimed.

"My uncle adored it. The loo was his treasured place to contemplate his special treasure. But elsewhere there were drawings by Annibale Carracci and Holbein and Cézanne and pastels by La Tour and Liotard. Do you know Liotard?"

"Yes! He's great!" Olivia cried. "Especially the pastels in Geneva and the quintessential one in Dresden of the young maidservant carrying a tray of hot chocolate."

'Hmm. You do know your Liotard. More than I do. One of my earliest favorites was a Botticelli—tiny, six by four inches. *The Annunciation*. My father bought it for my grandfather to honor his sixty-fifth birthday. When I was nine or ten I'd sneak down at bedtime, pluck it off the wall, and take it to bed with me. I think I had a thing for Botticelli's young Madonna. But then, it could have been that cute little angel . . ."

Olivia raised her eyebrows. When he was being amusing, the hazel points in his eyes seemed to sparkle. His were looks one could get used to, she reflected.

"By the time I got to Harvard, I was more of a seasoned connoisseur than many museum curators. I may, of course, be stretching the point, but sometimes I think ten percent of what I saw projected on the slide screens in lecture halls was owned by someone in my family. In graduate school, a troop of curators at the Fogg Museum would slaver over me, seeking my influence in garnering loans or possible gifts. I know at least one professor who gave me an A for a so-so seminar report on Hans Baldung Grün—whom I happen to adore—because, for the greater glory of Harvard University, he hoped I'd persuade my father to hand over ours. I own that picture now. It's hanging over my bed in Washington."

"What's it like to be fabulously rich?"

"Well, we're not fabulously rich," he answered in a serious tone. "At least not like the Rockefellers or the Mellons—or Jonathan Cresson, for sure! We don't fly around in our own jets or cruise in J. P. Morgan–type yachts. I've got a small boat—a thirty-six-foot ocean racer, a Bristol—in the Chesapeake. My family's quiet, preferring art, travel, living in pleasant places like Giverny, Paris, Rome, Amalfi. I own a small villa in Sicily which I bought in 1957 when I was learning to become an archeologist. Did you know that I came very close to becoming a professional archeologist? No, of course not. How could you? That's one of my secrets. Halfway through graduate school I got sick of books, theory, color slides, and seminars and trooped off to Sicily, where I participated in the excavation of an ancient Greek city. It was near Piazza Armerina, the belly button of Sicily. I had the most amazing adventures and adored it. I almost took up archeology for life, then decided that the museum profession would perhaps be better. I sometimes regret the choice. I spent much of the time being taught how to read Latin fluently by the director of the dig, who had this unique method of teaching. It got so that I could speed-read the language. In fact I still do it today and enjoy picking up Pliny or Tacitus or Vergil or Tertullian. Sorry, I sound like I'm boasting. You know, it occurs to me that I really ought to visit my house in Sicily more often."

She shook her head slowly in astonishment. Despite herself she was captivated by his ingenuous charm.

"What's it like to be rich, truly?" He pondered the question. "When I was young, six to twelve, we spent the summers on an estate near Southampton, Long Island. My father got rid of it, unfortunately. It's called the 'Harbor of Lost Men' and had been constructed in the twenties by a partner of John D. Rockefeller's. We bought it from him. The main house had fifty-three rooms, including a dining hall called the Refectory, natch, big enough to seat two hundred for dinner. On one wall hung a huge ship's wheel. It was from a clipper wrecked in the nineteenth century on our beach—hence the romantic name, 'Harbor of Lost Men.' The guest house had twenty rooms, all decorated differently. I remember the Whaler Room, the Geisha Room, and the Haunt Room. God, how I loved *that* one. It looked like something out of Edgar Allan Poe. There was a great, brooding four-poster and a mirror hanging slightly askew with the mercury painted in trompe-l'oeil so that if you looked into it from a certain angle, you'd swear you saw a ghostly face! When I was seven I'd go crazy in there."

Andrew leaned forward, his face close to hers. He took her hand. "Within the main house there was an Olympic-size swimming pool

—in marble, no less—entirely enclosed in glass. And under the house there were at least two miles of underground passages, big enough to travel through in electric carts. And off those tunnels, Turkish baths, a ship-model museum, gun rooms, laundries. Overlooking our man-made saltwater lake was a concrete replica of a captain's cabin in the stern of a Spanish galleon—used primarily for cocktails.

"More fabulous than anything, for me, was our garage. I remember counting dozens of vehicles. There were four Rolls-Royces, a Hispano-Suiza, a couple of old wooden-sided Ford station wagons, a grandiose Packard with the roof open where the chauffeur and footman sat. Father, seeing that I was getting edgy—I was eleven —took me to the garage and like a foreman on a ranch 'cut' out of the pack a brown Chevy pick-up truck. He built up the clutch, brake pedal, and accelerator with wooden blocks, taught me to drive in a couple of hours, and let me loose on our three-thousand-acre shooting preserve. I painted my truck with a fanciful emblem —like the Forest Rangers'. Imagine the looks on the poachers' faces when I would screech to a halt and jump out of the truck with a .22 rifle under my arm! And it was loaded too. I was a deadly little kid!"

"You sound like my little brother, who just loved his .22," she mused.

"My second stepmother thrived on nonstop parties. She'd invite two hundred for a ball which might last for days. A hundred or so guests with their servants would actually stay on the place. I'd be up every night almost until dawn, sneaking around, blacked out like a commando. I'd spy on everything, and I mean *everything*. God, when I think I actually crept around under the great refectory table during dinner . . ."

"And under certain beds at night, I suppose," Olivia added softly. "Is that where you got those eyes?"

"I actually got those from my Scottish nanny," Andrew responded with a wink. "What's it like growing up rich, you ask? Easy. But it was also tough. There were daily inspections of hands and fingernails when I was young, and shoes and dress, later on. When I transgressed—not too often actually—my father would beat me with a cricket bat with holes bored into the spade so that it'd fly through the air faster and hurt more. I had four 'mothers'—

three, really, because my actual mother died when I was two. Those stepmothers seemed right out of Cinderella—or Alice in Wonderland at times—though now I see them as much as I can. Those three witches each give me loads of advice, plus unbelievable dirt about the other two."

"Andrew, is there anything you ever craved and didn't get?"

"When it comes to cravings, my mottoes are 'One step at a time' and 'What have you done for me lately?' But right now," he said, gazing fondly at her, "I'm seriously reconsidering those two philosophies. Well, I shall now be completely truthful. My answer is: damned little. But now it's your turn. What's your special craving?"

Luckily for her, the waiters brought their dinner. They silently toasted each other, his unanswered question hanging in the air. He could not wait to bring it up again.

At 1 A.M. Andrew Foster returned to his hotel elated by his performance, thinking only of Olivia Cartright. He smiled when the concièrge informed him that London had been calling repeatedly, "a woman named Holcomb. She is awaiting your reply."

He raced to his room and called Brown's Hotel on New Bond Street.

"Rebecca, what's up?"

"Andrew, hi! There was a sensational story in Candy Swanson's column yesterday about Olivia Cartright. She makes her a heroine, some sort of goddess! How was she really?"

Andrew chuckled. "I fed that story to Swanson."

"For God's sake, why?"

"Believe it or not, to damage her reputation."

Rebecca Holcomb started to laugh. "Andrew, do me a favor. The next time, before you leak a story to 'damage' an opponent, please call me first. What happened?"

"She was brilliant. And don't tell anybody, but I just had dinner with her. She's fascinating."

"I see," Rebecca murmured.

"She's cool, devastating, an expert manipulator."

"I see."

"She's going to be one tough competitor."

"Did she tip her hand about the painting?"

"No," he replied wanly.

"Did you, Andrew?"

"The painting, actually, never came up."

"I see."

"Fascinating."

"Andrew, these one- and two-word sentences will get us no-where. Olivia Cartright sounds like a subject for later discussion. Meanwhile, I have some exciting news. Peter Grundy told me, in confidence, that what he calls the 'beautiful lady' came in from the Richfield estate late last night. And you can see it—you know, 'see,' but not examine. Grundy's still working on his intractable peer to get us special permission to study it."

"That's great. When?"

"First thing tomorrow."

"Okay, I'll get to London as close to noon as I can. But I might not get there until later. Better fix the appointment for around four in the afternoon."

"Andrew, I don't think that'll work. Grundy said, very emphatically, that early morning would be best. I think he means it's the only time. Is there a very early plane?"

"I seem to remember there's one at six. Christ! It's almost one thirty! Fix the appointment for later. Peter always gives me a break. We've done a lot of business together."

"You don't care about losing the edge?"

"Rebecca, this picture is going to be at William's for many weeks. It is not about to change," Andrew replied impatiently. "As you know, I like to proceed with a pre-conceived plan, step by step. I don't want to be hurried. The worst way to see a painting is to be tired."

"Fine," she said at last. "I'll try my best with Sir Peter. See you tomorrow!"

"Rush, rush," Andrew grumbled. He picked up the phone and dialed the Ritz. Olivia, luxuriating in a hot bath, was startled by the phone ringing near her ear. She picked it up at once. "Did you make it up to your room safely?" he asked. "I was worried you might get . . . well, waylaid."

"In the Ritz?"

"Or perhaps lose your way? I was hoping you'd need me to find your room."

Hearing his resonant voice, Olivia felt a growing sexual warmth rippling through her. Then, perhaps because of the unexpected suddenness of the feeling, she snapped back into consciousness. Laughingly she said, "I did make it all the way to my room. On foot. I needed the exercise after that divine dinner. You're a dear to call."

"I'm really calling," he said, "because I want to apologize. I may not be able to have dinner with you tomorrow. Something's come up. I've got to be in London by midday. I really should be there by nine, but what the hell! And I simply don't know my schedule well enough to be sure I can get back until the last plane. So let's have lunch, or maybe breakfast, the day after. But if I *can* work it out in London and get back at a decent hour tomorrow, I'll call you. We could have a late supper and go dancing. How does that sound?"

Say no, Olivia told herself. Get out of this. Cut it off. Foster is a competitor, a resourceful, charming one. Play it smart. *This man wants you and he wants your job!* Obviously, he'd been called to London to examine the Velázquez. It must have come in from the Richfield country estate and he's got a special 'in' to see it. Damn!

"Dancing," Olivia murmured, splashing the water in her tub. The image eased her anxieties. Dancing was the obvious next step.

"What's that?" he asked.

"Water. I'm having a bath."

"You're in the bath?" he asked, mimicking an adolescent tone of voice.

Olivia laughed. Instantly, she knew she had to gamble, hoping she could win both throws of her dice. "Andrew, it's very late. Do call me tomorrow. Make it in the late evening. We'll see."

"You're not sure?" he asked glumly.

"I hope to be here," she said, weighing down the words with doubt. "I shall most certainly try."

Olivia rang the concièrge and instructed him to book her a seat on the 6 A.M. flight to Heathrow. She was banking on the fact that she could call Peter Grundy at home in the morning and somehow talk him into showing her the picture. Although Olivia recognized that seeing the *Marchesa* before anyone else didn't really matter, getting the first glance—certainly before Andrew Foster—would impress Ayn Steyne. But could she make it in time?

10 MIRROR IMAGES

WHEN OLIVIA TELEPHONED PETER GRUNDY at his country house just before boarding her plane in Paris at five thirty in the morning, Sir Peter struggled to gain consciousness while attempting to converse with her genially, as if being awakened in pitch darkness was a social treat.

"What else, my dear, am I here for? To help, to oblige, to succor, to ease the troubled lives of friends and possible clients. If you come this morning, will you be able to see my very beautiful *Marchesa?* Let me see. The day is already fully booked. I attempted to reach Ayn Steyne, but she has yet to reply. You see, I have decided to allow potential bidders—am I to assume you are to be one of that privileged group? But I suppose I shouldn't probe—to have three hours each with the lady. I must tell you that your phone call this morning is most fortunate. The picture arrived here the night before last just before midnight. You well may be the first member of the public to view it. Since you are enterprising enough to be arriving so bright and early, why shouldn't you have the honor of seeing her first? We have parties confirmed from nine all the day through, and the nine o'clock probably won't make it, so you might have the full three hours. That will do? Excellent! Ta ta."

Sir Peter telephoned the night security guard at the gallery, instructing him to admit Olivia and give her a large cup of strong tea.

By the time Sir Peter arrived at seven thirty, she was purring.

"Olivia, my dear, you look divine!"

She smiled her thanks as he escorted her to the ancient elevator, which creaked its way to the fifth floor. He led her down a narrow corridor with moisture-stained walls to a tiny room empty except for three chairs, a rickety table, and a large easel on which was set a massive canvas obscured by a linen curtain.

"I will now leave you to your work and your dreams, Olivia," Sir Peter said with a smile. "But before I unveil the painting I must remind you that you are forbidden by Lord Richfield to study it with anything more than an ordinary hand-held magnifying glass. These are not my rules. The owner has insisted upon them, for everyone. I know how irregular this restrictive procedure seems, but he's adamant. And there will also be a guard in the room at all times. He was hired by Richfield. That is also part of the arrangement."

"What's he trying to hide?" Olivia asked tautly. She reached into her purse and dangled before Sir Peter's eyes a small magnifying glass.

"Nothing," Sir Peter hastened to reply, nodding his head at her unprepossessing loupe.

"It does give one the unfortunate impression," she persisted, "that there's something His Lordship fears in not allowing a possible bidder to study the painting the way any auction house would allow almost anybody off the street."

"Oh, come now. The directive is eccentric, I admit, but there's no need to blow it out of proportion. I promise to redouble my efforts to persuade His Lordship to be more reasonable. And, please, Olivia, tell me honestly what you think of it."

"Peter, you can't expect me to tell you what I really feel. First, may I be allowed to take measurements?"

"Oh, all right."

He removed the linen curtain from the painting, then slipped out of the room, gently closing the door. A stocky young man, dressed in a black pinstripe suit and vest, nodded his head deferentially and primly took a seat in a corner of the room.

Olivia had disciplined herself not to give the painting so much as a flicker of a glance until she was settled and absolutely ready to scrutinize it. She moved a chair to a point about six feet from the picture, which was illuminated by two large gooseneck lamps and by the daylight cascading from the single window. Then she closed her eyes, sat down carefully, turned her face in the direction of the painting, and opened them.

Her immediate impression was a surge of life and light, a spark of electricity, the subtle excitement generated when an important person—a presence—enters a room. Olivia was so astonished that she leaned back abruptly in her chair with a small gasp. My God! The thing *was* alive. The face was composed, yet alert. She was both saucy and self-conscious. Eager and afraid. The way the young woman held her right arm across her breasts yet hiding none of the flesh was a brilliant stroke, showing reticence and sexual hunger at the same time. Her eyes were steady but soft. The lips seemed prepared to speak. What might she say?

For the first hour, Olivia gazed at the magnetic image of Velázquez's *Marchesa* without moving from her chair. She forced her eyes over every millimeter of the nude figure, enthralled by the vitality and energy that exuded from what she had to remind herself was "merely a painted surface." What a miracle it was!

The flesh tones, slightly more ruddy than she had expected from the photograph, had been applied in such deft glazes that they did not just seem to be skin, they appeared to possess the temperature of human flesh. The eyes themselves were poems of artistry, so limpid yet so penetrating that you could easily mistake the dabs and blobs of paint for the incandescence of life.

Olivia spent the second hour examining the surface of the picture not with the simple loupe she had dangled before Grundy but with her powerful eyeglass fitted out with the miniature camera, in an agonizingly slow perusal of the subsurface of the work. When she'd begun, the guard rose in alarm and ventured over to be sure that she was not touching the canvas. But when he saw that she kept the glass inches from the canvas, he relaxed and returned to his perch. Olivia had brought with her a small bottle of xylene, a harmless cleaning fluid, and a cotton swab, but she did not dare take them out to clean minute passages of the painting. If the guard had not been there, she would swiftly have done it. But her intense scrutiny was nearly as effective. It was amazing what the trained human eye, aided by magnification, could perceive.

At first the colors seemed far too brown, the brushstrokes murky. Her examination revealed that the painting's varnish had yellowed drastically but evenly. That was a good sign, a solid piece of evidence that the varnish was original. Later applications frequently became gummy wavelets on the surface of the paint. The surface she was looking at was smooth but a little opaque. The yellowing effect had also turned the once-sparkling taffeta coverlet on which the sensual woman lay into a bilious greenish brown. And the neutral silver-gray of the background over her head had toned down to a lower-keyed dove-brown. But under the discolored varnish the whites looked like freshly fallen snow, crisp and crystalline.

At first Olivia had totally missed the clues. And even when she had studied the upper part of the canvas a second time, it had taken several minutes for the irregularities to register. There seemed to be mysterious letters—written backward—deep beneath the surface of the paint! Suppressing her excitement so as not to alert the guard, she gazed upon her discovery. Just under the surface glazes, barely visible to even the most penetrating eye, was an inscription on the back of the canvas and which had managed over time to seep through to the other side. It took Olivia nearly ten minutes to decipher the elusive script, to write down each word, and then translate the archaic Spanish inscription:

> I, Velázquez, have for a fleeting moment of eternity again borrowed life from my goddess, my desire, and have given that life to dull paint. The 16th of June, 1650, Roma.

Olivia had to stifle a cry. It was a monumental discovery.

The inscription was not the only revelation. She was now positive the painting had never been relined. The minute peaks of the brushstrokes had not been flattened, as would have happened had a fresh canvas backing been pressed by a hot iron to the back of the painting.

Olivia sat there, reveling in the work, scanning its surface with her eyeglass, pausing over key details—particularly the eyes. Trembling with anxiety, she dared to take the first picture with her concealed camera. Thank God, the guard didn't notice the muffled click of the shutter. He was lolling back in his chair near the window with his eyes half closed. Olivia took five more. That would be the end of the film. The only problem with the instrument was that it needed to be reloaded every eight pictures. The ones she had just made, plus the two at the Louvre, had expended the roll.

Cautiously she reached into her handbag for another. Where are they? Her hand scrabbled around in the bottom of the bag. Nothing! She must have left the other rolls of film in her suite. She sat absolutely stunned. Because of her carelessness, she had failed in the most vital part of her mission. Would six pictures be sufficient to convince the Met's board of the desirability of the Velázquez? Olivia was so disgusted with herself she almost burst into tears. The six photos she had taken would simply have to suffice. Luckily she had focused in on the Marchesa's glowingly beautiful face and her gleaming eyes. Her chronic impetuousness had caused her to commit what might be a monumental blunder. She rose to her feet, pulled out her metal tape measure, and recorded the dimensions in her notebook: forty-eight by eighty-one inches.

Olivia thanked the guard and departed with a quick goodbye and fervent thanks to Peter Grundy. She was happy he was on his way to an appointment, for she was afraid that with more time she might have let slip something that would alert him to her discovery. She had no doubts at all that the painting was authentic—and magnificent despite being filthy. Any professional permitted to examine the canvas the way she had would rapidly arrive at the same conclusion. So why the restrictions, the barriers, the unseemly presence of the guard? For an instant Olivia's mind was filled with doubts. Could her eyes have been playing tricks on her? She reread her notes. No, she had not been mistaken, for there were the words of the hidden inscription which proved the picture was by the master. Confused, exhausted by the tensions of her risky exploit, she fell asleep in the taxicab on the way back to Heathrow Airport.

Once back in the Ritz, she placed a call to Don Ciccio and revealed what she had found at William's, Ltd. She left out nothing —even her annoyance at herself in forgetting to bring along sufficient film. The Count listened avidly and asked a dozen questions about the condition of the painting and the nature of the inscription. But when Olivia tried to find out from him if there was anything about the Velázquez he might have discovered that might help her, he became reticent, saying only that he would talk to her about the matter face to face in Naples. And that was when Olivia realized that an invitation to his palatial villa was a command.

• • •

By the time Olivia was striding into the Ritz, Andrew had just arrived at William's and was beginning to raise his voice at Sir Peter Grundy, who found it difficult to remain unflappable.

"What the hell do you mean, I can't see the picture? It was all set, Peter. I mean, I fly all the way from Paris because I was told to come and now you have the arrogance to inform me that I can't see the thing!"

"Andrew . . . me, arrogant? I told Miss Holcomb to tell you that you could see the painting *only* first thing in the morning. This afternoon is absolutely out of the question. I have ceded that time to Roy Bentley and Sir Michael Fairless, who is after all the director of the Warburg Collection. You must understand this. Andrew, I beg of you, please calm yourself. It's not a question of your persuading me. I cannot show you the painting today. That's that."

"Just two minutes, Peter? I just can't go all the way back to Paris without a quick look. Please. And I apologize for being tardy."

"This is not a picture you simply blink at. Why not come back the day after tomorrow and give it the careful scrutiny it deserves? I can promise you four hours late in the day."

Rebecca Holcomb slipped her way into the conversation. "Excellent. Why not stay over? That's almost as good. You won't be the absolute first, but so what?"

"Can't do it, Rebecca," Andrew said. "Got some pressing business in Paris. I'll come back. But I don't know just when. The *Marchesa* isn't going to vanish."

"Andrew, now you're being eminently reasonable," Sir Peter said smoothly. "But please, please let me know long in advance. Who knows, Lord Richfield just might cut down on the time available for scholars to examine his treasure. He's so mercurial. Anyway, the honor of seeing the *Marchesa* first—if the honor matters—has already been won. By a most surprising connoisseur."

"Who?" Rebecca shot back. "Frobisher of the Getty?"

"No. A member of the opposite sex."

"Private collector? Museum type? A museum type!" Rebecca concluded, seeing the look on Sir Peter's face. "Why, that can only be Olivia Cartright from the Met."

"Indeed. I must say I was surprised when she called early this morning," Sir Peter remarked with a short laugh. "Amazing.

Somehow she learned that the painting was here, and rushed over from Paris."

"Olivia Cartright was here *this* morning?" Andrew was flabbergasted.

"Before the place was open," Grundy replied. "Awakened me at home at dawn. Forced me to arise at an ungodly hour and even take a train to town—I didn't want to bother my chauffeur. Studied the picture for three full hours."

"Faked out! I warned you that Olivia Cartright's no pawn," Rebecca said sharply to Andrew as they left William's.

"I never denied it," Andrew said with a laugh. He found himself both vexed and delighted at her maneuver. She was quite a woman! His fear now was that Olivia might not have returned to Paris, might not be available to see him, might not want to see him.

"You're worried about the painting, aren't you?" Rebecca asked, seeing the expression on his face. "Is it normal for an auction house to be so rigid about displaying a work of art? I don't know this field all that well, Andrew, but don't you find all this hocus-pocus strange? I mean, if they've got something to sell that's worth eleven million pounds, wouldn't it serve their interests better to allow anyone with a buck to see the thing—even if they wanted to bring along a nuclear reactor?"

Andrew smiled. "Usually, yes. But another way of 'marketing' a precious work is to play it this way—tight, restrictive, and at a distance. Somehow, then, the work elevates in importance. As you can see from my reaction, I've become even more excited because of the mystery."

"You should stay a day or two, Andrew."

"I can't. I have something vital to find out in Paris. I'll see the picture in plenty of time. In fact, I think it might be wise to go off and look hard at all the other great Velázquezes and then see this one. After that my eye will be a lot more receptive and fresher than my competitors'."

The other contenders came dutifully and paid homage to the work in individual ways.

Roy Bentley slipped into the tiny room and stepped up to the *Marchesa* as if extending a challenge to a duel. Then, positioning himself firmly in the chair, he brought forth from his green canvas bag several dozen black-and-white glossy photographs of the Rok-eby *Venus* and spent more than an hour comparing them to the painting. He was so absorbed, looking from one to the other, that he failed to detect the inscription.

"Not bad actually," he commented sourly to Sir Peter as he was about to depart.

The *Marchesa* was simply the finest painting of the seventeenth century he had ever seen, and most surely one of the most vibrant Velázquezes. But Bentley was also annoyed, for it was going to take a lot of work and clever subterfuge to capture it.

"Peter, why don't you send the picture over to the Gallery—say, next Monday, when we're closed. I'd like to look at her side by side with our portrait."

"Roy, that's utterly out of the question."

"Right! But you'll do it, won't you? If the Ministry politely—and staunchly—asks."

"Never! Sorry!"

Bentley stamped his foot on the sidewalk outside the auction house in vexation. There was no doubt he would have to pursue the masterpiece strenuously. As soon as he could, he would launch a campaign to discourage all potential bidders.

Sir Michael Fairless, distinguished professor of art history and keeper of the vaunted Warburg Collection, was so taken with the portrait that he paced in front of the "remarkable image of feminin-ity," as he called it, for half an hour, marveling at its vitality, at the subtlety of its glazes, moved by humanity revealed in the smolder-ing eyes of the young woman. As he made one of his passes in front of the picture—he had learned long ago that moving inces-santly before a painting somehow made him see more—for an instant he thought he saw something unusual in the upper back-ground. What was it? An imperfection? Deteriorating paint? No, it was nothing, he decided at last. His eyes were beginning to play tricks. It was time to go. For Sir Michael, examining a picture for longer than thirty minutes was dangerous. After that time, one began to imagine things. His report to his employers would be glowing.

• • •

For the next viewer the police had demanded such stringent security precautions that Peter Grundy had decided to close William's for the rest of the afternoon. The Russian delegation had demanded total secrecy and announced that only two people would show up for only fifteen minutes. But no less than six arrived—Ludmilla Tcherninka accompanied by the cultural attaché from the embassy and four expressionless young men who seemed more like dancers than bodyguards but who, by their contemptuous glances at the somewhat cowed guard in the *Marchesa*'s sanctum sanctorum, flagged their true vocations.

Not wanting to miss the historic event, Sir Peter politely insisted that he would accompany the party. Tcherninka grunted her assent. She lingered far beyond the requested fifteen minutes, remaining for close to an hour. Grundy was greatly amused to see that the attractive director positioned herself directly in front of the canvas and stood, rigid in concentration, with her arms folded tightly across her chest for the entire time.

"It has a certain merit" was her only comment.

Andrew tried several times to call Olivia from Heathrow with no success. Nervous though he was that he would not be able to see her that evening, all the way back to Paris, whenever he thought about being outmaneuvered, he would burst into laughter, causing the man sitting next to him to edge further away. He finally got through to her upon his arrival and implored her—why was she so reluctant?—to join him for a late dinner at Le Relais.

They met at ten o'clock and she was radiant. He wondered if he could get her to admit she had been in London. It would be a test of her feelings toward him and the true nature of their competition.

"Busy day?" he asked her.

"Oh, just dashing here and there."

"Go to any good shows? See any decent art?"

Instantly Olivia realized he knew. She wondered if she should make a clean breast of her surreptitious trip to London. Damn! She should have instructed Peter Grundy to keep it confidential. All of a sudden the game was becoming serious and the anxieties she had about the curious restrictions surrounding the painting surged back into her mind. Wouldn't it be better to deal with Andrew directly? For the moment she decided to stall and see whether she could get away with not telling him.

"A few. And you? Busy?"

"Flying here and there," he answered with an infectious grin. Why wasn't she telling him? Should he force her hand? "Gloomy weather, though."

"Gloomy? I found the weather sparkling," she said.

As Olivia looked at him, lolling back in the comfortable booth and sipping his glass of wine, she felt a stab of apprehension. Silly, but she could not help thinking there was more to the affair of the *Marchesa Odescalchi* than the selling of a masterwork. The smell of conspiracy was in the air. Olivia felt frightened and, without analyzing why, leaned toward him for protection. She would tell him.

"Andrew, we musn't fence around like this." She reached over to touch his hand. "We're friends as well as competitors."

He took her hand tenderly. "Right. Business and friendship. Gets mixed up, hard to keep 'em separate. Difficult, sometimes, to know what to say."

"What was your impression of the *Marchesa?*" she whispered.

"Didn't get to see it. I was supposed to go in the morning, but got lazy. You picked up my slot. Clever, not to mention opportunistic. My fault."

She shook her head. "Look, I'm determined too. In my position I've got to be. You should know that."

"Every time I see you I gain a little more respect for that determination," Andrew commented, a smile once again coming back into his face. "And the painting? Good? Bad? Indifferent?"

"I'm not going to tell," she said flatly. She noted his look of dismay. "I'm not being perverse . . ."

Andrew remained silent.

"I'm not going to tell you . . . until after you have had the chance to see it," she added.

"I suppose that's fair," he said reluctantly. "Now it's time for friendship. I know this great place—are rivals allowed to dance together?"

"Dancing around is what they're supposed to do," Olivia said, with a straight face.

Andrew laughed. "It's a quiet disco, minutes away."

On the dance floor Andrew's touch was tentative, teasing—slow movements, light caresses. He could hardly contain his excitement. But he knew he had to play it slowly, a waiting game, just like the pursuit of any art treasure.

"We must meet tomorrow. Where do you want to go? Let's make it the Jeu de Paume. I have a few things to show you. The luscious *Olympia*, for instance."

Olivia laughed and then said with genuine sadness, "I can't. I've got an appointment with a trustee. You know what that means. Then I have to travel around for a couple of weeks."

"A couple of weeks! God," he moaned. He steered her back to the table. "Are you really going after the Velázquez?"

"Perhaps."

The spell was broken. Glumly, he paid the check and they left the club.

He deposited her at the doors of the Ritz. "Good luck," he murmured, deeply annoyed, more by his inability to communicate to her the seriousness of his offer than at her intransigence.

"Oh, we'll bump into each other in a few weeks. In London, no doubt," she said, trying to make it sound light. But then, in a voice far sadder than he expected, she added, "We really must."

As soon as Andrew had returned to his hotel he called his contact at the CIA and described the information he needed—airline and hotel bookings for Olivia Alexis Cartright over the next three weeks, certainly for London, possibly for Madrid, Rome, and Vienna. The callback came within fifteen minutes. The operative informed him where Olivia was going and where she planned to stay in Madrid, Vienna, and London. When Andrew had finished jotting it down, he sauntered down to the desk and, with a tip large enough to make even the testiest concièrge break into a smile, instructed him to book different flights but the same hotels beginning with the Sanvy in Madrid two days hence.

Smiling to himself, Andrew returned to his room, collapsed on his bed, fully clothed, and fell instantly to sleep.

11 PROMISES, PROMISES

OLIVIA WOKE AT DAWN with an annoyingly lingering yearning for Andrew Foster and stretched back on her luxurious bed sighing with pleasure. She simply had to see him again; it had been silly of her to attempt to play games with him. A contrived coolness would never work for her. Though reserved on the surface, she was a passionate woman, tempestuous. She decided she wanted Andrew Foster. The question was how to get him and win out over him? She had to remain near him, and therefore had to know where he was going to be in the next weeks. Olivia had determined to change her travel plans and follow him—at a discreet distance, of course. There was only one person in the world who could supply her with the information she needed, the omniscient Count Nerone. Despite the early hour, she placed a phone call to him in Naples.

"Darling Olivia," his smooth, musical voice rang out. "I'm so pleased you called. . . . Too early? Not for me. I've been motoring myself around my gardens since first light. I must know exactly when I can expect you in Naples. We do have some unfinished business. . . . In two weeks? Excellent. You have neglected me. How can I repay my debt to you, how can I help you if I see you so infrequently? And see you in your new dazzling reality."

"I will, I will," she said. How had he learned so much? She decided not to probe and launched, instead, a challenge. "I have so much to ask you about the Velázquez."

"My dear, I really know little about the painting, other than the obvious—what everybody knows. I'd like to assist you," he replied after a pause, "but . . ."

"I need whatever help I can get on who might be seriously going after it. That's the kind of information you always seem to have at your fingertips.''

"This painting's becoming more than slightly mysterious," the Count said with a small laugh.

Olivia, puzzled by his apparent evasiveness, decided to attempt a jest. "You haven't thought of bidding on it yourself, have you?''

"Dear Olivia, I have other artistic interests at the moment, and besides, I want you to have the *Marchesa,* if you want it.''

"I do. I knew I could rely on you," she replied, wondering why he was sounding so reserved. Or was she imagining it? "I'm positive I know who is going to be my most serious competitor. Andrew Foster. Everything you told me about him so far has the ring of truth—he's rich, he chases women, and I don't doubt he's employed by the CIA. How did you find that out? But now I'm desperate to know what he's up to, for the next few weeks.''

"Very well, my dear. Hold on a moment while I ask my assistant, Marco Migliorini, to put an immediate trace on him.''

He came back on the phone and chatted with Olivia about the status of the art market and the latest rumors about who might be the front-runner for the directorship of the Metropolitan. It seemed like mere minutes before he interrupted himself. "Here, I have managed to glean some up-to-the-minute information for you," he said.

Olivia wrote down what he told her. Andrew was planning to go to Spain. He had booked a different flight to Madrid the same day as hers. Moreover, he had reserved a room at the Sanvy Hotel, the same place where she was going to stay! She didn't have to follow him. He was obviously trying to follow her!

"I have it. Bless you," she said. "How do you do all this?" It was an impulsive question, one she really didn't want answered.

"Someday you may be allowed to know. When you come to see me, perhaps I shall have even more information on young Dr. Foster. *Addio.*''

Compliant as he seemed to be, the Count seemed incapable of dealing with life in any other way than as a trade-off of debts and favors. Not for the first time was Olivia uneasy about her friend.

• • •

Shortly after nine o'clock Bruce Thompson rang insistently on the doorbell of her suite, to join her for breakfast. He was barely through the door when he asked breathlessly, "What's the painting like—really?"

"A triumphant masterpiece in pretty good condition," Olivia responded eagerly. "I don't think the picture has ever been touched by a restorer, at least in modern times. It has the bloom of life." Olivia almost told him about the astounding inscription she had discovered in the background of the picture, but decided not to. There were certain things she thought wise not to impart to Thompson, with his penchant for gossip.

"Splendid!" he said.

"And she throbs with passion," Olivia raced on excitedly, recalling vividly the sensuality of the Marchesa. "Bruce, it's more than a great work of art. It's a highly complex icon of all aspects of love, from the spiritual to the wanton. What I find so marvelous is that there's no hint of self-delusion, no inner echo of sadness or even self-hatred that you sometimes see in those portraits of legendary beauties of history. Take that warped Emma Hamilton, for example, so gorgeous on the surface in the Gainsborough portraits, so crude and depraved below the surface, so willing to hasten her own degradation."

Thompson's face reflected his growing anxiety. "I may be overreacting, Olivia, but do you think the *Marchesa* could be looked upon in any way as objectionable? I mean, is there any chance that the stuffy members of the board might turn it down because the lady's too raw? When it comes to naked women, the Met can rival the Vatican. Manet's *Olympia* was rejected years ago, as everyone knows. I realize these are modern times, but could there be a problem in trying to acquire a work some scholars believe makes Manet's courtesan look chaste?"

"In a sense, the Marchesa's totally objectionable," Olivia mused. "But then, in another, she's utterly pure."

Thompson grunted.

"The woman seems to have mystical properties," Olivia went on. "To me, she's one of those magical images that mirror the nature of the person looking at it. I mean, if you are chaste, she— this naked object of desire—will look chaste. If, on the other hand, you are sexually obsessed, debauched, whatever, she will appear lascivious. She's sacred and profane love in one image. My only hope is that a sufficient number of the committee will see her virtues of the spiritual and artistic kind and will want—"

"Will want to spend the institution blind? Olivia, I personally find your, ah, theory of reflected images or spiritual transmittal, ah, fascinating. But will the committee? I know some of those dullards pretty well. They won't begin to understand. And Ayn Steyne or Roland McCrae, what will they see in this creature? What will they make of the staggering price? And the fact that we already have the *Juan de Pareja* and the other Velázquezes?"

"Bruce, if anyone on the committee wants to kill the acquisition, they can come up with a dozen excuses. But I'll bet I can talk them into going after it. Of course, I'll need support, both in votes and in money, from key people like yourself."

"Olivia, forgive me for saying it, but are you quite sure it's a wise course? I mean, it is going to be horribly expensive. As you know, I'm on my way back to New York and I'll be happy to talk it up, but do we really need it?"

The intensity of her response caught Thompson by surprise.

"If we don't get this picture, it will mark the beginning of the end for the Metropolitan, do you hear? The very moment when the Met gave up. The exact time it stopped striving. Damn it! It's only money. This is an incomparable treasure that some dotty English lord is giving up without a thought. *We must get it!* If we don't we flag the world that we're finished as an institution. Collecting is what it's still all about. The Getty may have the money, but they buy second-rate stuff. We can't sink to their level."

"Jesus, Olivia. I'm not the enemy. Don't get on me when I say this, but are you sure you're going all out for the institution, and not just for . . . for your own career?"

She regarded him coolly. "Both, of course. Why not?"

Bruce Thompson smiled appreciatively.

"As we discussed," she said emphatically, "the acquisition of the *Marchesa* is my only hope to get to the top of the museum world. And it's your opportunity to stay on top, particularly considering your present tightrope walk with Steyne and McCrae. We've got to get this picture. And ward off forever Andrew Foster's chances of becoming the next director of the Met."

• • •

After Thompson had departed Olivia telephoned Ayn Steyne, eager for the first time in her relationship with that severe woman to confide in her, to receive encouragement. The more the labyrinthine path toward the Velázquez proceeded, the more ambivalent Olivia felt. At times she was supremely confident, at others fearful she was getting in way over her head.

"Tell me about the picture. Spare no details," Steyne instructed her curtly.

"First, the academic description," Olivia exclaimed, "and then the poetry. It is a decently preserved example of the master's mature period. The coloration is blonder than his earlier paintings. It possesses that distinct lyrical aura so marked in the second Roman period and is better, I think, than the later works such as *Las Meninas*. Now for the poetry. It's a smash, a power-packed act of genius, one of the most gripping portraits ever painted by anybody—better than the portrait of Innocent X. I adore it. We must, simply *must* have it!"

"Impressive. But what's the latest estimate?"

Olivia told what she had learned and launched into a colorful description of how she had wangled her way into the auction house ahead of Andrew.

"That's something I might have expected of him." Her voice had grown cool. "What do you plan to do next?"

"Go to Madrid, Vienna, possibly to Rome if I have time, and finally to London before returning to New York. I want to examine as many other Velázquezes as I can before my final report to the committee."

"Proceed—but be cautious. Goodbye." The phone clicked off.

And there it was, like the word from some ancient oracle, delivered laconically, coldly, enigmatically. The comfort Olivia needed would never come from Ayn Steyne. She huddled on her bed overcome with depression, then jumped to her feet and began to pack frantically. If she didn't rush, she might miss her plane to Madrid.

12 THE RUN-AROUND

THERE WERE FEWER THAN A DOZEN visitors in the rambling galleries of the Prado as Olivia wandered through, reveling in having the place to herself. She had arrived two hours before her appointment with the director, the charming and gregarious José Sánchez, so she could soak up the works of Velázquez. She strolled in awe past the phalanx of masterworks—*The Surrender at Breda, Las Meninas, Las Hilanderas*, the equestrian portraits of Philip IV and Prince Balthazar, the drunken sheepherders suddenly visited by Bacchus, the affectionate portraits of the Infantas.

She was fascinated to see that Velazquez's most famous works did not surpass the *Marchesa*. Indeed, some—even the most renowned—seemed almost feeble compared to the flamboyant young woman. But perhaps she was deluding herself in the hope that the painting she coveted was finer than reality would allow? But then again, wasn't the face of Bacchus faded? Weren't the draperies in *Las Hilanderas* slightly muddy? Weren't almost all the flesh tones of the Velázquezes in the Prado grayish?

After this, Olivia concentrated solely on flesh tones. Brilliantly painted as the surfaces were, delicate as their colors seemed to be, made up of manifold levels of subtle glazes, layered almost like real flesh, they possessed a marked pallor when compared with the *Marchesa*. Only *Las Meninas*, which had been cleaned years before by one of the leading British conservators, was equal to the *Marchesa* in its delicate and unerring application of paint, some passages so transparent that the oils seemed like diaphanous washes of watercolor, imparting what was almost a tangible body temperature to the painted image.

Was she dreaming or making it all up—indulging in wish fulfill-ment? Did she so much need a personal triumph that she was willing to delude herself? "For Christ's sake, you dummy, look again!" she ordered herself through clenched teeth.

But intense scrutiny only convinced her that she was right, that what she had seen in that dingy studio at William's Ltd. was one of the world's most sublime treasures. In his *Bacchus*, Velázquez had endowed the mythological scene with a cosmic significance—intending it to be nothing less than the universal symbol of what is godlike in humanity and what is human in the gods. In his *Marchesas*, he clearly wanted to create the universal image of woman-hood. That explained the potent admixture of feminine qualities from the trivial to the sublime, from spoiled child to earth mother.

As she stood motionless, sorting out the heady ideas rushing through her mind, out of the corner of her eye she spotted Andrew Foster, sauntering through a portal four or five galleries down the central corridor. She felt a rush of relief, and, just as quickly, a rush of desire. Thank God he had actually come! Olivia had asked for him at the hotel as soon as she had arrived and was crushed and confused to be told that no one by the name of Foster was expected. Had he seen her? Clearly not. Excellent! She quickened her steps to the administrative offices. She simply had to see Sánchez before Andrew could.

With a courtly smile, the Spaniard greeted his young colleague and gently chided her. "What could possibly bring you to Madrid so precipitously? And why must you depart so soon—for Vienna, you say? And if I am not being too forward, may I say how beauti-ful you have made yourself! What a boon to the otherwise dull-looking museum profession!"

Olivia laughed. "Don José, as always, the very spirit of the chiv-alry of Spain! I'm here on a secret mission—to study your Veláz-quezes so that I can decide if I want to bid eleven or twelve million dollars for the *Marchesa*. Should I? How does it compare with yours?"

"So, we are to be competitors," Sánchez observed with a wry smile. "For reasons purely of national pride our Ministry of Culture has decided that we must make a bid. But of course, we shall not win her. But the public bid will be a measure of how highly we consider this picture. I saw her once some fifteen years ago at Lord Richfield's. She needed cleaning. But she's beautiful—almost too beautiful."

"As beautiful as his pictures here?"

Sánchez hesitated a moment. "Better than most," he said sadly. "The story should never get out, but some of our great Velázquezes are damaged."

Olivia gazed dumbstruck at him.

He sighed. "During the last decades of the nineteenth century we had a restorer who was a zealot, not only in his work but, most regrettably, in what he proclaimed were *moral* aesthetic issues. It was an unfelicitous combination of assets! He 'ameliorated' many of our Velázquezes. During the seventeenth century, you see, it was fashionable in the royal court to rouge women's—and some men's—cheeks in bright, elliptical patches. And Velázquez painted that makeup just the way it was. This restorer's technique consisted —and this is not a jest—of rubbing his thumbs vigorously and incessantly over the surface of the paintings."

"What?"

"It's true! No chemical solvents for him. The soft pressure of his thumb was more effective. As he rubbed, millimeter by millimeter, month after month—mind you, it took three years just to rub clean one picture—the old varnish would come together in little warm balls of resin and would drop from the canvas to reveal the paint below. His diaries tell of miraculous moments when he would reveal the sheer beauty of original paint. But leaving well enough alone wasn't sufficient for him."

"I don't think I want to know what he did," Olivia remarked tensely.

"Being a moralist, the man waged a crusade against those rouged cheeks and forced his thumb deeper than he should have and eradicated them. Some of our paintings are now pale and a bit distorted. Not, thank God, the truly great ones like *Las Meninas*, which today is still radiant. Compared, however, to some of our other Velázquezes, the *Marchesa* must be in superb condition. She ought to be even better than your great *Juan de Pareja*, which was slightly damaged by folding, was it not?"

"God, what a tragedy!" Olivia burst out. "To think that even one Velázquez here was damaged! What about others?"

"A great many of his works outside of Spain may also have been tampered with—either too harshly cleaned, or slightly skinned by conservators who delved too far below the original varnish or, worse, squashed the robust landscape of the pictures' surfaces with hot irons and wax. In all, maybe only a dozen paintings are virtually untouched—a handful of ours, the six marvelous ones in Vienna, the portrait of Innocent X—and, possibly, the Richfield *Marchesa.*"

"Moral aesthetics!" Olivia snorted in disgust. She paused a moment. "Don José, are you absolutely sure that the Richfield portrait is by the hand of the master? There's no chance it could be a copy, is there?"

"No copies exist," Sánchez said flatly. "Except for his own second pair, which are, of course, not really copies. Personally, I'm convinced that the Richfield picture and the *Venus* in London are Velázquez's own first pair."

"Maybe the Pope's pictures will show up."

"Olivia, I suppose miracles can happen, even these days. But documents do seem to suggest that they were destroyed."

"Documents?"

"Yes. They're in Rome—in the Academy of Saint Luke. Years ago, I saw them."

"Do you remember if there were measurements of the pictures?" she asked excitedly.

"No. It was years ago."

"Oh, I hope I can find them! How can you be certain you're looking at an authentic Velázquez?" she persisted.

"For me, it's the eyes. And also the quality of the white paint. The master's white always has a trace of blue in it—*never* yellow, red, or brown. Never! His white is a splendid hue, sparklingly pure."

"Tell me, has anyone else been here to pick your brains?" Olivia asked lightly.

Sánchez laughed. "One other suitor. A private collector, Kurt Krassner. A German. Naturally, I told him nothing."

"There's another suitor downstairs right now," she said with a frown. "Andrew Foster."

"What a nice young man! Perhaps my secretary could fetch him . . . or would you find that an inconvenience, Olivia?"

"Right now, yes. For him. I wouldn't want to surprise him like that. It's better that I leave. But you could do me a great favor. I certainly don't want to ask you to do anything you'd feel awkward about, but if you could simply say something to the effect that you were expecting me in Madrid today, but learned, just now, that I had to return suddenly to New York."

"Ah! The chase for a great work of art is full of twists and turns. Why not?"

"But please don't tell him—unless he insists, naturally—about that terrible restorer or, please, about the documents in the Academy of Saint Luke."

"Unless he asks," Sánchez repeated gravely. "I assure you, Olivia. Shall we meet at the auction?"

"I'm not sure. The Metropolitan works in mysterious ways."

Andrew couldn't imagine why José Sánchez was so remote, even forbidding. It wasn't like the genial scholar at all. He had sat taciturn at his elaborate Victorian desk until Andrew finally goaded him into admitting that the picture at William's "seems to be a sound enough example of the second Roman period." His reticence could only mean one thing: the Spanish government had decided to make a run for the picture.

"I suppose you've been inundated by collectors, museum directors, and curators since the news of the auction," Andrew said, trying to keep the conversation moving.

"At this moment, only you," Sánchez said, his voice becoming suddenly more lively.

"What? No one from the Met? I understand they're rabid for the picture."

"The Met?"

"Oh, I'd have expected Olivia Cartright here already," Andrew remarked with a casual laugh.

"Perhaps the Met's ardor has cooled," Sánchez observed in a low voice.

"How so?"

"Miss Cartright—I find her an exceptionally bright young woman!—was due to come. Today, in fact . . . but called my secretary to say that she had to rush back to New York. Twists and turns . . ."

"New York? Today? I can't believe it," Andrew said in astonishment. "You don't suppose . . . she couldn't have checked in and then left? You must forgive me, Don José—"

"Leaving so soon? Without asking me any more questions?" the director teased, a flicker of amusement in his eyes.

"I do apologize!"

Careening back to the hotel in a taxicab whose driver took his message of "a life-or-death hurry" as a challenge, Andrew cursed himself for having instructed the concièrge not to tell *anyone* that he was staying at the hotel. Had he lost her again?

The three gifts she found in her room struck directly at her heart —exactly as they were intended. She gasped with delight. Nestled in the summit of a mountain of yellow roses was a handwritten note, another was propped up against an iced magnum of champagne, and still a third was tucked beneath a box wrapped in purple velvet. Olivia gently opened the box, not daring to breathe. On a bed of white satin lay a perfect Athenian gold coin of the late sixth century B.C. struck with a representation of Aphrodite Anadyomene. It had been made into a pendant, on a delicate gold chain. The note rambled, but with fervor:

Surprise! I saw it and was at once reminded of you, the ever changing image of love. I have booked a dinner for us this evening at Horcher's. I paid off the manager, who told me you were planning to dine alone on the patio tonight. So I figured that you had no logical excuse. After the heady joys of the Prado, you'll want to unwind. I have followed you from Paris—just for dinner. Phone me at once!

She put it on immediately, admiring it in the mirror of the vanity table.

The second note had more style:

These yellow beauties fade before the radiance of your hair. But they will do. Aphrodite, please look next—if you have not already—at the note next to the purple box. Purple is for . . .

· 145 ·

The third note was even more blunt:

A few seconds before the stroke of nine, I shall knock twice on your door and enter to open the champagne.

Olivia fell back on the couch. How foolish she had been! Would he forgive her? As she got up to call him, she heard a loud knock on the door. Andrew! She opened it slowly and there he was, leaning casually against the opposite wall.

"You were very naughty," he said with a broad grin, taking both her hands in his. "You gave me a heart spasm—and ruptured my relationship with Don José forever."

"Tit for tat."

"How did you know I was here at the Sanvy?"

"Easy," she said. "You seem to be following Diego Velázquez."

"And you."

"Me? How did you find where I was going?"

"Simple deduction," he drawled. "Same way you did."

"I'm glad you finally revealed yourself," she said, grinning.

"I mean, how did you really find out, Olivia?"

"Not telling."

He leaned back to admire the gold coin against her black silk blouse. "You two Aphrodites do look alike, you know. Olivia, how *did* you learn?"

"Don't worry, you fooled me at first. But your nervous friend, the manager, was most certainly not going to allow your assumed name to impede my getting your sweet messages."

"God, I really believed you'd gotten an alert from New York and took off."

She fondled the coin and whispered, "Thank you, Andrew. I adore it."

He kissed her quickly on the cheek. He had an almost uncontrollable desire to pick her up and carry her into the bedroom. But, with a self-conscious laugh, he let his arms fall to his sides. They gazed at each other longingly.

Andrew broke the spell, abruptly clapped his hands together, and busied himself with opening the champagne. He took elaborate pains to allow only a whisper to escape from the cork.

"Those who know say it's considered gauche in champagne country to let a cork actually pop," he said.

"I don't suppose you own a vineyard near Dizy or Bouzy or Epernay or Ay or Rheims, by chance?" Olivia remarked gaily.

"Aha! You know the area," Andrew murmured, caught up in the serious task of judging the champagne. "You know everything. Sometimes I've no idea how."

"I told you I studied in Europe one summer when I was a graduate student. One October, I happened to go up to Rheims for the *vendange.*"

"Alone?" Andrew poured a glass of champagne and handed it to her. "This is passable."

"Passable means exquisite!" she whispered. "To you."

"*Us.*"

"To us. I went alone. I was a loner back then, seeking the solitary romance of the harvest."

"Did you find it—romance, that is?"

"The harvest was glorious."

"Harvest? That's all?"

"I did meet some charming members of the Henriot family."

"Aha! Finally, romance! What did they want?"

"Can't you guess?"

Andrew cocked his head.

"One wanted to marry me."

"*Oh?*"

"I declined."

"A mistake?"

"Perhaps."

"Really?"

"Well, he's turned out to be far from the indolent playboy his father warned me he'd be."

"French daddies are always chauvinists when it comes to their children marrying foreigners."

"Not at all. Daddy wanted me for himself. He fancied young, blond California types."

"To marry?"

"Instantly."

"Were you in love with him, Olivia?" Andrew asked, his eyes glittering with impertinence over the edge of his glass.

"Tempted."

"Ever been tempted after?"

"Of course."

"Ever do anything about it?"

"Always the right thing," she said softly. "I was brought up properly."

"Me too!" Andrew laughed, and walked slowly toward her.

At that delicate moment, Olivia hooked her arm lightly in his and guided him to the door. "Don José was right about you, you are a nice man. I must get myself ready for dinner. Come back for me in an hour."

They strolled in silence down the crowded Paseo Serrano, drinking in the beauty of the luminous evening. When they arrived at the restaurant Andrew had selected, Olivia expressed her surprise. She had expected a typical Spanish establishment, specializing in "Madrilena" cuisine. Horcher's was hardly that.

"The place is pure Austrian," Andrew explained. "The Viennese family who owns it fled Hitler during the Anschluss, came to Madrid, and opened up what has got to be the best restaurant in the city. Has been ever since it began. Pressed fowl is the specialty. I took the liberty of ordering partridge. I hope you don't mind."

"Mind? I love it."

"What an admission from Olivia Cartright!"

"I bow to your expertise—when it comes to subjects you really know."

"A crack about my abilities as an art historian! I'm so misunderstood," he said with a resigned sigh.

"It's just that I hear you're more the museum administration type than a connoisseur."

"Not so. I'm brilliant at both."

"Perhaps I'm being a little harsh," she confessed. "You did seem to appreciate my Corot. Or was that a charade?"

"The truth, I swear."

"The naked truth?" she asked.

He threw his head back and laughed. "What a peculiar evening that Donors' Gala was! There I was skulking around trying to lay down a careful path of disinformation. Which fooled no one. A total failure."

"Poor boy," Olivia said softly, and reached out to touch his cheek. "Andrew, what was your first, split-second reaction when you saw me at the Met that evening?"

"I didn't recognize you at first. I saw a tall, athletic, attractive woman with marvelous carriage who . . ."

". . . looked like a 'librarian.' "

"You are a most amazing creature. No. Well, yes. When I saw who it was, I wasn't interested. But when I got closer, it was during that nutty interview with Connie Winthrop, I was struck by how beautiful your skin was."

"True?"

"Yes."

"I thought you were horrid at the gala."

"A bit stiff perhaps."

"Arrogant."

"You want to know what went through my mind when I saw you at UNESCO?"

"Yes."

"Again, I didn't recognize you at first. I recall thinking that only in Paris could one encounter a woman like that, someone sexy, chic, tomboyish, athletic, gorgeous, bright . . ."

"I like that. Should I believe it?"

"Sure. You know, the perfect 'librarian' type."

"In Paris you were manipulative—slippery. What about now?"

"Do you say that to all the guys?"

"You're changing." She couldn't quite disguise her anxiety. "Aren't you?"

"Totally."

"I wonder."

"I hereby offer a blanket apology for all my failings, dirty tricks, sundry abuses, arrogances."

"Perhaps I am wearing down that famous arrogance."

"My external hauteur is a mere husk. You know that now." He took her hand and brought it to his lips.

"Do you have any weaknesses at all?" she asked.

"Actually, I'm a failure."

"To say it that way is a form of arrogance," Olivia observed wryly.

"I'm serious. I'm convinced I should've aspired to something more creative in life than running a museum—painting, writing, poetry. Something more fulfilling than mere connoisseurship—"

"Mere?"

"Come now, Olivia, beneath the skin of almost every museum drudge there's a frustrated artist. Cliché, sure, but I'm beginning to believe it. When I was a kid out at our summer place I'd climb up into a favorite tree and settle on a branch way up high and listen to voices reciting poetry. And I'd see images—painterly images. So I tried to become an artist. But not for long. I guess my upbringing didn't have much to do with courage or—"

"Not charging ahead and getting what he wants doesn't sound like Andrew Foster."

"Oh, I tried. I studied a year at the Art Students League in Manhattan. Then I showed my work to an art critic, an acquaintance of my father's, and he said, 'Give it up!' "

"*You* believed an art critic!"

"This one happened to be right. My work was hopeless."

Their conversation took a lighter tone. They talked about exhibitions they had seen over the years and gossiped about personalities. Andrew kept edging toward the subject of the Metropolitan. Olivia, just as deftly, steered away until Andrew thought she had formed an impenetrable defense. At that moment Olivia unexpectedly attacked head-on.

"I've been told they've asked you to interview for my job," she said in a sweet voice.

He winced.

"For the Met, you have to be an artist—of a sort. Or a con man. You might like it."

"Look."

"It would be easier than the National Gallery," she purred.

He grinned. "I suppose every art museum is the same, fundamentally."

She nodded. "The same thirty-five trustees."

"That many? Any of them kind of temperamental?"

"The lot."

"Well . . ."

"The same one hundred and fifty curators."

"What?"

"No less."

"And every one a prima donna?" he asked meekly, "Look, I'm not sure if I want the post, unless I can get guarantees that the atmosphere will be, you know, more or less contemplative."

"Certainly! There are only twelve board meetings a year—each with a full rehearsal. Plus only twelve finance committee meetings. And twelve executive committee meetings. And at least six acquisition committee meetings."

"With probably some crisis meetings thrown in from time to time?"

"Usually four. Then there's the usual rich ambience of academe at the Met."

"You mean the jealousies, infighting, hypocrisy, and paranoia?"

"My, you do know the place," Olivia said with a gentle whistle.

"I'm not sure I want to know more," he said, gazing at her.

"Unlike the tumultuous National Gallery with all its financial difficulties and enormous staff," she teased, "at the Met it's like a monastery. Every one of the twenty-three curatorial departments yearns to spend buckets of money—from the same source. When five curators set their teeth to acquire something, it makes the Byzantine Empire seem like summer camp."

"Whoa. I'm beginning to rethink all this."

"And at budget time, with everyone bustling around for more money, it's like Napoleon's retreat from Moscow."

"Warm and friendly, you mean."

"Then there's the fun part—the incessant fund-raising, the union bargaining, the ongoing lawsuits."

"I withdraw!"

"You musn't, Andrew. We need you," Olivia cried. "Please reconsider!"

"Well . . ."

"We need your connections, your social standing . . ."

"What about my eye?" he protested.

"That too, I guess. But it's more your get-up-and-go. You know, the way you charged off to London."

"Aha!"

"And that marvelous way you would 'bring a sense of tasteful populism to the place without catering to the mobs.' "

"Hey, that's what Howard Olines wrote about me! In that case I'll do it. I'll become your director."

"Great!" Olivia exulted. "But, remember, no art."

"How's that?"

"The real job is one hundred and twenty percent administration."

"Good. Come to think of it, I detest art. I happen to revere administrative affairs."

"I'll bet you do." Olivia gazed at him, an impish smile coming to her lips. "I've heard those aren't the only affairs you revere!"

"Things of the distant past," he said, reaching over to stroke her hair.

For the next three days they saw each other virtually every waking moment. They parted company only late at night—at her door —with an elaborate politeness at first which became a faintly mocking ritual of voluntary abstinence. Olivia was confident she was reading all the signs correctly. Andrew had become infatuated with her and it was more, she knew, than physical longing. Andrew was equally convinced that Olivia was falling deeply for him.

As their affection grew, the joust continued. Try as she might, Olivia couldn't quite suppress the desire to use his feelings for her to her advantage. She wasn't sure enough of herself to press. Perhaps his interest in the Met was really as offhand as he had bantered about it. As for Andrew, the only thing that marred his happiness was the thought that kept creeping into his head that if he let matters run their course, she might eventually give in to his charm not only physically but professionally. He loathed himself for the thought, but it wouldn't go away.

In a dozen clever ways, Olivia made him aware how determined she was to land both the *Marchesa* and the job. They haunted the Prado, spending hours in the Velázquez galleries. Andrew deftly impressed her with his feelings for the work of the master and then casually suggested, "Why not buy the Richfield picture together?

Pool our money and get it for both our institutions—for both our publics and the nation."

"What? Share it? Ship it back and forth?"

"It's not as radical as it sounds, you know. You know more about the condition than I do. Could it conceivably travel?"

"It could conceivably do almost anything. Most of all be snatched up by the Getty or seized by the director of the other National Gallery, Roy Bentley, which is all too likely."

"Would you ever be willing to discuss the idea—unofficially— with Ayn Steyne and the board?"

"When you have your interview, wouldn't that be a perfect opportunity?" she countered.

"Didn't I give the job up?" he laughed. "I forget. You have this way about you that makes me forget everything but you."

"Dear Andrew," she replied, tenderly squeezing his arm. "If I promise to discuss with my board this peculiar idea of sharing, will you promise to withdraw?"

"Withdrawal's not my style."

"You haven't changed."

"I'm a totally new man—where you're concerned."

"Well, that much is true, and I love it."

During their visits to the Prado they maintained a more or less professional air. But as they wandered through places where they were confident no one would recognize them, they began to hold hands. By the time they visited the Santa María de la Florida to view Goya's paintings on the ceiling and sauntered through the empty galleries of the Academia, they had succumbed to caresses and an occasional kiss.

On Olivia's last night in Madrid they walked through the city until midnight, clinging tightly to each other. In the Plaza Mayor they sat on the steps of the great equestrian sculpture of King Philip by Tacca, hugging each other in the chill.

"I'm crazy about you. I want you. You feel the same way. Of course we're frightened about an entanglement. But we can have each *other*. . . . No, don't say anything. I want to make love to you. I *need* to."

Olivia returned his kiss with equal passion. "Don't you know what's happening to me? You look at me and I shiver. You come close and I can't stand it. Dozens of times in the past three days I've almost fainted when you got close. But I'm fearful that our professional relationship . . . oh, call it what it is—our competition —will wreck us. Andrew, that we must be in competition is a fact. It won't ever go away. I think maybe it shouldn't. But my fear is that our attraction will somehow work against us, against our careers."

"It'll work out. I'll make it work. I've never failed. And it's time we made love."

"Yes! But now? Andrew, you know I have to leave for Vienna in four hours."

"Take a later plane."

"Don't you see, for me there is no later plane."

"I'll come with you."

"Oh, yes! Please!"

To Andrew's rage, he learned that during the off-season flights between Madrid and Vienna were sparse. Olivia's early-morning flight was totally booked, as was the only other one later in the day. The best he could manage was to get on the waiting list for early morning the day after. The train would take virtually as long.

They stood before Olivia's door, their caresses growing more ardent. "Stay," he implored. "We'll both go in two days."

"I want you, I want you . . . but I have to go. To see the Velázquez in the Kunsthistorisches Museum. You see, if I don't go, it means . . ."

"It means that our personal attraction will threaten your professional life. I understand. Much as I hate it, I agree. It's a short time, isn't it?"

"No, it isn't!"

13 TALES OF VIENNA

OLIVIA STOOD, bristling and impatient, in the gilded lobby of the Imperial Hotel as the manager tried to reassure her. A problem had arisen in processing her reservation. (A hitch at the Imperial? Unheard of.) There was, the suave manager explained, a handy solution. If she would agree to occupy a suite for a few hours, then she could move into her proper room. To be shunted around was a bore, but what could she do?

Olivia instructed the porter to send up only a light bag. She planned to nap awhile and then go directly to the Velázquez gallery at the Kunsthistorisches Museum. The manager escorted her to the door of her temporary quarters and, curiously, disappeared after unlocking the door and handing her the key. What was going on? When she entered the foyer of the suite, she gasped. It looked like a stage set from *Der Rosenkavalier*. Every table, console, and breakfront was decked with vases of tulips—red, yellow, purple, white. The sun-dappled suite was ablaze with color.

And there was more. It was not so much a presence of someone, but the feeling of a presence. Olivia could almost smell it, a heady, deep human odor, definitely male. Andrew! Impossible! He could never have beaten her to Vienna. A bit fearfully, she poked her head around the corner and looked into the bedroom. No one, she saw to her deep disappointment. Then, in the closet, she saw a row of men's suits. His! A dozen ties, neatly arranged. Definitely his!

"Andrew! Where are you?" Olivia called, and spun around. Not a soul.

At the Imperial the doorbell makes a discreet buzz. So it was only after Andrew had locked his finger on the button that she finally heard the bell and ran to the door. There he stood, at attention, holding a single red rose. Olivia fell into his arms.

"How did you . . . ?"

"I was able to charter a small jet," he replied matter-of-factly, and kissed her. "You were right, it would have been an eternity."

"Are you really perfect?" Andrew asked when, at last, she walked slowly toward where he lay stretched out on the bed.

"In fact, not quite," she said, slowly peeling back the coverlet. She burrowed next to him. "I've got a mark like a small bullet hole in my left buttock. See?"

"Jesus, is it?" Andrew asked.

"Of course. Would I lie to you? My twelve-year-old brother put it there accidentally with his .22."

"It's cute."

It took hours for Andrew Foster to complete his first amorous exploration of Olivia Alexis Cartright. No false starts or weaknesses for this practiced Don Juan. Into early evening Andrew made love to Olivia. And she, delighted with his skill, acted as he wanted her to—entirely selfishly. Later Olivia took the long-distance runner to paradise and then briefly to sleep with a series of kisses, tastings, and caresses. After midnight supper before the fireplace they made love until dawn.

Slow motion was the order of the next two days. Late rising. Loving. Muted voices. Breakfast at eleven. Lunch at three. In between, a foray to observe a majestic painting, a bold sculpture, or a noble example of architecture somewhere in the radiant city of Vienna—which, as if programmed for lovers, remained cold and clear. Nap time. Love time. Champagne. Bath. Midnight supper. More champagne. Night into day.

To Olivia, even more delicious than the physical pleasures, which grew more intense and more subtle each time they made love, was watching Andrew change from a man of implacable confidence to a human being not in the least bothered about displaying his vulnerabilities.

"I've never been able to lie and get away with it. I can bullshit and dish out the malarkey, but I can't somehow, lie. If you ever hear me say 'I assure you' you'll know I'm attempting to lie. Which, of course, I shall never do to you. I did lie to you once—and to

friends in the Gallery—about the Metropolitan. They did approach
me. A few days before the gala. I met Ayn Steyne clandestinely at
my lawyer's office in Washington, and she told me that the search
committee was eager to interview me."

Although she wasn't surprised at the news, it still came as a bitter
shock. But her feeling of disappointment was overcome by her joy
at hearing him reveal his secrets. She was positive it was the first
time he had done that with anybody.

Andrew sprawled back on the bed and took her into his arms.
"But wait. Don't be anxious. Ayn Steyne did say that the power
structure at the Met would definitely not make up its collective
mind until after the sale of the Velázquez. She said they're going to
see how both of us handle the situation and then decide. Olivia,
how will you handle it? What should I do? Is there something we
should both do?"

Olivia kissed him as if she hadn't heard a word, stalling what
could only be a difficult answer to a series of puzzling questions.
Was he toying with her? What was he actually saying? How should
she react? In his casual and laid-back way, Andrew was telling her
something of great import. But she wasn't absolutely sure what the
message was. Were his defenses completely down? Or was he
trying to make it look as if they were? She was almost sure it was
real. Should she reveal herself? Tell him everything she knew?

A doubt lingered in her mind—minuscule, yet indelible. Perhaps
if she were older, or more experienced, or more elevated in her
position in life, she would not be so unsure of herself. But for the
moment Olivia decided it would be dangerous—no, "dangerous"
was an exaggeration—it would be not in her "best interests" to
reveal all to Andrew Foster. Suppose he was, after all, only infatuated with her?

Andrew had left behind any cynical male sexual greed. It was
not that he believed Olivia had succumbed or that he figured himself the dominant force, it was that he saw she was an equal. The
moment he had entered the suite he made the discovery that he
would give up everything for Olivia. Oh, perhaps a little at a time
but, eventually, everything. He would give her everything she
wanted. But in time. For someone who had never lost, surrender
was, suddenly, fitting.

Foremost in his mind was loving her. But he also wanted to

educate her. Olivia was brilliant but inexperienced. He pondered carefully how he could teach her without appearing to instruct—or patronize. As he loved her with his body his mind raced, trying to figure out how to handle his lover not just minute after delicious minute, but in the days and weeks to come.

One of their cultural expeditions had been to the Albertina Museum to examine the splendid collection of drawings. As they wandered through the galleries Andrew confided to her an astonishing secret he had learned from a former curator of drawings at the institution who had become indiscreet at the end of a long dinner with many courses and much wine. To foil possible thieves and ensure that the masterpieces on fragile paper would never deteriorate, every one of the master drawings on exhibition—works by the Master E.S., Dürer, Martin Schongauer, Rubens, and Watteau —was a brilliant reproduction. Olivia was astounded. When she scrutinized the individual pieces, she began to recognize the ruse. But why hadn't she even suspected the copies before, during earlier visits, no matter how good they were? Her lack of perception worried her. Her thoughts leaped to the *Marchesa*. Could she have made a similar oversight with the Velázquez? No. Certainly not! A painting was totally different, she tried to assure herself. After all, she had been correct about the condition of the Velázquezes in the Prado. But Andrew's seemingly offhand revelation disturbed her nonetheless. He was instructing her, she realized, but delicately.

They haunted the galleries of the Kunsthistorisches Museum, perhaps the single finest repository of paintings in the Western world. Together they viewed the six portraits of the royal family by Velázquez, but exchanged not a significant word, most certainly not about how the masterpieces compared to the *Marchesa*. They lingered a full hour in the hall with the nine Pieter Breughels, slowly touring the earthy paintings, pointing out to each other an especially striking figure among the hordes of characters populating the village fiestas or gluttonous feasts. In awe they gazed at the cruel citizenry trooping up to Calvary as if on a holiday, following a tortured Christ, some jeering him, others indifferent to his suffering.

"Want to see my favorite of favorites?" Andrew asked, guiding her to the door of the Rubens gallery. "There, on the far wall, in the right corner. It's not exhibited correctly. I wrote a paper about her in graduate school. Rubens placed her in his home in such a way that visitors would come in and casually glance toward the back of the house and there she'd be. The canvas hung so that it rested on the floor. Everyone thought Hélène Fourment was just passing through from her bath, naked, except for that marvelous fur she's wrapped herself in. "I love it," Andrew went on. "It's got to be one of the sexiest paintings ever created—along with the *Marchesa Odescalchi*. Am I right?"

Olivia did not rise to the bait.

Andrew left Olivia just once, for an hour. He had checked in with the local CIA office and was contacted immediately by an operative who said he "had to discuss something—in person." The meeting took place in a narrow, dark room of a third-class hotel on the Ringstrasse, "Where Harry Lime used to mix up the batches of bogus penicillin, from the looks of it," as his jovial contact described the place.

"Okay, now keep your hat on. This is about that bloody Velázquez masterpiece. And has nothing to do with the Agency. It's a request that comes from the National Security Adviser himself. Bass wants you, as director of the National Gallery and as a loyal, patriotic employee of the United States' intelligence community, to pull out from bidding on the picture."

Andrew was flabbergasted. "What in hell is this really all about?"

"Simple. It seems that the President wants to negotiate with the Soviets. He wants to make an impressive goodwill gesture to the Party Chairman. He has been informed through the backchannel at the Soviet Embassy that Ermenentov has been persuaded by his mistress Ludmilla Tcherninka—as you know, she's the new Minister of Culture—to ask for this thing as a gift. Or bribe, as I'd call it."

"Incredible! But with the National Security office mixed up in this, I suppose I shouldn't be surprised. You know, a gift like this is more than a mere gesture. That painting could cost over thirteen million dollars."

"Christ!" the officer exclaimed. "National Security won't fork over anything near that."

"Who knows?" Andrew remarked. "Anyway, if I find the picture as great as some people seem to think, I have other plans than making it part of some bribe for that Russian tyrant or a bauble in the private collection of his mistress."

"Well, think it over. Now, this is no directive. I was instructed to let you know, that's all. Perhaps nothing more will come of it. You know how many hot schemes are cooked up in the White House, which then disappear. Are you really serious about trying to buy this painting?"

"Not yet sure. I'm in a kind of developing partnership. Are you going to report this to the Agency?"

"You know I must."

On his way back to Olivia, Andrew mulled over the peculiar request. He suddenly felt anxious. It was a command.

That evening they attended a performance of Mahler's Ninth Symphony, savored a late dinner of venison at the Auf die Drei Hussarn, and spent several raucous hours in the Bar Rentz, a strip-tease joint on the Zircusgasse, where Andrew tried tipsily and vainly to persuade Olivia to participate in one of the "exotic dances open to amateurs," as the master of ceremonies described the affair. Later they snuggled on the floor of their suite in a quilt Olivia found in the closet. He nuzzled her neck and casually asked, "What's she like? What did you think of her? Isn't it time to tell me?"

Olivia raised herself up on an elbow and looked into his eyes, reaching out to stroke his temple. "I may be the only person on earth to know what she is. Velázquez depicted his young lover as Venus. And he, offstage, unseen, approaches her—as Mars. She's young, but not girlishly young. She's a woman in that extraordinary, exciting, never-again-to-be-experienced moment. About to be fulfilled. Mars was older, a bit grizzled. He had known war, bloodshed, danger—not fear, since gods never felt fear. But a young woman, even Venus, perhaps thought it was best to appear as if a goddess could experience fear or, at least, anxiety."

He moved close to her and longingly drew the tip of his tongue across her brow, down over her nose. and around her lips into her mouth.

"Wait!"

"Mars is ready."

"Hush!" Olivia nipped him on the ear.

He lay still, mesmerized by her.

"Venus has an unworldly beauty of flesh, but its fulfillment must await the pleasure of the god. Sexual hesitation—that's a great deal of what this painting is all about. Womanly hesitation, respectful hesitation for a divine lover. The young unbelievably ripe Venus—*amor et fecunditas*, 'ripeness and steam'—sees her lover approaching. He casts aside his armor. His manly defenses are down. He is beginning the ritual of offering himself to her. He is alert, eager, and vulnerable."

"Delicious!" Andrew inched closer.

"She is hiding herself and offering herself. Like this." Olivia pushed Andrew back gently and cast aside the quilt. "Venus reclines on the couch of love, both withdrawing herself—she covers her breasts just so—and offering herself . . . just so." Olivia edged toward him, her lips close to his. "Venus is sacred love and profane love, eager and uneasy, hungry and reticent, passionate and motherly, wise and innocent. All! Shameless and a little shameful. Wanting and waiting. This painting has nothing to do with our times. There's no hint of rapid overtures. It's like what is happening to us, something unexpected yet predestined. Something full of celebration, eagerness, sexual discovery! Andrew, the painting is exactly how I feel about you. My love letter in paint. Ah, I absolutely adore you. And, like Velázquez's Venus, I want it to go on and on."

He allowed her to sleep until almost noon. Then, very gently, he arranged the breakfast tray at her side and awakened her with a kiss. Then he broke out the cheerful news.

"Time to move on. We're going to Rome."

"Rome?" Olivia said sleepily. "Why not? There's lots we can do in Rome."

"More than you would ever believe," Andrew said with a grin.

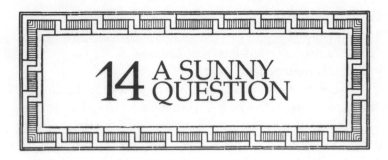

14 A SUNNY QUESTION

THE FLIGHT OVER the Alps was majestic, cloudless, and unexpectedly smooth. Moreover, there were no strikes at Leonardo da Vinci Airport. Their bags came tumbling out of the carousel first. The unexpected efficiency of the operation prompted Olivia to observe that the ancient gods must not be displeased with their behavior. When they emerged from the terminal into the bright sunlight, a uniformed young man darted up to Andrew and deferentially shook his hand. It was, Andrew explained, his caretaker, who had driven his car to the airport. Andrew slipped behind the wheel of the Jaguar and drove swiftly and easily through the crowded midday traffic of Rome to an underground parking lot on the Via Zandanarelli.

"Come," he said, taking her by the hand while the caretaker followed with their luggage, "to our place, my hideaway on the Piazza Navona. For me, the heart of Rome."

In an elevator Andrew described as "so old it probably dates to the time of Victor Emmanuel, but it works," they creaked to the top floor and entered a small flat—no more than three rooms furnished in striking black and white Art Deco furniture. The apartment looked down on Bernini's Fountain of the Four Rivers.

The spectacular view and the crisp purity of the decor were stunning.

"I yearned to live in the Piazza Navona," Andrew said. "It took two years, but when my agent finally showed me this apartment, I fell in love with it. It's like the royal box at the opera," he added buoyantly. "Olivia, a silly art history test. Do you remember who commissioned Bernini to make the fountain?"

"Our own dear Pope Innocent X," Olivia replied, hugging him.

They lunched at "his" restaurant, the Mastro Santo Stefano next door, where the proprietor fussed over them and hauled a large table into a sunny section of the sidewalk. The sun was warm, and after lunch they sat for an hour holding hands, watching the colorful human drama of the *passeggiata*.

"I think I could sit here forever," she said.

"I won't let you," Andrew laughed, and pushed back his chair. "We have an appointment."

She shook her head as if to say he was crazy, sprang to her feet, put her hand in his, and followed.

He led her down the Corso Agonale, into the Via dei Stradevari, and finally through the Piazza San Eustachio until they reached the Piazza della Rotonda and the Pantheon.

"To me, this is one of the most beautiful buildings on earth." Andrew gestured to the stolid portico of the antique edifice. "It proves that the ancients really did produce fundamentally better architecture than we can."

"And where Velázquez exhibited his *Juan de Pareja* for the first time," Olivia added.

"True. But that's not why I brought you here." He escorted her through the pair of great bronze Hadrianic doors. Inside the cool interior they gazed upward raptly at the vault of the rotunda soaring high above them and at the oculus through which burst a golden column of sunlight. Andrew gently pulled her over to the edge of the shining circle of light.

"When I was a kid in Rome one summer I used to come here every day. I'd dreamed that this circle of light was the portal to another world and if you were willing to give yourself to the future, and have full trust, you could step into it and get what you wanted. If you weren't, you'd disappear."

Suddenly he lifted Olivia in his arms and carried her into the shaft of sunlight. He deposited her directly in the center and kissed her.

"So, we're still alive and in one piece. I guess we know what we want. At least I do. Olivia, I brought you here to ask you the most important question I've ever asked anyone. I want you to be my wife. I want to marry you now, here in Rome. I love you. I want to have children. I don't care about the Met or the painting, I care about you."

She gazed at him in amazement.

"We can get married in Rome," he said quickly. "I've already looked into it. My lawyer here has investigated the documents we need, the posting of banns . . ."

"You already discussed it with your lawyer?"

"From Vienna. That's when I was positive, although I think I knew in Paris."

Tears of joy welled up in her eyes. "Yes. Oh, yes," she whispered, embracing him tightly. "But now . . .? In Rome? It's too fast. I mean, think of our careers! And your father—won't he disinherit you? I'd get fired. You might too. Who knows? Of course I'll marry you. I adore you. But don't we . . . shouldn't we wait until after the auction? I've been preparing, thinking for so long. Right or wrong, that picture's become the heart of my professional life. Oh, please, let's wait and do it right. Just four weeks, just that tiny amount of time? I'm a little scared."

He hugged her, laughing. "You're right. I was thinking we'd elope, marry without telling a soul, here in Rome. But damnit, you're right. At least I'll have you with me all of the time. We can work together, plot together about the auction. Okay, we'll make it the grandest wedding New York has ever seen!"

He took her back to his apartment. On the terrace looking down on the fountain, Andrew poured her a glass of wine.

"Andrew, it's not just infatuation? Or the thrill of the chase?"

"I said I want to marry you. Doesn't that prove it?"

"Andrew, in the Pantheon you happened to say . . ." She hesitated.

"I said I don't care about the Met or the painting. I want you to have them. I mean it."

"Yesterday, you talked about us buying the picture together, sharing it between the Met and the National Gallery."

"I meant that too," he said firmly. "Take it if you want. But if you wish to share it I've got it all worked out, point by point. If the condition is as good as you think, then there's no reason why we can't share it, say every four years, with maybe a year in between to send it to some worthy museum elsewhere in the country. So many more people in America will have the chance to see the masterpiece."

"Do you really believe our trustees would ever agree to such a novel scheme?"

"With our talents for manipulation, if the two of us can't manage that simple task, well . . . Shall we try?"

"Yes. But we must tell no one else. Who knows, maybe we'll turn up the missing pair."

He laughed. "It's the day for miracles, why not?"

As soon as she could invent a plausible excuse, Olivia slipped away from Andrew and went to the Academy of Saint Luke. A suitable tip to the custodian allowed her to browse for several hours in the archives devoted to Roman painters of the seventeenth century. It was there that she hoped to find the file on Diego Velázquez, and she did. But, to her annoyance, it contained nothing new—no information about his second visit to Italy, nothing about the stunning exhibition in the Pantheon when the *Juan de Pareja* was first displayed, not a word about the two pairs of portraits of the Marchesa Odescalchi, and not a trace of the measurements. Merely the standard, well-known historical data that could be found in any book on the master or the period. Olivia half expected she would uncover nothing new or startling. In retrospect, it seemed too pat. The scholar who had written about the Velázquez file at the Academy had invented it—not the first time that had happened in art history.

Olivia's former professor, Ulrich Seitz, who was in Rome teaching a seminar at the American Academy, turned out to be a virtual encyclopedia on the subject. Olivia and Andrew had arranged to meet him for breakfast. During his discourse, Seitz would pause from time to time, glance over at the pair who were taking notes on his remarks, and chuckle soundlessly to himself. The rivals were clearly in love.

"Velázquez in Rome," Seitz intoned as if he were launching into a lecture. "You probably know the story very well."

"Olivia does," Andrew said. "But frankly, I'm a little vague on the details. What happened?"

"Velázquez left Barcelona for Italy in January of 1649," Seitz began. "He landed at Genoa and went to the household of the Spanish ambassador, the Marquis de la Fuente, who had set up a round of appointments for him to look at pictures Philip IV might want to acquire. Promptly he went off to Venice and purchased a number of canvases by Tintoretto, Veronese, and Titian, which were sent back at once to the king by special boat. Then he proceeded on to Parma. There, Velázquez became obsessed with the works of Correggio, a passion superseded only by that of his royal patron. From Parma he went to Modena, spending days trying to buy Correggio's renowned altarpiece of the Nativity, *La Notte*, for his ruler. But the owner, the Duke of Modena, refused to relinquish the painting, even for the King of Spain."

Seitz described how Velázquez had finally gotten to Rome eager to see her art treasures and meet her renowned artists. No sooner had he arrived than he had to go to Naples to meet the Spanish viceroy and collect a sizable amount of money on behalf of the king.

"It was July before he was able to return to Rome and settle down. He stayed there, living well and very actively, for over a year. He took pains to meet all the eminent artists of the day and became friends of them all. And, of course, managed to acquire a young and beautiful mistress. The Marchesa. More of whom I will speak in a moment. There are notices in the documents in the archives about her."

Olivia glanced at him, surprised. Archives? Documents?

"During this period in Rome," he went on, "Velázquez painted only those bright Impressionist-like views of the gardens of the Villa Medici. Just when he became obsessed with painting Innocent X we don't know. All we have to go on is the report written some sixty-five years after the event by his biographer, Antonio Palomino. The account gives one a rare insight into what people actually thought about works of art in the seventeenth century.

"Before painting Innocent X he painted his traveling companion, Juan de Pareja, as 'practice.' You remember what happened. The likeness was so startling that when he sent Pareja to show it to some of his friends, they reacted with a mixture of 'admiration and amazement.' Palomino uses the word *asombro,* which implies fright mixed with surprise and admiration. Because, as Palomino writes, they didn't know, 'as they looked at the portrait and its model whom to address or where the answer would come from.' Then the portrait was exhibited in the Pantheon as part of a group of great paintings both old and new. There, the *Juan* was, and I quote Palomino again, 'applauded by all the painters from different countries who said that the other pictures in the show were art but this alone was "Truth." ' Because of this acclaim, Velázquez was elected to the Roman Academy.' "

"And the *Marchesa*s fit in here, is that right?" Andrew asked. "Don't some specialists claim they were painted at another time?"

"They do, but they are mistaken," Seitz snapped. "They are the keys to the great Roman experience of the master. You see, if the *Juan* was 'Truth,' she was 'Not just art, but the object of pure desire —the Naked Truth!' Palomino wrote only those words about her. But I found, some years ago, even more. Rather startling. I was rummaging around in the Academy archives and came across this description—a contemporary one—by a Flemish painter working in Rome, Andreas Schmidt. I happened to write it down. 'Of all the worthy masterpieces created by this genius, none it is said is more vivid and astonishing than the pair of portraits he made of his lover, the gracious Marchesa Fiona Odescalchi. When I was shown the paintings by the master, I fell back in admiration and amazement, so surprised was I at the comeliness of the young woman—a goddess. In one picture she reclines with her back toward you, on sheets of black taffeta, radiant with her soft, auburn hair, her guitar-like waist, the pink shining skin. But, ah, the second image which Velázquez then brought out! His goddess had turned to her lover, the very image of purity! Not only I, but every painter who saw the portraits applauded them as "the highest truth" of the painter's art that they had ever encountered.' "

Andrew laughed. "Quite an endorsement." Turning to Olivia he added, "Although it pales compared to some descriptions." Then, turning to Seitz: "But what about the Pope?"

"She may have been a cousin of the Pontiff," Seitz replied. "Obviously a favored one. She was, apparently, everything you see in her portrait—young, extravagantly beautiful, intelligent, and a bit melancholy. The documents in the Academy describe at length how she went to the Pantheon to see the art exhibit and fell in love with the *Juan de Pareja* and the artist who had created it. Now Rome was fairly immune to scandals of an amorous nature in those days, so when the young girl moved in with Velázquez, she seems to have had the approval of her family."

"And what did the Pontiff say?" Andrew asked.

"In those days, Popes were less concerned about morals than appearances—their own appearances, anyway. It's my theory that Innocent thought it was an amusing match and made up his mind to give the portrait commission to Velázquez after he saw how magnificently he had depicted her."

"Still, isn't the *Pope* a superior picture? Maybe we should negotiate with the family that owns *Innocent X*—the Doria Pamphilis—and forget about this damned auction and that eccentric Richfield!"

"No! The *Marchesa* should be even finer, it it's in equally good condition," Seitz argued. "The ideal situation would be if you could arrange to compare her to *Innocent*, which I believe is in mint condition. But I'm not positive. Every time I have asked the Doria family's permission to have the picture analyzed by a reputable conservator they agree, and then nothing happens. *Dolce far niente!* As for Lord Richfield, by now the entire art world knows about his peculiar restrictions."

"Ulrich," Olivia said, somewhat intensely, "are you sure there are no later copies of the *Marchesa*?"

"None."

"What about Velázquez's second pair—the nearly exact pair—how could anyone tell the difference between them?"

"The two pairs are described in detail—with measurements—in the Academy archives. But there's a problem there."

Olivia was stunned by his words.

"Ulrich, are you saying there are measurements of the different versions recorded in the archives?" Andrew asked. "Then all one would have to do is compare them with whichever *Marchesa* happens to be around—Richfield's or anybody else's."

"The measurements do exist—somewhere," Seitz said with a sigh. "I wrote them down years ago. But I lost them. This painting's jinxed. She's the Helen of Troy of art—beautiful but deadly, always causing chaos. That bizarre attempted theft which caused Lord Richfield impetuously to put the picture on the block initiated the envy, the greed, and now, more criminal activities."

"What happened?" Olivia asked sharply.

"Several weeks ago the file in the Academy of Saint Luke containing all the scholarly data, including those measurements, was stolen."

"What?" Olivia felt a shiver course through her.

"Hey, this is getting good," Andrew cried. "Nothing like a few intrigues to get me moving. Well, at least we know what we have to do. Talk our way somehow into the Doria Pamphili Palace gallery and subject *Innocent X* to a scientific examination."

"If Ulrich couldn't get the family to do it, how do you expect to pull it off?" Olivia asked in a puzzled tone.

"I have a plan."

When they left, Andrew took Olivia to Romolo, a garden restaurant in Trastevere near the Farnesina, where Raphael is said to have courted his beautiful mistress. Andrew particularly enjoyed the way the pergolas spread over each table like intimate canopies.

"What did you mean by a 'scientific examination'?" Olivia asked hesitantly.

"I have an appointment this afternoon with the director of the Doria gallery. I'd better go alone. I'm hoping he'll let me get close to the painting—behind that fence in front—so I can study it with a magnifying glass."

When Andrew arrived at the gallery, he was told that the director had suddenly been called out of town. He had expected he would be absent. And Andrew was not surprised at how he was treated. The assistant director, a wan, officious, grumpy man, permitted Andrew inside the ornate iron barricade that protected the magnificent painting. But far from allowing him to examine the picture, he wasted his time with idle chatter. All Andrew could see was that the varnish had yellowed, making the crimsons duller than they should be and clouding the white surfaces of the Pope's skirt. Whether the painting had ever been relined was impossible to discover. All the assistant would say was that the painting was "in good stability." When Andrew asked if he could scrutinize the work with a strong raking light to search for repaintings and repairs, the man curtly refused.

When Andrew told Olivia the story later, she was puzzled. "Why would they act like that? It's almost as if they were being rude on purpose."

"They were," Andrew muttered. "I wonder who paid them off? But I prepared for this. Their refusal to allow me to examine the painting will work to my advantage. Now we can give *Innocent* a really scientific look," he said with a smile.

"What now?"

"I planned ahead. When I want something, I get it. Through my lawyer I made arrangements some time ago for a clandestine look at the Pope. Inside the gallery. We go tonight. Totally unknown, of course, to the Doria Pamphili family or the director or the assistant director. I made arrangements for the superintendent to receive a sum of ten thousand dollars in Swiss francs deposited in a bank in Zurich. We'll go to the main entrance at midnight and we'll be able to examine the painting for two hours. If we need additional time, it's five thousand dollars more for each hour or fraction of an hour."

"Andrew, this is crazy! To risk everything to obtain some information that you might still be able to get legitimately!"

"I did so well a couple of hours ago, didn't I?" Andrew countered. "Time is running out."

"True. But what if we get caught?" Olivia asked nervously. "We'd go to jail. We'd get fired, get drummed out of our profession. What then?"

"What then? 'When in Rome . . .' We'll do what the Italians do —throw up our hands in guilt, cry out a few mea culpas, and wait for a week until the nonsense fades away. In Italy we'd be television heroes. If they hear about it in America, I just don't think people will care."

"Andrew! We're sure to be arrested."

"In Italy you can get married in jail."

The superintendent of the Doria Pamphili Palace gallery opened the door punctually. A chilled bottle of wine was waiting for the trespassers and the gallery leading to the special chamber where *Innocent* was installed had been illuminated by candles. As they walked down the corridor past a row of superb Italian Baroque paintings, Olivia whispered, "Nothing in my life will ever top *this* experience!"

He squeezed her hand. "Wait. Around the next corner you'll see more than art.

Even in the mid-seventeenth century, the epoch of manifestly theatrical artistic expression, the presentation of Innocent X must have seemed bold, even shocking. In the Doria gallery the painting was still exhibited just as it was when it was first displayed: within an alcove which seemed to be an audience chamber where a supplicant could approach the Holy Father himself. There were a series of mirrored doors so cleverly arranged that long before one turned the corner and entered the alcove, the reflected image of the brooding Pontiff came into view. In candlelight the image seemed to move and breathe.

Olivia grabbed Andrew's arm. "What's he going to say?"

"Certainly not admonish us for our sins. He'll boast about getting Bernini to create his masterpiece of a fountain," Andrew answered in a stage whisper. "But let's turn the conversation to Velázquez. And we'll have him say, 'That slow-talking Spaniard? A trickster. He painted his Moorish companion to entice me.' "

Olivia laughed.

"Then, next, we'll have him say, 'This Spaniard seduced my cousin, that paragon of grace, beauty, intelligence, and wit, which alerted me to his true talents. He painted twin portraits of her as the image of pure desire, naked truth—the sacred and profane. I urged him to paint a perfect copy of both portraits. The second pair, mine, was even more truthful. Only when I saw my pair did I allow the Spaniard to paint my portrait. Frankly, I dislike it; it's too . . . candid.' "

The superintendent has obtained the equipment Andrew had specified—lights, an ultraviolet lamp, a stepladder, even magnifying lenses fitted out with high-intensity lamps which slipped comfortably over the forehead. And, best of all, he had removed the heavy frame from the masterpiece. With Andrew's aid, he lifted the great canvas out of its sunken repository so that he and Olivia could see the back of the picture. It was perhaps the first time it had been removed since it was placed there more than three hundred years before.

Olivia spotted the inscription instantly. It was more faint than that on the *Marchesa* and was written on the upper part of the gray background just above the Pontiff's head. Andrew had not perceived a thing, which surprised her.

She was on the verge of grabbing his arm and telling him, but with a coldness that frightened her, she decided not to utter a word. As he began to busy himself with studying the surface of the canvas, Olivia moved around to the back. The words were faint, looking more like random squiggles of varnish than letters. Painstakingly she deciphered each word and, so casually that Andrew did not notice what she was doing, wrote the inscription in her notebook. With every word, she felt a bit cheaper, a little more angry at herself. But it had to be done—she had to have her protection, her advantage.

I, Diego da Silva y Velázquez, made this mirror of a domineering Lord of the Church who is no sinner, but no saint. 1651.

The painting was in superb condition and had been cleaned perhaps once, gently, in its lifetime. Andrew slipped a small vial of xylene out of his pocket, saturated a cotton swab with the liquid, and began to clean tiny passages of the picture, removing the varnish to reveal pure paint. He took a photograph of each area, pointing out what he called "passages of true genius," where the master had not applied pigment at all but had allowed the bare maroon canvas to create an impression of color and infinite space.

Andrew was jubilant about what he had found and told the delighted custodian he'd throw in an extra hundred thousand lire for having organized their illicit visit so well.

They exited furtively from the Doria Palace and hurriedly crossed the deserted Piazza del Collegio Romano. As they entered the narrow Via Lata, neither paid heed to the small, thin man huddled in the shadows of a portico. After they had passed, the man waited several minutes, then spoke in Italian into his radio transmitter. "*Signore Conte*, they just departed. They were in there three hours. They must have paid a lot for that."

15 THE "COMMON MARKET CONNECTION"

BACK IN THEIR APARTMENT above the Fountain of the Four Rivers, which glowed magnificently in the floodlights, they made love to celebrate their coup.

"Somehow, between tonight and the day of the auction, we're going to have to examine the picture at William's just as we did old Innocent," Andrew said, sighing. "With my notes and the photographs I took today, we have something unique. But there's one key thing missing. Someone out there has something we don't—those measurements. Damn!"

"And they could have a vital bearing on what the Richfield picture is really worth. The first version is clearly far more valuable, even if the copies are by Velázquez himself."

"Right," Andrew said. "Damn. But there's still more to do in Rome. I may have access to inside information on something that's always troubled me—the attempted theft at the Richfield estate. I have a friend in the *carabinieri*."

"Why bother?" Olivia asked casually. "Some amateur thief, an art nut, breaks into the Richfield house and, instead of stealing the Velázquez, walks out with a mediocre nude."

"Then, within two days, after he burns the thing, the police apprehend him."

"And he goes to jail," Olivia added. "So what?"

"I don't get it. The thief claims he's impassioned about art and has a special love for Diego Velázquez. If so, why the devil didn't he take the *Marchesa*? Why go to all the trouble of swiping a canvas of insignificant value and then burn it? It's almost as if he were trying to frighten Richfield so he'd panic and put the Velázquez up on the auction block. Well, it worked. Because that's exactly what he did."

"Andrew, does your mind always run in such convoluted circles?"

"Could the thief have also stolen the original *Marchesa* and cleverly put a copy in its place?"

"You're suggesting he could have stolen the other nude to cover his tracks? And you're suggesting that I—and everybody else—wouldn't have spotted the copy? Darling, you should write novels."

"You would have. I don't know about the others," he laughed. "But I'm still troubled. My *carabinieri* source, a certain Colonel Contarelli—he's the head of the Italian art theft squad—may offer a few leads. He's always in touch, worldwide, with art robberies. I paid his way to Washington a couple of years ago for a seminar on museum security. I'm going to try to see him today. This is one you'd better stay clear of."

"I intend to," she replied.

Andrew grabbed the telephone and within seconds heard the colonel's deep voice. How soon could they meet? Andrew asked.

"Come to my office right away. I shall send my car."

Colonel Contarelli was a trim, mustachioed man wearing a resplendent blue-and-gold uniform.

"*Dottore*, it's not you I'm wearing my dress uniform for, I'm sorry to say. I have to pose for an official photograph after your visit. What can I do for you?"

"Colonel, I need something that might be confidential," Andrew said conspiratorially.

"But of course."

"What can you tell me about the famous Velázquez—the one coming up for auction in London next month? I'm especially interested in the attempted theft."

"So are we," the colonel said with a tight smile. "This Fielding is a bumbling incompetent who has been in jail twice before, petty crimes mostly, but never for art theft. He gains access to the Richfield house and then, instead of stealing something of any merit, he takes an insignificant daub of the late nineteenth century, one of those fleshy nudes, and then burns it. Ridiculous! The mystery is that he seems to have been well briefed on how to enter the estate and exactly where to go. And seems to have wanted to be caught. He looks like an idiot, but if so, where did he receive his inside information? Strange."

"What do your records have on this character?"

"*Niente*," the colonel said with disgust. "I had hoped I could link this Fielding to a band of art thieves operating out of the south of Italy. But Fielding appears, so far anyway, to be a lone wolf."

"Why would you have suspected an Englishman to be a member of an Italian ring?"

"We call it the 'Common Market Connection,' " the colonel replied in an exasperated tone. "We believe the group consists of six Italians, some French, Germans, a Belgian, a Dutchman, and a Swede. And there may be an American."

"What have they done?"

"Last year they slipped into the Brera Museum in Milano—the very evening the alarm had been turned off for repairs—and selected two dozen Impressionists. The museum officials were fools. They didn't inform us; they went instead to the insurance company, which authorized a ransom payment. The paintings were returned . . ." He paused, looking pained.

"Something else?" Andrew asked.

"The thieves waited a week, revisited the Brera, and stole precisely the same paintings. Once again these misguided museum officials told us nothing and ordered their insurance company to negotiate. This time it took only a few hours, not days. After all, the value of the stolen property had been well established. The thieves had the temerity to demand fifteen percent more—and got it!"

"Colonel, other than making ransom deals, what the hell can thieves do with their stolen art? They can't sell the stuff. Not to anybody who knows. What do they do with it?"

"There are certain dealers and collectors who will buy anything for a low price. But stolen art is not intended to be sold. Most art is stolen by professional thieves on specific order. They smuggle the painting or sculpture or manuscript—manuscripts are very popular because of their portability—into Switzerland and take it to one of several banks whose officers ask no questions about legal title or provenance. These banks have the works authenticated and appraised and make loans up to about fifteen or twenty percent of the assessed value."

"Art is stolen for collateral?"

"Clever, yes?"

"But what happens when the loan comes due?"

"It is simply renewed," Contarelli explained. "It can go on virtually forever. So the statute of limitations doesn't matter after all. Tracking down art thieves is hampered because most victims—especially private ones—never report their loss. Once the authorities know, the government usually starts asking embarrassing questions about what else they own. Taxes, you know. So the owners swallow hard and keep silent."

"Stolen art used as collateral is virtually foolproof," Andrew said admiringly.

"Yes, and the techniques are becoming more sophisticated. We have recently learned of a case where the legitimate owner of a certain painting himself made an arrangement with art thieves to steal it. Negotiations were carried out with the insurance company and the ransom was paid. The painting was returned. So the owner now has his painting back and a healthy share of the ransom. For the truly enterprising art collector there's a nice twist on this—we call it 'variation two.' The real painting is copied, the copy is stolen, and after the insurance company pays off, the copy is returned to the owner. The original is hidden for a while and then sold, perhaps in America. For the unscrupulous owner and his hirelings, 'variation two' means a double profit—the insurance and the fair market value of the original masterpiece. With no taxes, of course."

"Could this have happened with the Velázquez?" Andrew asked sharply.

"It could have. But from what we know, the Englishman had no connections."

"Tell me more about this art theft ring," Andrew said.

"It has proven to be my greatest burden. The members are damnably discreet. Just when we believe we may have identified one of them, that person produces an impeccable alibi. We suspect that the ringleader is a member of one of the oldest families in Naples."

"Mafia family?" Andrew asked.

"Apparently—and also a noble family," Contarelli replied, "or what remains of the old nobility. His name is Don Ciccio Nerone, the Count Nerone."

"A count? Head of an art ring?" Andrew exclaimed. "Wait a minute, I've heard of this guy."

"Count Nerone is a connoisseur of considerable magnitude as well as a collector himself. We've spotted known art thieves coming and going at his palazzo outside Naples. We have been following Count Nerone for some years with no results. We can do nothing more. This is, after all, a free society. All we hope is that he makes that one tiny, fatal mistake."

"Maybe he's bribing the police."

"Not possible, I assure you," the colonel said unctuously.

"You mentioned an American. Any idea who that might be?"

"Only theories. But just between us, we think it might be someone who works for an American museum."

"You're kidding!"

"No. Of course, it's only speculation, but the individual we suspect seems closely associated with Don Ciccio. In the investigative stage I cannot, of course, reveal names."

"I understand." Andrew paused, then said smoothly, "Colonel Contarelli, I'm thinking of organizing another international seminar on museum security. I wonder if you might be able to attend. This time the meetings will be shorter, so that participants can spend more time traveling around the United States."

"*Signore,* I would be most deeply honored. Of course, I must examine my schedule. Life can be demanding in the *carabinieri.* The same honorarium? . . . Ah, *double*? I think I'll be able to arrange things. . . . In six months? Yes. What an honor!" He beamed. "Is there anything we can supply for you while in Rome? My aide is a former vice-squad lieutenant. . . . No? Well, anytime . . ."

"Sometime, I'd like the name of the American you regard as a suspect."

No sooner had Andrew Foster departed the ornate office than the colonel slipped a raincoat over his dress uniform and exited through a side door. He walked rapidly two blocks to a telephone kiosk.

He dialed the Naples number from memory. And then, when Don Ciccio Nerone came on the line, he gave a brisk report on his meeting with Andrew Foster.

"I commend you, Colonel," Don Ciccio replied. "You see, although he doesn't know it, I plan to become better acquainted with Andrew Foster. Tomorrow, at my palazzo."

When Andrew entered the apartment, Olivia embraced him almost frantically. "I had two close calls while you were out!"

"Close calls?"

"Two people telephoned."

"Uh-oh!"

"The first was your secretary in Washington. I pretended I was a servant who could just barely understand English. It is 'vital' that Roland McCrae see you when you next come to New York."

"Oh, God. The interview! How do I handle that?"

"In your usual impeccable way," she said, leaving it at that. "And Rebecca Holcomb also phoned. I managed to fool her too. She says it is 'imperative' that you get to London."

"She's right. I've got to see that damned picture."

"Andrew, I've got to get to London too."

"I'll book us at Brown's," he said.

"We can't stay together. The whole art world will be in London."

"But where will we meet?" he asked.

"Can we afford to?"

"Why not. Let's make it Duke's Hotel in St. James's. The assistant manager is an old friend. He'll take care of us."

"When would you like to leave?" she asked.

"Tomorrow."

"Why not the day after? An old friend called, inviting me to Naples tomorrow, just for the night. You must come with me. He's utterly discreet and has a fabulous collection. You'll enjoy seeing it. Anyway, I can't get out of it. He's sort of an uncle."

"An Italian uncle?"

"Well, uncle in quotes. I acquired him in a rather unlikely manner. While a graduate student I lived here for almost a year at the American Academy. I studied twelve hours a day but in the evening I roamed the city, mostly alone, and dined at one marvelous local restaurant after another. One evening I was in a modest *locanda* near Santa Maria in Trastevere and an entourage of half a dozen men entered with a tiny creature—barely four feet tall. He was almost a dwarf, but beautiful. I couldn't help staring at him, although no one else dared to. The waiters fawned over him and one of them confided to me that he was a nobleman and very powerful in the south."

Andrew looked at her fixedly.

"The group devoured platters of those sublime doves, in season that time of year. Suddenly I heard an utterly panicked cry—a squeak, really—and I looked up to see this elegant little man flailing his arms in the air. Everyone froze. His minions simply sat there, eyes popping. The man was choking to death. I'll never know how, but I ran over, swept him up, and gave him the Heimlich hug. Out popped this bloody piece of bone. When he came to, and when at last he could speak, he told me I had saved his life and that for the rest of mine he would give me anything he was capable of giving. His name turned out to be Don . . ."

"Let me guess," Andrew moaned.

16 HACKING AROUND

THERE ARE DAYS in the early fall when even Naples, a once noble city that long ago lost the struggle to maintain its beauty, offers a visitor sweet vignettes suggestive of earlier glories. The begrimed architecture, those neglected piles of a more affluent epoch, seems to rise up proudly in the bright sun. The commotion in the streets and alleyways has all the appearance of a bustling day at the turn of the eighteenth century, a romantic image, undiminished by the numbing filth of modern times.

On such a day, safely enclosed in a gleaming, midnight blue Rolls-Royce that Don Ciccio had dispatched to the airport, Andrew and Olivia felt insulated from tawdry reality. The roof of the luxurious convertible slowly began to furl as they were driven away from the core of the city at a stately pace, up the precipitous switchbacks, stitching their way toward the Nerone palace in the hills north of the bay. As if on a guided tour, the taciturn chauffeur, dressed in light gray livery, slowed the car from time to time and eased over to the side of the road to afford the couple dreamlike views of the glittering coast below, a sunlit crescent of beauty that nothing—volcanic eruptions or even modern warfare—had managed to tarnish.

Within an hour the limousine came to a halt before a high black-and-gilded iron gate crested by a stylized emblem of the sun. The driver sat impassively. A half-minute went by and then, with scarcely a sound, the gates edged open, somewhat tentatively at first, and then swooped back like wings.

The car proceeded up a wide, steep drive, flanked by bountiful gardens with dozens of paired potted orange and grapefruit trees sunk into pedestals of mounded earth, all sculpted with the distinc-

·180·

tive emblem of the sunburst. The trees sparkled as if coated with fresh varnish. As the car approached, dozens of jet streams of water would start up, bathing each tree. It was as if an ethereal regiment of misty soldiers, arranged in an honor guard, were saluting the guests.

Two butlers and a squad of female servants greeted them with eager smiles, plucked their bags from the car, and swept the couple into a grand foyer. A barrel vault hovered more than fifty feet above their heads, where, at the apex, a fresco depicting a vivacious congregation of the Muses seemed to beckon them up the broad steps of a grand Baroque staircase. They climbed to the *piano nobile* and were ushered into a lavish suite comprising a private sitting room, a bedroom, and an art gallery which would have graced either one of their museums.

The suite glowed in golds and light blues reflected from the eighteenth-century Pompeiian Revival paintings on the ceilings. There were lush purple, gold, and saffron Fortuny wall hangings, elaborate silvered Rococo furniture, and, covering a spacious terrace outside the chambers, lustrous green and aquamarine tiles depicting a myriad of sea creatures. Andrew could not quite disguise his awe.

The terrace, which afforded a spectacular view of the Bay of Naples, seemed as wide as Park Avenue and was festooned with dozens of miniature orange trees. Dominating one end, set into a niche, stood a life-sized Roman bronze which to Andrew's amazement had retained all its ancient gilding. The statue depicted a young athlete looking up with pride as he lifted the laurel crown of victory to his brow. The way the sculpture merged the ideal with sensuous naturalism was so striking that both Andrew and Olivia looked at it agape as they ambled toward it. Partly hidden behind a colonnade adjacent to their quarters lay a swimming pool, its undulating surface gleaming like sapphires. Caught up in the unabashed paganism of the scene, their eyes met, they shed their clothing, and dove into the shimmering, cool water.

An hour and a half after their arrival, they were informed by a butler that cocktails would be served at nine o'clock. Andrew grumbled to Olivia that, with their schedule, nine seemed a bit late. But she pointed out that Don Ciccio preferred to meet someone for the first time in candlelight.

• • •

Count Nerone's entrance was hardly in keeping with the majesty of his extravagant villa. Severely crippled, he half-dragged his tiny body across the grand salon, greeting the couple with effusive compliments. Andrew admired the performance, particularly since the diminutive figure gave no indication that he was in any way aware of his bizarre appearance. It took Andrew several minutes to get used to the apparition. He hoped he had been able to disguise his initial surprise. But his reserve broke when Olivia bent down to peck the Count on the cheek and then, to Andrew's astonishment, lifted the doll-like figure into her arms and carried him to a high-backed chair.

"My affliction is not contagious," Don Ciccio hastened to say, settling himself into his chair. "My family, an ancient one and a noble one—whatever that means today—habitually arranged marriages between not-distant-enough cousins. And this lamentably conservative policy would from time to time foster hopeless cripples in body and mind—*or*, in rare instances, crippled geniuses. *And*, in extraordinarily rare cases, beautiful geniuses. The beauties in my family were usually delightfully bright—just as they needed to be. Here! I'll leave it to you to decide which type I am."

"Sir, I think I know already," Andrew said quickly.

"How gallant. Some champagne! A toast to the most surprising couple I can imagine. When Olivia told me you were coming, I could scarcely believe it. The very notion that Olivia, such a typically American woman, so eager to prove herself, would fall in love with her strongest competitor . . . well! Then I thought, Of course, how logical! The American way. 'If you can't beat them, join them.' Right?" He beamed at them. "Now what are you two really up to? And what can I do to help?"

Hesitantly at first, and then unguardedly, Andrew explained. "I guess you can say that Olivia and I are involved in a . . . a collaboration to win the Velázquez. Either she will buy it, or both of us will buy it—I can't tell you which. Right now, I don't know. If you find this a bit confusing I can only say, so do I. To me, the picture seems to be surrounded by enigmas."

"How so? I just received the sales catalogue from William's and it seems straightforward to me."

"Well, for one thing, Velázquez made a second pair for Pope Innocent X; they eventually came into the possession of a certain Cardinal Aquaviva, Pope Innocent's cousin. This pair has been lost. Or so they say."

"That sounds straightforward to me," Don Ciccio repeated. "Although things are rarely what they seem to be."

"And perhaps even more puzzling," Andrew continued, "there's the bizarre circumstance of that theft at the Richfield estate which triggered the sale. Why in God's name would a thief—by the way, I'm told his name is Fielding and he's now clapped away in Dartmoor, an amateur apparently—why would he go to all that trouble to steal a paltry picture and not the *Marchesa*? Maybe some incredibly clever bunch of . . ." He paused. "To compound the confusion, Lord Richfield won't let anyone get close enough to the *Marchesa* to give it a decent look. So how will one ever know what's going on?"

Count Nerone turned to Olivia and with a hint of exasperation asked, "Olivia, give us your opinion."

"The picture is gorgeous," she answered quickly. "Despite the silly restrictions, I had a fair chance to look it over. Oh, maybe a tiny doubt sticks in my mind; I'm a little bothered by the fact that I didn't see any repainted passages, places where he had changed or corrected a line—those all-important *pentimenti* which prove beyond a doubt that a painting is a true original. But on the whole, I'm satisfied."

"Then, so am I," laughed the Count.

"Me too," Andrew chimed in.

Later on Olivia planned to reveal to Don Ciccio everything she had discovered—the startling inscription which virtually guaranteed that the *Marchesa* was authentic, the inscription on the back of *Innocent X*, and the clandestine photographs she had managed to take.

After an excellent dinner the Count took them on a tour of his art collection—Greek and Roman antiquities, seventeenth-century maps, Baroque paintings, and a group of superb Hellenistic cameos. Never had Andrew seen such satisfying treasures as the cameos. Each was small in size, but each represented a universe of activity: dynamic athletes, ripe gods and goddesses, occasionally a pornographic scene of astonishing vivacity. One, barely an inch across and only half an inch high, represented the triumphal procession of a Hellenistic king with such realism that Andrew imagined he could hear the blare of the trumpets, the clang of swords on shields as hundred of troops applauded their victorious leader enthroned on an elephant dragging along a score of prisoners. It was not Alexander but, as Don Ciccio pointed out, "an even more effective ruler, Ptolemy I."

"These cameos are wonderful! The best I've ever seen," Andrew exulted.

"I'm so happy to hear your enthusiastic assessment. I have winnowed my collection down from hundreds—no, thousands—to these perfect twenty-two you see before you. I bought, sold, traded, always striving for perfection. Ah, perfection! *I worship perfection!* In art and in life. Someone with my physical affliction would, of course. Yes, I worship perfection, but never allow it to become an obsession, like a certain infamous perfectionist in your country."

"Who?"

"Surely you've heard about the ardent stamp collector in New Orleans who searched the world for a Three-penny Black, the only piece he wanted? . . . No? Well, now. He offered to pay eight hundred thousand dollars. An incredible price—well above the market value. But since there were supposed to be no Three-penny Blacks for sale, there was no market. Well, at length, such a stamp surfaced. It invariably does when the word gets out. The vendor traveled to New Orleans. Our indomitable collector examined the beauty carefully, proclaimed it authentic, and gave him a cashier's check for the entire amount. "There are just two Three-penny Blacks in the world,' he proclaimed. And then he went to his safe and with his tweezers removed the other—*his!* Before the eyes of the astonished vendor, he calmly extracted his cigarette lighter and burned it! 'Now,' he said proudly, 'there is only one—and *it* is perfect!' "

"*Hideous!*" Olivia exclaimed.

"Vandalism!" Andrew snapped.

"That's an obsessed perfectionist," Don Ciccio observed ruefully. "And it would also be fitting if I were able to show you, hanging on my wall, one of the Velázquez *Marchesa*s. The picture *might* logically be in my collection, for Cardinal Aquaviva was a member of the Baranello clan—as am I. I am, incidentally, also a descendant of that gifted collector of the seventeenth century, Antonio Ruffo, the Sicilian nobleman who commissioned Rembrandt to paint *Aristotle Contemplating the Bust of Homer*. Olivia, when the Met bought that picture for so much money, world art theft began to flourish."

Andrew laughed. "See, Olivia, I told you the Met was a bad influence." He reflected for a moment and then seized the opportunity to ask his host a question that had been weighing heavily on his mind. "Speaking of art theft . . . Count Nerone, you may think what I'm going to say is dreadfully rude but . . ."

Olivia looked at him with an expression of fearful expectancy.

"Dr. Foster, I suspect you were referring to the rumors that I am a *capo* in the Mafia and chief of a ring of art thieves. Yes? To that I can only answer, *Cosi e s'e vi pare*."

"Pirandello," Andrew observed.

"Precisely. 'It is as it appears to be.' I adore Luigi Pirandello. Much of my personal philosophy is based upon his writings. He was, I'm told, a distant cousin of mine. But, of course, what appears to be is not always so. I have evolved a philosophy of life which is a reverse Pirandello. Or, to put it another way, in Pirandello's brilliant play, all about sheer appearances, a number of people observe very differently the same phenomenon and all of them believe firmly—and correctly—that they have observed truth. Now I seem to be a cultivated, well-educated dwarf, the last of a long chain of petty nobles in a historically distinguished family, the Count Ciccio Nerone. That is true."

Andrew just stared at him.

"I am also, just below that surface, an entrepreneur, an exporter, a financier, and a researcher of sorts. Yes, that too. And below that it appears that I am also a 'don' of organized crime, the shifty manipulator of stolen works of art, the *maestro* of art thieves, a middleman between my gang, our victims, and their insurance companies." His eyes widened. "But that is not as it seems. In truth, I've got nothing to do with the Mafia. Nor am I a thief or a broker for thieves. I generate these rumors myself and encourage them to float around. People believe them. Even the Mafia believes them. The *carabinieri* too. So you see, I've turned the story around. As it appears to be, it is not."

"But why this elaborate charade?" Andrew asked incredulously.

"For safety," the Count replied. "In a land where there are an average of four kidnappings a week, three killings a month, a maiming every day, to appear to be a thief in Naples is equivalent to a suit of armor. And to seem to be an important 'don' in the Mafia is to be an impenetrable tank. My carefully contrived persona is useful to the *carabinieri*. From time to time I act as their 'mole' in the art theft underworld. In a country where last year there were over fourteen thousand thefts of works of art, I am a necessity. That way I can avoid being kidnapped or assassinated. Even the Red Brigades keep their distance from me!"

"You seem to have convinced Colonel Contarelli of the *carabinieri*," Andrew said, shaking his head in wonder.

"To encourage the illusion, I bribe him of course," Don Ciccio replied casually. "Not directly. To his parents, who are proud that their boy is corrupt. The only vexing problem with my elaborate camouflage is that certain people who are close to me tend to be thought of as part of my 'ring,' the nonexistent ring. Even Olivia must be on his list of suspects."

Andrew turned to Olivia and gave her a relieved grin.

After the tour they were served port of such fragrance that Andrew thought he might faint into the bottom of the glass. Don Ciccio lolled back amid a dozen cushions spread over an antique Roman bed and said, "Andrew, you may have heard that Olivia saved my life. Twice, really. Olivia, even you are not aware of this. That evening at the restaurant in Trastevere when I almost choked to death, I had already made up my mind to end my life. I was monumentally bored. By forcing that bone from my gullet you saved me. Later that evening as I was commencing the ancient ritual—the deliciously hot bath, the contemplation of the straight razor as it lay on the edge of the tub honed to an edge so fine that pain would never have intruded—I saw your face floating in front of me and suddenly I decided to face life again. So I am doubly in your debt."

The Count saw the couple to their suite, embraced them fondly, and apologized for not being able to see them off in the morning. "You see, Andrew, because of my condition, it takes me hours to rise and get on my feet in the morning. By the time I would feel comfortable greeting you, you will have long departed." He turned away with a sad smile, then, as if an afterthought, said to Olivia, "Oh, could you see me for just a minute or two in my chambers before your departure? It's about what we discussed over the telephone—an insignificant matter. Bless you, Andrew, and farewell."

He thereupon retired and walked painfully to his private elevator. Once inside, he collapsed onto a cushioned chair resting for a full five minutes before he gained the strength to push the button that would guide the elevator into the basement. As the elevator began its descent he inhaled deeply three times, shook his head, and reached down for a telephone concealed beneath the gilded chair.

"*Azzione!*" he commanded.

The elevator, as soundless as the works of a handcrafted Swiss watch, swiftly dropped six flights into the depths of the palace. The elevator halted a few seconds at a steel fire door, and then, at another signal from the Count, continued downward. The descent, which became progressively more rapid, continued for a hundred feet until the elevator abruptly slowed and came to a gentle halt. The doors hissed open and the chair detached itself from the elevator and quietly rolled toward a pair of open portals.

The chair, now a compact electric vehicle, glided around a corner and into a brightly lighted tunnel that led eventually to an intersecting tunnel, where it came to a stop before a tiled wall. After a momentary pause the Count was swept through a hidden door. Once inside, two servants greeted him and lifted him from the chair and into a hot whirlpool bath. There he relaxed as the whorls and rivulets of the heated water flowed pleasurably over his body.

After his servants had dried him and draped him in a cotton djellaba, Don Ciccio once again mounted his mobile chair and propelled it down a corridor some fifty yards into a niche faced by a travertine wall. He opened the left armrest of the chair and punched a combination of twelve numbers and letters on a keyboard. Quietly a portion of the wall gave way, opening onto a vaulted grotto decorated with five superb mosaics of the first century depicting the Labors of Hercules, which he had excavated from the subterranean passages of the ancient Roman villa which lay at the foundation of his palace.

Once inside, banks of lights came on in sequence, illuminating the cavern in a soft crescendo. He guided the chair toward an enormous Ruhlmann desk fashioned in Makassar with ivory inlays and punched out another series of letters and numbers. The wall above the desk rolled upward to reveal a thirty-foot bank of computers and terminals.

Three terminals were operating. With a wry little smile, Don Ciccio typed INT-OP-ADVIC-T.S.56754.CRIM-ART-CENTRAL, an access code into the top-secret files of Interpol in their concrete bunker on the outskirts of Paris. The word VERIFY appeared on the screen. He typed, "Request information. Art thief, W. Fielding, Dartmoor Prison." He was instructed to stand by.

The Count had by no means been candid with Andrew and Olivia. He was far more than a brilliant entrepreneur and dedicated connoisseur. His true métier was espionage; he was the world's most skillful computer spy—an electronic trespasser or "hacker," as the breed had come to be known. In years of intensive labor, starting when data processing was in its infancy, he had succeeded in clandestinely invading and browsing about at will in the digital never-never land of some of the most powerful computers and data banks of the world. His technique was devilishly simple. It involved essentially a series of basic decoders and bypass mechanisms which any graduate student in cybernetics could have devised. And, from the very birth of printed circuitry, Don Ciccio had painstakingly purchased every electronic card, every piece of commercial software and computer logic available on the market. It had been amusingly simple to analyze—or "reverse-engineer"— each one of the devices and even easier to familiarize himself with the subsequent improvements. The result after nearly thirty years was that he had acquired a massive library of codebreakers and entry systems into the long-distance telephone network that made computers function. And he had managed to perfect his entry systems long before anyone had devised sophisticated internal-security warning devices.

Don Ciccio, though not a member of the Mafia, was indeed feared by criminals of all stripes. He had trespassed into the electronic files of organized crime and, in addition, into those of virtually every legitimate bank, business, insurance company, and real estate firm through which the Mafia and other criminals wove their subtle alliances. Don Ciccio was far from what Orwell had predicted "Big Brother" would be. No tyrant or police chief of a repressive government, he was an opportunistic watchdog of the industrial world, a secret scrutinizer of the innermost cybernetic activities of crime, business, finance, government, and defense. To his amusement, he sometimes found it difficult to distinguish between the categories.

If he needed news before the world heard of it, he plugged into the word processors of reporters while they were filing their stories. To decide where to invest was simple: he trespassed into data banks containing the most privileged financial data of the Fortune 500. For truly cosmic investments—and profits—the Count reserved a special "window" on his hacking board for the Pentagon, thereby learning months in advance where billions of dollars' worth of defense contracts would be awarded. He had one bank of computers set aside specially for his personal finances. He was worth billions, a wealth that increased geometrically day by day. He made far more in a week than he could possibly spend in a lifetime.

At first the Count had found it supremely fascinating to creep into the electronic brains of every institution not immune to telephonic relay, institutions as diverse as the Sony Corporation, the Retribution Attack Division of the Soviet Missile Defense Bureau, William's Ltd. auction house, the Prestige Escort Service in Beverly Hills, the Pentagon, AT&T, Crédit Lyonnaise, IBM, the FBI, Interpol, the Sûreté, the Brooklyn "Three Families," and Richard Nixon's hard disk drive. But the fun paled after a while, and he established a system of automated sweeps so that he could indulge in his favorite pastime—reading the classics—while his computers did all the work, probing ceaselessly. Alarms alerted him to only the most compelling and fecund batches of information.

World conspiracies tended to thread their way along linear paths, and the Count's computers, in infinite step-by-step patience, harvested a bounty of information. Just that morning he had learned of two egregious violations of the U.S.–Soviet Arms Agreement triggered by Party Chairman Leonid Ermenentov. The Pentagon had knowingly allowed it to happen. Why? He was sure he would find out—in time. The French government had decided to increase the manufacture of the Lycet missile by twenty-five percent. He noted with dismay the covert arrest of twenty-eight conspirators in a plot of Shiite fundamentalists to assassinate President Fuad el Orabi of Egypt. Although he was pleased to see the coup quashed —he greatly admired the resourceful Egyptian—any kind of plot in the Middle East was troublesome. He chuckled at learning of the secret printing of eighteen hundred dismissal slips by an American corporation which had a week earlier announced that it was initiating a significant expansion because of the development of a "promising new product."

"Sell!" he ordered his "Broker" computer. Sell it did, and within minutes his commanding share of Senior & Vegas vanished—with a lavish profit to him.

An Interpol file flashed on the screen and Don Ciccio scanned the information greedily. The full name of the thief was William Fielding. Court records were available—twin asterisks indicated that one could view the complete court transcript by the insertion of Code DX4. None of the information interested him until he saw a paragraph labeled FAMILY RECORDS. That one he pored over word for word.

> William Fielding has no known record of theft. His only known relative: a brother known as Roger Field.

Don Ciccio next checked up again on Andrew Foster through the files his assistant Migliorini had discovered. First, the FBI. He expended thirty-eight minutes hacking his way into the dossiers of the FBI's most elite files, smiling at the adolescent nature of the security blocks the agency had placed in their programs. Once the virgin information banks had been laid bare the Count moved to his third computer system, a custom Amdahl model with a memory capacity approaching the number of stars in the Milky Way. There he analyzed the FBI's series of preventions to see if the coded obstacles were not ruses to make a hacker believe he had safely broken through the defenses. No. He was precisely on course. He mused that perhaps he should get his friend Congressman Bill Leonard to inform the FBI how to devise a more effective defense —one not so clever that he alone would not be able to penetrate, of course.

The data, which he already had, included Andrew Foster's meager salary at the National Gallery, an expense account that equaled it, an estimate of his net worth at $50 million. And the notation that Foster was a part-time agent for the CIA. Quickly Don Ciccio penetrated the CIA's computer files. It took him barely five minutes. He had long before programmed a virtually instantaneous codebreaker into the majority of the Agency files. He had discovered that an abundant share of America's business activities seemed to be linked to the intelligence-gathering enterprise. There was something new.

Andrew Foster: update 7906AP: in Vienna he demonstrated an unreceptive attitude toward a possible mission, involving the "gift" to the Soviet Union of the Marchesa Fiona Odescalchi by D. Velázquez to be auctioned November 21 at William's at 112 Portman Place. Foster is no longer permitted to have access to sensitive material.

Don Ciccio threw back his head and laughed heartily, suddenly realizing why his old friend William Leonard had so urgently tried to find out his intention in the forthcoming sale. He would have to warn Olivia.

Next, as a routine precaution, he checked up on Olivia. On a sporadic basis Don Ciccio surveyed all his employees and friends. He poked into the files of the Metropolitan Museum of Art, noting with a sardonic laugh a confidential memorandum from chairman and trustee Ayn Steyne to another trustee named Roland McCrae.

I can assure you that O.C. is, to me, UNACCEPTABLE as director of this museum. I also heartily concur that, at over ten million dollars, the Velázquez is ridiculous. I shall not say a word to Cartright. She will simply be voted down by the search committee.

Neither the CIA nor the FBI data contained a word on Olivia. And that was what the Count expected.

Now, what to do about Diego Velázquez? He typed out the artist's name. Harvard University was listed as a major research source on the master. Although it was two thirty in the morning and his eyes were smarting at the flow of data on the pastel-colored terminal screens, Don Ciccio dialed a final set of instructions and trespassed easily through the intercontinental TELNET modem into the files of the Fogg Museum of Art in Cambridge, Massachusetts, Harvard's renowned teaching museum and the repository of a sophisticated information system with most of the world's knowledge of art history.

He found a profuse catalogue raisonnée of Velázquez's works, worldwide, compiled by a Professor Howard Broadbent. The references to the *Marchesa Odescalchi* were numerous, but contained nothing he did not already know. On a hunch he decided to find out if the private files of the professor were linked to the scholarly inventory, something that would have saved the professor considerable money. Not to his surprise, they were. And there he found a morsel.

We all know the likelihood that the master produced, probably for the Pope, an exact copy of the original pair of portraits. The history of all four pictures from the end of the eighteenth century is obscure. It is said that Velázquez's second version of the pair was destroyed by fire. That may or may not be. There were intriguingly coincidental activities in the Office of Suppression of Immorality of the Roman Inquisition. It just might be that the paintings were not burned, and in actuality were hidden from the clutches of the Inquisition. One might like to pursue this coincidence (if only I had time!). Finally, an amusing little circumstance. There is supposed to be "a Velázquez Fiona Odeschalchi (sic)" in a most unlikely place, in Fiesole, Italy. This "Marchesa" —no one seems to know whether it's a front or a back—is owned by a Brazilian importer and designer of jewelry, Joao Viva, who claims to be a descendant of the family of Cardinal Aquaviva (in whose family a Marchesa Odescalchi by Velázquez is recorded in the late 17th century). I, for one, am intrigued, since I'm fairly positive that no one else knows about it. Someday when I have time I might look the man up and have a glance.

The Count fell back in his chair. Should he tell Olivia? No. Instantly he plunged his fingers onto the keyboard of his chair and sent the vehicle rolling down the battery of terminals to one that was colored jet black and set apart from the others. Rapidly he entered the code FLO-RED, RED, ANSBCK. GIORGIO. And then typed "Proceed NOW—before dawn—Fiesole, Villa Joao Viva. Secure painting (17th c.) by Velázquez depicting a young exceptionally beautiful naked woman. INSTANT REPORT." He then closed the file with the instruction FLO-RED, RED, ANSBCK. O.C. 355786.

The last act of computer piracy committed by Don Ciccio that early morning was a foray into the electronic files of William's Ltd. There he encountered an entry in the Velázquez file which caused a smile to cross his face.

There is good reason to expect a fine feast on the *Marchesa*. The Met is just in. We believe Jules Bramet is coming in. The National Gallery is hotly pursuing the Met. The competition between the heads of these institutions appears to be building into a vigorous pattern. At the moment an even more serious contender seems to be the Louvre. Officials there have discussed with us the placement of a $13.1 million bid. But even more intriguing is the information that the London agent for Kurt Krassner has made discreet enquiries about the increments of bidding. Why Sir Michael Fairless should be so interested is puzzling. His institution has no money at all! Yet unlike him to perform outside appraisals. The *Marchesa* is changing everybody who comes into contact with her. Still in contention is the Cleveland Museum; the Prado will submit a symbolic bid. As to the decision of the Getty Museum and Robert Symes we know nothing at the present.

Don Ciccio spent a half-hour typing multiple instructions for his staff ("PROMPTLY!") into a file labeled CARTRIGHT/FOSTER. Among them was a command to search all existing intelligence departments of the Soviet Union for any reference, however veiled, to a painting of a woman by Diego Velázquez. It took his Amdahl only minutes to slip flawlessly through the complicated electronic traps, gins, deadfalls, and snares surrounding the personal records of the party bosses and particularly Chairman Ermenentov. The effort for the machine, he knew, was monumental, even with its astonishing capability of 75 million calculations every thousandth of a second. What his miraculous machine churned up made Don Ciccio roar with laughter despite his fatigue.

The Count managed to gain his room only minutes before Olivia gently knocked on his door. It was a half-hour before her departure. Over pungent cappuccinos the Count informed her of the latest addition to Andrew's CIA file. She looked mildly stunned. In Vienna? She recalled he had left her for a couple of hours in the afternoon. What did it all mean? The Soviet Union? It sounded dangerous, and suddenly she was afraid.

"I just don't know what's going on. All I know is that I love him
—totally." Then she told the Count what she had discovered, adding, at the end, what Ulrich Seitz had said about the curious theft
of the files in the Academy of Saint Luke.

With a sly little smile the Count reached back and extracted a
manila envelope from the headboard of his elaborate bed.

"Then I am sure you will find this intriguing."

Quickly she opened the envelope and shuffled through the papers—all Xeroxes. When she had digested what they were, she
raised her head and stared at Don Ciccio in stunned surprise.

"The files from the Academy of Saint Luke!"

"Read them on the plane. They have interest. Lots of gossip
about the Marchesa, who doesn't seem as pure or as entirely faith-
ful to Velázquez as legend would have it. But nothing is what it
seems to be. What is really important are the measurements. They
are in palms, but I have translated them into inches and centimeters
for you."

Olivia saw that Velázquez's first pair of portraits measured exactly seventy-eight by forty-five inches. The second pair, for the
Pope, measured eighty-one by forty-eight. In an amusing aside, it
was noted that Velázquez had taken pains to make his second pair
of portraits larger "so that His Eminence could never claim he had
not obtained the more important works." Eagerly she snatched her
notebook from her purse and consulted her notes. The Rokeby
Venus measured eighty-one by forty-eight. It had to be Velázquez's
second version. And the Richfield painting was the same. So what
she had seen in William's was the Pope's version! It was a breath-
taking piece of information which shattered the accepted scholarly
assumption that the Rokeby *Venus* in London's National Gallery
and Lord Richfield's erotic masterpiece were the pair of portraits
Velázquez had originally made for himself and his lover. And the
information also proved utterly wrong the accepted theory that
the pair of *Marchesa*s painted for the Pope had been destroyed. The
further implications of her discovery made her heart pound: if
the Pope's pair of nudes still existed, the first pair, which no document had ever claimed had been destroyed, must have survived
also. Would they ever turn up?

"I'm not sure I understand. These files . . . Did you? I . . ."

"It is not as it appears to be. Believe me," he said affectionately.

"I shall tell you more later. Be at ease. All will work out, I can assure you. Now, you must hasten to London. At the time of the sale I shall meet you there."

"You mean you'll attend?" she said with more than a hint of nervousness in her voice.

"Of course. I am sure you will be needing me most at that moment."

"Yes," Olivia said. It was a whisper, almost sad.

"Be trustful. Have I ever hurt you?"

"Absolutely not. Oh, I am giving you the wrong impression, aren't I? Absolutely not!"

"Well, good. My darling girl, you must be off. There's only one other bit of information I hope you will be able to make use of."

Olivia leaned forward tensely.

"Over the grave objections of many of his advisers, the Party Chairman of the Soviet Union, Leonid Ermenentov, spurred on by the entreaties of his mistress, formerly the director of the Pushkin Museum and now Minister of Culture—"

"What! Ludmilla Tcherninka?" Olivia gasped.

"Yes, indeed. Well, the Chairman has decided to ask the National Security Adviser to buy the Velázquez and then give it to the Soviet Union as an inducement to bring him to the summit."

"Oh, my God."

"And this you must know. Sir Michael Fairless—you, of course, know of him . . ."

Olivia nodded.

". . . will be ordered by the Russians to examine the painting."

"Ordered?"

"Yes. Not at all curious. Sir Michael is an espionage agent for the USSR. Use this, Olivia," the Count said emotionally. "Somehow *use* it."

Olivia parted in confusion, elated at the knowledge that she knew more about the Velázquez than anyone on earth but deeply concerned—frightened—that Count Nerone might be more than an idle meddler. How could he have learned so much? What was he going to do with the information? Suddenly he seemed to her to have become more than a little dangerous. She needed Andrew more than ever before. And just when she did, they would have to be apart.

17 STARTLING IMPRESSIONS

A FEW MINUTES AFTER DAWN the plane carrying Olivia and Andrew took off from Naples for Rome. They arrived late and their departure for London was delayed two hours, causing an increasingly fidgety Andrew to grouse that their luck was changing for the worse.

"Annoying!" he complained as they tried to wend their way through the crowded corridors of the jammed airport. "But most annoying is not having you!"

"Darling, I won't be away every minute of the day—or night," she assured him. She gripped his hand tightly. But, to herself, Olivia looked forward to being on her own.

Not that her love for Andrew had diminished. It was just that she relished the chance to pursue the masterpiece by herself. So far, with the aid of Don Ciccio, she had achieved miracles, and she had come to believe that she alone was destined to solve the mysteries surrounding the enigmatic painting and that she alone was fated to decide who the next owner would be. And she needed time to reflect on how to adjust to spending her life with Andrew. The effect of marriage on her career was a question that nagged. She had spent years training to be an art historian and the investment was too valuable to fritter away. Andrew did not intend her to become a member of high society, dashing from one fashionable part of the world to another. Although she looked forward eagerly to being financially comfortable, Olivia feared that when she married him she would become a slave to a bewildering amount of property. He had mentioned no less than five family homes—in New York City, Washington, the estate on the Hudson, in New

Jersey, and on Hobe Sound. And what about the additional *pieds-à-terre* in Rome, Hong Kong, Kyoto, and Sicily?

And she had found herself wondering, too, whether she could hold on to him. He was careful, steadfast, collected. She was intense, instinctive, impulsive. Their opposing temperaments might be attracted initially. But forever? Would they become in time like oil and water? What about his penchant for beautiful women? And what about his ambitions? Try as she might, Olivia could not dispel the thought that his career was far more important to him than he was making out. Finally, what about her work, her ambitions? Underlying everything were those burning questions.

At Heathrow they decided for the sake of prudence to leave the airport for their hotels separately. Andrew would go on ahead to Brown's. Olivia would lag behind to make a few phone calls. Their parting was lingering and emotional. For a moment as Andrew's taxi drove off, she half expected it to return to fetch her. But the vehicle was swallowed up by the congestion surrounding the terminal.

An hour later Andrew checked into his hotel and was handed a fistful of messages. Rebecca had called to say that she had to see him at once. His father had called. Another message, marked "urgent," was from Andrew's former stepmother, Elmira. There was a note from the assistant manager of Duke's Hotel asking him to call, and another from Sir Peter Grundy. Finally, there was one from someone he'd never heard of before, a Marco Migliorini.

Duke's Hotel was the call he returned first, and he was furious to learn that no room could possibly be available for him for at least a week. No matter how much he implored his friend, the assistant manager, nothing could be done. He could, of course, seek out another hotel, but that would be too risky. The staff at Duke's was the only one he was positive would be completely discreet. When Andrew called Olivia at the Westbury to convey the bad news, he was told she had not yet arrived.

Then he called his father, who was just having breakfast in New York.

"Is she as luscious as I've heard?" his father asked.

Andrew felt stricken. How on earth could his father have learned about Olivia?

"And what about that woman at the Met? Is she going after the painting too? I hear she's an aggressive bitch."

Andrew sank back on his bed with a relieved grin and gently slapped his forehead. The blood rushed back into his face.

"I haven't even seen the painting yet, Dad."

"Just as well," his father replied in relief. "I'm worried about this painting and your involvement with it. I don't want you to get burned. I had dinner with Bill Leonard last night, who kept saying it would be a political disaster for you to buy this extravagant thing."

"Dad, I appreciate your concern. But I'm not in politics . . . and I think Leonard's getting a bit old and frayed. You might want to know that Jonathan Cresson wasn't swayed by Leonard's feelings. I know he's a friend but—"

"Friendship has nothing to do with it. Just so you know what the political—and public—reaction will be. What are you doing other than running around after the world's most expensive painting? We've not seen each other in so many months. Have you looked up the indomitable Elmira? She knows Richfield and that gang. Hell, son, I won't beat around the bush. I've heard rumors about you cavorting around Europe with some blonde."

In a flash, Andrew decided to tell him. He gulped hard, gripping the telephone receiver as if he were trying to squeeze moisture out of it, and stammered, "Dad, her name is Olivia Alexis Cartright." He paused and in a strangled voice continued, "Yes, the 'bitch' from the Met."

His father chuckled. "A little dirty work, eh?"

"Dad, *no!* I met her a little over two weeks ago in Paris but . . . Look, I've got to tell you something important. With you, I've never known quite how to begin. But this is kind of vital . . ."

"Son, just come out with it."

"You mustn't tell anyone. And I mean *anyone.* Do I have your word? . . . Good. How do I do this so that I don't sound like a teenager? Father, Olivia and I met in Paris, fell in love, and I've already asked her to marry me."

"*You what?* The words came out in a plaintive howl. "To a social nobody? And a competitor?"

The initial outburst was followed by a tirade, in which he threatened to cut Andrew out of his will, and muttered that he might be "chopped from the family tree." The emotional explosion diminished quickly. And when it did, Andrew began to reason with his distraught parent. When he felt a slight dig might be in order, he threw in a pointed reference to his father's own complex marital history. Within minutes, the elder Foster was almost tractable.

"She's everything I ever imagined, Dad. Intelligent, gutsy, beautiful. I know it's a shock. I can understand you're angry because you weren't told. The trouble is . . . I'm not altogether sure I've been told. She hasn't agreed to a specific time."

His father exploded again. "What the hell does she want, anyway, a prenuptial agreement? Money. She's after your money!"

Andrew patiently explained that what Olivia really wanted was the Velázquez and the directorship of the Metropolitan and that this posed certain problems.

"At least that makes her sound like she has some character. When am I going to meet this paragon?

Andrew sighed heavily when, at last, he could put the receiver down, not quite certain what his father truly felt. He decided he wouldn't say a word about the conversation to Olivia.

Next on the list was Elmira. The "urgent" news was that she had heard from someone at William's—"I've forgotten the name"— who had slipped the word that the Metropolitan Museum was carrying on secret discussions to consign for later sale a flock of paintings in a desperate attempt to raise the money for the *Marchesa Odescalchi*. The acting director of the Met, "an unattractive, ambitious woman," was trying to engineer the deal over the violent objections of the majority of her board. Andrew earnestly thanked his stepmother for the tip.

Suddenly inspired, he asked, "Elmira, can you arrange a meeting with Lord Richfield?"

"Nothing simpler. I know him rather well. Would tea or drinks do?"

"Drinks would be perfect. Sometime this week? At noon? Just the three of us?"

Andrew now tried Olivia again and to his increasing puzzlement was told that Dr. Cartright had not yet checked in. He next telephoned Sir Peter Grundy.

"So, back in town?" Grundy said. "And, of course, you want your crack at the masterpiece . . . Now? No, not possible. Andrew, why, oh, why didn't you take my advice and make an appointment to see the painting weeks ago? Today is the last day Lord Richfield will allow individual examinations. Tomorrow it goes to conservation for varnishing and then into storage before the public showing just before the sale."

"My God," Andrew cried out between clenched teeth. "Surely there's an hour sometime today."

"The whole day is booked. . . . Who? Frobisher, Symes, and Waters. All signed up long ago."

"You mean I, a potential bidder, will not be allowed to study this thing until the public sees it?"

"Richfield is adamant."

"And crazy. I might be the top bidder, Peter."

Grundy sighed heavily. "Come tomorrow morning," he said. "I shall see to it. Two hours. No more."

"Bless you, Peter. I knew you'd do it. I can't wait."

Grundy rang for his secretary. "Please inform Mr. Frobisher that I shall escort him to the inner sanctum right away." With a grand smile he emerged from his office to confront the director of the Getty Consolidated Museum of America.

"Ah, dear Frobisher. Good trip? Well rested? . . . Excellent. Once you cross the threshold of her chamber, you'll never be the same man again," Grundy intoned dramatically.

Robert Frobisher entered the room where the *Marchesa* was exhibited, looking around nervously as if he were concerned about being followed. He seemed to draw back when he was introduced to the guard, and then sat silently in the chair that was placed a yard or so away from the picture. Frobisher gazed at the canvas in a torpor, terrified, as he almost always was when he encountered a work of art that he had never seen before and knew little about. The picture shimmered before him as if in a blur. He wrung his hands. What should he think? He didn't have any idea. Frobisher recognized that he possessed a less than exacting eye and had been able to disguise his failing to his board of directors by clever repetition of technical art-history verbiage. His trustees interpreted his reluctance to acquire certain works as the sagacity of a professional. His colleagues in the museum world knew better, recognizing that he was incapable of distinguishing between the good and the mediocre. They were delighted. What if the superwealthy Getty had at its helm—and in control of its enormous treasury—a true connoisseur?

Frobisher twisted uncomfortably in the chair. He tried to compare the painting in front of him with the ones he had examined two weeks ago at the Prado. But individual pictures all seemed to merge into one indistinct canvas with earth colors, gray backgrounds, and ruddy flesh tones. If only someone had written a learned treatise on the *Marchesa*, then he would know how to react. Frobisher studied the painting for an hour and a half—mostly for appearances—and left, putting on a show of casual confidence.

Robert Symes, the ebullient private collector from California, arrived an hour early for his appointment and drove Grundy to distraction pacing the floor of his office as he nattered on about the American art market in his wheezy soprano. When finally he could enter the room where the Velázquez was hanging, he glanced at it, and fell deeply in love. She was far more radiant than the first time he had seen her. He spent two full hours marching back and forth in front of the steamy young woman in total silence, coming as close as was permitted by the guard and then agilely springing away.

Symes had virtually devoured the painting with his eyes. And left with the firm impression that it was in good, if not superior condition. He had failed to detect the inscription. Symes did not have an eye for subtleties. It was a go! The only question was for how much.

James Waters of Cleveland had encountered Symes in the narrow corridor and managed a thin smile at what was obviously put-on sadness on Symes's leathery visage.

"You're next, Jim. I'm not at all sure about it," Symes told him. "But maybe you will be able to see clearer than I through the yellow fog covering the surface of the picture. Big it is, but is it any good? You museum chaps have less to lose. I'm treading carefully."

Waters initiated his examination by leaning casually against the opposite wall and, as if conducting a ritual which involved a precise timetable, moved from corner to corner of the room, muttering under his breath. "Is it any good? My God, it's overwhelming!" He could not possibly have imagined from the photographs how much energy the *Marchesa* possessed. It was almost as if she could reach out to him and caress him. In a thousandth of a second prudent James Waters became reckless. "Awesome!" The master had never been more penetrating or sensitive! But then, perhaps he had never been in love before. James Waters had never fallen so much for any work of art in his career. As he gazed, rapt, at the masterwork he began to feel a longing. The more he looked the more complacent he became, as his nimble mind rationalized what he had already decided to do. In buying the Velázquez for what he was certain would be the highest price ever in history—a scandalous price— he wasn't stepping out of character. He hadn't been prudent or, as he knew some of his colleagues called him derisively, "weak." It was simply that he had been waiting for that one surpassing moment, that once-in-a-lifetime opportunity that only truly great connoisseurs could muster the patience for. What he was going to do would put him in the history books forever. God, she was lovely! He chuckled to himself and completed his long study by lying down and squinting at the picture for fifteen minutes, then scrutinizing the tantalizingly beautiful young woman on tiptoe.

He returned to Grundy's office and asked his secretary for the use of a typewriter. After he had typed his message, he waited patiently outside the auctioneer's office half an hour to see him.

"Peter, may I submit a sealed bid?" he asked calmly.

"Of course. We accept them from time to time." Grundy said evenly.

"This one is slightly different," Waters explained. "When the bidding reaches twelve million pounds, you may open the envelope. You must not open it at all if at any moment in the sale you see me shake my head. If I don't, you must read what I have written with the utmost care and proceed exactly as I have instructed."

"It is a novel approach. But why not," Grundy affably assured him.

Strolling back to his hotel nearby on Regent Street, James Waters was exhilarated by his courageous action. There was no turning back and the thought didn't faze him. If he had felt stronger physically he might have scampered down the street in sheer joy. He was right, so very right. He had seen it all in a flash. He chortled to himself in the delight of being the only human being on earth to know who would win the divine *Marchesa*. He, James Waters! He had to be the victor—with a bid of the dimensions he had committed to Grundy. What a shock it would be to the art world! By God, he'd show the callow young generation of collectors that the older crowd could do it. He whispered out loud his top bid and laughed.

His heart pounded as he quickened his steps. Suddenly Waters felt an attack of vertigo. He searched in his pockets for his pills. Why hadn't he carried them with him as his doctor had ordered? He simply had not got used to the ugly reality of his heart condition. Perhaps he was imagining the dizziness. As he walked along studiously, the feeling of instability began to wane. Waters felt a little silly. A false alarm.

He exhaled in relief, approached the street corner, and looked to the right and left to be doubly sure it was safe to cross. Just before the light changed James Waters allowed himself a spontaneous, wild little dance of victory. What a triumph! As he did, he felt his body being engulfed in a rush of heat. His head seemed about to explode. He jerked up as if hit by an electric current and collapsed in front of an onrushing bus. Hours later, in the city morgue an autopsy revealed that James Waters had been the victim of a massive cerebral hemorrhage.

Olivia did not waste time registering at the Westbury. She dropped off her bags and drove directly to Wilton's for lunch. Owing to the midday traffic, she was already late for the appointment she had made from Heathrow after Andrew's departure.

Roy Bentley was waiting impatiently at a table in the corner of the elegant dining room. From time to time he glanced approvingly at his sleek image in the mirror opposite. His eyes would dart from there to the entrance, scouting like a hunter for young men who might happen in. A half-hour late, Olivia was escorted to his table, offering her apologies.

"You look quite brassy," Bentley snapped. "What have you done to yourself?"

Olivia laughed. If Roy Bentley considered her "brassy," she knew the transformation was effective. They chatted for a few minutes about trivialities, then Olivia confronted him directly.

"Roy, dear, what are you going to do about the Velázquez?"

"You first, darling. What's your move?"

"For me, the painting is problematical," Olivia said convincingly. "I had come prepared for bells ringing, chorus singing, fireworks. It's great, but not . . . you know. I can't get close enough to it to make up my mind. That's where I need your advice."

"Even if you were one of my favorite little students that summer —oh, when was it?—yes, six years ago, don't expect me to help you. You see, no one can. Surely you remember what I tried to drum into your brain in my course: 'When you're going for a work of art, you're a thousand miles closer to it than anyone else in the world. Listen only to your own instincts.' "

"Are you telling me you're not interested in it?"

"As a government employee subject to the Official Secrets Act, my dear, I could be severely censured even for mentioning the name Odescalchi," Bentley said archly.

"If I were you, Roy, I'd not be obsessed with this sale."

He simply stared at her.

"There must be many important treasures Great Britain needs more," Olivia added gently.

"Dozens. All critical." He threw up his hands. "And all coveted by Mr. Dollar or Herr Mark or 'Gettem' Getty. The responsibility I bear is such a burden." He sighed and shifted in his seat. "You really won't wrest a thing out of me, Olivia, much as I adore you— and I do," Bentley added with a small laugh.

She reached over to pat his arm.

Bentley examined his fingernails and with a sly grin asked, "How are they treating you at the Metropolitan? Are you to be their choice as director?"

"I'm still only a candidate," she said. "There are others. But I'm working hard on it. Have you heard anything?"

"Nothing of substance." He cocked his head and said cunningly, "But it seems to me that you might subtly pressure your board regarding the antidiscrimination issue. I would have."

"Roy, you have all the finesse of a street-fighting politician!" Olivia cried delightedly.

"How did you think I made it to the top of the greasy pole at the National Gallery? Fight on with all your weapons, my dear."

"I intend to. I may have given my trustees pause by sending a letter actively requesting the position."

"Thereby making it a women's rights issue? Capital!"

"You continue to amaze me. Come on, I can keep a secret. As an old friend, tell me, are you going to be bidding at the sale?"

"Of course not," he retorted. "Why should I bother? If I wanted to capture this picture, the last thing I'd do is bid. Under British law I'm allowed to sit on the sidelines and then petition the Board of Trade to grant me the funds to purchase the thing. At my request Parliament must block the export of the painting should some foreign institution seek to carry it away. I can block it for a month, six months, even longer, to raise the money. I can easily obtain the funds from some commoner eager to snag a knighthood or from the Exchequer, which usually bends to my will eventually, or from our own sizable funds—that acquisitions trust fund a very special American friend gave to us years ago. Until then, if my stay of exportation is about to expire, I simply ask Parliament for an extension. Why, then, should I go to the auction? Why should I bid and fight against myself? I can stall the *Marchesa's* departure from England for . . . generations!"

Olivia slumped in her chair. "But you must raise the money, mustn't you?"

"Yes! I could . . . if I wanted. For great things. Not for every petty landscape, still life, or precious little watercolor that comes along. But, Olivia, in the case of this Velázquez, I don't choose to."

Bentley leaned forward and in a stage whisper asked, "What if I were to tell you that I wholly agree with your opinion. I, too, think the picture is second-rate. I was granted special permission to study it. Would you believe me if I told you I had the painting removed to the Gallery for one whole day last week—on the day we're closed to the public—and will be allowed to examine it once again, side by side with the Rokeby *Venus,* a week before the sale? I asked for it only to be absolutely certain of my opinion that the painting has suffered grievously."

Olivia left the restaurant convinced that Bentley was lying to her.

Lord Richfield would never have allowed him to remove the painting from William's Ltd. And Grundy couldn't do it on his own. Olivia was sure Bentley would wait until after the sale and then pounce upon it.

As soon as Roy Bentley left Olivia, he phoned Lawrence Wright, the art critic of the *Telegraph*, and invited him to his club for dinner that evening.

Throughout the meal Bentley was subdued, serious, a demeanor which annoyed the journalist, who had come prepared for the usual fusillade of biting and witty comments fired at everyone in the world of art. But Bentley seemed genuinely guarded and unsure.

Finally he blurted out, "I don't want to, but I simply have to tell someone. Swear you never heard this from me."

"Of course, Roy. Would I break your confidence?" Wright said smoothly.

"It's about the Velázquez. I fear it's no good."

Wright started to protest, but Bentley hushed him.

"Please, not here. Anyone could be listening. I tell you, the picture is a copy, possibly even a fake."

"What a revelation!" Wright said, and began to rise from his chair. "Are you one hundred percent sure?"

"Would I be wrong about something like this? I've seen the original."

"How shall I break this? I can, can't I?"

"How could I possibly stop you?" Bentley remarked piously.

18 AGAIN, PIRANDELLO!

OLIVIA RETURNED TO THE WESTBURY after the cat-and-mouse meeting with Roy Bentley. She checked in and took a long nap to be at her best to meet Andrew for a late supper and dancing at Annabel's, a fashionable private club on Berkeley Square. She smiled when she saw he had called her three times.

At the club he hugged her tenderly and guided her to the candlelit dining room, gleaming with the soft reflections of a hundred mirrors, then to his special corner table. The maître d' fawned over him and nodded appreciatively as Andrew ordered a bottle of Krug.

Olivia gazed around the room. "Would it hurt my image to say, 'Ah, finally to be in Annabel's!' "

"You're the first woman I've ever brought here who had the gumption to say she's impressed. And by far the most beautiful," he said, giving her a fond kiss. "I have some bad news. My friend at Duke's tells me that the only way we're going to get in there is to rub out a couple of the guests. No rooms for at least a week. I just don't trust anybody else."

"How about—oh, dear. It's been a whole day and I was lonely without you."

"Marry me tomorrow. I can cancel my visit to the Velázquez."

Olivia raised her eyebrows.

"Yes. Finally I'm to see it in the morning. Guess who came in to William's today? Frobisher, Symes, and Jim Waters. I'd love to know what each one of them thought."

"Let's dance," she whispered. And the evening passed deliciously as they danced, dined on cold quail, and danced some more. Works of art and the tangled world of art museums were far from their minds.

They left shortly after three in the morning and strolled around Berkeley Square toward the Westbury, a block and a half away.

"It's late enough," Olivia said softly. "Come up and tuck me in. No one will see us. Those who do won't care and won't talk."

"If I do, I'll never get out of there."

"That's the point."

He suddenly froze. She wondered if she had somehow offended him.

"There's someone over there," he whispered in alarm. "In that doorway. In the shadows. Watching us."

They were standing in front of the windows of a fashionable luggage shop on the corner of Conduit and Bond Streets. To Andrew's astonishment, a rapier-thin young man emerged from the doorway, waved, and ran nimbly toward them across the deserted street.

"What the hell is this?" Andrew muttered.

"*Signore,*" the man began in a polite voice, "I apologize. My name is Marco Migliorini. I have a message for you from your friend Don Ciccio."

He handed Andrew a manila envelope.

"My *patrone* said to be sure you both receive this. It's important. And, once more, I am sorry if I alarmed you. One must be wary, you know."

Then he saluted and strode off in the direction of Regent Street. But before he turned to go, so deftly that Andrew took no notice, Migliorini slipped a small envelope into Olivia's hand. Quickly she placed it in her purse. She looked at the manila envelope.

"Open it," she urged. And he tore the envelope apart.

Dear Andrew and Olivia,

I trust this letter finds you in the best of spirits. Marco Migliorini is one of my most treasured people. He will be constantly in touch.

I have discovered the following:

(1) Robert Symes has told his bankers that he has decided to bid for the painting. Tentatively fourteen million.

(2) The Getty Museum will bid to thirteen.

(3) The decision of the Cleveland Museum is unusual. The

director has given Peter Grundy a sealed bid. No one knows how much.

(4) The Louvre is definitely in. The Ministry of Finance has been ordered by the President to commit fifteen million.

(5) I'm still tracking Herr Kurt Krassner. I'm positive he will bid.

"Olivia, how does he get such specific information and so fast? Could he just be making it up?"

"I've never known him to be wrong."

The hall porter on duty at the Westbury hardly bothered to look up as Andrew breezily wished him good morning and, with his arm around Olivia's waist, escorted her to the elevator. Once in her suite, they fell into each other's arms.

At dawn Andrew awoke and started to dress.

"Come back here," Olivia commanded.

"Darling, if I stay one more minute, I'll never walk again," he protested.

At the door he blew her a kiss. "Annabel's again tonight? Around ten? I adore you."

Olivia's great faith in Don Ciccio was not unfounded. She was not surprised to find her envelope contained additional information that was even more privileged.

I have discovered something unexpected about William Fielding, the thief who did not steal the *Marchesa*. He is the brother of a man who works for Harold Greenway, Lord Richfield's solicitor. Greenway handles every detail of the Earl's financial affairs and made all the arrangements for the sale of the Velázquez. Fielding's brother, Roger, is the security guard who watches over the *Marchesa*. Interesting, no?

But even more startling to her was the second item:

The National Security Adviser is most determined to purchase the painting in order to offer it to Chairman Ermenentov. Every possible effort to dissuade potential bidders from entering the auction and every possible technique of disinformation about the picture will no doubt be forthcoming. Andrew's position is going to become more and more difficult. The CIA has been ordered by the National Security Adviser to obtain Andrew's absolute promise not to participate in the sale. What else they will try to urge him to do is unclear. You might expect some exceptionally curious behavior on his part, behavior that might seem out of character. The pressure is sure to be intense.

Olivia studied every single word of the letter. She wasn't at all sure what to believe anymore, but whatever might develop in the murky game surrounding the *Marchesa*, she knew that Andrew would tell her the truth—in time, anyway. Although she had no great right to complain, it bothered her that he had chosen to remain silent. She could only hope that once he saw the picture, he would make up his mind what to confide in her and then they could work together as true allies.

"Bless you, Don Ciccio," she said aloud.

Andrew looked forward to seeing the portrait with growing excitement and tension. Despite his fatigue, his senses were alert. His only concern was that he might have worked himself up into too nervous a state of expectancy.

Sir Peter Grundy greeted him effusively. "At last!" he cried, extending his arms.

"Can't wait!" Andrew exclaimed.

"Lucky you. Andrew, you're the last to view the masterpiece before the auction. His Lordship's representative closed off the room, just after Michael Fairless was here this morning. It will stay sealed until the sale."

On the way down the corridor Sir Peter explained yet again Lord Richfield's peculiar demands. No one would be allowed to examine the work with anything more sophisticated than a pocket magnifying glass. The painting could not be touched. He would stay in the room, acting as a guard.

Andrew nodded.

When Sir Peter threw open the door, Andrew made a beeline toward the picture but then fell back, as if struck by a force surging from the depths of the canvas. The image of the young woman was startling, just as Olivia had described it. Yet, as he gazed mesmerized, the image seemed somehow not in perfect focus. It was as though his view of her were glazed. Andrew shook his head, pulled out his checklist, and began to devour the picture in front of his eyes.

First, the immediate reaction. He wrote the words "Hot! Not in focus." On to the next item.

Second, describe the object in painstaking detail. Andrew forced himself to write down a detailed description of the portrait. "A young woman, in her early to mid-twenties, portrayed reclining on a couch covered with what looks to be a gray-green mantle and a crimson pillow, half-covered by a fur wrap. The woman has soft, milky skin (blurred by the ancient yellowing varnish) through which one can detect what I suppose is a series of bluish veins. Her face is round, but not moonlike. She is naked and holds both arms over her breasts in a gesture that seems to imply chastity and sexuality at the same time. Her hair is a lustrous black—or must be underneath the gunk of the old varnish. Her eyes are doe-brown. Her legs are long and graceful, knees clamped together, apparently on purpose. Or are they about to part? Puzzling, this picture! The background is a neutral, and rather disappointingly flat, gray-green. Flecked into the upper right surface of the background are curious squiggles."

Three, the condition. Andrew drew his chair as close to the painting as he dared and began to pore over it with his magnifying glass. The surface of the picture looked decidedly murky. A series of soft, blurred glazes seemed to obscure the whole surface. But were they glazes? The more he directed his glass over the picture, the more he became convinced that the blurred appearance was the very fabric of the painting itself. Trouble! Andrew wrote in his notebook, "Close examination seems, initially, to point to the fact that there is no old varnish. All surfaces appear to be similar, and have wispy, feathery qualities one would not expect in a painting of the seventeenth century."

He broke off from his intense scrutiny, his eyes smarting from the effort, and sighed in frustration and puzzlement.

"Something's strange," he said to himself. If he didn't know better, he'd say that it could not have been painted in the mid-seventeenth century. What was he looking at?

He went back to his examination, forcing himself to study every square inch of the large canvas. His eyes coursed back and forth, from top to bottom, side to side, as a farmer plows a field.

It was time to go through the rest of his checklist. Four, does it have a use? Not applicable. Five, what is the exact style of the object? Andrew got up from his chair, stretched elaborately, and studied the painting from across the narrow room. The style? It was Diego Velázquez, of course. But really? Superficially, the style of the great painter was apparent; but, linking his distance view with his close-up study, Andrew could readily see that the style was softer, less crisp than anything he remembered of the master's other works.

Next steps. They were automatic and simple. Six, subject matter —a naked young woman. Very sexy? Not after a more contemplative look. The more time passed, to Andrew's increasing befuddlement, the Marchesa began to look placid, even matronly. Seven, inconography. Not applicable. Eight, the history of the work. Obvious. Or was it? Nine, the bibliography. Published a dozen times despite the fact that no scholar had ever been allowed to examine the work scientifically. Ten, obtain outside advice. The hell with that! He didn't need an outside expert to buttress what he was already thinking, that the supposed masterpiece, the "treasure of Velázquez's middle period," was not an original Velázquez at all. Despite the repeated assertions that no copyist had made a replica, Andrew was gradually becoming convinced that he was gazing at an amazingly clever copy of a Velázquez original. A brilliant copy, but a replica nevertheless. He rocked back in his chair. The first thought in his mind was, how could Olivia have been fooled? Olivia, of all people! The second thought was, how was he going to tell her?

Step eleven, scientific analysis. Impossible! Under normal circumstances a serious client for a bona fide masterpiece that might fetch a world-record price would be permitted, even encouraged, to subject the work to all the most modern scientific implements— microscope, X-ray, infrared, ultraviolet, spectographic analysis, and a host of other delicate probes. But not the Richfield *Marchesa*. And, to Andrew, the reason was obvious. It had nothing to do with Lord Richfield's eccentricities. The old thief was afraid that even the most primitive scientific tool would reveal that the picture was a mere copy.

He was stunned by the realization, but proud of his acumen, convinced that he had made the astonishing discovery solely because he had followed a rational process of investigation—and also because he had not rushed to see the *Marchesa* before preparing himself by examining other works by the master. Well, after what he had unearthed, all the books on Diego Velázquez would have to be rewritten. He now presumed the vaunted Richfield *Marchesa* had been painted by a professional copyist, probably in the eighteenth century. The presence of a copy confirmed for him the story that the pair of paintings made for Pope Innocent X had been destroyed. A pair of replicas had obviously been made just before the calamity. How should he break the news to Olivia? What would her reaction be? He would tell her directly. That was the only way.

But before he departed, he looked down at his notes. Words of caution leaped out at him from the checklist. "Always look again!"

Could it have been the lighting? At his request Grundy helped him position a spotlight to illuminate the painting sharply from the left side.

For a second the *Marchesa* once again became flesh and blood. Andrew felt almost a sexual stirring as he stared at the naked young woman. He pulled the light closer and sat down to contemplate. He forced himself to draw his eyes over every millimeter of the canvas. The painting, once again, weakened and became a shadow of a masterwork.

"Dammit, I was right!" he said to himself triumphantly.

He turned to Grundy, winked, and moved slowly toward the painting. "Peter, you don't mind if I carry out my checklist—to the letter."

"Proceed," Grundy said tonelessly.

Andrew removed a small vial and a cotton swab from his pocket and ostentatiously held them up so that Grundy could see what he had in his hand. The auctioneer stood still, for a moment confused.

Andrew opened the bottle, dipped the swab into the substance, and started to wipe the surface of the painting near the Marchesa's right breast.

With a cry, Grundy rushed over and seized the bottle and swab.

"Andrew, really! You Americans can be so forward." Sir Peter tried to sound severe but was unable to suppress his amusement. "You know the rules!"

"Peter," Andrew explained, "it's only harmless xylene. I'd like to clean your picture just a jot."

"After the sale and if you win, you may clean it all you want. Which reminds me—do you want a reservation for some seats at the sale? Or will you send an agent?"

"I'll take one seat," Andrew replied. "But remember, Peter, a seat doesn't guarantee that I'll bid."

Back in the hotel Andrew holed up in his room and brooded, his mind churning. How puzzling! But the picture was no enigma. It was a copy, plain and simple. How Olivia could have failed to recognize the obvious truth was beyond him. It couldn't be lack of experience, it must be lack of perception.

Suddenly Andrew realized he wasn't only disappointed in the painting.

Olivia had arrived at Annabel's early and was ushered to a cheery chintzed alcove to the left of the bar. She asked for a bottle of Krug and casually studied the two dozen portraits of pet dogs that decorated the walls. It was an amusing and successful attempt to blend a continental and English country look. The champagne made her deliciously alert and giddy at the same time, suffused with a warm longing for Andrew. Olivia had been eagerly awaiting what he would say about the *Marchesa* when she had first entered the elegant establishment, but after a glass of the superb wine such pressing matters as the painting, museums, and the petty conspiracies of the art world faded far back in her mind. The only thing that was real—and vital—was Andrew and her life with him.

And there he was! For an instant, as he turned the corner into the alcove, he looked preoccupied and older—suprisingly so. It was nothing, really, she decided quickly—perhaps only the subdued lights in the room.

When he spotted her, his face brightened. He kissed her, taking her hand and squeezing it affectionately. He whispered, "I love you so," and led her to the darkened area of the dance floor illuminated only by strings of tiny winking lights sunk into the floor.

They danced without talking for hours and then ambled back toward the Westbury. "May I escort you, madame, to your hotel?" Andrew said lightly.

"And then to my room?"

"Absolutely!"

"You may," Olivia whispered.

They made love with a quiet intensity and fell asleep in each other's arms. Then Olivia awoke and saw Andrew gazing at her in the semidarkness. She drew herself closer and hugged him, kneading the tight muscles in his back with her strong fingers.

"I want everything in the world to be the best for you, my darling," he began. "And I want you to get everything you want."

"Sweet," she murmured.

Andrew fell back on the bed with a sigh and Olivia gazed at him lovingly. His eyes looked softer than she had ever remembered.

"All right," she said teasingly. "You've been avoiding her all night. I won't let you get away with it for another second." She snuggled tighter to his body. "Tell me, for God's sake. I'm dying to know. What did you think of her?"

"Art." He spoke the word in exasperation. "Do we have to speak about a work of art? You're the piece I want. Come!"

She squirmed away from him and lay on her side just beyond his reach. "Not until you tell me."

"What a day!" he said, trying to remain composed. "Grundy called me—thank God I had just gotten back to my room—to ask if I wouldn't mind postponing my appointment until after lunch. It seems that Sir Michael Fairless had developed a sudden passion to examine the picture, and since he is the head of the famous Warburg, I had to move to the side again!"

"Darling, you don't seem to have much luck with the young Marchesa, unlike all your other ladies," Olivia said lightly, beginning to move toward him. She had a pang at hearing that Fairless, the Soviets' agent, had such keen interest in the work. "Tell me!"

"I was surprised by what I found."

"What's this?" she asked with a half smile.

He averted his eyes from hers, then slowly turned on his back and stared at the ceiling. "Olivia, I don't want you to misunderstand, but I didn't see the *Marchesa* your way."

She didn't seem to hear him. With her eyes shining like jewels, she came to him and suspended her body over his, gave him a quick kiss, swaying her breasts above him provocatively. "How then? Pure or earthy?"

"Darling, I'm afraid I didn't . . ." He looked away. It was going to be far harder than he had imagined. "I mean, didn't the picture seem a bit bland? Weren't there passages that appeared to you . . . well, flat? I mean murky, compared to the vibrancy of the *Pope*?"

Olivia studied him intently, looking into his eyes to see the now familiar sparkles of mischief. But the smile wasn't there, and his gaze was hesitant.

"Murky?" she repeated. "Of course the thing needs cleaning badly. You're not kidding me, are you?"

"Dear, no jokes. I wouldn't do that. I found it somewhat hazy . . . I mean, it seemed dirty."

"Yes, I said that," she said.

"It seemed to me to be indistinct, out of focus, and, well, kind of like a giant watercolor." He sat up. "Diego Velázquez never painted like that! Olivia, think back. You saw it quite a while ago. You've seen a lot of the master's works since then. Doesn't she seem inferior—in retrospect?" He took her hands and squeezed them as if to implore her to make a confession. Olivia pulled back abruptly.

"Andrew, what are you saying? What are you trying to do to me? Is this some sort of game? God, we're together in this! Surely you saw the inscription?"

"Inscription?" His eyes darted away.

"Look at me!" Olivia said, her voice rising. "There was an inscription coming through from the back of the canvas. The letters looked like they were written backward, but you could read them, *if* you had really studied the thing!"

He could not have been more distressed. What was this fantasy?

"If you really had looked at the painting and if you're not trying to trick me for some reason, you couldn't have missed it. I memorized it. 'I, Velázquez, have for a fleeting moment in eternity once again borrowed life from my goddess, my desire, and have given that life to dull paint. The 16th of June, 1650. Roma.' "

"I must have missed it," he said, his voice now sarcastic.

As she looked at him in growing confusion, the thought that he was dissimulating—lying—seared her mind. He couldn't be, but he must be. What else? He could only be lying to her because he had been lying all along. He wanted the painting, her job, and her downfall. The loving words, the subtle change of personality—my God, even the proposal—were all lies. All Andrew's deft mimicry came vividly to her mind. He was, she said bitterly to herself, the true, devious CIA man. But her heart told her his distress was real.

"Andrew, why are you doing this to me?" she said, drawing the sheet around herself.

"Clearing the air, that's all. I have to tell you straight. Look, let's forget this picture. There's a curse on it. Ulrich Seitz was right. The *Marchesa* is Typhoid Mary. We don't need it. We've got each other. It didn't turn out to be the dream you thought it was. That can happen. Let's just drop it." He reached for her.

Olivia pulled back. "Let me clear the air for you! That painting's a work of pure genius. One of the world's greatest. And the inscription shows that there's not a shred of doubt about its authenticity. You're wrong. You had a bad day. Maybe your eye wasn't in tune."

"Oh, come on, Olivia, an eye doesn't need to be 'tuned.' It's experience, that's all. Years of looking. I mean—and I hesitate to say it—that some of us are more seasoned when it comes to the Old Masters. Forget it. There're always other works of art. I remember the first time I was crushed when a work I had believed to be radiant just slowly slipped away."

"This isn't going to work, you realize," she said coldly. "This inept attempt at disinformation doesn't faze me. I'm going after that painting, no matter what you say."

"Olivia, maybe you thought the *Marchesa* was so great because you wanted it to be—or because you were unconsciously trying to impress me."

"I hardly knew you then," she said. "And I still don't. You're wrong, or worse, deliberately trying to destroy me."

"Stop it!" he cried. "You *wanted* to find a masterpiece. You were, as usual, impulsive. I wasn't. I studied it dispassionately."

"And you're really telling me that I've got no eye."

"Well, perhaps—but I understand, for God's sake—I'm saying that your eye may not have the necessary years of seasoning yet. I don't want to argue with you. We've got each other, our lives. Let's not allow a little mistake to get blown up. You can have the painting, I already told you that. I'm only trying to save you from making a serious mistake."

"You didn't see it. I suppose that shouldn't surprise me," she said, almost to herself. "You missed the inscription—also coming through from the back—in Rome on the *Pope*. I was going to tell you."

"If there was, then why didn't you? Why didn't you share this—this miraculous inscription during your dramatization of the *Marchesa* in Vienna?" he said angrily.

"Frankly, at that point in our relationship I had to hold something back because I couldn't bring myself to believe that you were being fully candid with me. And, obviously, you weren't and aren't."

"Why not in Rome when I asked you to marry me? Olivia, what are you trying to do to me?"

"Find the truth."

"I'm convinced I have it," Andrew said, pleading with her. "The *Marchesa* cannot be an original by Velásquez. Olivia, dear, a lot has happened since you saw the picture. Maybe, back then, you so wished the *Marchesa* would be magnificent that you . . . well, transformed it into something better than it is. In art, that can happen."

"You're telling me my eye is flawed?" She spoke the words coldly and drew further away from him. He cringed. "You're saying I've deluded myself? Oh, Andrew, you're the one who's wrong, or trying for some reason to throw me off. Is there something you're keeping from me? Why? If not, maybe it's your eye that's flawed. You failed—twice—to perceive the true nature of a masterpiece underneath a thick layer of yellowed varnish. The *Marchesa's* every bit as good as *Innocent X*. What's wrong with you? Is this some conspiracy to push me out of the sale? Did you measure the picture?"

"No!" he snapped. "I can always get details like that later."

Olivia desperately wanted to tell him what she had learned about his background, about what she knew of the National Security Adviser's attempt to drive him out of the sale, to reveal what she had learned about the measurements, the existence of the photographs she had taken of the *Marchesa* that would establish beyond all doubt that the painting was an authentic Velázquez. But now all she could think of was how to hurt him.

He lay there bewildered at her stubborn opposition to the facts. What could he do? Just repeating over and over his belief that the Richfield "masterpiece" was filmy, weak, and unresolved, despite the undeniable skill with which it had been painted, would be fruitless. After all, everybody else had apparently been fooled too. Or had they? Andrew had no reason to think that the message from Don Ciccio, supposedly recounting what the other competitors were planning to do, was anything other than a masterly fraud concocted by a man who was probably exactly what the rumors claimed—a Mafia Don. For the second time since he had known Olivia Cartright, Andrew felt deeply disturbed. All he wanted was to have the *Marchesa* actually be what Olivia was trying to claim it was. Then all he had to do was to help her get it with all his resources. What if he did, and then the truth came out, as it inevitably would? What then? Disaster.

"Darling, there's no conspiracy," he said softly. "I'm no conspirator. You know me by now. I saw what I saw. I'm convinced you didn't see what you thought you saw. It was early in the morning, you were tired, and perhaps you let your professional feelings get confused with your personal feelings . . . about me."

"I hardly knew you then," Olivia repeated. "And I'm beginning to think I never will."

He reached lovingly for her. "Oh, come. Who cares? It's only a painting."

"Right there is the source of all your failings, Andrew Foster. You're so privileged, so jaded, so rich and self-assured. You've got my job sewn up. You could buy this picture out of your own pocket money, if you cared. But you don't really care about anything. Life is a gameboard. But this painting is not a move in a game for me. It's life itself. Remember, once I told you that it symbolized my love for you? I think it's genuine and you believe it's a fraud. That says it all."

"Olivia, you are mistaken about this painting. Why you persist in this fantasy, I don't know. Either you deliberately want to wound me . . . or you really . . . really have no eye."

That, as Andrew instantly and to his despair recognized, was not the thing to have said to Olivia Alexis Cartright.

"Get the hell out of here!"

"Willingly!" he snapped. But as he was buttoning his shirt, he allowed his hands to fall weakly to his sides. "Olivia, let's stop. Think. Act reasonably. Suddenly there's a lot we've got to talk about. You're suspicious of me, I'm worried about you."

"Worried?" It was a shout of rage. "Well, I'm not worried. I'm furious! Get out!"

"Reason with me."

"Reason with a liar? You've shown a side of yourself that I detest. Suspicious of you? Not at all! I know you've been using me. I hate you for it. You could have made a mistake on this picture—that's forgivable. But to manipulate me for selfish or careless or covert motives—I'll never forgive you. To dismiss me so easily and to suggest . . . You've ruined everything. You've blown it!"

"Maybe you have too, Olivia. Your eye isn't as perfect as you think. Or your manners either. You're afraid to admit it. And who's really trying to trick whom? Oh, hell." He stalked out the door.

She collapsed on the bed and burst into tears, then she lay there for hours, her arms behind her head. The more she analyzed his reaction to the *Marchesa*, the less convinced she became that he'd been acting out some sort of duplicitous drama. He seemed positive he was right. His genuine surprise, his unaffected anger at her response, could not possibly have been feigned. Or could it?

Andrew had steered directly for the bar at Annabel's. He couldn't understand why she had so strongly defended her view that the Richfield *Marchesa* was a real Velázquez. Incomprehensible. And why had she called him a liar? What did she really know about his double life?

Climbing up on a bar stool, he ordered a double Cognac. And another. When the liquor had calmed him, he went to the phone booth and called her. He would beg to come over and talk. There must be an explanation for why two people, each a trained connoisseur, had such opposing views about the same painting. But the phone kept on ringing, and Andrew fumed once more. He was sure she was just lying there, listening to the phone ringing on and on, knowing it had to be him. He returned to the bar and downed another double Cognac. And a fourth.

When he awoke late the next morning, he could not remember when or how he had gotten to his room.

19 CAUGHT IN THE ACT

OLIVIA HAD WANTED to reach out for the phone each time it rang. She longed to talk to Andrew, mollify him, perhaps even apologize. But she was still so stunned by his hypocrisy and cruel words about her professional ability that she could not bring herself to pick it up. What did she have to apologize for, anyway? He ought to beg her forgiveness!

Early in the morning, twisting sleeplessly, she for a moment considered slipping over to his hotel. But the echo of his harsh words put an end to her momentary feeling of tenderness.

She was so upset that she even thought of canceling her luncheon with Lord Richfield's niece, Lady Eleanor Swift. But she steeled herself to press on. The more she dwelled on it, the more convinced she was that the *Marchesa* was a masterpiece. It was triumphant, easily in a league with Velázquez's other Roman masterpieces. Nothing could change that, no matter what Andrew might think or what his motives might be.

Lady Eleanor turned out to be far from the generalist that Professor Ulrich Seitz normally produced. She was the classic example of an art historian with an eye, an interest, and a sensitivity only for her own narrow field of study. When Olivia asked her what she thought of the painting, which Lady Eleanor must have seen so many times hanging on the third-floor landing at Richfield House, the young woman answered as only a specialist would.

"I must admit that I have no opinion at all," Lady Eleanor replied hesitantly. "I never got around to looking at it carefully. Really. Was not in my field."

"Surely there's something you can tell me," Olivia persisted.

"You see, it was always just there on the stairs. Of course when I was very young, I knew it was Velázquez, and famous, and valuable, I suppose, but . . . Later on, when I started to study art history I became a scholar of Mannerism, the . . . ah, as you know the antithesis to Velázquez. So I'm afraid I ignored it. I'm sorry I can't be more helpful. There was a copy around too."

"A copy?"

"Not a very good one."

"I see. What can you tell me about the condition of the original?"

"I recall it as being yellowed, a sort of beige, brown, and gray patch on the wall."

"I see," Olivia remarked, clearly disappointed.

"I'm not much use to you, I'm afraid. I'm so terribly sorry." But then Lady Eleanor brightened. "I did bring a notebook that might intrigue you; it's something of a curiosity. It contains, I find, a number of references to the Velázquez. My uncle doesn't know it exists. He's so eccentric!"

"I won't tell anyone I have seen it," Olivia said diplomatically.

It appeared to be a logbook containing anecdotes about many paintings in the Richfield collection. As they picked away at their food, Olivia scanned the pages, noting that the journal had been written in several neat hands and was mostly of the early nineteenth century. She could find no mention of major damage or significant repair to the *Marchesa*. That was gratifying. Moreover, it seemed that it had been cleaned only once, lightly, in 1807.

Skimming the book, Olivia suddenly came across an entry that flabbergasted her. In 1818 two frames had been fashioned for what was described as "the pair of portraits." Measurements were given for the two paintings and, to her astonishment, they were virtually identical to the measurements cited in the documents she had received from Don Ciccio, the copies from the archives of the Academy of Saint Luke. One portrait was eighty by forty-eight inches—close enough to the precise eighty-one by forty-eight from the archives. That one had to be the Richfield and the papal painting. The other portrait mentioned in the notebook measured seventy-eight by forty-five inches—exactly corresponding to the first pair of portraits Velázquez had created for himself. What was going on? Had someone in the Richfield family, long ago, somehow managed to find Velázquez's first, smaller frontal image?

Quickly Olivia leafed through the pages of the slim volume, excitedly seeking confirmation. And there it was—in an account of an artistic soirée at which two paintings by Diego Velázquez— obviously two frontal views—had been exhibited side by side for a coterie of appreciative guests.

On the evening of September 16, 1832, the two pictures the master Diego Velázquez painted of his comely Marchesa Odescalchi were shown together, the larger on the left. The guests amused themselves vying with each other to describe which image was more provocative, the smaller or the larger. Everyone agreed in the end that the master had painted his beloved mistress with equal beauty.

Olivia felt a wave of elation. The acceptance of both frontal portraits as authentic masterpieces by Velázquez at a party long ago might not be counted as absolute proof that they were indeed the master's own. Yet the information was more than intriguing! And the differences in their measurements—precisely the right ones— might be evidence that the pictures were genuine. Why would a copyist have painted a reproduction in a different size than the original? A copyist's intention, after all, is to deceive. Besides, how would a copyist have known of the archives in the Academy of Saint Luke?

Eagerly Olivia turned the final pages. But there were no further entries. She placed the book on the table, leaned forward tensely, and asked, "You say there was a copy of the *Marchesa* in your uncle's collection?"

"Yes."

A flush warmed Olivia's face. "Why do you say it was a copy? Could it possibly have been Velázquez's own first version? He made two pairs, you know. The second pair larger than the first. Could what you now remember as a 'copy' possibly have been authentic?"

"Oh, that would be romantic," Lady Eleanor replied. "I stumbled across the second portrait in a storage bin in the cellar when I was searching for some silver that my great-aunt had willed to me. The picture lacked that clarity one expects from a master's work."

"Could it have been just dirty?" Olivia persisted.

"It was. But it's too much of a romantic notion to believe it's by Velázquez himself," Lady Eleanor said, offhandedly. "It must be a copy."

It was obvious that Lady Eleanor Swift was not dissimulating and was convinced she was right in her assessment of the painting. Romantic though it was, Olivia was equally convinced that she had discovered the original version of the *Marchesa*, one that some member of the Richfield clan had found, on the Grand Tour someplace, not a copyist's replica of Velázquez's frontal portrait of his lover. The guests at the party, even though they weren't trained art connoisseurs, would have known the difference between a signature Velázquez and a copy.

Whatever the second *Marchesa* was, Olivia was convinced it had to be the painting Andrew had seen at William's. A switch had been made! When? By whom? He had been right! He hadn't been lying to her. But what had she said to him in her anger? Terrible things. She must rush to him at once. But first, there was an even more important thing to do. Pleading an engagement that she had been forced to make at the last moment, Olivia hurried her guest through the rest of the lunch. She had to get to William's and have another look at the painting. She would go at once to pay a call on Grundy, and beg his permission to examine the *Marchesa* once more.

She prayed she wasn't too late. She remembered that Andrew had said Lord Richfield had ordered the room sealed off until the day of the auction. Was that when the switch was made? Olivia was confident she could persuade Sir Peter to open up the gallery for one brief examination.

Who could have engineered the switch? Grundy, acting under the orders of Lord Richfield? No, not Grundy, she reflected. He was slippery, but incapable of that kind of chicanery. It had to have been Lord Richfield himself or someone in his employ. Her mind leaped again. What about that solicitor of his? What was his name? Greenway. Don Ciccio had informed her that Grundy had hired as the security guard William Fielding's brother, the brother of the man who had tried to steal the Velázquez. Suddenly she was afraid. What if the guard was on duty?

• • •

When Olivia arrived at the auction house she was told, to her frustration, that Grundy had left for the day. She glanced down the corridor toward the private elevator. The door was ajar. Approaching cautiously, she found it empty. She entered without being seen and pushed the button for the fifth floor. The ancient lift rose slowly. It halted, at last, with a jerk. When she opened the sliding partition there was a loud metal screech. But no alarms rang out; no guards appeared as she walked down the narrow corridor toward the room where the Velázquez had been.

Olivia put her ear against the door. Not a sound. Gingerly she tested the knob. To her shock, the door was unlocked. She opened it silently, getting ready to confront the guard sitting in his accustomed chair by the window. She would have to have some excuse for him. Just to buy a little time. All she needed was a lightning-quick look at the painting. But there was no guard. He had gone out and left the room unlocked. Olivia slipped across the threshold and shut the door behind her.

The large canvas was on the easel, shrouded by its linen covering. She took the fabric in her hand and whipped it aside. Within a fraction of a second she knew that what she was looking at was not the painting she had seen before.

But what was it? Was this painting the Richfield "copy" or something else? The game was getting more and more ominous every minute. She realized in her growing anxiety that this time she might not be able to appeal to Don Ciccio for help. This was a mystery she would have to work out for herself. The thought of independence calmed her. She could do it—and would. All at once Olivia felt utterly in control of herself and the situation. It was a marvelous feeling!

Quickly she extracted from her purse a ruler and took the measurements. They were virtually identical to Velázquez's own first portrait of his lover recorded in the archives of the Academy of Saint Luke! My God, could it actually be . . . ? She had to obtain proof. Olivia lunged at the canvas to examine it, to clean it, but before she could get her bottle of xylene out of her purse, she heard someone cough. She wheeled around in surprise and saw a man in the corner of the room in the act of donning his coat, looking at her with an expression of bewilderment. She almost fainted.

"Was gibt's?" the man muttered.

Olivia hurriedly covered the painting with the linen. Coolly, she calculated what to say. She tried to smile casually and said, "Have you finished?"

"I was just about to leave," the man replied.

Desperately wanting to flee, Olivia nonetheless found herself returning his stare.

He was tall, erect as a military officer, and slender. A great mane of coarse silver hair fell over his brow. His eyes were an electric blue. His face seemed perfectly proportioned, the nose aquiline. He might be in his early sixties.

As she gazed at him, she felt herself flushing. "I'm sorry, I didn't know . . ."

He smiled and started toward the door. He had extraordinary magnetism. Olivia was more than a little stunned by her reaction to him.

"Are you one of Grundy's assistants?" he asked in a German accent.

Olivia swallowed.

"I believe you are not. I have seen your face before. Of course. You are Olivia Cartright of the Met. Aren't you?"

Looking into his penetrating eyes, she found herself incapable of avoiding an answer. She nodded.

A brilliant smile broke across his face. "May I introduce myself. I am Kurt Krassner. Might I have a word with you about this painting?"

She just stared at him.

"I shall not ask how you got in here, but are you thinking of trying to purchase it at the auction?"

She nodded, recovering her composure.

"Running after this painting could become difficult and, well, dangerous," he said evenly.

"That sounds rather like a threat, Herr Krassner."

"I do not intend to threaten you. I would never try anything so crude with such a clever—and attractive—young woman. All I mean to say is that I intend to bid heavily. I am a wealthy and determined man and usually get what I am after. If you plan to bid, it will only be a waste of your time and for me an annoyance since you might cause me to spend a bit more."

"I find this conversation wholly ridiculous. The Met is not without resources either, you know."

"Does your distinguished institution have as much as fifteen million?" His teeth looked like white fence posts. "And there may also be danger. I just heard on the radio. The director of the Cleveland Museum of Art—you probably know him, James Waters . . ."

"What about him?"

"He died this morning near Piccadilly. They say it was a heart attack. But, to me, it's suspiciously unlike a heart attack. Do you recall, some years back, that there was a killing on exactly the same street corner?"

"That's a ridiculous remark!" she exclaimed.

"Waters's death is a tragedy, but at least it cancels one potential bidder. Now if I could only persuade you to back off."

She coldly contemplated the man and his words, and swept out the door.

She walked quickly back to her hotel. Her heart was pounding; she was absolutely positive that what she had seen in that brief moment at William's was not the *Marchesa* that had so thoroughly captured her weeks before. But what was it, an original or a clever replica? She suspected it was the former but couldn't be certain. If only she had had more time! She had to find out whether her suspicions were correct. She would, she knew. It was her destiny to find the truth about the *Marchesas*. And now it was time to tell Andrew. To her bitter disappointment he was out.

The phone rang, startling her. Andrew! Olivia threw herself across the bed to answer it.

"Kurt Krassner here. I hope you don't mind, but by simple deduction I found out your hotel. Would it be possible for you to have dinner with me this evening? I would like very much to continue to discuss the affair of the *Marchesa Odescalchi*. I have some information I'm sure you'll find interesting."

"Certainly not!"

"All right then. May I ask you a question?"

"Oh, I suppose so," she said, furious that she hadn't simply slammed the phone down.

"I might remind you of the favor I did you by not informing Peter Grundy of your unauthorized visit to the *Marchesa*."

Olivia made no reply.

"Don't be afraid. I am not an ogre."

"The question?"

"If you were in my place, what would you do about the *Marchesa?*

Olivia almost burst out laughing.

"Please tell me."

"I would say, Herr Krassner . . ."

"Yes?"

Olivia whispered sweetly into the receiver, "Do go near it. Don't bid. Follow your instincts and your eye. You know the painting looks, well, muted, hazy. Stay away. That's what I intend to do."

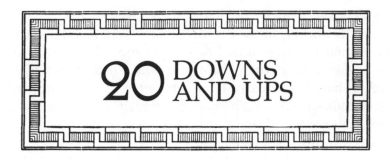

20 DOWNS AND UPS

AT JUST THE MOMENT Olivia had set out for lunch with Eleanor Swift, Andrew was dragging himself out of bed to dress for his meeting with Lord Richfield at the townhouse of his former stepmother. The throbbing pain in his head almost impelled him to call and say that he was too ill to leave his room. But he drove his aching body through the motions. Then, abruptly, the flesh gave out. He sank back limply on the bed and started to drift off to sleep, his stomach turning over, when he was startled by the rude jangling of the telephone. He grappled for it. It has to be Olivia. To his astonishment the caller was Ayn Steyne.

"The search committee," she started briskly. "The members would like to meet you tomorrow. At five thirty. The Union Club. There's the new evening Concorde from London tonight at eight o'clock. I can tell them you'll be there?"

"Certainly!" he managed to say. "But you must tell them that on such short notice I will hardly be prepared."

Yet Andrew was fully prepared. He had been quietly accumulating data on every aspect of the Metropolitan from annual reports and financial papers available to upper-level members for almost two years. His information was prodigious. Despite his hangover, he danced around his room doing jabs and uppercuts. Would he put on a show!

Elmira de Santangelo Walker Heinemann Foster sallied into the capacious foyer of her Regent's Park townhouse looking as though she were dressed in a tent made of Persian carpets. She landed a wet kiss on Andrew's cheek.

"Why so downcast? A matter of the heart? Or a hangover?"

"Both, I fear, Elmira," he replied with a pained smile.

"Lord Richfield is in the drawing room," she said, lowering her voice. "I must warn you that he isn't overjoyed to meet you. He growled like a bear when I told him why I had invited him. He seems to have expected just me. He gets somewhat worked up when it comes to the possibility of an amorous encounter. So try to charm him, my dear." Andrew sighed.

"How's your snake of a father?"

Andrew groaned. "Look, Elmira, if Lord Richfield is put off, I can slip away now. I'm not sure I feel up to meeting him, anyway."

"Bosh! Come in, have a drink, and start talking."

Andrew followed her docilely into the spacious, cheery room.

The Earl was exactly what Andrew expected. He was tall, thin, and bulgy-eyed. He tilted his head back at an exaggerated angle and thrust his hand forward—straight as a swagger stick.

"Robby," Elmira exclaimed in a voice that carried a note of command, "Andrew, my favorite stepson, is vexed that he hasn't been able to study your Velázquez painting. I realize that you can't allow crowds to come rushing in, pawing it—but he's a bona fide scholar and such a nice young man. Now, both of you, sit, have your drink, and try to talk this little problem out."

The Earl cleared his throat nervously. "I find immense satisfaction in insisting that the prospective suitors for my *Marchesa* examine it the way my ancestors did. Looking at it with their naked eyes. None of these modern pieces of equipment—X rays, infrarays, spectro-rays, or computers! Just the human eye, a simple glass, and intelligence. Traditional connoisseurship."

Andrew found it hard not to smile. "Sir, I do agree with you. Yet you must understand today's museums. We have so much invested in sophisticated equipment that we'd feel cheated not to be able to use our toys. And besides, the art world has changed since your ancestors began collecting pictures. Art has become a bit more expensive. Your *Marchesa*, for example, may even reach a truly astonishing sum—perhaps in the area of nine million pounds."

"Come now," Richfield admonished mildly. "The picture has to fetch much more than that. My solicitor, Harold Greenway—and Grundy of William's as well—have assured me that my reserve price of ten million pounds is realistic."

Andrew maintained a poker face, although he was amazed that the peer had so casually revealed his reserve price, something that normally remained a closely guarded secret. The man was more than an eccentric, he was a loon!

"Your Lordship," Andrew said earnestly. "I'm not a private collector seeking a bargain. I'm a steward on behalf of the American public and I have to act prudently. I must be certain that your painting is one of the original portraits of the Marchesa and is in acceptable condition. New evidence suggests strongly that a copy was made of the picture—perhaps in the eighteenth century. I have to be absolutely certain of what is coming up at the sale." He halted to assess the Earl's reaction.

Lord Richfield allowed himself a hollow laugh. "You're saying my painting's some sort of copy? A fake? Well, it ain't!"

"You must understand, Your Lordship," Andrew said gently, "I cannot take anything for granted."

"To be blunt, Foster, I can't say I've ever examined the canvas very closely myself except during the age of masturbation. But experts have assured me that the picture's prime. After the attempted theft, my solicitor suggested that I get rid of the damned thing since prices for Old Masters were increasing dramatically. Greenway has handled everything about it. He's an exceptionally clever young man and I leave all my legal and financial affairs in his hands."

"Lord Richfield, I'm a little surprised that you didn't at least try to arrange a deal with your government. Wasn't it possible to negotiate with, say, the National Gallery and obtain a tax concession?"

"Bugger the government! Taxes don't concern me. I need some cash for a real estate investment Greenway's keen about. If the painting reaches my reserve, I shall be in a very solid position."

"It might not. What then? You must have read the article this morning in the press that some scholars believe the condition of the *Marchesa Odescalchi* is flawed."

"Rumors!"

"Auctions are decided by rumors," Andrew retorted.

"True, dammit!"

"Frankly, I personally believe that something's wrong with the picture. But I have an alternative to the volatile setting of the auction room. May I suggest a highly favorable arrangement for you—and me?" Andrew said in a low, urgent voice. "I know of a way of guaranteeing your reserve—quickly—without having to pay the auction house a percentage."

The Earl's bulging eyes glistened.

"Withdraw the picture from the sale. Let me examine it for a few hours with my conservator. If I change my opinion and am satisfied with its condition, I'll pay you ten percent more than your reserve. In cash. I shall hand over to your bankers a registered check at the end of the working day, eleven million."

Lord Richfield angled his head toward the ceiling and waited.

"All right, I shall make that eleven million five hundred thousand pounds," Andrew added.

"You'll examine it for how long?" Richfield asked, and lowered his head to gaze fixedly at Andrew.

"Half a day."

"How so?"

"Magnifier, hand-held, plus spot cleaning with a harmless solvent."

"Something like dry cleaning?" the Earl brayed.

"Something called xylene. Quite harmless. My conservator dabs a little of it on an ear swab and presto."

Elmira sidled over and plucked the Earl's glass from his hand. She walked slowly to the sideboard, filled it, and replaced the glass in his hand, giving his arm an affectionate squeeze.

"Now that I think about it," Andrew said, "let me round out my offer. Twelve million!"

"Now, that could be interesting. Although I must say I never involve myself in haggling. Do you mind discussing the details with Greenway? I shall call him. Could you talk with him today, just after lunch? His firm is Rust, Waites, and Greenway. At the Temple."

"I'd be delighted. Might I assume we have a tentative deal?" Andrew asked. "That is, if the picture stands up to my scrutiny," he added with a tone of skepticism. "I must warn you that I have very strong doubts."

"The deal you describe seems acceptable," Lord Richfield replied gravely. "Your doubts will be dispelled."

"How splendid, gentlemen!" Elmira cried. "I just knew if I got you together you could work it out. Congratulations to you both!"

As he promised, Richfield made an appointment for one thirty at Greenway's office. It was perfect! Andrew would return to his hotel, pack, call upon the solicitor, and wrap up the deal.

He almost danced back to the hotel, so elated was he to be able to come to grips with the troubling painting. Finally, to be able to study it scientifically! To be able to prove without a doubt that he was right. To be able to stop Olivia from making a terrible blunder, one that would almost certainly destroy her career. Then he stopped dead in his tracks. What about the painting? Could he have so misjudged it? Richfield was so confident. Olivia was so confident. Deep down he knew she had the sharper eye. But he had analyzed the picture, he had subjected it to his checklist! Andrew was disturbed. He was doubting his abilities to perceive. Was he beginning to transform the painting in his mind to something it wasn't? He hastened his steps.

He was buoyed by the realization that the beauty of the deal he had just made with Lord Richfield put him in the perfect position either way. If the picture was a later copy, then cleaning it, even in part, would provide proof. It he had been wrong and the portrait was an original, he would be able to get it. He stopped again. What if it *was*? He would never obtain permission to export it from Great Britain. Roy Bentley would do everything he could to block the move. How horribly ironic!

Then in an instant a simple, brilliant solution to the export embargo came into his mind. Having just removed the painting from auction, he'd start a new auction. And in the new auction, he would bid against himself. That no one had thought of the ploy before amazed him. But it would work!

He turned the moves of his scheme over in his mind to be certain he was right. Once he had presented his registered check to Richfield's bank, he, as legal owner, would apply for a formal export permit from the Board of Trade. The National Gallery would block the request. The Board would allow—as it almost always did—a period of perhaps six months for the Gallery to match the purchase price. That would be a difficult task, Andrew knew, even considering their acquisitions trust fund. Yet, even if his price was equaled, it didn't matter. Andrew could simply offer to pay more to Lord

Richfield. There was nothing in the export rules or Board of Trade regulations to stop anybody from jacking up the price he himself had to pay—and the National Gallery had to match. If Bentley somehow managed to match Andrew's second price, then all he had to do was raise the ante again. He had figured out the only loophole in the complicated set of laws governing exportation of masterworks from England, almost without thinking about it. And it was foolproof.

Back at the hotel there were several messages for him, but none from Olivia. Harold Greenway's office had called confirming the meeting at one thirty. Edward Lassiter had left instructions to meet at a pub near Fleet Street at five. That message spelled trouble! Lassiter was his primary European case officer at the CIA.

Andrew tried to call Olivia. The operator told him she was out. He left yet another message. Damn her.

Promptly at one thirty Andrew was ushered into the oaken interior of Greenway's offices in the Temple. He was the stereotype of an elegant solicitor, gracious, reticent, and well groomed. He spoke in a mellow, modulated voice.

"Lord Richfield has given me all the details of your conversation with him," he said. "But I hope you won't mind going over your proposition just one more time for me, so I can be positive I have digested it accurately."

"Not at all," Andrew said with a confident smile. "In a few days, let's say three, I am to be allowed access to the *Marchesa Odescalchi* with my conservator for half a day. I will study the picture with proper magnifying glasses and be allowed to carry out some spot cleaning with xylene. If I am convinced of the authenticity of the picture and its condition is good, I shall immediately prepare a cashier's check for the account of your client in the sum of twelve million pounds. At that time I shall receive the legal title. The painting will be withdrawn from auction. Then, jointly and at the appropriate time, we'll make the announcement. That's it."

"That is substantially what Lord Richfield told me," Greenway said. "Uh . . . when did you actually see the picture?"

"Yesterday afternoon. It's a question of more time and a more professional manner of examination."

"I see."

Andrew smiled and started to extend his hand. "Will you draw up the necessary papers, then? I'd like something in writing now —even before I tell you that I'm satisfied with the painting."

"Oh, I think not, Dr. Foster," the solicitor murmured.

"Well, okay. I suppose it's not life or death. But I must have a written agreement as soon as I verbally inform you that the check is being drafted."

"I think not."

"What?"

"There will be no agreement, sir, because I cannot allow such a sale."

"What's this?"

"I cannot recommend such a transaction. And I have informed Lord Richfield, who agrees with me fully."

"Have I missed something here?" Andrew said in confusion.

"Yes," Greenway said with a cool smile. "You may be angry with what I say. But after listening to your offer I advised Lord Richfield that it would be unwise to conclude such an agreement. Accordingly, I have been instructed by him to let you know that there can be no such 'deal,' and that the painting will appear on the auction block in two weeks, on schedule."

Andrew whistled through his teeth.

"His Lordship somehow failed adequately to alert you to the fact that I am . . . well, the significant factor when it comes to decisions on his behalf."

"I don't get it, Greenway. What's going on here, anyway?"

"Nothing but a sound business decision."

"I wonder. Say, this isn't some elaborate con game, is it?" Andrew tried to sound jocular, hoping that the solicitor might explain his reasoning.

Greenway was firm. "I do sympathize with you, Dr. Foster," he remarked calmly. "But his Lordship sometimes gives the impression that he has agreed, when he is, in effect, merely noting someone else's proposal. It is my responsibility to advise him of what— actually—to do."

"I still don't get it," Andrew said with a pained smile. "You're supposed to be clever. You've done well for your client. But it is hard to believe that you would turn down a hard cash offer of two million more than the reserve. You both know the picture's not going to exceed that by much. Face it, this sale may not turn out to be all that great. Besides, you have to pay the seller's percentage to the auction house. I'll even sweeten the pot. I'll throw in an additional amount equivalent to three percent of the reserve."

"The auction house will surely ask for a penalty fee if we withdraw," Greenway mused.

"I'll throw in fifty thousand dollars more," Andrew snapped. "But I insist upon examination rights. A half-day."

"I'm sorry," Greenway replied brusquely. "But I simply cannot recommend this course of action to my client."

"You're crazy and so is Richfield," Andrew said angrily, trying to keep calm. "You're making the biggest blunder in the history of art auctions. You'll see!"

At a quarter after five Andrew entered the Blackfriars Pub and settled himself into the third booth on the right of the main entrance, just as he had been instructed. Edward Lassiter slipped in beside him so quickly that he was surprised.

"Ed, for God's sake, what's up?" Andrew whispered.

"I know it seems melodramatic, Andrew, but I have to order you not to bid for the Velázquez at the forthcoming sale." Lassiter, a balding, thin-faced six-footer, cleared his throat nervously. "This is a most serious matter. It comes straight from the National Security Adviser himself."

"Give me a break, Edward," Andrew muttered in an exasperated tone. "Since when does the Agency give a damn about the National Security Adviser and his political minions!"

"Listen, will you?" Lassiter ordered. "Roger Bass wants to present the painting to Chairman Ermenentov as a 'gift.' Bass realizes he can't influence many others who may be bidding. But you, as the head of one of the richest museums in America. . . ."

"Is Bill Leonard behind this?" Andrew asked bitterly. "I know he tried to pressure another collector, who, thank God, isn't bidding."

"The President of the United States is in on this one," Lassiter snapped.

"Uh-oh."

"Andrew, I'm smack in the middle on this. You're an employee of the federal government both at the Gallery and the Agency. I'm passing along a presidential order. You love your country, don't you?"

"Ed, don't wave the flag at me. I've worked, pretty effectively too, for fifteen years on and off for you guys, and I've never been asked to carry out any mission that was not rational and obviously of great benefit to the country. But this is degrading! There must be other ways of bribing this dictator. Send him a helicopter, or a computer game. I refuse to knuckle under to Roger Bass."

"Andrew, I'm in a terrible bind. Bass had a tantrum when he heard you wouldn't play the game. Threatened to have me sacked."

"He did? After what you have done for him? What a cheap bastard! So why doesn't Bass bid? It's a free market. Surely, the all-powerful National Security Adviser can get the money. He can have the thing for only eleven million or so."

"He doesn't do things that way."

"You're right, as usual. Ed, it happens you're in luck," Andrew said. "It so happens that this hyped-up Diego Velázquez is not an original. I studied it for two hours and I'm almost totally convinced it's a copy of the eighteenth century." Andrew explained in detail what he had discovered.

"Well, that beats all!" Lassiter exclaimed. "That's great. Let Bass buy a fake. Just desserts. We followed orders. It's not as if the son of a bitch bothered to ask what you thought of the 'masterpiece' after you'd looked at it. The Russians won't be able to do a thing. After they've got it, I'll drop the word to them that the picture's a copy. Think of their embarrassment! They'll get Bass for sure. You know how Washington works. Bass will take the fall."

"Even if it's a questionable picture, I hate to see the Agency buckle under to a political hack like Bass. But I suppose you're right. I'll go along. But, Ed, I need something in exchange. I'm flying to New York tonight. I have an important meeting at five thirty tomorrow. I need some information—totally unauthorized information."

"I'm listening."

"I need everything you've got—from your most secret file—on Ayn Steyne. There's bound to be some juicy stuff."

"You sure don't mess around with the lower classes, do you?" Lassiter said. "Why Steyne?"

"A matter of the heart. I'm in love with Olivia Cartright, the acting director of the Met . . ."

"We know."

"I need information about her boss."

Lassiter took a long sip of his stout and looked at Andrew. "How are you planning to use this material—if there is any material?"

Andrew smiled. "So there is something."

"You don't intend to leak it to the press, do you?"

"Never! This is an affair of the heart. I'm no muckracker. I want my girl back. And the only way I can think of doing it is to give her a present . . . something unique. All I want is enough damaging stuff to, well . . ."

"Scare the hell out of Steyne? Blackmail her? For love, huh?" Lassiter sat for a long time, staring at the opposite booth.

"Okay, Andrew. Just for you, and for all the years, and the Velázquez, and my job. You've got to protect me. Use this information only once and only for your private affair."

"I swear."

"The information will be handed to you tomorrow afternoon. Where will you be?"

"At five fifteen, the Union Club at Seventieth and Park Avenue."

"Count on it."

"After this I want to resign from the Agency."

"But, Andrew, why quit now? You like the work, don't you?"

Andrew returned to his room with a sense of anxiety and deepening frustration. He still could not reach Olivia on the telephone. Where could she be? Had she disappeared? No, she hadn't checked out, he was assured by the reception desk. So Andrew sat down and poured his heart out in a letter. He told her that he loved her and trusted her and begged her to trust him. He was going to New York for three days to appear before the Metropolitan's search committee and would come directly to her room when he returned. When he finished, he didn't give it a second glance.

Andrew's spirits rose when the hall porter assured him that his letter would be delivered straightaway to Miss Cartright's room, "without fail." By the time he had gone out to Heathrow and boarded the Concorde he was feeling optimistic that Olivia would accept his gifts and return to him. The plane roared down the runway and burst through the haze shrouding London. There were few material things on earth that gave Andrew Foster more of a thrill than flying the luxury aircraft. Soon he fell into a deep, peaceful sleep.

21 ANDREW LETS GO

ANDREW PEERED UP at the brown-brick and limestone façade of the Union Club squatting on the corner of Park Avenue and 70th Street and had to grin. It was the perfect choice for the initial rendezvous between the august search committee of the Metropolitan Museum of Art and its prime candidate for director. The place was the epitome of calmness, gravity, and reserve—a perfect no-man's-land where candidate and committee could feel each other out in the first steps of an elaborate courtship.

Shoulders squared, he entered the canopied portal and introduced himself to the majordomo guarding the entrance. He was handed over to a black functionary garbed in a chocolate-brown uniform and docilely followed him up an imposing staircase that was just a shade too pompous for its space and along a broad oak-paneled corridor hung with a series of yellowed portraits of the club's founders, most of them dating to the time of the Civil War.

The five members of the search committee awaited him in the deserted salon bar. Andrew was relieved to see Bruce Thompson among them, although the normally demonstrative trustee merely nodded. Roland McCrae stood off slightly to the side at the end of the informal receiving line. "I am so very pleased to see you here, Andrew—if I may be permitted to use your first name. I am looking forward to hearing your words of wisdom." Squeezing Andrew's elbow for an instant, he added, "Be sure to let yourself go, young man. This is not the Star Chamber. You're among friends. Be frank."

They seated themselves in a tight circle of enormous leather-upholstered chairs, each one flanked by a small side table on which sat a carafe of ice water and a glass. All eyes turned to the chairman of the group, Gregory Smithers, a financier whose art collection was rather modest for a Met trustee. He had secured his place on the museum's board owing to his good fortune in having married a woman of great wealth who had conveniently passed away six months after the nuptials. Smithers opened the meeting with words that are a virtual formula when a search committee has decided on a candidate in advance.

"Dr. Foster, please consider this meeting informal. Off the record. Think of it as a pleasant opportunity for us to hear the viewpoints of a highly qualified expert concerning possible directions the museum might take in the future. We are aware that you have not had the time to prepare and realize that it's a little unfair to ask your opinions about a complex institution whose inner workings you cannot be expected to know. We are more interested in your general observations—your overall philosophy about art museums."

"Of course," Andrew said with a compelling smile. To the members of the committee and to Roland McCrae he made precisely the right impression—assured yet humble, at ease yet obviously deeply impressed with having been asked to appear.

"As a matter of fact, on the way over on the plane," he remarked, "I jotted down a few notes."

The committee members settled back comfortably in their overstuffed chairs, awaiting the usual measured, cautious litany. Andrew's opening words fully met their expectations.

"The greatness, the stature of the Metropolitan is fundamental to the history of the international museum world. Its landmark acquisitions, including the first Impressionist master to come to the United States, its world-class exhibitions, its educational programs reaching out broadly to all—from the youngest children to senior citizens throughout the land—have made history. Rightly so. It is undeniably one of the most superb institutions in the world—except, of course, for a certain National Gallery in Washington . . ."

He smiled and glanced at the circle of members. He took a sip of water and continued.

"In recent times, however, that glowing reputation has unfortunately, as you gentlemen know better than anyone . . . well . . ."

Andrew paused. He shook his head as if deeply reluctant to continue. "But, naturally, this happens from time to time . . ." He allowed his voice to trail off.

Roland McCrae spoke up. "Young man, please express yourself directly. If you feel you must lay on the table a few criticisms, please do so."

"Thank you, Roland," Andrew said with a convincing sigh of relief, delighted to see that the older man was taken aback by the use of his first name. With a man like McCrae that alone would make him suspicious of Andrew.

"Yes, go on, Andrew," McCrae urged. But there was more than a hint of frigidity in his tone.

"Okay, I will," Andrew said firmly. "What I have to say is nothing that everyone in the museum profession doesn't already know. The Metropolitan has become moribund." He halted as if the words were difficult to form. "Everybody talks about how sad the situation is. How run-down the buildings are. How shabby the place has become. How flaccid the special exhibitions are. How the once-vital educational programs have almost died out—slashed as much as thirty percent—"

"Twenty-five percent," Smithers broke in, his voice strained. "I wonder, Dr. Foster, if this line of . . ."

Andrew chose to ignore him and plunged onward. "I mean, why are three of your most distinguished curators looking for jobs elsewhere?"

"What? What is this, Mr. Chairman?" one shocked member asked.

"You mean you didn't know?" Andrew exclaimed.

"I, for one, didn't," Roland McCrae said. "Why are they contemplating such drastic action?"

"Simple. You're taking so long to choose the next director that they feel the museum is falling into a state of lassitude and chaos," Andrew replied.

"Is this the place, Mr. Chairman, to bandy about mere rumors?" another member of the committee objected.

"These are hardly rumors," Andrew interjected coldly. "I am personally negotiating with two of your top curators to come to the National Gallery."

"Well, during times of transition there are bound to be certain . . . how shall I put it . . . indecisive moments," Smithers commented lamely.

"Sirs," Andrew said, so quietly that the committee members had to lean forward in their chairs to hear him. "These are not 'moments,' these are fundamental weaknesses. Deep wounds."

"Wounds?"

"Yes," Andrew said firmly. "And you suffer from a few diseases in addition. Possibly fatal diseases. For example, the lawsuits . . . and the ugly union business."

"What's this?"

"You must be aware of the legal scandal that's about to break over your heads," Andrew said wonderingly. "Friends in Albany tell me that two suits are about to be filed with the New York State Human Rights Commission. Apparently over the years you have endorsed a policy of promoting your women employees far less frequently and paying them far less than men. Less by some fifteen percent. You are bound to lose the suits. From what I hear, you're guilty."

"Guilty?" McCrae cried.

"Oh, yes, Roland. You must also be aware that your guards' union is about to call a strike. And I'm sure you have plans how to handle the attempts of some of your curators to form a professional union." Seeing the astonished looks on the faces of the committee members, Andrew quickly added, "You didn't know?"

"Dr. Foster, this is all quite unexpected. I'm not sure this is the moment to air . . ."

Andrew's voice took on a tone of palpable disgust. "I find it difficult to believe, sir, that you would avoid discussing—frankly and openly—some of the festering problems facing your institution. These are plain facts. And I'd suggest that, if you are seriously looking for a director—a manager, not a figurehead, then you will address these problems." Andrew's voice had taken on a penetrating chill.

"Why have these problems come about?" a member asked.

"Essentially, I think the problems can be traced to a board of trustees that has stopped thinking how to make the museum a better place for the public and the staff. The impression in the field is that the board thinks only of how to use the institution for its own purposes or for the sake of its intimate friends."

The members of the committee sat like a cluster of stones.

Bruce Thompson finally broke the silence. "Andrew, what would you do?"

"Settle all discrepancies in women's salaries—immediately," Andrew replied. "And talk to the union at once."

"But that might cost several million!"

"Probably around four or five," Andrew replied airily. "But the peace it will buy will be worth it."

"What else do you recommend, Foster?" It was Roland McCrae, speaking harshly.

"A third of the present board should resign," Andrew said without hesitation. "Recruit younger trustees from a broader slice of society. Get more than just great-grandsons, cousins, and nephews from the same families that founded the place. Get more than just lawyers, investment bankers, and socialites. Elect some board members from the community at large."

"This could lead to . . . to some sort of a revolution," someone was heard to say.

"Much needed," Andrew commented. "Launch a public relations campaign to reach out to the people," he went on, his voice brightening. "Draw up architectural plans to redesign the space. Hire the toughest management consulting firm in the country and allow it six months to expose the flaws and weaknesses. Open up. Grow. Haul yourself into the twentieth century."

A stillness had descended on the room.

"Obviously, you should let your new chief executive—make it a chief executive instead of just a director—select a prize advisory committee. Say, five members from the existing board, three new trustees, two staff members, plus a representative from the management consultant firm. Ask them to recommend fundamental changes in the constitution and bylaws of the museum so that you can guide it into the modern era."

Roland McCrae spoke out in acid tones. "Foster, I will not insult you by saying that I neither admire your glib bluntness nor believe a word of your advice. I appear to be your target, the focus of your slanted 'argumentum ad hominem.' That is grossly unfair. I do not sit on this board or this committee. Mine is only an elderly—and I hope, mature—voice of conscience which seeks balance and harmony."

"High time we faced some hard truths around here!" Bruce Thompson piped up. "Some of us have been suggesting just such reforms for years. Mr. Chairman, why don't you find out if Foster would like to become our next director. That was the original plan, wasn't it—much as I was opposed to the candidate at the time."

"Thompson, you never know when to hold your tongue, do you?" Smithers snarled, dropping his pretense of gentility.

"Oh, just find out. Go ahead, ask!" Thompson retorted in exasperation.

Smithers looked around him in confusion and then asked somewhat hesitantly, "Dr. Foster? What are your intentions?"

"Gentlemen, I have no intentions. I do not want to be the director of this thoroughly muddled institution. No thanks. I'm not sufficiently diplomatic, I guess. My advice is to look for fresh blood. Aggressive blood. Guts and fire." With that Andrew rose to his feet, shook the hand of each astonished member of the committee, and started to amble out of the hushed room. "And if I were you, I'd hurry up about it too!"

Bruce Thompson followed him out into the corridor and almost hugged him.

"Andrew, I'm not utterly sure I believe this. What an act! And, of course, I have a certain suspicion why you've done it."

"Let me tell the lady first, Bruce. In an hour or so, I'll have this whole thing pinned down."

"What a fine lad you are!"

"Tell that to Olivia," Andrew remarked with a hollow laugh.

A small foreign car was parked on the corner when Andrew exited the gloomy interior of the Union Club and went out into the dazzling sunlight. The driver motioned him into the front seat. Once inside, he handed over a bulging manila envelope and drove slowly uptown as Andrew eagerly digested the contents.

"Amazing!" Andrew exclaimed. "It's all here. Please thank Ed Lassiter for me.

• • •

Andrew entered Ayn Steyne's residence on Sutton Place and was guided by an impassive servant into a spacious salon with its walls decorated in red velvet on which, in ostentatious frames, were hanging four paintings by Chaim Soutine. To Andrew's amusement, one was patently a forgery. Ayn Steyne sailed in like a man-of-war, wearing a full, tight-waisted black silk evening dress.

"What game were you attempting to play at the meeting of the search committee? I just got off the line with Roland McCrae. He is livid. Self-righteous candor is so boring, Andrew. Couldn't you have waited until you secured the job and then manipulated your reforms quietly? It's going to be hell to put this all back together!"

"I only want to help the Metropolitan," Andrew replied modestly.

"So, it was a bargaining ploy. I admire that. Now let's get back on the track."

"Mrs. Steyne, I really don't want the job," Andrew said. "I meant what I said to your committee."

"What are you up to?"

"You see, I have a candidate who'd be better than me."

"Be serious. Andrew, we're in a bind. The selection process has been going on far too long. Criticism is mounting."

"I want Olivia Cartright to be offered the job."

"Cartright? Absurd! That woman seems to gather up the most peculiarly diverse group of backers. Bruce Thompson and now you. Why? At least Thompson had some strange idea that he wanted to marry her."

Andrew's eyebrows rose. But he said nothing.

"She's bloody bright, I'll admit that," Steyne mused. "And if she put her mind to it, could make herself fairly attractive—with tasteful advice. She's determined too. Ambitious. But her parents were nobodies. We need someone at the pinnacle of society, someone who has entrée into every right place in America. Old money. Social standing, as you well know, is two-thirds one's curriculum vitae in the art museum profession. And, anyway, the Metropolitan is not ready for a woman."

"What about Olivia's record as a scholar, a connoisseur, and a negotiator?" Andrew asked calmly. "And don't forget her performance at UNESCO!"

"I repeat, I am looking for someone who has executive ability and, above all, is socially well connected. Olivia can never attain those heights."

"She's about to become very social, and exceedingly rich too," Andrew remarked offhandedly, enjoying immensely his role as spider.

"So Olivia has decided to marry Bruce Thompson," Steyne said. "That won't make any difference. Thompson is second-level. He doesn't enter into my plans. I think it's time to ask him to resign from the board. Roland McCrae is wholly with me on this. Roland really does admire you, Andrew, despite your outrageous comments at the meeting. He looks upon you like . . . well, like a slightly spoiled nephew. He'll forgive you. You'll enjoy working with him—and me."

"Aren't you a little concerned with legal issues if you summarily dismiss Olivia as a candidate? A civil rights suit may grow out of that move."

"I'm not interested in legalistics—or civil or women's rights issues, either. We retain a competent team of lawyers. No one, least of all Olivia, will harass us with threats of litigation. It would be years before anything came to court and by that time she'd be broken."

"Mrs. Steyne, my request is simple. I want Olivia Cartright to be the next director of the Met with full executive as well as administrative powers."

"Are you mad? I'll tell you what I intend to do. Not only am I not going to make Olivia director, but I'm going to can her. And why, may I ask, are you bothering to support her?"

"I have asked her to marry me. That may just help out her social standing, wouldn't you say?"

"Marry? Olivia? You're a fool. What nonsense! What a puerile attempt to pressure me! Do you have any idea who you're dealing with?"

"Of course." He paused to stare at her. "You are the principal stockholder of Pan-Oriental Oil Company. You also own the controlling shares of Aetna Oil. And that, as you know, is the drilling company in Sicily which is secretly linked to the Amoebina Society, the covert rightist organization in Italy whose vice president recently committed suicide because of an investigation into his embezzlement of government funds—to the tune of two hundred and fifty million dollars. But there is something like two hundred million dollars more still missing, isn't there? You must know, because you have an account at Bank Leu in Geneva."

"Crap!"

"No crap at all," Andrew said with a broad grin, admiring her fighting spirit. Then, in rapid succession he enumerated specific account numbers and amounts which only Bank Leu and Ayn Steyne could know.

She sat down abruptly, shrugged as if she had not a care in the world, and said, "So I made some money investing in oil. So what?"

"Oh, I know your manipulation of Aetna Oil assets may not be outright fraud," Andrew went on, "but consider the news stories! After that amount of press it might just be a bit tough to remain on the Metropolitan board. And I'm sure that a couple of congressional investigating committees might have to probe the issue. Yet another government might fall in Italy. Why rock the boat? Think of what you'll be gaining—the most capable chief executive in the world for the Met. And you can even take credit for it."

Ayn Steyne swiftly analyzed her options. She had none. Andrew Foster had managed to unearth some chillingly specific information even if he hadn't gotten the whole story. The Aetna Oil transfer of a quarter of a billion dollars was only the beginning. Once that came to the surface, other links in the chain of corruption might rupture. And the other links, worth hundreds of millions more, led to the highest echelons of the United States government.

A thoughtful Ayn Steyne tallied up the pluses and minuses of the situation, calculated the chances of a scandal, and said simply, "I see your point. I shall not stand any longer in Olivia's way. But you must understand, I don't have total power. Roland McCrae has actually more to say about who will become the next director than I."

"Crap!" Andrew snapped.

"Listen to me, young man," she said angrily. "I'm still convinced that you are the best choice for the Met. Andrew, talk Olivia out of her fixation on the directorship. Once married, won't she want to live a little? Do you really want a career woman? A rival? Think of your life together with a career girl, bustling back and forth between New York and Washington."

He chuckled at her appeal to his presumed chauvinism.

"Olivia's really better as a connoisseur," Steyne said in exasperation. "She'd get bored by administration. I've noticed that in her already. I'll tell you what. Let's do nothing for ten days—there'll still be two weeks before the sale—then let's discuss Olivia's proper role at the Met again."

"That would give you just enough time to remove the money from Bank Leu and bury it elsewhere," he said. "No deal."

After a long silence Steyne said quietly, "I shall not block Olivia's election. I'll submit her name in nomination. I usually get what I want. Although there's no guarantee. It'll be hell dealing with Roland!"

"Get rid of him. He's trashing the place," Andrew remarked in a clipped voice. "For someone who can deal with a secret slush fund of the dimensions of this one, firing an ex-trustee and hiring a director seem like child's play. And please don't try a double cross on me."

"May I ask you something?"

"Don't bother to try to find out how I know about the fund."

"I wasn't born yesterday, young man. Your patronizing attitude in this victory of yours is quite annoying. I've another question. What did you think of the Velázquez? Will you be bidding?"

Andrew's mouth twisted into a sly grin. "I have my suspicions about the picture. By the way, Olivia adores it. But that's her business. As for me, I'm out—definitely out."

"You are, young man, an intriguing mixture of truth and falsehood."

"Something you seem to know a lot about, Mrs. Steyne."

Andrew flew to Washington and over dinner told a relieved Jonathan Cresson that he had resisted the blandishments of the Metropolitan Museum and had recommended to an "intrigued" Ayn Steyne that Olivia Cartright would make the best choice.

"Sir, you wouldn't take it amiss if I held a press conference to announce that I have no desire for the Met job?"

"Nothing would give me greater pleasure, my boy. But keep it discreet. Tell me, are you absolutely positive about the Velázquez?"

"I'm pretty certain it's a copy," Andrew said disconsolately, and then added hesitantly, "From my first examination—"

"Shit!" Cresson spat out. "Dammit, boy, are you sure?"

"I think so," Andrew said, stunned by the uncharacteristic outburst of profanity.

Cresson clenched his fists. "Shit! I so wanted to beat the Metropolitan!"

Andrew conducted his press conference in the paneled board room of the National Gallery. After cocktails had been served, Andrew assured the reporters from the *New York Times*, the *Washington Post*, the AP, the UPI, and CBS Radio that his statement would be brief—and highly newsworthy. He hadn't invited any television correspondents—he wanted to hold off TV coverage until London. With luck he could spill the beans to the BBC just in time for the morning news so that Olivia might actually see him make his gift of love.

"Okay, here it is," he began crisply. "I've just been asked to become the director of the Metropolitan Museum of Art. I've made my decision . . ." A long pause. "Which is not to take the job."

"What the hell," said the *Times* reporter. "That's the most sought-after museum job in the United States! Why?"

"Two reasons. One, I like what I'm doing at the moment and, two, I have a feeling that I'm not qualified for this extremely difficult job. That museum needs a fighter, a daring, tough, creative, steel-willed, diplomatic, money-raising administrator."

"You're not?" the reporter from the *Post* asked.

"Oh, I suppose I could do it—it's just a job for someone else, or at least I think so."

"Who?" they asked in chorus.

"Someone closer to the action."

"That would be Olivia Cartright," the *Times* reporter said.

"Right."

"I won't print the answer to this one," the *Post* reporter said, "because I don't approve of gossip sullying the arts, but I have heard that you and Olivia Cartright have been seeing each other. Is it true? And if so, has a possible, ah, amorous relationship influenced your decision?"

"I respect Olivia a lot. But I'm sure you'll understand that whatever comment appears on that, she'll have to make it."

"Is the National Gallery going to be seriously bidding on the Velázquez next week in London?" the woman from UPI demanded.

"Not sure. I think maybe not," Andrew replied.

"Why not? Can't Jonathan Cresson afford it?" asked the AP correspondent.

"Easily. It's not the money. It's my opinion that the quality of the picture may not be up to the standards of the National Gallery of Art."

"Dr. Foster, this couldn't possibly be a convenient way of transmitting a message to some potential competitors for the painting via the front page?"

Andrew smiled. "Now you must excuse me, I've got to return to London."

22 ENTENTE CORDIALE

ALTHOUGH SHE WAS virtually certain that she was about to pull off a major triumph, Olivia had felt no elation, convinced that Andrew had walked out of her life forever. The very thought made her despair. Then his passionate—and enigmatic—letter was delivered to her. What was he really trying to say? His letter was certainly a declaration of love, but there was still the competition and conflict. His ardor delighted and reassured her. But the news that he had flown off to New York to be interviewed by the Met's search committee upset her.

Would he accept? She desperately wanted to call Ayn Steyne to demand an explanation, but realized that such an impulsive action would seriously damage whatever slim chances she might still have. Besides, she already knew what the explanation would be. All Steyne would say was that the committee had a right and an obligation to interview as many candidates as possible. Asking directly what the outcome was likely to be would be the worst thing to do. And maybe, just maybe, Andrew was going to . . . Don't think of it, she admonished herself. Deep inside, Olivia felt like a child.

She shook herself out of her confused state of mind and prepared to move into action. How to solve the identity of the *Marchesa* that Andrew had dismissed as a copy and she had seen too fleetingly to assess properly? She simply had to go back to William's and examine the picture once more—this time with the permission of Sir Peter Grundy. How to accomplish that she had no idea. But she had been invited that very evening to the auction house for a reception and buffet dinner launching a sale of Oriental ceramics. She would think of something by then.

The cream-white, ornate Adam reception rooms of the grand old house crackled with the kind of energy generated when rare, fine objects of art and wealthy collectors come together. But this evening was unique. For the first time since the most recent political upheavals had tipped Mainland China smartly to the right, the newly emerged entrepreneurs were rubbing shoulders with their capitalist colleagues from Hong Kong and Taiwan. It was clear that the preening nouveau riche gentry from Peking, Shanghai, and Canton were mesmerized by the thought of snatching lavish examples of their traditional art back to the homeland. As Peter Grundy surveyed the soignée crowd, he beamed with delight. The sale would be yet another dazzling feather in his cap. With the *Marchesa* William's had already stood the art world on its head— and now this!

Grundy's philosophy was that fine art looked finer surrounded by beautiful women, and there were more than Olivia had ever seen in one place. To her satisfaction she was clearly considered one of them. The men glanced at her appreciatively, and one slim, copper-skinned young Chinese with hair as black as diorite shadowed her for minutes. Just as he was about to make his approach, Olivia veered away and almost bumped into Kurt Krassner.

"How amusing!" he said, gesturing at the crowd of Chinese peering at the vases. "To think that some of these Orientals were probably Red Guards back in the good old days and are now ardent capitalists and budding art collectors is too amusing. Bravo, I say! Would you join me for dinner this evening? I still have things to tell you about that forthcoming sale."

"I'm sorry, I can't," Olivia said. "I made plans to stay here for the buffet."

"Dine in an auction house?" Krassner said in genuine amazement.

"It's business," she replied.

"Oriental porcelains? Or still trying to chase down the Velázquez? A vain pursuit. Who can help you now? It's in the lap of the gods—and the very rich."

"Maybe I can talk Grundy into removing it from the sale in exchange for some highly coveted works of art." She hoped she sounded convincing.

"Ha! Anyway, Grundy has nothing to do with it. I shouldn't be telling you this, but the *Marchesa* is not under the control of even its owner. All arrangements have been made by His Lordship's solicitor, Harold Greenway. Especially the security arrangements. Try talking to him."

"If Greenway calls the shots, is he the one who let you into the room alone—without the guard?"

"You are most persistent, young lady. I do admire that in people. Actually it was Sir Peter. But he can no longer grant such special favors. Not even for you, Miss Cartright. Look, forget all this. When can we meet?"

"Why, at the auction of course."

"I'm going to outbid you, you realize that, don't you? I do not intend to take your advice at face value."

"Why should you be in a position to win?"

"Because I happen to have everything in order. I have, through my agents, been able to, ah, corner the market on everything pertaining to the Velázquez."

"Why didn't your agents engineer the removal of the Velázquez file from the archives of the Academy in Rome?" she asked in a soft, teasing voice.

"What?" Krassner stepped back, flabbergasted.

"Ciao," she said breezily, and went off to find Sir Peter.

Olivia discovered Grundy pinned to a wall in the corner of the room by an elderly collector who was berating him about how "crude" Chinese porcelains were compared to the glories of Longton Hall ware. "It is far superior, you know, to all this factory-made Chinese export paste."

"Interesting. . . . Quite so. . . . Fascinating. . . . To be sure. . . . Indeed yes. . . . Umm," Grundy mumbled in a polite refrain. Tonight any fool could be suffered. When he saw Olivia approaching, he cut the man off. "A client. Must talk to her."

Grundy took Olivia by the arm and led her toward the hors d'oeuvres. "Allow me to use you as an escape mechanism, Olivia."

"That's why I came."

"Delighted! I didn't know you were interested in Orientalia," he added, shooting a glance over his shoulder to be sure the Longton Hall addict was not following.

"Everything worthwhile and genuine intrigues me," she replied. "And you happen to be on the top of my list."

"I do like flattery—so very, very much!" A faint blush came to his face. "Have you decided what to do about the *Marchesa*? International interest mounts every day."

"Peter, I've decided not to bid."

Grundy dropped his spoon into the mound of caviar.

"Instead I'm going to write a novel about her—a mystery story."

"Olivia, you do amuse me! Do you have a plot?" What could he learn from her? What was she after?

"Oh, yes. The basic characters are a man, somewhat like Andrew Foster, and a woman, somewhat like me. Disguised, of course. We are bitter competitors, but then because of an amusing series of circumstances, we decide to work together and buy the painting as a team—for both our museums so that more Americans can see it."

"How fanciful," Grundy exclaimed. "And how good for business! With the two of you bidding together, I'd be forced to charge double the estimate—which, by the way, my dear, has climbed to the unheard-of but deliciously welcome level of fifteen million dollars."

"What's nice about fiction is that you can make up anything," Olivia said. "Even such an outrageous price."

"But that's not fiction," Grundy replied cheerily. "That's real life!"

"Fifteen million! You think it will reach that?"

Grundy smiled broadly.

"Forget the real world, let me go back to the nicer reality of my novel," Olivia said. "My characters will encounter a little problem with the picture. One of them will be convinced it's brilliant; the other will be equally convinced that the thing is a damnably clever later copy—not by Velázquez at all. Together they manage to sneak undetected up to your fifth-floor room. They bribe your ever present guard to examine it, even remove it from its frame." Olivia looked at him intently. "The guard will, of course, be in secret a member of a gang of thieves."

"Not bad."

"And what about this twist, Sir Peter? The copy was always in the collection of Lord Richfield."

"Certain experts are convinced that is, indeed, a fact," Grundy said, his voice lowering conspiratorially.

"They are?" Olivia said, unable to conceal her astonishment.

"Of course. But they say nothing about it, hoping that His Lordship will part with the wrong picture and they can buy his original —actually the copy—for a song."

Olivia stared at him wide-eyed. But Grundy didn't seem to notice her reaction. He whispered, "And several switches are made." Then he laughed. "Oh, no. That's not very good, is it? Olivia, I fear I'm not very gifted at inventing plots for thrillers."

She exhaled in relief. "I like it, Peter. Why *not* have a switch? Here's how it can be done. Unknown to the auction house, the guard is in cahoots with an unscrupulous character who . . ."

"*That* would never happen at William's," he protested. "Surely!"

"Surely not," she agreed.

"A truly novel twist of the plot," he mused. "Why not inject a little real life into it? Your guard shouldn't be an employee of the auction house. Make him like the young man who at present watches over the *Marchesa*. He's not one of my employees; he's actually—keep this to yourself—an employee of Lord Richfield's solicitor and financial adviser, Harold Greenway. And that *is* nonfiction."

Olivia's eyes glistened. Just what Don Ciccio had told her.

"In the novel," she said, "I could make the brother of this guard the thief who broke into Richfield's house."

"Very good!" Sir Peter cried. "You do have a most facile imagination! That way it becomes a devilish inside job. Very good stuff."

"Let me tell you about another inside job, Peter. I slipped into your private elevator the other day while you were out and sneaked into the room where the *Marchesa* is kept. No one saw me. Except for one person. Not the guard, he wasn't anywhere in sight. The man in the room with the painting, alone, is standing over there—Kurt Krassner."

Grundy stiffened but said nothing.

"What would happen if Lord Richfield's solicitor learned about such a breach of security?" She whispered the words.

His mouth opened and closed abruptly.

Olivia held up her hand. "I shall say nothing. If . . ."

Seeing the steady, cold look in her eyes, Grundy muttered, "I assume you've come down to earth from your flights of fancy."

"Quite."

"What is your 'if,' Olivia?"

"I'll say not a word, *if* you give me an hour with the *Marchesa* alone tomorrow evening. Late. After closing. Only you will be here to let me in. No guard. I insist on being alone with the picture. If not, I shall reveal what I know."

"I say, you are serious, aren't you? Do you realize what you are asking? If Greenway or Richfield found out, my contract to sell the painting would be ruptured. It might even destroy the firm."

"I only care about examining that painting again."

"You'd actually tell? And ruin me?"

"Count on it."

"But, dammit, you've already inspected the picture longer than anyone else!"

"I need more time. Alone."

"This is blackmail," Grundy said through clenched teeth.

"I call it equity."

Grundy's head sank to his chest. His ears gradually became a shade of vermilion. For an instant Olivia feared he might be having a heart attack.

"I'll tell," she said with chilling finality.

He lifted his head and looked straight into her eyes. "All right. What else can I do? Be here tomorrow night. You shall have your pound of flesh."

"Good! I'll call if there's a hitch in my schedule."

"Hitch?"

"I might be a little late. I'm planning to go to the country tomorrow. I hope to return in plenty of time."

Grundy sighed. "Olivia, you're incorrigible!"

"I have my ways," she said, and smiled brightly.

Olivia felt so sure of herself that she easily restrained her temptation to break away and race back to her hotel to call Don Ciccio. She lingered on for an hour reveling in the pageantry of the evening.

Back in her room Olivia conversed for the greater part of an hour with her mentor, asking him to obtain everything he could on Sir Peter Grundy and Lord Richfield's solicitor, Harold Greenway. Exhausted, she fell into a deep sleep.

She was awakened just after dawn by Don Ciccio, who hastily recounted his discoveries.

"Sir Peter Grundy, despite a fondness for conspiracies of minor significance, is an honest, ethical man, free of vices. We cannot find even a peccadillo that can be said to mar his image. He can be trusted."

"And Greenway?"

"Completely untrustworthy. Sinister. And very clever. Do be cautious," Don Ciccio warned. "He's living a double life. In one, he's a respectable, sedate, rather plodding, member of the London bar. Has a farm in the country and dabbles in livestock. Adores puttering around in his garden. Is married to a docile woman. True blue."

"And his other side?"

"The classic English gentleman cad. On the sly, Greenway's an ardent gambler and a connoisseur of beautiful young women. Among his clandestine financial interests is a sixty percent owner-ship of a modeling agency, which is rather more like an escort service. He dabbles extensively in the merchandise during the eve-nings he stays in town."

"Expensive tastes?"

"Massively! His gambling brings him big losses. And he lavishes gaudy bibelots on his young tarts. But, still, he's rich. You see, he's one of those people who worship money."

"What about his peculiar employee—the guard at William's?"

"Alas, nothing more than you already know," he replied.

As soon as she was off the telephone Olivia had a thought. She went downstairs and told an eager-to-please but puzzled concièrge what she wanted to do. Efficiently he went about his task of discov-ering what the visiting hours and regulations pertaining to visitors were at Dartmoor Prison.

"Visitors' hours are from two thirty to four—every day except Mondays. There are convenient trains from Victoria Station. The trip takes only one and a quarter hours. Shall I make the booking? . . . Yes, madame."

The journey, although comfortable, was as bleak as solitary con-finement. As the train approached the station, the handful of pas-sengers getting off huddled deeper into their coats, not wanting anyone to observe them.

Olivia marched into the grim portals of the castlelike prison and announced that she was an American journalist preparing an article about international art theft and was interested in talking to William Fielding. She assured the constable that she had obtained the permission of Fielding's solicitor to interview his client.

"Well, ma'am, once in here I suppose it's pretty much up to him. But I don't think he'd want to lose the opportunity to meet a looker the likes of you." Olivia shot the officer her most winning smile.

A half-hour later a sallow, handsome young man was led into the visitor's cage. He took a seat and winked at her lewdly. "Nice bird. Like to stay the night? Nice place, this hotel."

"I'm researching an article on international art theft," Olivia began in a businesslike way. "And I simply had to talk to you. Because you're so, well, famous and exciting!"

He preened.

"You really must tell me how you do it."

"Why me? I'm a regular," Fielding said indignantly. "No art stuff for me. Whatta ya do with the junk?"

For an instant Olivia had the sinking feeling that she had chosen the wrong person. "You *are* the William Fielding who was arrested after breaking into the Richfield estate, aren't you?"

"I guess. Say, let's talk about you."

"But you're so much more fascinating. And mysterious. That appeals to me."

"Coo."

"I mean, why, as a 'regular,' a 'pro,' did you steal a mediocre picture and then . . ." It was almost a plea.

"I'm an art lover, is all," he said. "I've a secret passion for art. I've got this 'ere hobby, you might call it—to rid this world, which is so full of ugliness, don't you agree, of mediocre pictures. I had to do it. I had to burn it. It was a very bad nude. Fat face, fatter bun, tiny titties. You know, 'connoysership.' I think of my work as for the benefit of mankind. Anyway, I'm getting out shortly. It was all a sort of good-hearted, impetuous act. Sometimes loving great art can lead a body astray. Now, that's a story for you." He paused, dragged his eyes over as much of Olivia as he could see behind the cage, and got to the point.

"American, are you? Are you going to be around in two weeks when I spring? There's bound to be a roll of parties, all to be remarked upon in the *Tattler* and *Harper's and Queen*. Tell me where you're staying and I'll be sure to send off the engraved invitations."

"What did your boss have to do with this 'impetuous act'?" Olivia asked calmly.

"Boss? I'm a lone wolf."

Olivia pressed on. "By the way, I met your brother not too long ago, at William's auction house, guarding the painting of the *Marchesa* by Velázquez that I'm sure you know a great deal about."

"I know a lot of art, but I don't know that one, Missie," he said, looking straight into her eyes. His gaze was malevolent and, despite herself, Olivia had to look away.

"This is how I see it," she said. "Your boss—his name is Harold Greenway—learns somehow that there's a copy of Lord Richfield's Velázquez on the premises and dreams up the idea to make off with Richfield's authentic painting. He gets you to substitute the copy for the original, but something happens. You panic, maybe. As a cover, you make off with another nude—an inferior one. You destroy it. You're caught, as you and Harold Greenway have planned all along. A bumbling thief is apprehended, the stolen picture has been burned, and Greenway, no amateur when it comes to the law, sees that you're given a slap on the wrist. Am I right so far?"

William Fielding's lips curled. "You'd better be careful, lady. This kind of rotten talk could cause you a pack of worries. You follow?"

Olivia ignored the threat and plunged on. "Greenway suggests to a panicked Lord Richfield that his valuable Velázquez had obviously been the target and advises him to put it up at auction— fast. His Lordship readily agrees. Greenway forces the compliant William's Ltd. to agree to the restrictions, especially the one that spells out that Greenway handle the security arrangements. At first the original Velázquez is put on view. Then after every potential buyer has had a look, the copy is substituted for the sale."

Fielding laughed—but his eyes were ominous.

Olivia looked at him directly. "The clever, nearly foolproof plan goes awry because your employer doesn't realize that the head of the auction house, Sir Peter Grundy, can't say no when certain old friends beg him for a special look—alone, without your little brother hanging around. Even if Greenway and your brother have the run of William's, it is a busy, almost frantic place. They can't slither back in and make a switch every time they suspect that sweet, never-say-no Grundy is going to allow someone a quick look. I'd love to know what Harold Greenway will say when he learns that two of the richest potential purchasers actually studied the copy."

Fielding leaned forward and spat on the counter. "This is what you'll be if this fantasy of yours sees print."

"Of course, this is only fantasy," Olivia continued. "Let's say the copy sells for millions of pounds. Perhaps slightly below expectations, but certainly not below the reserve price, which Greenway has control over. Later the original is sold to some unscrupulous collector at a grand price. Almost everybody wins. Lord Richfield wins. Greenway wins. You win. The institution or collector that has been conned either never finds out or chooses to keep the blunder a secret." Olivia paused to take a deep breath. "I think you are geniuses."

Fielding twisted his stocky frame forward in his chair, placed his elbows on the counter in front of him, and moved his face close to the wire screen between them. "You're going to get yourself into big trouble. Doesn't that worry you?" he whispered.

"Frankly, yes," Olivia replied coolly. "Above all, I'm afraid that Greenway or your brother will attempt to destroy the original. If they try I shall . . ."

"How could you stop them? Guess who's coming to see me early tomorrow? My solicitor, a close friend of Mr. Harold Greenway."

"I shall reveal to the police—and the press—certain photographs." She explained how she had hoodwinked his brother by taking clandestine photographs of the painting.

Fielding's body drooped back a little in the hard metal chair. "But who'd give a shit about your precious story or little photos."

"Plenty of people would care. No matter what happens, that original mustn't be touched. Your boss, Greenway, must guarantee that no matter who wins the painting now at William's, I shall get the original."

"Piss off. You're way over your head."

Olivia got up to leave and said grimly, "When you get word to Greenway tomorrow of my visit, be sure to tell him who I really am. I'm not a journalist. I'm a member of the staff of the Metropolitan Museum of Art in New York. And when it comes to art fraud the police and the press will believe what I say."

"Speaking of frauds, I should have you arrested," Fielding burst out. "Hey, Constable!"

At the shout a police officer entered from a side door. Olivia had just enough time to whisper her parting words. "And tell Greenway I'm under the protection of a certain gentleman named Don Ciccio Nerone. *Personally* under his protection. I shall be contacting him soon. Nothing should happen to the *Marchesa*."

William Fielding's face grew ashen and he nodded weakly.

Olivia returned to London on the next train and took a taxi directly to William's. Sir Peter was waiting for her alone and escorted her to the fifth floor without a word. He unlocked and opened the door, and motioned her in.

Olivia wasted no time. As soon as she heard his footsteps recede down the corridor and heard the clanking of the departing lift, she went to work. She extracted a small bottle of xylene from her purse and a number of cotton swabs. At certain passages of the painting, especially the transitions from one color to another and where the contours had been painted with emphasis, she cleaned ever so slightly and examined the section. At each, she took a photograph. She took particular care so that no one would detect her cleaned passages unless they used a high-powered magnifying glass.

Again and again she pored over the small areas she had cleaned. The true nature of the painting was becoming clearer to her by the moment. Once more she went over her notes, making sure that she had written a description of every passage she had touched with her cotton swabs, double-checking that she had a photograph for every part of the painting she had cleaned. Finally she stepped forward and rechecked the width and length of the canvas. Almost exactly what Velázquez's original image measured. Again she scrutinized the hazy surfaces of the picture and then focused in with her magnifying glass at the tiny, almost imperceptible, areas she had cleaned. There was simply no doubt about it, beneath the cloudy outer surface of paint—and it was paint, she was certain, not merely old, blurred varnish—there were areas of startling clarity and purity, just like the first *Marchesa* she had seen. Cloudy and pure all at once. The fact hit her like a revelation. It was then that Olivia realized that she was close. There was one more thing to be done. One more risk.

She knew that she would have to subject the Rokeby *Venus* in the National Gallery to a similar scrutiny, and do it without the knowledge of Roy Bentley. When could she get the opportunity? That was the problem. The room where the *Venus* was displayed was very popular with the general public. She remembered from her summer working as an exchange student and docent in the Gallery that a guard was positioned nearby at all times. It would be impossible to sneak up to it during public hours and surreptitiously spot-clean it. To ask Bentley for permission would spoil everything. Reckless and foolhardy though it was, Olivia knew that the only way she would obtain final answers to the questions that nagged her would be to hide out in the Gallery after the place had closed. And manage to evade the night watchman—somehow.

Olivia prepared for her secret visit to the Gallery all the next day. She purchased a bottle of aspirin and another of allergy tablets. If things went awry and she was caught, she planned to say she had been overcome by a respiratory attack. If she were apprehended in the act itself, her career would be over. She shuddered at the thought, but didn't allow her fear to deter her.

Taking pains to change her clothes each visit, Olivia made two reconnaissance tours of the Gallery to scout out her hiding place and follow the route leading to the hall where the Rokeby *Venus* was exhibited. The women's lavatory on the same floor was spacious enough and did have a small antechamber where an attendant usually sat on a chair. The place seemed ideal. She sauntered along the route from the lavatory to Hall XIV where the *Venus* was exhibited in isolated splendor. She counted the steps carefully, trying to listen over the hubbub of visitors how much the wooden floor creaked. It did, but not alarmingly. With the attuned eye of a museum professional she scrutinized the ceilings and baseboards for signs of hidden television cameras or acoustic or electronic scanners. None. Thank God the National Gallery was still, after so many years, technologically backward.

She entered a third and final time at four o'clock, when only a handful of late-afternoon visitors were making their way into the museum. Clad in denims and sneakers, her head draped in a scarf, she made one last journey from the lavatory to Hall XIV and walked back slowly among the crowd of people on their way out of the gallery. She darted into the ladies' room, entered the stall farthest from the door, and sat down to wait. Several times just after the clanging of bells and the far-off shout of a guard, "Closing time!" she almost got up and rushed out. But, clenching her fists and shutting her eyes, she tried to regulate her rapid breathing. After fifteen minutes of silence, she began to relax.

For a moment she was overcome with a new terror. Might there be patrol dogs? The Metropolitan had tried them years ago but had dropped them after finding them too expensive to keep trained. By one hour after closing time, her anxieties had vanished. A guard made a noisy and entirely perfunctory inspection of the lavatory. He threw open the door, walked in, spat loudly into a washbasin, grunted, and walked out.

At nine o'clock the guard again opened the door a crack and allowed it to slam shut. Silence. Half an hour later, Olivia made her move. She walked to the door and gingerly opened it. The Gallery seemed deserted. She made certain that the door didn't have an automatic lock. With her heart beating at a frightful pace she slipped out into the corridor, which was illuminated by amber nightlights placed at intervals on the baseboards. She cautiously inspected the one nearest her to be doubly sure that it contained no electronic scanner or electric eye. No. Cushioning her steps, she began to tiptoe toward her goal.

Suddenly a loud, rasping cough cracked the silence. She froze. The guard must be a room or two away, far too close. He blew his nose and muttered something to himself. Abruptly, a voice began to speak. Olivia almost screamed.

"For the second selection, we have a vintage performance of Sir Thomas Beecham in a recording of 1944. Brahms's Third Symphony."

The BBC! God, what a relief! The radio would drown out any creaking from the floors. Making her way through the five galleries leading to the *Venus*, she made certain that other security officers had not been posted along the path. Incredible though it was, the entire main floor of the National Gallery seemed to have been entrusted to just one sentry.

When she had reached Hall XIV she took pains to scout several rooms beyond to assure herself that no guards were stationed there. Then she huddled in a dark corner behind a couch and waited to see if the guard would make a round. She had no idea if it would be a well-timed routine or totally at random. At the Metropolitan she knew it was standard procedure for the chief of the night security staff to roll dice to determine the chance hours when the galleries should be inspected. After an hour and a half Olivia was fairly sure that the guard would make no inspections at all. Apparently, once the nightwatchman had determined to his satisfaction the place was empty at closing time, he retired to his fixed post to listen to the BBC. Incredible!

Confident that she would not be disturbed, Olivia approached the *Venus* and with the aid of a small flashlight began to examine it inch by inch through her magnifying glass. The condition was good except for a large—and superbly stitched—repair all the way down the Marchesa's sinuous back. Olivia knew from her research that the repair had come about in 1914 after a suffragette, apparently offended by the Marchesa's sensuality, had slashed her.

Right away, Olivia detected the first of what she counted were more than a dozen small passages which were distinctly duller than the rest of the canvas. The blurry areas looked like parts where a careless restorer might have neglected to clean. She took a sufficient number of photographs to be sure she had recorded the phenomenon. Finally, she took careful measurements of the painting. They were, as she'd suspected, virtually identical to the painting she had first seen at William's.

Silently she padded back to the lavatory and collapsed, listening to the music, which seemed to be amplified in the emptiness and stillness of the galleries. She must have dozed off several times, once when the guard walked past the door, this time not even bothering to open it. At six o'clock in the morning, wide-wake and growing impatient for the moment when she could stroll out among the anonymous crowds, Olivia heard the words that changed her life forever.

"That concludes our hour of Handel," said the BBC commentator. "The continuation of the program will take place two days hence, starting at four A.M. Now, before the morning world news, we present our regular cultural information. There appears to have been an unusual announcement from the United States. At a special press conference held yesterday, Dr. Andrew Foster, the director of the prestigious National Gallery of Art in Washington, D.C., stated that he would probably not be bidding at the forthcoming sale at William's Limited for the notorious nude portrait of his lover by the Spanish master Diego Velázquez . . ."

Olivia sprang to her feet and gripped one of the washbasins. Dumbstruck, she stared at herself in the mirror. Then she clapped her hands over her mouth to suppress a shout of joy.

"The effect on the sale is not expected to be significant, according to Sir Peter Grundy, the president of the auction house. 'There are,' Grundy affirmed, 'many other vital contenders that will guarantee a world-record price for this masterpiece.' "

The commentator was heard to shuffle some papers. "In another development, Dr. Foster announced that he has withdrawn from the race for the coveted directorship of New York's Metropolitan Museum of Art, generally considered to be the world's largest and most prestigious art museum. Foster stated that there were two reasons why he turned down the offer made by leading officials of the institution."

"Oh, Andrew!" Olivia cried, and with a rush of longing heard his voice reverberate through the galleries.

"One, I like what I'm doing at the moment and, two, I have a feeling that I'm not qualified for this extremely difficult job."

The commentator continued, "Dr. Foster added that the Metropolitan 'needs a fighter, a daring, tough, creative, steel-willed, diplomatic, money-raising administrator.' So, in New York City, at least," he concluded, "running an art museum appears to be something of a struggle."

Olivia collapsed onto the chair, stunned. How Andrew had presented her with a unique wedding gift and where she learned that she had gained the most cherished dream in her life would be a precious story to someday tell to their children. At the crack of dawn—hiding out in the ladies' lavatory in the National Gallery of

Art in London! Hiding out! For an instant Olivia thought of simply leaving, walking up to the guard, telling him who she was, and asking his assistance in leaving the building. But, of course, she couldn't. She spent an impatient two and a half hours, hoping anxiously that she could make it back to the hotel before Andrew arrived from the airport. How could she explain her all-night absence? She wasn't yet ready to tell him what she had found out about either the second *Marchesa* at William's or the Rokeby *Venus* at the Gallery. The perfect moment to present him with her own special wedding gift would soon come.

It was not until several women had used the lavatory that Olivia reckoned it would be safe for her to leave. Shortly after ten o'clock, frantic that she would not make it back to the hotel before Andrew got there, she escaped.

Andrew had not yet come. With a beatific smile on her face, Olivia lay on her bed and waited for him.

23 PACT WITH THE DEVIL

ANDREW BURST into the room and Olivia smothered him with kisses. In a catharsis of lovemaking all the agonies, anxieties, fears, and terrible doubts of the tumultuous week were swept aside.

"Never, never, never in my life could I have dreamed of anything like that!" she cried, hugging him. "Suddenly I hear over the radio . . . I was so stunned!"

"Am I forgiven?" he whispered.

"Oh, yes. I'd forgiven you. So many days ago!"

"I was such a fool," he said, shaking his head.

"So was I. I do adore you. Darling," she said, "I have so many extraordinary things to tell you."

"Me too. And I insist on telling you first," he said, grappling her back onto the bed. And then, gazing intently into her eyes, occasionally stopping to give her a kiss, Andrew Foster told her what he had done in New York.

Olivia sounded shocked. "You blackmailed Ayn Steyne? For what?"

"For you."

"But how?"

"Dearest, there's something about me you don't know and perhaps it's time you did. I revealed to Steyne that I knew certain things about her activities that might prove embarrassing."

Olivia looked anxiously into his eyes.

"I am the director of the National Gallery and, uh . . . at the same time I'm an employee of the Central Intelligence Agency."

"Andrew! You? A spy?"

"Not a spy. An information-gathering agent. Not really very romantic. Call me a junior member of the club. Have been since I got out of graduate school. All I do is keep careful notes on whatever country I'm in when I travel around the world for the Gallery. It's an effective cover. On occasion I might meet a contact someplace or memorize a special message."

"Why did you get into this?"

"Love for my country. But I'm going to quit—very soon."

"Is it dangerous?" she asked.

"Only the dangers that come with bureaucracies. Here's a state secret for you. You won't believe it but you've got to, because it's true. Roger Bass is trying to get his hands on the Velázquez so he can offer the thing as a bribe to Leonid Ermenentov, to get him to come to a summit meeting with the President. I swear it," he said emphatically.

Olivia succeeded in looking surprised.

"He pressured the Agency to force me to drop out of the sale. I did. It wasn't hard. After I saw the painting, I told my control officer that it would be amusing to let Bass and the Russian tyrant get a fake. Ha!"

"What? Was that a hard promise?"

"Sure."

"What if I change your mind?" Olivia asked quietly.

Andrew smiled and shook his head. "You can't, I'm afraid. The trade-off was not to bid in exchange for some information about Ayn Steyne. That was the blackmail."

"I have a few things that will change your mind, Andrew darling," she said, cuddling up closer to him. "I shall start with the 'problems' surrounding the painting."

"Olivia, must you? That damned thing almost destroyed us."

"You were right," she said.

"I know I'm right."

"I said, you *were* right."

"I don't get it."

"You were right when you thought the *Marchesa* was dull and murky. And so was I when I believed it magnificent. We were both right about the picture. Because there were two paintings of the *Marchesa* at William's."

"What?" Andrew jerked himself upright on the bed and listened avidly as Olivia described how she had made her way up to the gallery in William's, unnoticed, after her lunch with Richfield's niece and had discovered the second painting.

"Once I learned that there was another *Marchesa* in the Richfield collection, I just had to get into that room upstairs and see the picture. Whatever it is, the painting you saw—"

"Is a copy," he interrupted triumphantly. "So I wasn't nuts!"

At that instant Olivia decided not to tell Andrew about her visit to the auction house for a third time and nothing about her adventure in the National Gallery. Not yet. Those sagas would be recounted when she was in a position to present him with a gift equal to his.

"Your eye didn't deceive you," she said. "You saw a muddy, hazy *Marchesa*. It was not the same one I saw."

"God, I wish I could see the original!"

"You can. For a start, here are six photographs of her face," Olivia remarked offhandedly. "I took them when I first saw her." It was not the time to show him her most recent photos. Not yet.

"How the devil did you get these?" Andrew said with unfeigned admiration.

"With this. It's clever. A miniature camera and magnifying glass." She handed the instrument over to him.

Andrew shook his head and chuckled. "Talk about spies!"

"We each have our special talents," Olivia said. "The slides are minute but I think they show everything you need to know."

Andrew delicately cradled the transparencies in his hands. Each was about a quarter the size of a regular 35-millimeter slide. He took them to the window and held each one up to the daylight for a long time.

"This is utterly different from what I saw! How right you were! The woman's alive! Those eyes! Amazing! Those lips! The hair! The skin radiates! My God, what a masterpiece!" he exclaimed. "For Pete's sake, Olivia, the night of the argument, why, oh why didn't you just pull these out and show them to me?"

She gazed at him. "You're right! I could have. Yes, they were there, just over there in the drawer, all the time. I could have. I looked right at the drawer where they were and for an instant thought of showing them. But I was so furious, so hurt, so frightened at what I thought you were doing to me—I just couldn't bring myself to do it. I just couldn't trust you." Then she came over to him and pushed her face close to his, adding saucily. "You should have believed me anyway."

He threw up his hands in surrender. "But where is the original now?" he asked.

"Darling, Harold Greenway has to have it, and that's what makes me scared. I asked Don Ciccio to find out everything he could about Greenway's activities. I learned that he's a double-dealer. Lives two lives. Runs a prostitution ring. Gambles. Guess who hired William Fielding to break into the Richfield estate?"

"Greenway."

"And guess who Fielding's brother is?"

"The security guard at William's?"

"Absolutely."

"Neat. Unbelievable. We got him. Now it's up to us to close Greenway's trap, find the painting, and somehow convince him to sell it to us."

"Really?" Olivia said skeptically, and then her face grew long. "But I'm terribly worried about what they might do to the painting. I warned Fielding. I told him about my photographs and I dropped a name that kind of slowed him down."

"Don Ciccio's? Ha! Greenway must be in a sweat, waiting for you to make a move. We'll have to show our strength—soon."

"But how? In what way? God, I've wracked my brains on how to handle this."

"Leave it to me. I'm going to telephone Greenway, bait a hook, and then reel him in," Andrew said confidently.

"Telephone him? And say what?"

"I'll start by telling him about us."

"Andrew!" she protested.

"Watch me," he said, and went to the phone. "I'll make you a bet that within five minutes he'll be begging us to join him for dinner this evening." He shot her an impish smile. "Ah, he's coming on the line," he whispered, cupping his hand over the receiver. "Greenway, Andrew Foster here. . . . No, this is not about the Velázquez. I have something else I want to discuss—something highly confidential. As you may have heard, I made a public announcement about my feelings regarding your employer's Veláz-quez. . . . No, sir, it was no ploy."

Andrew looked up, winked, and took her hand in his.

"Why? No matter. I don't want to waste your time with idle chatter over the *Marchesa*. I'm calling to find out if Lord Richfield might consider selling some of his other treasures—directly. I can make it worth his while."

Olivia covered her mouth in surprise.

"Interested? . . . Good. Look, Greenway, as you know, I'm not the kind of man who likes to sit still. Are you free tonight for dinner?"

She suppressed a laugh.

"Impossible? Too bad." Andrew's voice fell. "I would have been bringing with me a most intriguing and charming young woman— someone you'd have wanted to meet. Who? Olivia Cartright. . . . Yes, the acting director of the Met."

Andrew paused for only about five seconds, looked up at Olivia, and nodded his head.

"Excellent! Dinner at eight, your house. Number Twelve, Totten-ham Mews. In Kensington. Good. We shall be prompt."

"What did he say? *What?*"

"He covered up his shock smoothly," Andrew said admiringly. "When he heard your name he turned jovial. You're the mark, all right."

Olivia shuddered.

"Don't worry, darling. I'm developing the perfect scheme. Let me get it down on paper and have Harold Greenway sign it this evening. Think of it this way. We can confront the bastard with what we now know and force him to sell us the *Marchesa* in secret and let our competition break their butts over the copy at the sale. Caveat emptor. That's what the big-time auction market is all about."

"Wouldn't I love to do that," she remarked. "But, seriously, how can we force him to return the original?"

"Olivia, I am being serious. We deserve the original, don't we? After everything we've done and you've discovered. Do you really want all our competitors to have a shot at the real thing? Do it my way and we can get the original for just the reserve price—ten million—and let Bass and the Russians get their just deserts. It'll work. What could go wrong?"

"Our reputations for one thing. My God, you are serious. This time we'd get caught for sure. The escapade in Rome . . . well, that was a clever game. This is fraud. A criminal conspiracy."

"Darling, after all the struggle, you'd let the masterpiece get away?" he protested weakly.

"Of course I don't want it to get away. I just want more. I don't want to get caught in some . . . confidence game. Let me explain . . ."

"You're worried that the copy might be spotted immediately. It won't. If everybody assumes it's Velázquez's masterwork, then it will be. Who really looks at the works of art on auction day, anyway?"

Olivia gazed at him, an expression of infinite sadness clouding her face.

"Perhaps you're right," he said. The last thing he wanted was another argument. "Reputation. The risk. Okay. I told you I'm no good at scheming. But it'll work, you know. Of course, ethical is best. We'll force Greenway to return the original. Fair's fair."

"Good." She smiled. "But—as a gesture—a tiny thing. Let's make him give us the copy."

"For what?"

"A souvenir. It was the thing that drove us apart—and brought us back together."

"You got it."

She kissed him with a combination of tenderness and hunger.

Precisely at eight o'clock Andrew escorted Olivia up the steps of Harold Greenway's imposing townhouse. A butler showed them into a handsome paneled room where several Victorian paintings were hanging in rather ostentatious lighting. The furniture was grand—almost too flamboyant for the setting—and the decorative objects, mostly art nouveau bottles and lamps, were just a little profuse. It was the lair of a man who had not collected by instinct but who was striving to impress. Greenway greeted them cordially, appearing to be utterly unfazed at seeing them together. They engaged in polite small talk over a glass of sherry. Dinner was proper, stodgy, and a shade overcooked.

"I have talked with Lord Richfield," Greenway said at last. "About your novel suggestion that once the hurly-burly of the sale is over we begin discreet discussions about some of his other art properties. I am relieved that you are not bringing up the Velázquez again. That seems to be settled, once and for all. Although, I hasten to add, I can't quite believe that you'll truly be out of the bidding. But that's your affair. Anyway, His Lordship has instructed me to inform you that his small Canaletto and the large Jacob Jordaens might become available. The Canaletto is valued at three million. And the Jordaens, a mere two million two hundred thousand."

Olivia looked at him without expression. She had to admire the sang-froid of the man.

Andrew frowned as if in minor vexation. "I believe I've seen the paintings in question in several publications. Excellent pictures. But I was hoping that the prices might be a little more realistic."

"I'm sorry," Greenway said sympathetically. "You see, these pictures have been in the family since the late eighteenth century. Now, such an illustrious provenance validates the prices—which are, I admit, slightly over the market."

"Not for me," Andrew replied with a sigh. "We might as well return to the issue of the Velázquez."

"I know this sounds silly," Olivia chimed in, "but before it's too late can't we still make some sort of special arrangement? Sell it to us? Andrew and I have joined forces. We'd like both our institutions to share the masterpiece. What we want is simple. The *Marchesa* that I saw."

Harold Greenway tilted his head back and laughed. "Forgive me, I'm not very good when it comes to American practical jokes. Please join me for coffee and port. I do hope you will forgive me . . . it has been a most trying week."

"Of course," Andrew said calmly. They retired to the sitting room, where the butler served them coffee and set down a bottle of port. "Mr. Greenway, do take the time to peruse this document, which I'd like you to sign before we leave."

Greenway waved off the paper Andrew held out to him. "All this has gone too far," he remarked evenly.

"Fine," Andrew said. "Then we'll just have to go public. You know from your employee Fielding that Olivia has got to the bottom of your conspiracy."

Greenway snatched the paper from Andrew's hand and read it

rapidly. "You actually have the temerity to demand that I sign my name to this flimsy document that forces me to return what you call the 'first' *Marchesa* to William's Ltd.?" His voice seemed to rise with each phrase.

"That's it, but there's more too," Olivia said in a low voice. "And you must give us the second version, the one now in the auction house."

"Preposterous! I know nothing about a 'first' or 'second' version."

"Difficult to believe, isn't it, Greenway?" Andrew remarked. "Our evidence is all circumstantial. Nothing more than the shifting winds of conjecture. But as an attorney, you must agree that's sometimes the best kind of evidence."

Greenway stared at him sourly.

"Here's how I figure it," Andrew went on. "You've gotten yourself into a few financial scrapes—possibly gambling, maybe girls."

"My gambling is serious, but not critical," Greenway cut in. "The girls I can easily afford."

Andrew started to speak, but was silenced by a wave of Greenway's hand. "You understand that there's no proof at all that I engineered a theft and then a substitution of my client's Spanish masterpiece . . ."

"None at all," Andrew replied.

"But if I don't sign this paper and manage to deliver the 'first' Velázquez to William's," Greenway reflected, "you will simply go to the Earl and tell him that one of you saw one *Marchesa*, a very beautiful one, and the other saw a replica."

Olivia eased into the conversation. "Yes. And at just about the same time Andrew is talking to Richfield, I will be holding a press conference at William's—on the morning of the reception the day before the sale—in front of the substitution and inform the world about it."

Greenway seemed not in the least concerned. With his hand held to his chin, he walked a tight circle in the middle of the room. "There's a flaw in your amateur scheme, don't you see it?"

Andrew cocked his head warily.

"If no one can find more than one painting depicting the Richfield Marchesa, who will believe you?" Greenway said.

"Oh, come on! The whole story has been carefully transcribed and is in the hands of my solicitor," Andrew said sharply. "He has instructions to break the news tonight unless . . .!"

Greenway shook his head slowly. "Habeas corpus. How can you prove the existence of the other body?" He looked up slyly.

"I can," Olivia said. "The first and second paintings are recorded in these photographs. These are prints. Andrew's solicitor has the original transparencies."

"Who'll believe this? You'd have to be an art expert to tell the two apart. This is a house of cards—about to fall."

"Stop stalling," Olivia said through clenched teeth. "Shown side by side—the photographs blown up to an enormous size—with the testimony of someone like Roy Bentley, our circumstantial evidence will prove telling. The press will have a field day. You'll go to jail."

"Precisely what do you want me to do?" Greenway asked sharply.

"First, take us to the real picture," Andrew commanded.

The building where Greenway had deposited the *Marchesa* had been well chosen, being two doors down from the delivery entrance at William's Ltd. The room where the picture was stored was on the first floor, and it was cozy, containing an easel covered by a linen drape, a series of spotlights, a large table, a telephone, a leather sofa, a number of comfortable armchairs, two nondescript Victorian landscapes on the walls, and a well-stocked bar in the corner.

"There she is. Switch on the lamps. There are several high-powered magnifying glasses in the drawer of the table."

They went about their examination swiftly.

"This has got to be the single most startling work of art I've ever encountered," Andrew said. "She's really alive. Majestic. Humble. Sexy. Defiant. Compliant. Dreamlike and utterly natural, all at the same time. Just like you told me, darling!"

"Remove the canvas from the frame," Olivia ordered.

"As you wish," Greenway replied.

In a minute Greenway, aided by Andrew, had removed the painting from its ornate gilded frame and set it on the easel. Andrew moved one of the spotlights around to the back. Thousands of holes lighted up through the fabric.

"Remarkable how thinly Velázquez painted, isn't it?" Andrew observed. "God, how rare to have a grand seventeenth-century painting that hasn't been relined! Olivia, show me the inscription."

"Here! It says: 'I, Velázquez, have for a fleeting moment of eternity again borrowed life from my goddess, my desire, and have given that life to dull paint. The 16th of June, 1650. Roma.' " She paused. "That's odd. What are these broad washes crisscrossing the back of the canvas? Are they varnish? Obviously recent. There seems to be hundreds of tiny white threads embedded in them." She turned to face Greenway with a puzzled expression on her face. "Was some sort of backing put on the painting?"

"No backing. What you see is the web with which I draw you in," he said in a sibilant whisper. "But unlike any other spider with its prey, I don't intend to eat you. I need you, as you need me. It is not checkmate, as you assume; merely a draw."

"I've had as much of this nonsense as I can stomach," Andrew burst out angrily. "Olivia, let's call the police and start Greenway on his way to Dartmoor to join William Fielding."

"But that could trigger a disaster," Greenway said softly, "an artistic disaster of monumental proportions, one that could make you two bright young people look like imbeciles."

"Greenway, you're bats," Andrew said, moving quickly toward the telephone. "The only responsible thing to do now is to get the original back at William's Ltd. so the auction can continue. And call the police."

Greenway laughed. "Before you bother Scotland Yard with such a fantasy, do me the favor, first, of listening to my proposition and watching an experiment. Examine that small landscape over there on the left wall. Remove it. Both of you. Hold it up to the spotlight."

Andrew was about to refuse, but he was suddenly made wary by Greenway's inexplicable calm. He plucked the canvas from the wall.

"Bring it here," Greenway said with a smile. "Turn it over. Olivia, you notice anything?"

"The exact same broad strokes of a sort of clear varnish. And dozens of tiny whitish filaments embedded in the varnish. What is this?''

''Now, Andrew, if you will,'' Greenway said solicitously, ''remove the little painting from its frame. Place the canvas in the grate of the fireplace.''

''We haven't all night for this little drama, Greenway.''

Greenway turned to Olivia with a faintly pained expression.

Grumbling, Andrew leaned the picture against one of the fire-dogs.

''Both of you, observe.'' Greenway pulled from his vest pocket what seemed to be a small calculator. He flourished it briefly before their eyes and then depressed one of half a dozen buttons.

The canvas in the grate burst into a blue flame—instantly—and just melted. It took less than a second. In ten seconds its wooden stretcher glowed, flamed, and was consumed.

Olivia gasped.

''My God!'' Andrew shouted. ''How the devil—?''

''The Richfield treasure, the world masterpiece, the glorious Marchesa Fiona Odescalchi,'' Greenway warned, ''will disappear in exactly the same way. Quicker!''

''Vandal!'' Olivia cried.

''Butcher!''

''Oh, come now,'' Greenway remarked with a shrug. ''The landscape fetched fifteen guineas at Christie's two weeks ago. I hardly think the world of art will long grieve its passing.''

''But you also wired the Velázquez, You . . . you . . . Oh, Jesus!'' Andrew shouted.

''Hush up!'' Greenway commanded. ''Yes, I did. And it will work, too. The device is as simple as one of those instruments that open garage doors. The radio impulse triggers the wires on the back of the painting—and *poof!*''

''Jesus!'' Andrew muttered.

''Calm down,'' Greenway said with a casual wave of a hand. ''Now listen.''

Andrew retreated to one of the overstuffed chairs and stared moodily at Greenway.

''Instead of moving pictures around all over again—this time I might get caught and the game would really be over—I suggest I agree to allow you to buy this picture, the original, for the reserve price of ten million."

"And then you'll incinerate it, I suppose."

"Not if you two follow my orders," Greenway said. "On the day of the sale, you—one or both—will hand over to me, for His Lordship, a registered check for ten million."

"And then?" Olivia asked.

"And then you'll have to bid—convincingly—on the copy of the *Marchesa*. Why? Someday I may have to explain to His Lordship why two pictures fetched less than double the one."

"Why don't you bid on it yourself?" Andrew asked.

Greenway suddenly erupted. "You may think you can toy with me, but you can't! I will destroy that masterpiece over there, and its destruction will be on your hands. I don't care a jot about it, but you do. You have chased after it, you will pay an enormous sum to preserve it for your public. Your very lives are at stake. I personally don't give a damn." He brandished the instrument which could cause Velázquez's gorgeous *Marchesa* to disappear in seconds "Believe me, this threat is real.

"I have nothing to lose. You do!" Greenway continued. "Through blind luck, you alone have the opportunity to secure a world masterpiece—without competition and for very little money. Why should you care if some doltish collector or imperceptive museum buys a copy of a Velázquez? Your obligation, I presume, is to find great treasures and secure them for your museums for the benefit of the general public. Everybody else be damned! Do what I say or I will burn the picture. And don't think others are not wired too!"

Olivia looked at Andrew frantically, imploring him not to goad the man, who seemed eager to carry out his threat.

"We give in," she said quickly. "But please . . . please consider making just one more switch. One more, so the original will be at the sale."

"I told you *no* once before. I am getting more than a little impatient with you, young lady."

"We give in," she repeated hastily.

"That's better," Greenway muttered almost to himself. "Now, here's the agreement. If the copy doesn't make the reserve, you will pay the full ten for the original. I shall tell His Lordship that I was able to find a buyer after the sale. I want you to feel satisfied about this arrangement."

"*Satisfied*?" Olivia cried. "About being party to a fraud?"

"It's your choice, you idealistic . . . you fool! Choose between what I am suggesting or the destruction of some of the most beautiful pictures on earth."

"All right," Olivia sighed.

"As an incentive and, of course, for your promise of eternal silence about this affair, I suggest . . . that for each million the copy sells over the reserve, I return to you half a million. If the copy goes for eleven, then I shall return to you half a million. If the copy reaches the incredible sum of fifteen million, then you get back—let's see—"

"Two million," Olivia interrupted, barely able to conceal a smile.

"Exactly."

Andrew glanced at Olivia and whispered, "This will crunch Roger Bass."

"What's that?" Greenway asked harshly.

"Nothing," Andrew said, shrugging. "I was simply saying that we've got no choice. Greenway, we've got you but you've got us. Unless we bid vigorously and thereby balloon the price of the copy, then we pay the full reserve. The more we bid, the less we have to pay! And with us bidding, the painting on the block—the copy—becomes even more desirable! Ingenious."

"It's agreed, then? After all, we all know what will happen if we fail to agree."

"Diabolical!" Andrew said. "When will you remove the incendiary material?"

"At the end of the sale. It is an agreement, then?"

Andrew looked at Olivia, who nodded.

"You have us," she said grimly.

"Agreed, dammit," Andrew muttered.

"Silence forever?" Greenway added silkily.

"Absolutely. On both sides?" Olivia asked.

"Assuredly," Greenway replied with a smile.

Olivia glanced at him, looking crestfallen. She turned away; only then did she smile.

24 THE EYES HAVE IT

THE VISIT TO NEW YORK was a whirlwind lasting a mere four days, but Olivia felt she had been wrung through every emotion she had ever experienced in her life—anxiety, surprise, tension, fear, futility, hopelessness, the wild release of triumph, and jubilation tempered by second thoughts. Andrew sailed through it, barely ruffled. He raised ten million dollars and received permission from his patron Jonathan Cresson to share the Velázquez with the Metropolitan. For Olivia, her task was not unlike guerrilla warfare.

The conference room on the second floor of the Metropolitan Museum of Art traditionally used to decide upon new acquisitions was far from impressive. The table seated comfortably no more than eight. The room was decorated with appropriate sobriety, its walls painted the middle tones of gray with a tinge of lavender, a color believed to make most paintings seem more striking than they really are. But on the morning of the special meeting of the august acquisitions committee, there were no paintings or prints. Olivia had removed the Sisley landscape, the Monet *Peonies*, and the tiny Georgia O'Keeffe semi-abstract study of a white farmhouse that normally graced the room. She preferred austerity. It symbolized attention to duty.

At precisely nine thirty the members of the committee filed into the room, led by Ayn Steyne. The six men seated themselves like a judicial body at predetermined places at the table. Their positions, according to museum custom, never varied. Steyne, as chairperson of the board and ex-officio voting member of the committee, assumed the head of the table. Along the right side—in order of strict seniority—were Richard Baxter, a collector of Oriental porcelains, and J. Perry Wheeler, a financier and proud possessor of what most professionals agreed was the finest private collection of John Singer Sargents in America. At the end, opposite Steyne, sat Harry Wintermayer, an elderly (and canny) collector of English furniture, and Amos Fischbach, a painfully shy great-grandson of the founder of one of Wall Street's most illustrious firms and a collector of African art. On the left side of the table were Grant Osgood, who despite never having donated a penny to the museum in the fifteen years he had been on the board, was considered vital to its future because of the hope that he would eventually give even a morsel from a collection of Old Masters universally reckoned to be the finest still in private hands. Finally there was George Frothingham IV, a portly man in his early forties and a fancier of arms and armor, Greek and Roman antiquities, late Egyptian art—and power.

Olivia sat just to the left and slightly behind Ayn Steyne. Only one other person had been allowed in the room: Roland McCrae, who, while not an official member, had been granted the right as a former president to attend any museum committee he wished with rights to speak, but not to vote. Of course, everyone had always interpreted his spoken displeasure as tantamount to a veto.

Ayn Steyne opened the hearing by reading rapidly the requisite preamble.

"In compliance with paragraph eight of chapter one of the constitution and bylaws of this museum, I hereby initiate this executive session of the acquisitions committee. As you all know, in executive session all proceedings are to be kept confidential. Only notes will be kept, and I, as custom dictates, hereby indicate to you that I shall do so personally. These minutes may never be published."

She glanced around the room noting the perfunctory nods from the members.

"Thank you, I have a quorum. I have your formal assent. Now let the meeting commence." Steyne leaned forward and with a tight smile said crisply, "All right. Enough of formalities. These affairs are intended to be as frank and informative as possible. Our acting director has important news for you today about the Velázquez. Olivia."

Roland McCrae's watery eyes glinted malevolently.

"Thank you, Madame Chairperson," Olivia said. "I have for

everyone a folder containing black-and-white photographs of the painting, some facts about its history, as well as a transcript of my impressions after examining the painting in London. The transcript contains, in addition, a comparison of the *Marchesa Odescalchi* with all other surviving paintings by Diego Velázquez—and especially, of course, our own *Juan de Pareja*. I would like to direct myself to two matters—quality and money. How does this painting compare in quality to his other masterpieces? And, at the price it will probably bring, is it worth it?"

"I understand it's going to be a frightful price—something approaching eight million," J. Perry Wheeler blurted out in his wheezing voice. "What about that?"

"I suggest we put that matter aside for a moment," Olivia said brusquely.

She then launched into a rapid monologue that seemed to jerk each member of the committee up in his seat as if he had been yanked by strings. She was pleased that her deliberately blunt delivery had produced the desired effect. They might not like her for it, but they were damn well going to have to listen to her.

She had carefully studied the expressions of each member as they had filed in and glanced at her, seeing her for the first time since she had transformed herself. The reactions had been surprise and admiration. Amos Fischbach seemed floored when he turned the corner into the conference room and looked straight into her face. The others seemed to be more attentive than she had ever remembered them being. All except Roland McCrae, who assumed an air of studied nonchalance.

"Gentlemen, I shall not indulge in dramatics or histrionics," Olivia continued. "We all know what we are facing; you don't need emotion from me—just analysis."

Hearing these words, Harry Wintermayer prepared himself for a spell of theatrics and high emotionalism. Good. Great art needs great passion. How attractive she'd become, he mused. Although McCrae had convinced him to reject the picture, he just might change his mind. She was so vibrant, brimming with confidence and energy. What he'd give to be forty!

"Our great museum," Olivia went on, "has in its hundred and twenty-six years of existence invariably had the courage to acquire the greatest works of art, the finest pieces by the most illustrious artists of all time, works that stand on the veritable summit of artistic achievement, that sum up entire epochs of civilization or the entire spectrum of a master's creative life, that have inspired other artists and exalted the common man, works that are bright shining lamps of beauty, grace, and humanity.''

Roland McCrae shifted uneasily in his chair, wondering if he shouldn't attempt to look a little more interested. Amos Fischbach, who obviously had been knocked head over teakettle by Olivia's flashy appeal, had glanced down at him and, seeing his casual attitude, had scowled. But worse, McCrae saw she had won over Harry Wintermayer. The old boy sat mesmerized. But he concluded that to change his strategy would be to show weakness. So he determinedly maintained his pose of nonchalance. It didn't matter what they thought of him. His surprise witness would destroy Olivia Cartright's little show.

"And the *Marchesa Odescalchi*," Olivia said after a slight pause to look into the eyes of each member of the committee, "is all of that. It is one of the most beautiful, compelling, and human portraits ever painted. Not just to have survived, I say, but *ever painted*. It possesses a magnetic vitality, a universal comprehension of everything that womankind stands for. The *Marchesa* is the finest example of the creations of a historic genius, its sublimity unsurpassed. The moment you contemplate this human being, she is alive, breathing, sentient, thrilling. This is a portrait of someone Veláz- quez loved dearly, a masterpiece that ranks with the top five portraits in all history. And . . . it can be ours. Not without struggle or painful sacrifice. We are going to have to stretch our existing re- sources to a point beyond any we have conceived of before. But the effort will be worth it. The acquisition of such a masterpiece is an opportunity that might not come again in a dozen lifetimes."

When the meeting had begun, Grant Osgood, as usual, wished he were somewhere else. Or at least he had come to the meeting with a familiar sour feeling. Although he had never shared his thoughts, Osgood despised the political way the Metropolitan chose its purchases and decided upon what gifts to accept. Quality seemed the least of its criteria. Never had the curators of the insti- tution—and most certainly its jellyfish of a former director—

seemed eager to pursue only those precious few, triumphant things. All they wanted was what was acceptable to the consensus of curators, none of whom knew anything about any moment of history other than his or her own. In all his years on the board Osgood had opened his mouth no more than half a dozen times. On each occasion he had mildly criticized a work of art about to be purchased for an amount exceeding a quarter of a million dollars. It had thus been assumed that Grant Osgood was, in the words of the museum's treasurer, "taciturn, myopic, and cheap." His presence on the board and the acquisitions committee was tolerated only because anyone who owned four matchless Rubens oil sketches could be as taciturn, myopic, and cheap as he pleased.

When Olivia had started her speech, Osgood had sat leafing through the file, hoping to kill time. When he saw the painting he grunted with pleasure. How majestic! The hoopla in the press was, for once, justified. When the news of the auction of the "masterpiece" had first burst on the front pages, Osgood had automatically pooh-poohed the publicity. Looking at the photos, he ruefully admitted to himself how mistaken he had been. Finally something to struggle for, to spend the institution dry for! At that instant Osgood decided to make the first donation to the museum in his life. He sat immobile, waiting for the perfect moment to let his fellow members know of his largesse. He smiled to himself just thinking about how astonished they would be.

When Richard Baxter heard Olivia say ". . . great effort," he flinched. Obviously they were going to ask for donations and he was going to be trapped. How to look generous without having to spend a dime? His real estate empire was on the verge of collapse, and a pledge of even a hundred thousand dollars toward the painting—what Baxter figured would be the lowest possible offering any committee member could make with any dignity at all—would break him. Oh, God, what would he do? He was about to be exposed in the cruelest forum of all. What humiliation!

J. Perry Wheeler, who had been picking up rumors about Baxter's difficulties refinancing a routine debt, had been watching him surreptitiously and had not missed his reaction. He made a note to phone his broker as soon as the meeting was over and instruct him to dump from his real estate portfolio any property remotely linked to Baxter's companies. And Wheeler, too, began to calculate how much he would have to kick in for the painting. It was, of course, purely a question of prestige—an amount which would depend purely upon what that droopy bastard Amos Fischbach finally decided to come up with. Wheeler looked forward to embarrassing his younger opponent by giving more. The meeting was finally getting to be interesting—and to Wheeler's eye the painting wasn't so bad either, not that he really cared that much about art. But here was a painting he could understand—the young woman looked as if she was about to embrace a lover. Wheeler loathed any work of art without an explicit motif.

"But before I turn to financial specifics," Olivia sped on, "I must sum up my feelings about the picture, and the simplest way to do that is to tell you who else wants it. Everybody! Unlike other important works we've tried to acquire over the years, here we don't have just one or possibly two competitors. With a little sleuthing we have learned of at least eight competitors—the Getty, the National Gallery in London, the Louvre, the Prado, the Cleveland Museum (at least until the untimely death of the director), the Soviet Union (and that is gospel!), plus two private collectors, Robert Symes and Kurt Krassner of Germany."

Harry Wintermayer had been listening to Olivia with growing fascination until he heard the name Symes. He shook his head. Not true, he thought, Bob's out. Told me he's scared of the publicity. Wait! Could he be lying?

Olivia went into a detailed explanation about how the bidding would be conducted in increments of one hundred thousand pounds, virtually equivalent to dollars. Then, lowering her voice, she said, "And I think I know what some of those bids will be."

The private collectors, she asserted, would bid high, but probably not high enough—in the area of eight million pounds.

George Frothingham IV fingered his pocket calculator for a few seconds and looked up in alarm. The museum would have to go into debt for fifteen years to raise anything near that!

"And that's not going to make it," Olivia said calmly. "We have it on good authority that the Prado will go to three million dollars, the Louvre to as much as thirteen, and—Dr. Foster's press announcement notwithstanding—the National Gallery of Art has been promised at least ten by Jonathan Cresson."

It seemed for an instant that every member of the committee stopped breathing.

"May I pose a small question?" Amos Fischbach asked in a high-pitched voice. "Olivia, how do you go about obtaining such specific information as this? I mean, are you sure? How can one penetrate the security of the National Gallery in Washington?"

"If you keep your ears close to the ground, the true story always emerges," she said blandly, and explained that someone would always talk about what their institution was planning to do—mostly just to indicate to other people that they were on the inner track.

Outwardly Frothingham seemed to be pleased. He even nodded his head as he listened to the figures. But his mind was seething. The top bid coming to an astounding $13 million? That was madness! He'd vote this one down, for sure. Christ!

As soon as Olivia had finished her analysis of the bids, Roland McCrae waved his hand casually over the table, leaned forward in his chair, and asked silkily. "Would it be permissible, Madame Chairman, for me to say just a little word or two?"

Olivia smiled to herself. She had been wondering when he was going to strike. His timing was perfect—as usual. But she wasn't concerned. She knew she had made progress, even with the crusty Frothingham, who in earlier meetings had tended to block any purchase over $2 million. Judging by his benign smile, she was almost certain she had won him over.

"I admire the director's zeal and ability to lift us up to her levels of enthusiasm so swiftly," McCrae said with an ingratiating smile. "But I suggest a moment or two of deacceleration . . . reflection. Wouldn't another opinion be fitting? Another's expertise—genuine expertise—in this difficult field?"

Olivia at first thought that McCrae's interjection had lost him a few points. But she was wrong. McCrae had actually gained points. He had insulted her in such a reassuring tone and had smiled so engagingly that the majority of the committee members nodded their assent. Which expert would he quote?

"Splendid," McCrae went on. "I thought it wise to take the precaution of enlisting a world-renowned scholar to give his opinion about the painting. That individual is here right now—standing by."

"Standing by?" Olivia was flabbergasted. Should she interrupt and ask Steyne to overrule him? Olivia thought of pleading that the issue of whether or not to bid for the *Marchesa* was too complex, too much of a secret, for an outsider. But as quickly as she had thought of it, she realized she could not. Not knowing who the expert was, she was outmaneuvered. And there was always the slim chance that McCrae had blundered by calling in someone sympathetic to her.

"Olivia, surely you would not object to Sir Michael Fairless making a brief appearance before this committee as an expert witness," McCrae said with a sly smile.

At first Olivia couldn't believe what she had heard. Michael Fairless, the director of the Warburg Institute and a world authority on Spanish painting in its golden age, was really about to walk into the conference room and make some sort of statement about the Velázquez? She became alert, all her senses sharpened. Her instinct goaded her to reveal what Don Ciccio had told her about him, that Sir Michael, a cherished member of the British establishment, was, and had been for years, an espionage agent in the service of the Soviet Union, the unknown "fifth man" in the Philby-Blunt conspiracy of traitors.

But that would be the worst possible move. No one would believe her unless she could lay out on the table every fact—and name her source. And that she couldn't do. So Olivia found herself having to smile like a Renaissance Madonna and meekly reply that she was "honored by the arrival of a worthy colleague."

McCrae excused himself and returned to shepherd in the dour-faced, aristocratic scholar. Fairless smiled with slightly pursed lips and stood with his arms hanging down like tethers as McCrae extolled him as "the most experienced expert in Spanish painting of the seventeenth century in the world today and who has recently examined the painting of the Marchesa Odescalchi."

If ever there was a moment to attack, this was it. But how? Olivia thought. Fairless was the most formidable opponent McCrae could possibly have rounded up and he had no idea why. McCrae thought Fairless would carry the day because he was British, distinguished, and the possessor of a knighthood. Not because he had been hired to bad-mouth the painting. She had to do something!

When Sir Michael approached the head of the table, Olivia rose to her feet swiftly, thrust her hand out, and stared at him with a penetrating coldness, trying to impart as much enmity through her eyes as she could. He was shaken. Then, as if she were about to peck him on the cheek—a gesture which made him even more nervous—she whispered in his ear, "I know that you are working for the Soviets. I can prove it. Be careful. I want the painting. I will chop you to bits."

Sir Michael Fairless barely reacted and managed to take his seat with dignity. McCrae then urged him to present his views. With a curt nod he began.

"Of course, any painting that appears on the market that can legitimately be ascribed to the great master Velázquez is bound to excite us all. In the past two decades there have been, other than this, only two, the jester holding the glass, purchased by the Cleveland Museum, and your own *Juan de Pareja*. Both are estimable works. The jester was sold privately for five hundred and fifty thousand dollars. And you, as you know, spent what was then the highest sum ever paid for a seventeenth-century picture. The *Marchesa* is comparable. But it has attracted its share of detractors. Some have reflected—and I among them—that perhaps a responsible public institution might do well to consider if any painting is worth as much as it is rumored this one might fetch—from twelve to as much as fifteen million dollars."

Amos Fischbach, impressed by the dignity of the scholar, asked, "Sir Michael, would you advise that we just rest on the laurels of our *Juan de Pareja*? I mean, since we already have the best."

McCrae noted wonderingly that these were the first intelligent-sounding words he'd ever heard from the young idiot. Sir Michael had been about to agree, but had made the error of glancing into Olivia's eyes for a second. He became flustered. Ayn Steyne's keen eye had detected the exchange. Something was about to happen, but what?

"Not . . . necessarily," Fairless said, and hesitated.

Roland McCrae coughed into a handkerchief.

Fairless turned to look at McCrae and once more caught the fire in Olivia's eyes. He began to stumble.

"But, it is, after all, a matter of personal opinion. The Richfield

Velázquez is . . . an interesting painting and, uh, seems to me to be the original, as Dr. Cartright no doubt may have already told you in detail. There are said to be some four versions of the image in all, two frontal, two from the back. In the best work of the master one element is paramount. And that is the treatment of the eyes. The eyes must be piercingly clear, yet rendered with a seeming swiftness that can make them, up close, seem rather sketchy."

McCrae, who had started to shift uncomfortably in his chair, could no longer restrain himself. "Sir Michael, what does all this mean?"

Fairless appeared to have lost his bearings for several seconds. Then he continued in a subdued voice. "I have studied the eyes of this young woman . . ."

The eyes? For Christ's sake, thought Wheeler, Fischbach, and Wintermayer as one.

". . . and I must say . . . although this is, of course, a personal opinion . . . that, well, the impression of that sharp gaze through exceedingly clear eyes is, uh, perhaps a bit . . . I suppose the word 'clouded' is not totally inadequate."

At this, Fairless raised his hand to his brow and gazed absently down the length of the table.

"Sir Michael, should we bother buying this terribly expensive thing?" George Frothingham IV inquired impatiently.

The elderly expert could not avoid looking at Olivia. "Well, uh . . . of course, it is a decision that only you can come to in the wisdom of your deliberations. But if it were up to me, I, uh . . . I'd examine the consequences fully."

"That is exactly what we intend to do, Sir Michael," Olivia interjected harshly. She looked at every member of the committee and said, "You are seeing for yourselves why Sir Michael is not considered decisive in scholarly circles. Anyway, his quavering, personal biases about quality and value have nothing to do with what you—as the most responsible members of the institution—should do about the painting or our need to have it or our courage to acquire it. I personally resent the intrusion into this traditionally highly confidential matter of a man who is not only incorrect but deliberately lying."

"I object to this disgusting display of rudeness," Roland McCrae shouted. "Madame Chairman, discipline this—this impudent—!"

Ayn Steyne, who recognized very well the beginnings of a victory march, scowled at McCrae and looked coolly at Olivia as if to say, It's for you to prove. If you fail, you're dead.

Olivia gave Steyne a curt nod. "Excuse me for a few brief moments. Fairless spoke about the eyes—the key element of the eyes. Let me show you those eyes. Clandestinely—yes, secretly and without authorization—I used what I suppose you'd call a spy camera to take photographs of the face of the Marchesa. It was stupid of me not to have taken more. But, as you'll see, the proof of quality is indisputable."

The instant Olivia had departed Roland McCrae, with an equanimous smile, turned to Fairless. "Sir Michael, tell the committee what you told me yesterday."

The scholar sat frozen in place.

"You said clearly, and I paraphrase, 'You'd be fools to spend much time or money on this overrated masterpiece.' I do believe you said that."

The members of the committee, embarrassed, looked away from the pair.

Olivia returned and set up a slide projector, then dimmed the lights. The first slide appeared on the far wall. It was but a tiny part of the woman's beautiful face. At first, singly, the slides were meaningless fragments. But after projecting all six, once slowly and then again, explaining the details, the committee could get some idea of the burning intensity of the eyes of the Marchesa and the startling beauty of her image.

Olivia used the dimmer for the lights so that the slow crescendo of illumination came as a dramatic climax to her brief but powerful presentation.

Staring fixedly at Sir Michael Fairless, Olivia said softly, almost sympathetically, "There! The eyes have it. Clarity, beauty, brilliance. And, dammit, the rest of the painting is even better."

An electric silence had taken over the room. Again and again Ayn Steyne said to herself, Finish him off!

"Sir Michael," Olivia asked deferentially, "would you care to inform the committee whether or not you are working—in the matter of the *Marchesa*—for someone else, some other institution?"

"I . . . I am at the Warburg, a research institute. We have no desire to purchase works of art."

"Not the Warburg? Who are your clients? The ones to whom, I'll bet, you gave a glowing report of the painting."

The scholar, utterly crushed, cradled his head in his hands. Olivia dismissed him with a wave of her hand. All McCrae could do was to see his guest to the door, none too graciously. McCrae started to speak, but Olivia cut him off sharply.

"The Metropolitan is a very great institution now," she began. "With both the *Juan de Pareja* and the *Marchesa*, it will be sublime."

Grant Osgood cleared his throat loudly and started to speak in a penetrating monotone.

"For years I have silently suffered through deliberations of this committee on works of art that were no better than 'fair.' But now I want my voice to be heard. This Velázquez is the finest work I have ever seen—finer than the *Juan de Pareja*, which was itself a singular moment. But this! Unparalleled! I think we have an obligation to vote for its acquisition and address ourselves smartly to the business of raising the necessary funds—even if it comes to the astonishing amount of ten or twelve million—whatever it takes! When will we ever see its equal? We've got to move. And I should like to help—in a modest way, of course."

"Grant, I want to thank you for your timely and helpful words," McCrae said mellifluously. "But this is serious business. I may have made an error with Sir Michael. Of course, I had no idea . . . But I was, and am, trying to maintain a balance, trying to prevent the museum from acting rashly."

"But aren't we supposed to be seeking the best?" Osgood asked steadily. "I, for one, am willing to help as much as I can."

"I thank you, kind sir," McCrae responded with a supercilious smile. "But perhaps that won't be necessary."

It was another terrible blunder. McCrae in his wildest imaginings could not have dreamed of Osgood's response—nor could any of the others, except perhaps for Perry Wheeler, who winced at McCrae's patronizing words and unctuous tone of voice and said to himself, Old Grant isn't going to suffer that fool too long! The explosion came from deep within Osgood and grew in intensity. The museum would never be the same. Years later they were still laughing at what came to be known as "the avalanche."

"McCrae, will you have the kindness to shut the fuck up?" Osgood retorted in a cracked whisper. "By the constitution and by-laws of this place you shouldn't be speaking. As a matter of fact, you shouldn't even be in this room. And you, Ayn Steyne, as chairperson, shouldn't allow this kind of nonsense to go on. Under your biased leadership and the actions of that idiot of a director you dredged from some stew in England, in the past decade this museum has acquired the most mediocre junk imaginable. But now we're going to change all that."

Roland McCrae was nothing if not an experienced guerrilla in the never-ending wars that take place in the halls and boardrooms of every art museum. Interpreting Osgood's outburst as either self-defeating eccentricity or madness and fully expecting the man's vulgarity would destroy him, McCrae put on his best act. He smiled genially, almost as if Osgood had just presented him with an award for cultural excellence.

"I understand how passions can flare up in a discussion of works of art that happen to appeal to one personally. Mr. Osgood, in my time I suppose I've gotten excitable too. Now, I am trying to maintain balance. If I may be permitted to say so, I've hardly found your record of monetary support for this museum very encouraging."

"Oh, buzz off, McCrae," Osgood said. He looked over at Olivia. "From what I gather, thirteen or fourteen million will win the Velázquez. Right?"

"Fourteen will do it," she said firmly.

"So let's raise the fourteen," Osgood continued. "From my calculations the museum has about three million in purchase funds. Add to that another three million which we can take out of the Fletcher Fund, even though it was given some eighty years ago with the wish that we never spend more than one-third of the principal, my suggestion is that we use it all and repay it with income from the Rogers Fund over, say, fifteen years. That makes six million. Only eight to go."

"Very good, Mr. Osgood, I see you can do sums," Roland McCrae said sarcastically. "But can you also add?" At this he looked around, with a wink, assuming others would share his joke, but no one was looking at him.

"McCrae, that's the first attempt at a joke I've ever heard from you. My pledge—and surprise! I will make one!—is quite blatantly intended as a bribe. I'll give three million in cash toward the *Marchesa* . . ." Osgood paused.

A stunned silence ensued.

". . . on two conditions. One, that the committee at least match my pledge and, two, that Roland McCrae resign from this board of trustees as an 'emeritus' or anything else. Gets out and *stays* out! Soon I've got to make the decision where to leave my collection; it'll probably go to the institution which demonstrates the most guts. I reckon my collection today is worth . . . oh, roughly, fifty to sixty million. What do you say?"

The silence was broken by a braying laugh from Harry Wintermayer.

"I confess I have looked down on Mr. Grant Osgood. I interpreted his perennial silence as bad manners or ignorance. I have been gravely mistaken. I apologize to you, Osgood. I admire your guts. And now I'd like to make a pledge of half a million. I wish it could be more. My conditions are the same as Osgood's. Rolie, it's time to move on."

Roland McCrae's face paled. His voice broke as he rose to his feet and addressed the committee.

"So that is the measure of the regard and the thanks I get for guiding and counseling this great institution so selflessly for so many years. Osgood, you are an egotistical, twisted man. As for you, Harry, 'Et tu Brute.' Ah, but in time you will all look back on this sad day when you ignored my advice and you will recognize your fatal error."

"Unless you're going to make a pledge, McCrae, I suggest you get the hell out of this meeting. *Now*," Osgood growled.

McCrae glared at him and at every member of the committee. Then he stalked, stiff-legged, from the room, closing the door very gently. Even in defeat, museum decorum had to be maintained.

Ayn Steyne rose to her feet and studied the group. "As your chairman I may not always have acted with the proper degree of leadership. I have been—and still am—undecided about this painting, especially at the outrageous prices we're hearing. And, as some of you also know, I have not always been totally supportive of our acting director. But, Olivia, your presentation today was top-notch—particularly in the face of that awkward encounter. I am pleased to make a pledge of a quarter of a million dollars. I too have a condition."

Olivia groaned to herself. Here it comes. Andrew would be handed her job.

"My condition is that this committee elect Olivia Alexis Cartright the eleventh director of the Metropolitan Museum of Art—the first 'battlefield commission' in our illustrious history and so well earned." Steyne turned to Olivia. "I've wanted to do this for such a long time, my dear."

"Move it!" shouted Grand Osgood.

"Second," cried Amos Fischbach.

A chorus of "ayes" filled the room.

"Elected!" said Ayn Steyne.

It had happened so suddenly that Olivia lost her composure. "You don't have to . . . I won't . . ." She turned away from the others and had to work hard to hold back tears. When finally she could speak, she said demurely, "I accept —oh, with so much plea-sure."

"Done!" Osgood barked. "Now let's get the rest of the money. The Wintermayer and Steyne pledges makes it only four and a quarter to go. He studied the faces of those members who had remained silent. "Come on, gentlemen. Time to ante up."

"I'll go for two hundred and fifty," Frothingham said with a wry smile.

"Me too," Wheeler said with a shrug, looking right into Fischbach's eyes.

Fischbach gulped. "I guess me too." Damn! he thought. That prick Wheeler faked me out.

"Great! Only three million, five hundred thousand to go," Osgood chimed in.

Richard Baxter lowered his eyes and flushed. Then with a calm smile he said, "Put me down for a quarter of a million." As he uttered the words his mind was racing. How brilliant! That should dampen the rumors. Anyway, what difference would it make? In a week or two he'd be destitute. Might as well go out with a little panache. At Baxter's announcement, Wheeler crossed out on his memo pad his earlier reminder and jotted, "Buy shares in Baxter Corp." He ought to be able to purchase the empire for nothing and send the bastard to the poorhouse!

"Three and a quarter more," Osgood called out like an auctioneer. What about it, Madame Chairman?"

Ayn Steyne seemed to shudder slightly and shook her head no.

"It's only money, for Christ's sake," Wheeler blurted out. "Count me in for another million."

A quarter more from me," Fischbach said.

"That leaves us short only two million," Osgood grunted in resignation. "Well, good try, a damn good try, but I guess that's what we can bid."

"It's not enough!" Olivia cried out. "We *must* have the painting. Now listen, please. There *is* a way. It will take courage, but it will solve the problems of our lack of money and the likelihood of a great deal of bad press over the stupendous price the picture is sure to bring. We could buy the picture in partnership with the National Gallery of Art in Washington and share it, so that millions more people can see it. After all, we both want it. A partnership will save us money initially. With two determined bidders working together at the auction, the *Marchesa* could easily go for, say, only ten million."

"I know the National Gallery is interested," Ayn Steyne said. "Jonathan Cresson telephoned me last night and said that if we wanted to enter a partnership, he'd agree."

"Olivia, permit me to say that it's a creative concept, but am I correct in interpreting your true feelings about this kind of deal? You aren't personally convinced are you?" asked George Frothingham IV.

"Of course I'd much rather have it all for ourselves," she said. "And, who knows, we might," she added, so softly that no one heard her.

"What's the wish of the chair?" Fischbach asked.

"I'm dead set against joint purchases," Steyne replied. "What you have to realize is that in order to create the partnership, both sides must be able to raise an amount that will slightly exceed the knockdown price, say, fourteen million. In addition, half of whatever the winning bid is must be set aside by each institution for at least fifteen years as a special fund in case either institution wants to buy out the other. That is Mr. Cresson's wish. And we just don't have the fourteen million."

"I've got it!" Olivia exclaimed. "Here!" She waved a letter in the air. "From the Guardian Foundation."

The message from the foundation stated its intention to pledge the sum of $2 million toward the purchase of the *Marchesa* by the Museum and the National Gallery, with the absolute understanding that the strategy of the bidding and the precise bid be decided by Olivia Cartright and Andrew Foster—alone—on the day of the sale. Further, if the painting was sold to another party at the auction the funds raised by the Metropolitan had to be used for other purchases designated by Olivia Cartright.

"Isn't this all getting out of hand? What the hell is the Guardian Foundation?" J. Perry Wheeler asked, wheezing.

"A 501C-3 foundation," Olivia said, "which Bruce Thompson just set up. Exclusively for the Metropolitan."

"Thompson?"

"Jesus!"

"I'll be damned!"

"What the hell, we'll accept his money."

"Is it legal?"

"Absolutely."

"Will all this work?"

"I believe it will work," Olivia responded. "If we win, I suggest we exchange the painting every four years— assuming, of course, the condition warrants it. I'm sure it does. To be certain, every four years the conservators of each institution shall make a recommendation in writing as to whether or not the exchange should continue for another four years. If not, we should pay up our half of the cost of the painting and get full possession."

"Let's do it," Amos Fischbach muttered. "I move it."
"Second," Wintermayer added quickly.

A second chorus of "ayes" filled the room. Once the vote had been completed the members all came up to shake Olivia's hand and wish her well. When they had left, Ayn Steyne placed her hand awkwardly on Olivia's shoulder.

"That was a powerful performance. I've seldom seen the like of it, in business or in Congress. Will you ever be able to forgive me for my behavior these past months?"

Olivia studied her face intently. "No," she replied. "Ayn, if you were so moved by my actions, why didn't you put up the final money at the critical moment? You're so rich, you wouldn't have missed the money."

"Of course I could easily have given more. I didn't, out of pure pique. I'm not sure if I shouldn't follow poor Roland."

"You should," Olivia said quietly.

"Bruce gave two million dollars? Amazing. But why?"

"To spite you. Bruce gave it to me as a kind of wedding present. 'Funny money, to be spent in one place,' he told me."

"Do you really intend to bid in person at the auction?" Steyne asked. "Wouldn't it be more prudent to call in a professional representative? According to museum regulations, you're not allowed, actually."

"Break them," Olivia replied coldly. "I'll handle the bidding."

"But we've never allowed a staff member . . ." Steyne protested. "I mean, for someone not used to the pace of the high-powered sale room . . ."

"I shall do it, and that's that."

"But you have no experience. Sometimes these affairs can get very frightening."

"Only I can do it. And I no longer scare easily," were Olivia's parting words.

25 FACE-DOWN

THE RECEPTION at William's Ltd. the evening before the sale of the *Marchesa* was, even the competition frankly agreed, the most glittering that any auction house had held in half a century. Sir Peter greeted each one of his four hundred guests personally and spent most of the evening wandering among his list of "finalists," pumping them up in various subtle ways. The general feeling was that the portrait looked ravishing, though it was installed in a rather peculiar manner—high up in the center of a proscenium arch built into a wall of the famous hexagonal sale room and bathed in theatrical spotlights. A few self-appointed cognoscenti muttered that the varnish appeared to have bloomed, making the picture look a bit hazy. But no matter, that would soon be remedied once the picture was thoroughly cleaned after the sale.

"She's smashing, I'll admit it. But surely not nearly in the vicinity of twelve million pounds, Peter," the British art critic Armand Hollingshead complained in his soft, quavering voice. "Bet you a weekend in Cannes that you'll never make it!"

"Taken, Mandy," Grundy replied.

Robert Symes peered up at the painting and decided to elevate his bid two increments.

Roy Bentley pointedly ignored it.

Andrew and Olivia kept their distance from each other, having decided to dissimulate until the last. They pretended to bump into each other by chance in front of the painting.

"Greenway was right," he whispered. "The copy looks great! Caveat emptor, Roger Bass! But you're much prettier," he whispered. "Marry me tomorrow, after the sale?"

"You might not want to," she said. "Frankly, I don't think much of it. I tend to agree with those rumors I heard a few weeks ago that the thing was . . . well, flat, a bit muted."

"Yeah, I heard that some dumb museum director even thought this was a copy."

"Now that *is* dumb," Olivia said.

"I can't believe that stodgy committee of yours not only voted you the directorship but coughed up fourteen million! Pretty good. That gives you a lot to fiddle around with when you really hit the big time!"

"Enough for two," she replied with a secret smile.

"Who do you think will win the thing? God, I hope it's Roger Bass!" He chuckled. "Watch it. Here comes Kurt Krassner. Let's toy with him."

"Herr Foster, why are you here? I thought you had bowed out. Like me."

Andrew cocked his head. "You too have decided not to bid?" Andrew asked in surprise. "Herr Krassner, that doesn't sound like you at all."

"Sadly, yes," the German said with an elaborate sigh. "I have come to the conclusion that the painting—no matter how attractive —will be far too expensive for me. I am, after all, merely a beginner. Anyway, I have heard from certain experts," he said, looking at them slyly, "that there is something . . . peculiar about it. Although it seems striking enough now. I promise you, I'm out. So I leave the field to you," Krassner concluded cordially, and wandered away after kissing Olivia's hand.

"What do you suppose that meant?" Andrew asked. "And a hand kiss too. How pompous!"

"Damn. He's lying. He'll be in."

"Why do you say damn? I call it good. Less money we have to spend."

'True," she hastened to add. "Look at them all! The sharks are gathering." Olivia quickly changed the subject. "Baron von Thurn is in the next room chatting with Lord Richfield. He'll be in the thick of it."

"I saw Jules Bramet at the bar."

"Marvelous!"

"And Philippe le Grand. I hope he'll bid his conceited heart out."

"This will bring joy to your heart," she managed to whisper to him before they had to break away from each other. "There's a plump, gorgeous woman who looks Russian to me. And would you recognize Bass if you saw him?"

"He's here somewhere, heavily disguised," Andrew replied, muffling a laugh. "This is going to be great. All these characters—all helping us!"

The potential bidders were easy to spot. They paid homage to the painting, all the while maintaining poker faces.

Richard Warner, the art auction columnist for the Paris *Herald Tribune*, made his rounds, tailing every likely bidder, scribbling down every word he got, especially the flowery disclaimers. He overheard—and dismissed—the wave of denials issued by Kurt Krassner and his two aides, who were working the room like politicians. Philippe le Grand snubbed him, which he took as an affirmative sign.

The director of the Bavarian National Museums refused to comment, but did say that he was surprised ("furious" would have been more accurate) to encounter his colleague, the director of the State Gallery in Berlin. Both in early—and out early, Warner figured. He eagerly sought an interview with Ludmilla Tcherninka, the Soviet Minister of Culture and the director of the Pushkin Museum in Moscow. He was astonished to see the Soviet Union represented for the first time in modern history. He was not quite sure what to make of her statement that she would "most certainly not be bidding for something so wildly expensive" as the Velázquez, but was present only to study "Western auction-house techniques."

The director of Boston's Museum of Fine Art, Irving Fellows, blabbered on about the unfair way that Lord Richfield "deliberately kept every serious scholar from his picture." Warner put him in his "not serious" category. He sneaked up to Robert Symes and got a rise out of the millionaire by asking, "What's this I hear about poor Jim Waters of Cleveland placing a high sealed bid just before he died?" Symes sputtered and told him that "James was a fine scholar, but not much of a spender." Jules Bramet, upon seeing Warner edging toward him, fled.

To his surprise, Warner spotted Andrew Foster and Olivia Cartright exchanging agitated whispered comments to each other as they stood in front of the picture. They looked like lovers. Aha, the rumors were right. But as a good reporter must, he dismissed the peripheral issue from his mind. When he got to Olivia, she smiled and told him she couldn't say anything about her intentions. Andrew Foster was cryptic. "If I get involved, it'll only be from the sidelines." Now what the hell did that mean, Warner wondered. Roy Bentley had to be lying when he stated that "the one picture we already have of this young lady will suffice, thank you so much."

Just as Warner was about to leave and file his story—everybody would read his predictions the next morning—the delightfully unexpected occurred, something that would add spice to his tale. Flanked by two bodyguards and carried on the arm of a tall majordomo was the *eminence grise* of the art world, the consummate Neapolitan collector and, some thought, the ringleader of the world's most accomplished art theft operation, Don Ciccio Nerone.

At the moment of his flamboyant entrance, Irving Fellows of Boston, whom Andrew could not abide, was complaining to him, "Why I came to this display of wealth and social climbing, I don't know. Of course, I'd never bid on one of these media blockbusters. Although the painting doesn't look so bad. God! Who's that amazing-looking dwarf?"

"You, who know everything, don't know?" Andrew needled. "That's Don Ciccio Nerone, from Naples. Brilliant man. His collection, especially his Hellenistic cameos, is stupendous. Excuse me while I pay my respects."

"Hey, he's that Mafioso character!" Fellows said, his mouth falling open.

"*Cosi é s'é vi pare,*" Andrew muttered.

"And look at Olivia Cartright chasing after him—my God! She really looks delicious. Boy, I'd like to take her . . ."

"Make one move and I'll—You'll never get another loan from me in your life, Fellows," Andrew found himself snarling.

Fellows stepped back quickly and studied him in surprise. "Hey, this sale's getting very interesting. Have a thing going for your bitterest competitor, eh?"

"Don't be fatuous, Fellows."

Andrew went over to Don Ciccio and to the astonishment of the throng who were ogling the Count but trying to seem not to, shook his hand warmly.

"Don Ciccio, I've missed you," he said. Then, sotto voce: "Olivia has too. I got into a terrible fight with her over this sensual creature, but we are back in love again."

"I heard all about it. Olivia phones me every day."

"You will come to the wedding?" Andrew asked.

"Of course! In New York, I presume? Good. I have so many friends there. What do you think of the 'Naked Truth' now that you have finally seen it?"

"When my eyes were opened, I found her magnificent."

"I've seen better Velázquezes," Don Ciccio remarked with a grin. Andrew could see that he was not joking, but what he was trying to communicate totally eluded him.

Don Ciccio navigated his bearer through the throng, which parted in fascination as he approached. Several undercover members of Scotland Yard shadowing the Count followed closely, looking obvious. Don Ciccio instructed his bodyguard to proceed circuitously toward Olivia, who had stationed herself in front of the *Marchesa*.

"So, what is today's assessment of the *Marchesa Fiona?*" he asked in a conspiratorial voice.

"I'm still convinced I'm right. My opinion hasn't changed since I talked to you yesterday. Everything adds up: measurements, paint surface, and the different inscriptions."

"Does Andrew suspect anything?"

"Nothing. I had to save him from committing a felony, which Greenway solved—"

"Careful!" Don Ciccio nodded to his right. "There's that clever reporter from the *Tribune* with Sir Peter Grundy in tow," he warned. "Everything's in order, then? We shall meet at the Greenway flat as soon as the sale is over?"

"Oh, God, I hope so. I'm so nervous. What will Andrew think of me? Bless you. I would never have gotten this far without your unceasing help."

"You may go even farther. I might have a few surprises left," Don Ciccio remarked, a beatific smile illuminating his handsome face.

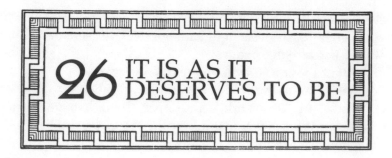

26 IT IS AS IT DESERVES TO BE

PRECISELY AT THE STROKE of noon, Sir Peter Grundy, attired in a pearl-gray morning coat, mounted the podium at the center of the stage in the sale room of William's. "My lords, ladies, and gentlemen, Lot 101, the *Marchesa Fiona Odescalchi* by Diego y Silva Velázquez. The bidding will start at five hundred thousand pounds and will proceed at one-hundred-thousand-pound increments, unless, of course, I am verbally instructed to do otherwise."

He passed his benign gaze over every part of the silent chamber.

"And now to begin," Sir Peter said softly, "at five hundred."

The first hand in the air was Irving Fellows's of Boston, who had sworn he was not going to bid. "Here!" What a clown. It was just not proper to actually say anything. A score of disapproving glances were cast his way, but to Grundy, this bit of American gaucherie was welcome at the outset, to get things moving.

"And I have from left center, at six!" Sir Peter smiled at Don Sánchez of the Prado. The early bids were almost always from those who wanted to be a small part of history but had resigned themselves to the gloomy realization that they had little chance of victory.

Bids of seven and eight and nine hundred thousand pounds followed like a machine-gun fusillade. Who would break through to the million-pound mark?

A languid hand stretched into the air in the far rear of the jammed chamber. All heads craned. A poker-faced Jules Bramet slowly lowered his hand. He knew he would never win the work of art he had come to covet so much. He could smell the avarice in the crowded hall. There were others, he admitted to himself in anguish, who were even hungrier—and wealthier—than he. He glanced at Kurt Krassner. The vulgar German might easily be the victor.

At Bramet's bid, there was a discreet clapping, causing Sir Peter to smile broadly. A few seconds passed without a sound. Grundy allowed the moment of quietude to linger and then looked up to the ceiling as if imploring the Almighty to help him. As he did the bidding started up again.

"And to the gentleman to my left, one million one hundred thousand." Sir Peter inclined his head at Robert Frobisher of the Getty. As he raised his finger, a cascade of confused thoughts raced through Frobisher's mind. Should he be bidding at all in this high-priced circus? Yet, even if the picture fetched twelve million dollars, how many Velázquezes could he afford? A thousand of them! Was the painting really all that magnificent? Oh, might as well buy it! What the hell was twelve, even thirteen million dollars? But if he did win, what effect would the scandalous price have on his shaky stewardship of the museum? He was both elated and depressed.

Grundy allowed himself a lightning-quick smile. "And from Mr. Robert Symes a bid of one million two hundred thousand." The big boys were finally coming in, earlier than he had expected. But there was still an air of caution. For a moment Grundy was concerned. Did the early entry of Frobisher and Symes mean that the sale might never soar to the heights? No. As he found a bid of one million five hundred thousand from the Louvre he could sense the mounting excitement. As soon as he marked the bid there came a muted cheer, accompanied by more clapping. Excellent!

Symes sat back smugly. How thrilling it was to be present at the biggest and most famous art auction in history, bidding for a great masterpiece! Way back during his orphanage days he never dreamed . . . Who was in and who would survive? Krassner. He was sure to enter any moment. The Louvre just did, though Symes had a hunch Le Grand would not last long. He had heard some intriguing rumors about the impending ouster of the imperious director. Baron von Thurn? Maybe. God, how he wanted the painting.

"There, on the left, one million six. That's very good, my lords, ladies, and gentlemen!" Sir Peter intoned. Splendid! Andrew Foster had just entered the bidding.

Quickly, Philippe le Grand raised his hand. "We now have one million seven," cried Grundy.

With these words, Kurt Krassner stood up and bulled his way back down the crowded center aisle. He was leaving! But once Krassner reached the back of the enormous room he turned abruptly, leaned against the wall, and raised his hand with a flourish.

"The bid is to you, sir, at one million eight," Sir Peter called out genially, and then wheeled to his right, snatched a bid from the aisle and announced almost in the same breath, "There! At one million, nine!"

The crowd let out a collective gasp. It was Olivia Cartright. She looked a little tense.

"I have an answering bid of two million from Dr. Andrew Foster across the room," Grundy cried out excitedly.

Andrew had wanted them to sit side by side, as if the two bitter competitors had by chance drawn adjacent seats. But Olivia had refused, saying that their bids might appear more convincing if they were separated. The truth was that she didn't want him anywhere near her when the bidding entered the final stages.

There was a lull in the bidding, which Grundy allowed to germinate for precisely fifteen seconds. He counted the seconds silently to himself like a orchestra conductor, wanting the action to solidify but not to deaden. During those moments several individuals thought deeply and sorrowfully about their prospects of obtaining the shining *Marchesa*. Baron von Thurn shrugged and decided he had been correct in not getting involved, although he was still, annoyingly, tempted. Then, abruptly, he changed his mind, raised himself iron-stiff in his chair, and signaled his bid. Two million one hundred thousand pounds.

"Two, two!" Grundy cried out, acknowledging Olivia's answering bid. A murmur ran through the crowd—she had just cast the precise bid with which the Met had won Velázquez's *Juan de Pareja* from the National Gallery in a world record.

A fine omen, Grundy thought.

With a grin, Andrew answered her bid. Olivia waved her hand in a salute and gave Grundy another signal. "Two, four!"

The crowd was becoming excited. Barely three minutes had passed since the bidding had begun. Sir Peter was flushed with the effort of concentration. Now that the world record for a Velázquez had been passed, there was no guessing where the bidding might end.

"Come now, let's make a real go for this masterpiece!" a harsh voice called out from the rear of the chamber. It was Kurt Krassner, in an unseemly breach of auction manners. He seemed to think he was at a sports event. But Sir Peter forgave the bumptious German when he heard his next words. "I bid six million pounds. I want to test the field for its courage."

A jump of 3.6 million! There were gasps, cheers, whistles, loud clapping and then the spectators fell silent with awe. Baron von Thurn smiled. He had been correct, as usual. But he wasn't through yet. Le Grand chewed on the nail of his little finger. Symes narrowed his eyes and recalculated. He decided to wait out a few more bids. When it got to ten million he would blow the dwindling opposition out of the fray. He shook his head in dejection. That was a prearranged signal for Grundy to watch him with special care. Grundy acknowledged the signal with the slightest nod.

"I have six million one hundred thousand, and two and three and, now, four, and . . .and . . . five!" Grundy's voice gradually rose to a shout as he pointed to Philippe le Grand at the conclusion of a rapid series of bids.

They are beginning to go mad, he thought. Good! He raised his arms to quiet the crowd, for a few people were starting to rise to their feet in an attempt to see who the bidders were. "Ladies and gentlemen," he appealed, "please respect the traditional decorum of the sale room." That would both calm down the spectators and allow the bidders to catch their breath.

Olivia raised her hand. Six million six. She thought of blowing Andrew a quick kiss.

Krassner answered her rudely. "Sorry, my dear Miss Cartright, I'll bounce you—to six, eight!"

Olivia answered with her own theatrics, making a gesture as if she'd been crushed. She hunched down in her seat, holding her chin disconsolately in the palm of her hand. It was the signal for Andrew to take over for a while. He jabbed his arm into the air. "Six, nine!" Peter Grundy cried.

Krassner boomed "And seven!"

In an unprecedented flurry of bidding, four bidders jumped to their feet and flailed their arms at the same time. It was Bramet, Robert Symes, a young man in the back whom Grundy didn't recognize—who was he representing?—and Robert Frobisher.

"Gentlemen, I must choose only one bidder at seven million one hundred thousand." Grundy was fairly purring. "I believe the bid is to you, Mr. Bramet. Now, one at a time, and at a gentle pace, please. We are now part of history and must act accordingly."

The crowd responded with laughter.

Robert Symes waved his program above his head. Seven million two hundred thousand.

Von Thurn topped it, at seven million three hundred thousand. But he knew he'd never win. He bid only to spite Symes, who, sure enough, turned to glare at him.

"Eight!" It was that damn Bavarian jumping the bid increments again. How vulgar! Baron von Thurn thought sourly. What a blitzkrieg of a voice! Yet he sensed an almost imperceptible deflation in the man. By God, could the upstart be through? Sir Peter leaned tensely over the podium. He was beginning to perspire profusely. "Yes. And . . . and . . . there's eight million one hundred thousand from . . . ah . . . from Mr. Bramet."

At that moment it was as if someone had thrown an incendiary charge into the room. The frantic acceleration of numbers exploded. Grundy was panting with physical exertion. He waved his arms over his head as he found a bid of eight, then eight five, a leap to nine million, followed by staccato raises to nine million one, then two, and three and four, then five, six, seven!

"Ten million!" Grundy cried out. The crowd cheered wildly. The bid had been Olivia's. Andrew jumped to his feet with a jubilant smile and threw up his arms in the champion's sign for victory. She grinned back. They had reached their safe plateau. The original was theirs.

Kurt Krassner answered with a bellow. "Twelve million pounds! That should do it!"

Great! Andrew said to himself. It was far from over. Robert Symes waved his index finger and Sir Peter intoned, "The bid is twelve million one hundred thousand pounds."

Even before the spectators could react, more bids crackled through the hall. With a grand bid of thirteen million pounds, Philippe le Grand gained the honor. But to Grundy's astonishment, Krassner vaulted over that lofty pinnacle. "Fourteen million, *ja-wohl!*"

Le Grand slumped into his chair. He was finished. He had begged those subhuman characters in the Ministry of Culture to give him a real amount of money! He threw in a special curse for that pig of a curator who had never stopped nagging him about the condition of the painting. He was finished and not just with the painting. Its loss would prove a bitter blow to France. They would remove him from his post. In the past several days he had smelled the acrid odor of conspiracy. That rotten woman minister! She was probably sleeping with that runt of a curator. *Merde!*

Now Olivia calmly raised her hand, indicating a bid of fourteen million one hundred thousand pounds. Andrew was stunned. Why was she back in? That wasn't according to their plan. What if she had won it! Jesus! But it didn't matter, for Krassner shot his arm up and called out, "Fourteen, five!"

Great! Andrew repeated to himself. They were home free and would walk off with their treasure for a mere four million—and, if the fools kept on bidding for the copy, perhaps for much less. Andrew leaned back to watch the finale of the circus, a loose grin on his face. But he was concerned at the incredible risk Olivia had taken. She easily could have been the final bid! He stood up and tried to catch her attention. But Olivia was watching Peter Grundy intently, waiting. In growing anxiety, Andrew realized that Olivia was contemplating another bid. Had she forgotten the plan? Lost her senses? Was it auction fever? He had seen it happen, especially to the inexperienced. He stood up, staring at her, mentally imploring her, trying desperately to make her aware that she was in a trance. How could he break it?

With a determined expression, Olivia made another bid. Fourteen million six hundred thousand. Krassner answered. The action was as rapid as exchanges at the net in the doubles finals at Wimbledon. As Andrew looked on in horror, Olivia matched Krassner volley for volley to sixteen million pounds, by far the highest bid for a work of art in history.

He would have to physically restrain her. Andrew struggled

through the crowded aisle toward her. She was already two million above the amount she had been voted by her committee. She was so headstrong, wanting to save some money. Please, oh, please, let someone even crazier make a bid so he could at least get to her side.

Robert Frobisher nodded his head rapidly.

"There! From the Getty Museum a bid of sixteen million five hundred thousand pounds." It was all Grundy could do to get the words out.

Olivia didn't move. Andrew felt enormous relief. She was finally out. Just the same, to be certain, he continued to make his way toward her.

Kurt Krassner hesitantly raised his right hand. "What is your bid, sir?" Grundy had to ask after a few seconds. "Failing to hear your voice, I take it your bid is sixteen million six hundred thousand. Is that correct?"

Krassner nodded glumly. His fire had all but gone out. When he saw Olivia raise her hand, Andrew stumbled and almost fell into the lap of a portly Dutch art dealer sitting on the aisle across from her. She had an odd smile on her face. Oh, God!

"Marvelous!" Grundy shouted. "That is sixteen million seven hundred thousand to the Metropolitan Museum of Art."

The crowd broke into shouts of encouragement. "No! No!" Andrew cried. But either Olivia couldn't hear him over the din or she refused to listen. He saw that she no longer cared about anything —only the picture. She was oblivious to him, transfixed as a stalking tigress.

Frobisher slumped and shook his head. He was done. Le Grand shivered in private rage. Krassner's face had become florid. *"Scheisse!"* he hissed, and stomped out of the room. Baron von Thurn's face was wreathed in a smile. Bramet shrugged and relaxed in his chair with an amused look. Grundy looked toward Robert Symes with an eye like a hawk's. There was a long pause. Finally, Symes shook his head. No. He, too, was out.

Grundy looked slowly around the room, like an actor in a Greek tragedy about to begin his soliloquy. "At sixteen million seven hundred thousand pounds, to Dr. Cartright of the Metropolitan. The bid is clearly yours. Is there anyone else?"

Andrew called out, "Cancel that bid!" Sir Peter raised his hands to hush him. It was too late. Olivia had bought—for the most money ever paid in history—a clever copy, worth perhaps five thousand dollars. As the enormity of her blunder began to sink in, he felt his legs weaken.

Grundy raised his hand in what looked like a benediction. "Are there any more bids? It is sixteen million and seven to you," he said, pointing to Olivia. "But I have a sealed bid—from the late James Waters of the Cleveland Museum of Art. I shall now open it."

He removed the letter from the envelope and perused it for several seconds.

Go, Waters, you son of a bitch! Andrew said to himself. Just this once in your life! Go for it!

Grundy looked up, shrugged, and said, "The bid from the Cleveland Museum is . . . not sufficient."

Andrew held his head in his hands.

"That is once . . . Dr. Cartright's . . . at twice!"

The spectators began to clap rhythmically until Sir Peter's stare silenced them.

"Twice, I said. And . . . at three times . . ."

Every one of the four hundred people in the room sucked in their breath at the same moment.

"That's—" But Sir Peter didn't have the chance to finish. The unidentified young man sitting way in the back who had bid earlier languidly raised his arm.

For the first time in his career, Sir Peter became flustered. "Please, sir, I apologize. But I must be sure. Your bid is . . . is . . . sixteen million eight hundred thousand pounds? Confirm that for me, if you will."

The young operative from the National Security Adviser's office nodded. "That's correct."

There was a long pause from Sir Peter. He had no idea who the man was. What if he were an imposter or a crank? Cool, detached, he simply had to be a solicitor representing someone or some institution of almost incomparable resources. Grundy didn't hesitate. Even if the man turned out to be a fraud, it wouldn't matter. Olivia Cartright's bid of sixteen million seven would hold up. But as he studied the calm demeanor of the young man, Sir Peter knew he meant it.

"Dr. Cartright, the bid is to you," Grundy said.

She made no response.

"If there is no further bidding from New York," Grundy continued almost funereally, "that is sixteen million eight hundred thousand pounds. Once!"

Andrew squeezed into the chair next to Olivia, elbowing an indignant art dealer into the aisle. "Darling, what's happening to you? I almost keeled over. You could have been clobbered!"

She grabbed his wrist. "Hush, Andrew. How far do you think that government guy will go?"

"What?" And then Andrew stared flabbergasted as Olivia calmly raised her arm.

Grundy had missed the gesture in his concentration to close the bidding. Before Andrew could stop her, Olivia stood up. "Is it possible to place a bid of sixteen million nine hundred thousand pounds in this auction gallery?"

"What, what?" Grundy stammered in momentary confusion. "Oh, yes. Most certainly."

The young man in the back lifted his arm once again.

"That would be seventeen million pounds," Grundy said dreamily.

Andrew reached over and took hold of both of Olivia's hands. She turned to him, smiled, and called out, "Seventeen million one hundred thousand."

The audience cheered and Peter Grundy had to shout. Repeatedly he called out to the man in the back of the hall, "The bid is to you, sir. Will you respond? Please reply!"

But the man sat, his hands folded in his lap, a stunned look on his face. Then he shook his head. It was over. Andrew heaved a sigh.

"That is seventeen million one hundred thousand pounds—a world record. Once . . . and twice . . . and three times! To Olivia Cartright of the Metropolitan Museum of Art."

The room erupted in cheers and whistles as the spectators surged toward Olivia and Peter Grundy. Olivia stood and embraced Andrew, almost crushing the breath out of him.

"I'm not really crazy. I hope!" she cried.

"You've just spent four million dollars over what your board voted you! And for a copy! Jesus!"

"It's only money. And anyway, Cresson pledged you ten million. We can use some of that."

"Olivia, I just don't think you realize what you've done." he said.

"I'll explain at Greenway's flat. Oh, God, I hope I've done the right thing."

Suddenly they were engulfed in the crowd. They worked their way to Sir Peter Grundy, who was mopping his face and accepting the congratulations of his elated staff. When he saw her, he grinned broadly and threw her kisses with both hands.

"You are a marvel, Olivia. I forgive you everything."

"Peter, there's something you must do, at once," she said when she had managed to get to his side. "It is a matter of the greatest urgency. I want this picture out of here, within seconds. It is mine now and I don't have to be ordered around by Richfield's guard or anyone else. Your security staff—not Richfield's—must deliver the *Marchesa* to the address I have written on this card within fifteen minutes or I shall not honor my bid. The place is just behind your building."

A bewildered Sir Peter extricated himself from the throng to dash off to make the arrangements. Olivia turned to Andrew and threw herself into his arms.

"Kiss me. Believe me. Tell me I've got to be right. Andrew, oh, Andrew, I pray what I think is there will be there. It's for you."

"What the devil is all this?"

"Either a triumph or a disaster."

"Do you realize how much money you're in the hole? You know you can't just bow out of this. When the hammer's down, it's down. God, this is terrible!"

"It's wonderful. If I'm right, we've saved a little and have received twice the amount for our money."

"I'm going mad."

"When you see what I have to show you, you'll be delirious."

"You already are."

"Let's run," she said. "Here comes the press."

Sir Peter had done an efficient job. Two workers flanked by a pair of guards were carrying the painting into the Greenway house as Olivia and Andrew arrived. Within minutes the picture had been hefted up on an easel in the middle of the room, inches away from a larger and far more radiant *Marchesa*.

Andrew approached the paintings, studied them silently for a few moments, and moaned, "Seventeen million one hundred thousand dollars for this . . . cloudy . . . mess!"

"Not at all," a cheery voice pealed out from the next room. "I'd call it an absolutely enchanting coup. If, that is, it is *not* what it appears to be."

"Don Ciccio!" Andrew shouted in astonishment as the Count rolled through the door in his mobile chair.

"Andrew, my dear friend, before you are carried off into the next world by a fit of apoplexy, perhaps Olivia should acquaint you with her various theories. And then confront us with the truth."

Olivia began a little tensely. "I have reason to believe I've found Velázquez's two frontal portraits of his lover."

"Quickly, let us see if your gamble was right," Don Ciccio said urgently.

"What now?" Andrew asked.

"A little archaeology," Olivia replied. Turning to Don Ciccio she asked "Is he here?"

"Of course. Allow me to present my chief conservator, Riccardo Agnello."

A string bean of a man entered the room, pushing a table on wheels covered with cotton swabs, assorted bottles, large magnifying glasses, and a couple of ultraviolet lamps.

"Wish us luck, Andrew," Olivia said.

He beckoned her over to him and cradled her in his arms. "I love you just the same. Madness!"

Agnello carefully adjusted his magnifying glass, then approached the painting, obscuring with his body the face of the *Marchesa* Olivia had just purchased. He picked up a piece of cotton, moistened it with a liquid, and gingerly began to clean. Within a few minutes he stepped back to reveal a sight Andrew could hardly believe. The dull, opaque face of the young woman now shone forth in unearthly beauty.

"My God! I did it!" Olivia cried out. "Andrew, look. Those delicate glazes, the glowing flesh tones, the gleam in her eyes. Isn't it a miracle? I was right! It's not a copy. It's the painting Velázquez made for himself. The Richfield 'original' is the version he made for Pope Innocent. And now I have them both!"

Andrew exhaled noisily.

"Takes my breath away too. I almost had a heart attack when I first realized I might be looking at Velázquez's first portrait."

"My God. It *is* by the master," Andrew said incredulously. "They both are. Olivia, you've made one of the most amazing discoveries in the history of art. How, when, did you first suspect?"

"When I began to stop brooding and being hurt about what you thought of the picture, when it struck me that you couldn't be trying to deceive me or drive me out of the sale."

"Why, for God's sake, did you think that?"

"I may be at fault, Andrew," Don Ciccio said quietly. "I was able to discover that you are employed by . . . you know, and that there were certain pressures from your government not to participate in the sale. I so informed Olivia."

"So, stupidly, Andrew dear, I thought that—"

"I was lying to you. Don Ciccio, how the hell do you come up with your information?" His words came in anger.

"In this instance, an old friend, Bill Leonard, phoned me some weeks ago to suggest that it would be in the best interests of the United States that I not consider bidding on the Velázquez."

"Jesus, you too?" Andrew had to laugh. "Were you thinking of bidding?"

"Of course. Until I learned that Olivia wanted the painting and, naturally, I stepped aside. But I believe I'm satisfied."

"So," Olivia said, "when I realized that you wouldn't lie to me, and after I had lunch with Lord Richfield's niece and learned that a 'copy' of the *Marchesa* had been in the Richfield family since the early nineteenth century, I knew I had to get back to William's and see if a switch had been made. When I sneaked back into William's, I measured the canvas. I knew then, for certain, that the original and what looked to me at first like a copy were different sizes. And it struck me as inconceivable that a copyist would not have copied the picture exactly. The measurements of this 'copy' and the first *Marchesa* I had seen were identical to those in the archives."

"Archives?" Andrew exclaimed, thoroughly puzzled. "I thought Seitz told us that someone had stripped the files!"

"Again, dear Andrew, I had something to do with that," the Count interrupted. "When I learned that Olivia wanted the painting I, ah, asked the custodian of the Academy, of which I happen to be a member, to put the pertinent data aside in my carrel at the Academy. I had photocopies made for Olivia. Tomorrow or the next day the files will be back in their proper place."

"You sure do get around, my friend," Andrew said. "You guys kind of wrapped up the competition, didn't you?"

"Aren't you pleased?" Olivia smiled sweetly. "Anyway, the measurements convinced me that both 'original' and 'copy' were by Velázquez. But why was one mucked up? I knew I had to study that 'copy' again closely. As I told you, Krassner was there, so I couldn't. But because of Krassner I was able to blackmail Sir Peter and get in a third time."

"Blackmail?"

"Yes, I told him that if he didn't let me see it once more, *alone*, I'd tell Greenway that Krassner had been studying the painting without a guard present."

"Risky."

"But it worked. Then I went to the National Gallery, examined the Rokeby *Venus*, and even managed to spot-clean it. I discovered that all three paintings had the same splendid surfaces but two had signs of muck on them. I was almost positive that I had seen three of the four original Velázquezes."

"How did you get Roy Bentley to let you in—and actually spot-clean the *Venus*?"

"He didn't. I am your pupil, Andrew. I hid overnight in the National Gallery. In the downstairs ladies' room."

"Olivia!"

"One must take risks," she added. "That's what you always say."

"Suddenly I understand why you tried so hard to get Greenway to switch what he—and I—thought was the copy, so that the original would be put on the block—and promise to give us the 'copy' as a souvenir! Olivia, for God's sake, why didn't you come clean with me? Why didn't you tell me all this?"

"First, I knew we'd get caught. And when that terrible Greenway threatened to destroy it I knew that I, and you, had to back off."

"By the way, my friends, the incendiary device has been deactivated," the Count said. "There is no longer any danger of conflagration."

"Second," Olivia raced on, "I didn't say anything to you because I wasn't totally positive I was right."

"I was convinced you had become hypnotized in the sale room. Buck fever. I was trying to get over to you and stop you." Andrew turned once more to the paintings. "So this 'copy' is Velázquez's first image. And Richfield's slightly larger one is the second, the Pope's. Okay, what happened to it?"

"Someone deliberately painted over it to make it seem like a copy," Olivia explained.

"Why the hell?"

"The *Marchesa* you dismissed for the best of reasons as a replica seems to have been doctored on purpose. Someone carefully painted over it with what looks like a combination of watercolor, gouache, and a bit of vegetable glue. I've no idea why."

"I believe I may have the answer," Don Ciccio said. "My files on art history record a number of similar cases, when original works of art were deliberately made to look like copies."

"But why?"

"To trick customs officials."

"Ah," Andrew sighed.

"Or to fool appraisers," the Count added.

"Clever," Andrew said.

"Or to avoid property taxes," Don Ciccio went on.

"Of course," Andrew agreed.

"Or to bilk someone out of an inheritance," the Count concluded. "And that, I think, may have happened in this case."

"Your inheritance, by any chance?" Andrew asked.

"A relative" was all the Count would say. "And now we will raise the curtain on our last act and see if a fourth painting that depicts our Marchesa, which I have acquired recently, is also by the master."

"Give me a break!"

"Don Ciccio, what *is* this?" Olivia said, bewildered.

The Count whistled two quick notes, at which two uniformed men carried into the room a painting almost exactly the size of the two before them. They set it up on a third easel.

"Friends, I have waited until this dramatic moment to learn whether I, too, have a masterpiece!" With those words Don Ciccio pulled the covering and there lay revealed what seemed to be a slightly hazy replica—a very accomplished one—of the Rokeby *Venus*. "Riccardo, attend to it. Tell us if we have the fourth genuine *Marchesa* or simply a daub."

"Your Excellency, it will take but a moment," Agnello assured him.

"Where the hell did this come from?" Andrew asked.

"I found it in the collection of a man named João Viva. Near Fiesole. It seems he is a descendant of the family—the Aquaviva family, who were related to Innocent X—who received the Pope's pair of paintings around the turn of the eighteenth century. Signore Viva is satisfied with the price I offered him. It seems he has something to hide from the Italian authorities, something that I know about. Like Harold Greenway, he may never be satisfied, but he is forever relieved."

"Your Excellency," Agnello called out in a quiet voice. "Observe. It is an original. No doubt."

"Thank God," Don Ciccio exclaimed.

"This is a dream, a beautiful, dangerous dream," Andrew said. "And it's all going to fall apart. What does Richfield know? What'll he do? What about Roy Bentley? He'll block the export."

"Allow me to put your mind at ease, Andrew," Don Ciccio said. "As for Richfield, he's made more money than he ever dreamed. From both his original and copy. His trusted adviser Greenway made such a fine deal for him. And I hardly think Greenway will say much about the Fielding brothers."

"Richfield's niece Eleanor Swift—she could expose us! Won't she figure it out?"

"She's so wrapped up in her own little field, she wouldn't even care," the Count assured him. "Anyway, the picture did sell for more than fair market value."

"Bentley. He's vicious," Andrew said. "How to get around him? Can't use my ploy of outbidding him any more. He'll block the export. And how to explain to our boards of trustees—and the world—how Olivia bid for one painting and came up with two. Oh, God."

"I have thought of that, of course, and have taken a page or two from my antecedent Luigi Pirandello," Don Ciccio said. He turned to Olivia. "My dear, you have a most unusual combination of masterpieces. You have both frontal portraits of his gorgeous lover by the genius Velázquez. And I seem to have acquired the back of the young lady—the one he made for himself. As my very special wedding gift, and as my final sworn gesture of thanks for saving my life, I would like to present you with my portrait. That way you will have the original pair. If you wish, you can tell your board members that you received a generous gift from an 'anonymous donor.' American boards adore anonymous donors."

"I can't do it! It's too much. Absolutely not!" Olivia protested. "That makes three paintings in all."

"Then we shall make an exchange. I shall give you my painting and you shall present me with your larger version of the front."

"But the first portrait is far more valuable. I mean, even if Velázquez himself painted the Pope's version, the first is more vital, fresher, filled with love . . ."

"You have little choice, my dear," the Count said with more than a hint of exasperation. "You must not deny me—you have no right to deny me—my responsibility to the honor of my family. In my land, in my family, there are such things as sacred obligations. What you did for me makes me honor bound—joyously—to render the appropriate thanks. Just because in the modern world so many people care nothing about honor, and grace, and the pleasure of giving something of great value, doesn't mean that I have to follow the herd. Olivia, I'm shocked. You, of all people, want *me* to be a part of the vulgar modern society that grabs and grabs and never gives?"

Laughing, tears in her eyes, Olivia rushed over and hugged and kissed him. "I accept!"

Then, turning, she walked slowly toward Andrew, stalking him —again the tigress. Her eyes flashed. "And now you, Andrew

Foster. I can tell you why I didn't tell you anything, refused to reveal what I had learned, deliberately, and with full knowledge aforethought did plan and scheme to keep you in the dark." She threw her arms around his neck and kissed him passionately. "For my wedding gift to you, in exchange for the directorship of the Metropolitan—that most glorious gift of all time—I give you what you so cherish, the two *Marchesas*!"

Andrew threw back his head and roared. "I won't even hesitate. I'll take 'em! With, of course, one little proviso. That we share them forever between the National Gallery and the Met, their true owners."

"Great! Every four years we exchange. You can have them first."

"And we'll split the payments right down the middle," he said. "The way I figure it, the 'original' cost us the ten million reserve, minus—let's see, it was to be half a million less for every million over ten—so that makes the cost only six and a half million, plus your 'copy'—'copy'! ha!—at seventeen million one . . . that's twenty-three and a half million. I got from Cresson ten million and you—God, you knew all this when you went to your acquisitions committee!—have fourteen. Precisely what we need."

Then Andrew's face fell. "But it doesn't matter. Bentley will wreck everything! He'll block the export of both paintings forever. The dream is smashed—the perfect dream."

"My boy, there is an elegant solution," Don Ciccio observed suavely. "The third painting—my painting—I shall lend, indefinitely and anonymously, to the National Gallery here. Bentley can hang it side by side with the Rokeby *Venus*, exactly where it belongs. That little gesture will dampen any desire to block the exportation of the two paintings to America. He's sure to get the knighthood he covets."

"We accept!" Olivia and Andrew cried out simultaneously.

"As soon as the pictures are in Washington, we should make a public announcement," Olivia exclaimed, "telling the world that we've acquired not one masterpiece by Diego Velázquez, but two. One at auction and another from a private collection, the Nerone collection. That will keep the tongues wagging."

"Excellent. After all, I did give you the picture. And I doubt if anyone will probe too deeply, knowing my reputation," Don Ciccio chuckled.

"What a way to launch your directorship of the Met, darling!" Andrew exulted as he hugged her.

"I want to share that too," Olivia said. "Andrew, you know I don't want to raise money, testify before Congress, negotiate with unions, mediate with the staff, assuage trustees, fight for building programs, goad the city government. I'm a connoisseur. I want to be a hunter of great art. I'll accept the directorship only if it frees me to deal with art and only art. As a matter of fact, I have it on the best of authority that Ayn Steyne will soon be resigning. That means the Met needs a new president, someone gifted in art history and administration. On an equal footing with the director!"

"What a team we'll make!"

"It *is* as it appears to be," Don Ciccio murmured.

"And as it *deserves* to be," Olivia added, beaming.